I MURDERED YOUR MOTHER, I THINK?

SECOND EDITION 2024

ROBERT BECKSTEDT

Copyright © 2024 Robert Beckstedt.

All rights reserved. No part of this book may be reproduced, stored, or transmitted by any means—whether auditory, graphic, mechanical, or electronic—without written permission of both publisher and author, except in the case of brief excerpts used in critical articles and reviews. Unauthorized reproduction of any part of this work is illegal and is punishable by law.

This book is a work of fiction. All names, characters, locations, and incidents are products of the author's imaginations. Any resemblance to actual persons, things, living or dead, locales, or events is entirely coincidental.

ISBN: 979-8-89419-404-2 (sc)
ISBN: 979-8-89419-405-9 (hc)
ISBN: 979-8-89419-406-6 (e)

Because of the dynamic nature of the Internet, any web addresses or links contained in this book may have changed since publication and may no longer be valid. The views expressed in this work are solely those of the author and do not necessarily reflect the views of the publisher, and the publisher hereby disclaims any responsibility for them.

One Galleria Blvd., Suite 1900, Metairie, LA 70001
(504) 702-6708

BOOKS BY ROBERT BECKSTEDT
AVAILABLE AT AMAZON.COM

The Great Great Aunts from Prussia

The Tributaries of Alex Beckham

Ian and Anton

THE DEDICATION

Dedicated to my family and friends who encouraged me to travel the world and accepted the changes within me when I returned. And I thank God for giving me the opportunity to experience all of this in good health and safety, while instilling in me love and respect for all I have encountered.

—Robert Beckstedt

"The world reveals itself to those who travel on foot."

—Werner Herzog

INSPIRATION

"I have a deeply hidden and articulate desire
for something beyond the daily life."
—*Virginia Woolf*

"Wherever you go, go with all Your heart."
—*Confucius*

"Within you there is a stillness and a sanctuary to which
you can retreat at any time and be yourself."
—*Hermann Hesse*

"To live is the rarest thing in the world. Most people just exist."
—*Oscar Wilde*

TABLE OF CONTENTS

Haiti - September 1916

1. The Hard Choices of Love 3
2. The Road to Emptiness in Santo Domingo...................................... 8
3. The Fate of an "X" 18
4. Goodbye Momma, Goodbye My Love.. 24
5. Voyage to the Unknown 28
6. The Resurrection 32
7. 1919–Innocence Lost and New Life Begins.................................... 41
8. The Family Chat 45
9. One Family Grows – One Family Goes 54
10. The Progression of the Gabriels 59
11. The Departure of Two Lifetimes.. 62
12. Raoul Bows to the Devil 67
13. Andrea's Decision for Eternity... 70

Balboa, Panama – 1995

14. The Demise of Andrea's Husband... 79
15. Oh Where, Oh Where Has My Little Boy Gone? 95
16. The Secret Hiding Place for Alejandro 100
17. Andrea Comes Marching Home 108
18. High Tide Begins to Recede on Andrea's Beach 115
19. The Politics Begin.. 119
20. The Shot That Falls on Deaf Ears.. 126
21. Let's Make a Deal Balboa... 134

22. The Ring Catches Fire Without an Extinguisher 148
23. Andrea Bares Her Teeth and Prepares for a Dog Fight 159
24. And the Wheels on the Bus Go Round and Round 167
25. A New Day but Not a Fresh One 177
26. Michael Rows the Boat Ashore 183
27. Generations upon Generations 195
28. Andrea Needs What She Needs When She Needs It 198
29. Gaze into My Eyes, Sweet Child 207
30. The Question is Revived – Why at Age Thirty-Five? 212
31. Gone but Not Forgotten 220
32. The Return of Royalty to Balboa 223
33. I Must Get This Baby off My Chest 241
34. Which Witch Way was Which? 257
35. Mother, the Time has Come and Gone 262
36. Let's Wrap the Package with a Bow on Top 279
37. History is Scattered on the Table 285

2017 – Twenty Years after Andrea's Death and the Family's Relocation to the US

1. Something Has Arisen from the Pit 299
2. He is a Writer - He Makes Stuff Up 312
3. On the Brink 316
4. Two Weeks before the Day of the Attack 331
5. Morning of the Surgery 337
6. One Week before Michael's Surgery 349
7. Out of OR 355
8. Tell Me Why, Mommy Dearest? 367
9. The Life of Which People Can Only Dream 376
10. The Book of Revelations 381
11. Love Comes in Many Forms 390

HAITI - SEPTEMBER 1916

THE HARD CHOICES OF LOVE

One-room shanties formed from creek rock and mortar, topped off by their rusted, galvanized roofs squatted like tombstones alone on the mountainside above the town, the land itself owned by Marinette, Voodoo goddess of the Earth. The dirt road traversed the mountainside, abutting some shanties, then continuing to form their flooring. The road was muddy in the rainy season, dusty in the dry, maintained only by the cart and foot traffic it provided for the mortals.

"Etienna Gabriel, inside the house right now and crawl under the bed. Hurry, scoot, but check for snakes and scorpions." whispered Jesula, Etienna's mother, with folded arms and a stomp of her foot.

"Why, Mama?" responded Etienna.

"American soldiers are stalking our streets like a pack of wild dogs. They're searching for teenagers like you. If they see you, they will capture you, strap your arms behind your back, and force you to work for them against the Cacos. You'd be toiling for the military fighting your father and the rebels. I 've told you over and over, it's not safe for you on the streets. Always stay close to the house. That's why you kids are not in school. If you set foot in the school, they'll seize you like a runaway Billy goat." Jesula's voice was strained with tears. "I'm not going to lose you to those animals the way I lost your brother."

"How can they do that, Momma? I mean, grab me, and take me from you. That's not right. That's slavery or plain kidnapping. What will they make me do if they take me, Momma?" asked Etienna with wide-eyed panic on her face.

"Crawl under the bed if it's safe. I'll tell you when to come out." Etienna saw nothing deadly, only cockroaches, so she squeezed under the bed. "By law, they're not permitted to enter our house, but they can linger in the streets as long as they want. They're like boas in the brush waiting to strike, and like a good-sized boa, they'll not let you go. They're lurking by Rosa's on the corner right now, their vermin eyes scanning the neighborhood. They abducted her son last week. She's talking to them in non-stop Spanish. She knows it frustrates them terribly, and they just want to get away from her. Just be still."

Jesula stood inside with the door cracked, keeping eyes on the soldiers. As she watched, she again spoke softly but sternly. "The reason they can take you is called 'statute labor,' a form of corvée. Our King Henri invoked it a hundred years ago, but it was only to last fifteen years. He built the Citadel to guard us against the French. But now our government has invoked it again at the request of the Americans who arrived last year. Our government allows them to take us and work us hard without pay. If we refuse, we are beaten severely, so severely, many of us die. The Americans need to get at the Cacos in the mountains, and they need workers to do it. They use our young men to chop through jungle and construct roads. They use you young girls to cook and wash their uniforms. And they also do…well, things we do not want to think about." Jesula gave Etienna a sad glance. "I'll find a way to keep you unharmed, my love. I pray to Saint Francis to shelter you from harm."

Etienna knew what the things were they didn't want to think about, even at age thirteen. She already witnessed her mother and Rosa, trained by their mothers and the Voodoo priestesses, place curses on men who raped and beat girls in the village. She also watched them cast protection spells on the innocent who were sick or in mourning, needing their love. Etienna observed from an early age how these curses instilled a deep fear among the wicked. Other than protection, no one wanted a doll on Jesula's or Rosa's altar.

The Americans saw Voodoo as nonsense. Kidnapping, forced labor, and sex trafficking represented a different problem for the Voodoo world.

The Priestesses became mindful that trying to curse these atrocities demanded too broad a scope. They were unable to pinpoint any specific individual to punish. These barbarities evolved into a way of life in early twentieth-century Haiti; only avoidance could render safety to the young and the weak.

Rosa's irritating tongue and nonstop Spanish garble caused the soldiers to slither off to search elsewhere. Outside the hut, Jesula stood crying. When Rosa saw her, she came to give Jesula a warm hug. "What is it, my dear?" she asked, reverting to her sweet voice.

"What am I to do, Rosa? You know what danger we are in. We have already lost our only sons, but Etienna? At her age, she is a main target for the sex traffickers and the Americans and the corvée. Even if she escapes both, I have a problem feeding her since her father went to fight in the mountains."

Rosa looked at Jesula with pity in her eyes, but she stayed quiet and let Jesula express her deepest fears.

"I know my husband will never return. I know he does not love me or his daughter. There is no schooling for Etienna. The Americans have ended that. What kind of job will she find with no education? She will be homeless, captured, or worse if anything happens to me. We are trapped. Perhaps death is our only way out." Jesula stared hopelessly into the heavens.

"Jesula, I'll not stand for any of that kind of talk." Rosa grabbed Jesula by the shoulders and gazed into her eyes. "My child, that is never an option. The Lord says it is a sin. Have you considered restavek for Etienna in the Dominican or some other country?"

Jesula's mouth dropped that Rosa would even suggest it.

"I know it is a form of slavery, but we have that here. The American marines invaded and have occupied Santo Domingo since May. They have taken over the government, although neither side wants us peasants to know. There is no resistance there, at least not an organized military one. The corvée laws have no need to be enforced."

"I'm not following you?" responded Jesula with a puzzled and pensive stare.

"The Americans are fighting a public relations war, wanting the Dominicans to think their occupation is beneficial. Because of the sugar shortage caused by the war in Europe and the destruction of the beet fields, our sugarcane has temporarily become invaluable. This occupation is about control of the sugar industry in Haiti and the Dominican; about a partnership formed among the governments and the plantation owners. Remember when I visited my sister in Santo Domingo a couple of months ago?"

"Yes." Jesula nodded, wiping her tears.

"Her husband landed a job on a freighter carrying sugar to the Panama Canal. He said companies are setting up trade businesses in Panama, and the Americans are looking for female domestic workers to serve both these executives and the military officers protecting the canal. In addition to the Americans, foreign embassies are being established by countries from all over the world. Panama is booming. Does Etienna speak English?" Rosa asked. Rosa learned a lot from her sister.

"She can speak some Haitian Creole, but mostly Spanish. Why?"

"If she can speak some Haitian Creole, not the French style, the English style, and being a smart girl, she will pick up US English in no time. She will be in demand."

"Keep going." Jesula was finally paying attention.

"She also has another advantage." Rosa paused, squeezing Jesula's shoulders. "Your daughter appears strong and healthy, but she is not pretty." Jesula pulled back. "I say that because that will be an advantage. If she has big breasts and a shapely ass, she could fall into the wrong hands. Most ladies of the house do not trust their husbands or sons around our 'little Negro girls,' as they call them. Has Etienna started her womanhood yet?" Rosa asked cautiously. She was being dreadfully blunt to Jesula, and Etienna was within listening distance, but Jesula knew good intentions stemmed from Rosa's heart.

"Yes, a few months ago. Her breasts are starting to swell under her blouse. They are noticed, not only by the boys, but those dirty old scoundrels parked on the benches." Jesula shook her head in disgust. "Let it be known to the gods, I hate men. Soldiers, traffickers, horny boys, creepy old men. You name it, I hate those bastards. I always store a few extra dolls to be prepared if, or should I say when, they attempt to debase my little Etienna."

"The beginning of her womanhood is nothing a baggy shirt won't hide for now anyway. We need to get her into the right hands. We must visit my sister in Santo Domingo and explore the domestic labor opportunities. I heard the Americans oversee this, not the Dominicans; that is a good thing. Want to try?" asked Rosa, lifting her eyebrows.

"Rosa," Jesula started to weep once again. "What choice do I have? It's a big risk, but I trust the Americans in the Dominican more than the Americans in this hellhole. But if she leaves the country, I will never see my baby again, Rosa. Oh, Rosa, where are the gods these days for us innocent people? I thought our Archangel Michael defeated Satan at the beginning of time. Where did the love and respect we had for each go after the Europeans and Americans invaded our island?" Jesula dropped to her knees, her face buried in her hands.

Rosa lifted Jesula to her feet. "I have a brother who works at the border. We will have no problem getting across. I suggest we leave town late tonight, so as not to be seen by the Marines. They are usually drunk and passed out on rum by then. And they are focused on the rebels in the mountains. By daylight, we will be out of town and approaching the border at Jimaní by noon."

Jesula looked stunned. "You mean tonight?"

"Every day your little girl is here, she is in danger of terrible, horrible things. Right now, she is hiding under a bed on a dirt floor with cockroaches crawling up her legs. And at the same time, she watches for snakes while she conceals herself from soldiers. Why not now, Jesula? Get whatever you want to take with you, but don't take much. And don't tell anyone what we are doing, and I mean no one. No goodbyes, no nothing. If the sex traffickers get wind of this, we will never make it across the border. They'd snatch all three of us up in Jimaní." Rosa's lips turned down in a grim expression. "We must only talk to the Americans once we arrive in Santo Domingo."

THE ROAD TO EMPTINESS IN SANTO DOMINGO

As the sun inconspicuously approached the horizon, and the first crow of the dominant cock in the distance, Rosa made her silently made her way to Jesula's door. Knocking gently with one knuckle, the latch scraped open slowly, and Jesula peeked out.

"Ready, my child? We need to be out of town before dogs or soldiers see us. Is Etienna ready?" asked Rosa. "We're right on schedule once we pass into the countryside."

"Yes, we're ready," Jesula whispered. "We've been talking most of the night, trying to accept all this." Rosa could tell by Jesula's swollen eyes she had been weeping.

Jesula grabbed her bag containing a few pieces of fruit and a mason jar filled with water. Etienna emerged first from the shanty. Jesula closed the door behind her, not making a sound. The three began their journey down the mountainside and out of the motionless, darkened town, to a destination that would become the end of life as they knew it.

They reached the border at Jimaní by midday without incident. Those of most concern on the road were still asleep from their debauchery the night before. But they would not be for long. Rosa and her brother connected easily. The patrol at the border was modest the men were more interested in drinking and playing dominoes than protecting a third world border. After a short chat, Rosa's brother kindly nourished them with rice and water, then prepared them each a thirty-day visa. It was a short dusty walk into the town of Jimaní. Rosa insisted Jesula and Etienna stay behind her and not say a word or make eye contact with anyone.

It was midday hot and steamy; no shade to be found anywhere. They shuffled their way into the dirty border town, a place lined with liquor stores, filthy restaurants, and sleazy strip clubs. Along the sidewalks were beggars with no legs or arms, people sleeping, or dead, propped against the buildings, (one couldn't tell which), and blind men and women jiggling their cups for spare change. As they made their way to the bus station, they were approached by unkept, unshaven men with the pungent smell of urine and body odor radiating from their very being. Etienna thought the men in her village smelled bad, but this was worse.

"Any of you hot little chicas wanna make some quick pesos and go with me to a little grind-fest down the street?" a hunchbacked man asked in a crusty voice, his head cocked sideways like that of a deranged buzzard. A disgusting rash poched his face along with a scabbed head of thin stringy hair. "How about you, little senorita? I could get you some steady work. But to get a decent price, I must try you out myself. You'll bring a coin or two more when those little titties come popping out. Your mommas ain't too bad neither. Look at those booties. And oh my, look at those shadows through them blouses. Can I have a peak?" said the pervert as he rubbed his crotch.

Rosa and Jesula glared furiously as the man gave a loathsome chuckle. "Kinda pretty faces when you don't frown. C'mon, give me a flash, chicas. I can get ya both jobs and a room to sleep in. C'mon, girly," he said to Etienna, "let me touch." He began circling them, his eyes moving up and down on their bodies. "You're still a virgin, ain't ya sweetie?" he said to Etienna. That'll bring a good price, at least once, if you know what I mean. How about lifting the skirt." The slimy pervert laughed in a nightmarishly way. Rosa and Jesula were across the line of livid, while Etienna had tears streaming down her face. She hid behind her mother.

"Touch my daughter, and you'll wish you hadn't, you gargoyle," screamed Jesula. "The God's will pay you a visit, and horses will chew your torso, little by little, until they see your bones and your bloody organs. They will follow you until you die a slow and horrible death." Jesula reach up and pulled a patch of slimy greasy hair from the pervert's scalp with her razor-sharp nails. "This will be on your own special doll by nightfall if you don't leave us. I assure you; you don't want that to happen, Freako." She squinted at him, but not once did she blink.

"Shit, that hurt, you loco bitch. You took a chunk of skin with it too." The freak whined as he rubbed his bleeding head. "Okay, okay. I'm going away. You Voodoo women are crazy. I don't want to die like my padre with boils and sores inside and out. You say you're gonna make me into horse food. Please, chica, give me my hair back. I'll leave all of you alone."

"You're not leaving just yet, cursed one. I'm keeping this little patch, and you will help us safely to the bus station. You are going to keep your other mutant friends away from us," said Jesula as she dangled the repugnant bit of bloody skin and hair in his face. He tried to snatch it but missed. She began talking in a language not even Rosa understood, then she switched back to Spanish. "If anybody bothers us on the way, you will never get this hair back. Now go, lead us to the station, you wretched piece of burro dung."

"Yes, yes, just don't throw down a curse on me," the pervert pleaded, his body shaking in fear as he escorted them to the station.

"Hey, buzzard man. You can pick your scalp up next to that pink house up there after our bus passes. I'll fling it out the window," said Jesula, staring at the heinous man with her rage-filled eyes. "Boils and sores are where I will start with you, like your padre. Your penis will rot off first. Then the horses will break bones. Pray I don't change my mind and keep this chunk just for fun." The man's eyes widened with fear as he imagined the horrible images she painted of him. "Now, stand next to that building where we can see you, and don't move until after our bus passes the pink house."

Rosa bought their tickets. They climbed into the ramshackle bus, making their way to their torn seat through chickens, piglets, and dogs. They crammed into one seat, Etienna in the middle. She looked at her mother. "Momma, you really scared that man with your Voodoo threat. Great bluff. Backed him off right away."

Jesula stared straight ahead. "I was not bluffing, child? If I can get a patch of hair, a piece of skin, even urine or spit, I can make a doll and curse them for the rest of their life." Etienna scrunched up her eyebrows. "But I never harm anyone directly, that is not my right. I make the family of Ghede aware of a wrongdoing and pray to them what I believe should happen. The gods then judge. They decide whether to grant my request or refuse it. Or they can change the punishment to be lighter or worse. Sometimes, I suggest an offender die, but not often. Most of the time, I ask that they be placed in pain and misery or confusion for a while. But sometimes they kill themselves to escape the pain and insanity. That's not my responsibility. People around here know our powers are real, and those who doubt won't take the chance. That is why I have tried to teach you the art of witchcraft early, Etienna, so you can protect yourself if I'm not around."

As they passed the pink house, Jesula threw a small piece of crumpled paper out the window. The three watched as the pervert crossed the street and snatched it.

"Momma," asked Etienna, "why is he yelling and shaking his fist at the bus? You threw his hair out. Why is he doing that?"

Jesula looked at Rosa, then smiled at Etienna. She pulled the mason jar from her bag, but it was no longer empty. It contained a patch of scalp. "He just discovered a moldy piece of bread in that wadded up paper. I picked it from the gutter as we boarded the bus. Now he is scared to death. He doesn't know what I'm going to do, and frankly, girls, I don't know yet. I think I'll leave it up to the family of Ghede and how hungry his horses are these days. Yes, that is what I believe I will do. Let them decide." Jesula and Rosa smiled at each other as they both hugged the innocent Etienna tightly smashed between them.

In that moment, Etienna understood her mother was not only teaching her to protect herself, but to protect others from evil as well. And that man was pure evil.

After four hours of dusty, pothole-riddled roads, the bus stopped in the center of Santo Domingo. Jesula, Etienna, and Rosa waited until the livestock exited so they stepped in nothing. As they entered the crowded streets, Etienna observed it to be like Jimaní, only with more people and chaos. The odor from the horse feces and slaughterhouses was overwhelming. Etienna's throat began to tighten, and her stomach rolled. Suddenly, she vomited. Jesula and Rosa ignored her first nasty taste of the big city.

"Just stay close together and look straight ahead. No talking to anyone. Just follow me," said Rosa. "My sister lives a mile from here. Once we get to the market district, this ugliness won't be as bad." Rosa looked around. "I have never seen this many American soldiers in the streets. At least they aren't approaching us. They don't have to. They don't need us. If they did, like back home, they'd just take us and have us later for dessert."

"What does? Etienna started to ask.

"Nothing, honey," Jesula answered as she frowned at Rosa.

The three weaved their way down the populous streets and through the market until they reached a dilapidated, eight-story colonial walkup. "This is where my sister lives. It looks bad from the outside, but it's cleaner and cooler than you would expect inside. She lives on the top floor, where most days, they feel a breeze off the harbor." Etienna lifted her gaze to the top. She tried not to show her fear. "And watch where you step. Parts of the floor and stairs are dry rotted, or the termites stopped holding hands and you'll fall through." Etienna giggled. Jesula smiled and gave her a hug. "Try to walk on the edges, not in the middle. And watch out for bare wires, or you will be electrocuted. And please, don't ask my sister about her face. Her husband is not a sweetheart, but he gives her and the kids a place to live and food to eat.

"That's more than our men," said Jesula.

"So, Jesula, no curses. My sister can be a bitch sometimes." Rosa looked at them with eyebrows raised. "They are my only family left."

Jesula nodded and said nothing. Etienna and Jesula ascended the eight flights, following methodically in Rosa's footsteps. Rosa arrived at a blue door, partially painted but mostly bare wood. She knocked.

"Who is it?" said a gruff voice from inside.

"It's Rosa, my love. And I have a couple of friends with me."

"No men, right? The kids are here, Rosa," her sister replied. "You can't bring men around here when the kids are awake." Etienna looked curiously at her momma.

"No, Nia, no men. It's a friend of mine and her daughter from my neighborhood in Haiti. We need your help."

Two deadbolts slid and the door opened. There stood a woman highly resembling Rosa, except for the crushed cheekbone on her face. The woman reached for Rosa. They hugged tightly.

"Come in little sister, and your friends too. All of you come, sit around the table, and I'll get you some water," said Nia.

They all walked to the kitchen table, but Nia turned abruptly. "Oh, praise the gods you're safe, Rosa. I've been worried sick about you, with the occupation and the Americans forcing labor and themselves upon you. I so love you, honey." She hugged Rosa once again. Rosa hugged back as tears streamed down their faces.

"They got my son last week, Nia.," said Rosa. Nia closed her eyes and held Rosa's hand to her damaged cheek.

"Oh Rosa, my love. He'll be returned safely. I'm sure of it. At least, you didn't lose a daughter." Nia felt she said something that should have been left unsaid.

Nia gathered a pitcher of water and four glasses. They took seats around the rickety table. "How about you, Nia?" Rosa asked. "I hear the American marines invaded and took over the city since I visited last. And not only here, but a few other towns in the Dominican. Did you lose a lot of soldiers in the battle?"

"Oh, bless you honey, not at all," her sister responded with a giggle. "They had us so outmanned and outgunned. They parked a huge battleship in the harbor, cannons aimed right the City Hall. Talk about a five-hundred-pound gorilla. Our army is so out of date. The president just surrendered."

"They didn't put up a fight?" asked Rosa.

"No, the president knows our soldiers sit around and get high all day. We have nothing that could even sink a canoe, not to mention a battleship. Those boys joined the army to get clean clothes, a room in the barracks, and a couple of meals a day. I'd am surprised they give them bullets. One boy shot himself in the foot while he was running away. It was planned by both sides from the beginning. It was a joke." Nia paused, rolling her eyes. Etienna reached for her mother's hand under the table, frightened by the

Nia's badly battered face. "I told you on your last visit, the Americans only want our sugar cane, and the president wants to sell it to them."

"So that's where Jose is now, working on a freighter?" asked Rosa.

"Yep, he's somewhere between here and Panama, loading and unloading sugar cane. The same ships that transport the young women who agree to restavek," Nia said nonchalantly as she filled everyone's water glasses again. Jesula was worried over the reddish-brown color of the water. Their creek water was clear back home.

"Well, Nia, that's why we are here," Rosa responded. "This is my friend Jesula and her daughter Etienna. We're trying to get Etienna out of Haiti. The Americans and the Cacos rebels are still fighting a guerrilla war in the mountains outside our town. The Americans made our town their military base, and our government reenacted the old corvée law to force our young men and women into labor."

"That's how you lost your son?" Nia confirmed with Rosa.

"Yes. I would suspect our government got as getting a pretty penny from the Americans for that. They have the kids chopping jungle and building roads so the Americans can get their cannons and weapons through. And frankly, as you know, they take the young girls for more than just cooking," Rosa whispered.

"How can I help?" asked Nia.

"We thought if we could find a legitimate way to traffic Etienna, preferably out of the country, with a restavek arrangement, she might be safe. She's not safe in our village. Jesula has a sister in Panama who was trafficked there about five years ago. She was lucky to get with a reputable trafficking firm, not sex traffickers. With the Americans here, we heard they need domestic workers in the Panama Canal Zone. Do you know anyone who can help Etienna and get Jesula a job?" Rosa pleaded.

Nia studied Etienna and Jesula, observing them closely. "Jesula, I'm afraid you're too old for restavek in Panama, but there might be other countries that will take you. Maybe an American family here in the Dominican. But the Americans and the Panamanians have agreed they'll only bring in girls from other countries under the age of fifteen. And these girls can only be used as low-level domestic workers. They get no money. They work for food, clothing, shelter, and education. Only older Panamanian women can oversee these girls."

"Why don't they hire the Panamanian girls?"

"The Panamanian girls are unreliable. They run off with their boyfriends or stay home and babysit for their mothers." It was a clever political move by the Panamanian working party."

"Will they let my daughter come visit?"

"No, honey, if you want your daughter to work in Panama, I'm you must let her go forever. But if she stays here, the sex traffickers will get her. It is a heartbreaking decision you must make."

Etienna came over, sat on her mother's lap, hugged her, and cried intensely. Jesula squeezed her firmly and cried even harder over the thought of parting. Etienna pulled back far enough to look into her mother's tear-soaked eyes. "I'm not going to leave you, Momma, I'm staying here with you. We can go back to the village and—"

"Stop, Etienna. If we go back to the village, you'll be taken from me there as well, either by the Americans or the rebels. You can only hide under the bed for so long. And when they take you, they'll not be kind to you. I can't take the thought of you being raped and beaten. This way, you have a chance, not only for you, but for the future of your own children and grandchildren. Haiti's will not improve. I have been praying for your protection for years. This is a unique opportunity the gods have offered to you to start your life new and safe. You must go, my child." Etienna left her mother's lap and dropped to her knees, buried her face in her mother's skirt, and sobbed. Jesula cradled Etienna's head as tears trickled down her face, the tears dripping onto her daughter's cherished hair.

Etienna knew her mother was right. She couldn't leave her house or go to school. She hid like a mouse always alert in a thatched roof. She embraced her mother, their bodies rocked together in grief.

"Rosa, you have come at the right time. The Dominicans are rounding up people with Haitian passports and sending them back to Haitian jails for breaking immigration laws. The Americans don't want rebellious Haitians here at all; none of you. Etienna would be plucked from the jails in Haiti. How did you get across the border?"

"Our brother, Pedro, let us through with no hassle," said Rosa.

"I forgot he was still there; I haven't heard from him in years. You came through Jamani;' smart move, honey." Nia was proud of her little sister's ingenuity. "If we make our move tomorrow, we have a chance. The Americans are fine if you leave the Dominican for another country. The don't want you Haitians here."

"The Americans don't like us, do they?" interjected Rosa.

"Not as long as your guerillas are shooting their soldiers." Nia continued to talk as she filled the pitcher of water once again. "In the past, it's been perilous to do what you want to do. Young girls are commonly sold by their families who can't afford to raise them. Some promise the family they have connections in the US or Western Europe who will gladly adopt their daughters. Or they offer them a restavek opportunity. But most are seedy sex traffickers taking advantage of desperate parents. Who knows where happens to these girls, but I've heard stories?"

Jesula and Etienna stopped crying, following Nia's every word with breathless stares. They were terrified. "How can I be sure that won't happen to my baby?" Jesula's voice was quivering.

"Just in recent months the Americans set up employment offices in Santo Domingo. I suggest tomorrow morning, we get Etienna cleaned up and visit their offices down at the harbor. They are legitimate. That's where Jose got his job. But before we go, completely grasp the difference—Jose will come and go, but Etienna must promise not to leave her employer until she's eighteen years old. She'll then be free, but with no money to return. She'll need to make her own way in Panama at that point." Nia waited silently for a response.

"Oh Rosa, you and your sister are sent from the gods. Etienna, all we can ask for is your safety. Are you okay with this, my precious?" asked Jesula, gently holding Etienna's hands.

"No, but I have to be, Momma. But why can't you go with me?" Etienna asked as she sobbed.

"Honey, you heard why. I'm too old and I have no money. But from your Voodoo teachings and what you'll learn from the Black Magic in Panama, we'll find a way to communicate. Now, let's get some rest. Nia, if you have a blanket, we're fine sleeping on the floor. I need to wash Etienna's dress. She can clean her shoes. All will be dry by morning from this ocean breeze. Then we'll visit the American offices. I so love you, Etienna, and our souls will always be together." Jesula and Etienna embraced again, each time a little longer and each time a little tighter.

"I love you, Momma."

"I love you, my brave Etienna."

3

THE FATE OF AN "X"

The four women crept carefully down the rotting stairs, emerging onto the street. The thick air created an immediate sweat on their bodies. The stench of recently cleared horse dung was pungent in their nostrils. The muddy streets were slippery from the evening rain.

People were sparse in the city at sunrise. The women made their way through the market, where the merchants were setting up their wares and displaying their livestock, preparing for their daily sales. As they approached the harbor, horse-drawn wagons pulled heavy sacks of sugar to the docks. Hordes of men like swarms of ants, unloaded the wagons, carried the sacks up the gangplanks and dumped them into the lower holds of the cargo ships. Fortunately, most of the beggars and traffickers were passed out in the gutters from their drug of choice the night before. The soldiers and police had not yet fully staffed the streets.

As they approached the American employment office, a line of thirty men and women left over from the day before sat in the muddy street. The doors were not open for the morning's interviews. By noon, the line would grow to five times its present size.

In the harbor, was the five-hundred-pound gorilla known as the *USS Prairie*, the warship that had delivered the American marines who invaded the city just a few months earlier. Not a single shot had been fired, defeating the Dominicans without a fight. The *USS Prairie* was a formidable reminder of who was now in charge of the island of Hispaniola and who should not be.

As a swarm of people mushroomed in front of the employment offices, three American soldiers appeared in full dress uniforms, wearing white gloves, standing at attention in front of the door. One had a clipboard in hand, the other two with rifles and bayonets. The one with the clipboard began to speak loudly and theatrically. "All those looking for work on the freighters, form a line in front of this man with the rifle. To do so, you must be a male between sixteen and forty years of age and in good health. All of you looking for domestic work in Panama, form a line in front of the woman in uniform directly to my left. "To be in this line, you must be female, under age fifteen, and with a parent or legal guardian. If your daughter is chosen, you will receive five dollars for her, when and only when she is securely on the ship and the ship has left the harbor. She will need to pass a physical, which you are required to attend with her." The soldier had barked these instructions a thousand times. "If she has tuberculosis, polio, venereal disease, a skin rash, or is pregnant, she will not be accepted. She must also be a Christian. No Voodoo backgrounds will be accepted. Do not waste our time if any of these are the case. If anyone gets in line behind you, tell them of these requirements." With that, part of the crowd walked off.

"Jesula, anything they should know about?" Nia asked.

Jesula looked at Rosa. "We are Christians, right Rosa? That Catholic priest came by our neighborhood and talked to us last week. And Etienna and I told him we accepted Jesus Christ as our sword and savior."

"Not sword, Jesula, Lord, Lord and savior." Rosa shook her head.

They all looked away from each other and almost laughed for the first time in days.

As the sun climbed higher as it approached noonday. No one yet entered the colonial offices as the lines continued to grow. "Is this for real, Nia?" asked Jesula.

"I'm sure it is, but this waiting is unusual. It went quick when my husband applied. The Americans know the Dominicans are not fond of them. Part of this employment thing is so we will like them. They're understaffed and lack the numbers, but they have the guns and cannons.

There's probably some sort of rebellion in town somewhere. We'll stay here in line all night if we must. Rosa and I will go up the street and get some bread and water. You two wait in line." Jesula and Etienna sat on the now dry ground and with no shade, waiting for the line to move.

At two o'clock, the doors finally opened, and one by one people entered. At three o'clock, Etienna and Jesula reached the front of the line. "Next," said the American guarding the entrance, still standing at attention, sweat running down his cheeks. Jesula and Etienna rose and walked their tired, soaked bodies through the ten-foot-high double doors. Once inside, they were dispassionately led to a desk, where they both stood in front of an old Panamanian man in a white shirt and dark blue pants.

"My name is Christian, and I'm from the country of Panama. We've made a treaty with the Americans, who are leasing our canal. We need young women to work as domestic servants for military officers, politicians from numerous countries, and corporate executives. Is that the reason you're here today? If not, we end this interview right now."

"Yes sir," said Jesula. "This is my daughter, Etienna. She's thirteen, and I'm concerned for her safety in our village in Haiti. You see, sir, there is—"

"I don't care why you're here, so save it. Have a seat, and we'll get started." Etienna and Jesula sat in the two worn wooden chairs in front of the interviewer's desk. He addressed Jesula. "My job is to recruit domestic labor to work in Panama. I will be brief, so you understand what is going to happen. We will ask few questions, then a physical examination will be performed on your daughter. Are you ready to begin?" Christian looked up from his paperwork at Jesula. She nodded. "You're her mother, correct? Can I see your identification and her birth certificate?"

"Yes sir, I'm her mother, but I gave birth to her in my house. She has no birth certificate. The Haitian government does not issue identification unless you're important." Jesula's hopes began to fade.

The clerk didn't look up. "Doesn't matter. She doesn't look over fifteen. Just give me some birthdate that says is under fifteen. If there is a problem, they'll turn her out on the street. I wouldn't worry about it. They need girls over there for many reasons. Let's keep going. I'll need you to sign this paper when I'm finished. It says you understand what's going to happen to your daughter." Etienna and Jesula sat on the edge of their chairs, holding hands, tears welling in their eyes. They both knew what he was about to say.

"We're taking girls under the age of fifteen to Panama. They will be purchased by Americans, Chinese, or other embassies, by high-ranking military personnel, of corporate executives to perform tasks such as laundry, housecleaning, shopping, and other petty domestic labor. She will receive no pay for these tasks or any other tasks. She will share a clean room with four to six other girls. She will be required to dress every day in a clean, unwrinkled uniform. She will be fed well. She will be taught to read, write, and mathematics through the age of eighteen. At the age of eighteen, depending on her quality of service to her family, she will either be offered a paying job with the family or be given three months to find a job in the private sector. Whatever job decision she makes at that point will no longer be the responsibility of the Panamanian government or the family involved."

He paused and looked at Jesula, who nodded her understanding. He then looked at Etienna, who did not meet his gaze directly but did nod her head.

"Let me make this clear, ladies, and this is where your signature is important. You understand this is in no way slavery. Slavery is against the law. It is considered human trafficking but is in no way sexual trafficking. Your daughter does, at any time, have the option to leave her domestic job, provided she pays back to the family her purchase price from the auction. She is free to enter the streets, work in the private sector or return here. But she will have no money, and Panama has strict laws against child labor. If she leaves her domestic contract, her only choice will be to work in the prostitution rings. And I assure you, that will not be a pleasant life. Is that clearly understood? Are you ready to sign our agreement? Or your X?"

Jesula looked at her daughter. The tears shining in Etienna's eyes were more than she could bear. "Do you understand, my love, if you don't follow their rules, you'll be worse off than you are now? Promise me you understand, and you'll follow their rules. I assure you, I'll get to you someday, and we'll be together once more."

"I do, Momma. I understand." Etienna started crying. She hugged Jesula. "Sign the paper, Momma, and let's finish this."

Jesula signed the paper and looked up at the clerk.

"Alright," he said, "I have a few questions." The clerk went through a list of basic questions. When Jesula finished answering, he looked at Jesula, "She will leave the day after tomorrow, on Wednesday, if she passes the physical. Is that a problem?"

Jesula shook her head no. The clerk told them to follow him. They entered a room that looked and smelled uncomfortably sterile. They were turned over to an overweight middle-aged woman. The woman's huge breasts strained the buttons on her all-white uniform. She wore a white hat, stockings, and shoes, along with a silver stethoscope around her neck.

"Thank you, Christian, you can leave us alone," the nurse said. "I'll bring her out to you when I'm finished." Once Christian was out of the room, the woman spoke to Etienna in an aloof and monotone voice. "Okay, young lady, take off all your clothes, lay on this table, and put your feet in these stirrups." Jesula helped her daughter's naked body onto the frigid metal table.

Once Etienna was in position, the nurse began her examination, continuing to speak in a tone as cold as the table. In fact, everything was cold, the table, the stethoscope, the floor, the instruments, and the nurse's heart.

"Has she had chicken pox, smallpox, measles, or any other kind of skin rash within the last three months?" the nurse questioned.

"No, ma'am," Jesula answered.

"Any fevers, coughs, dementia, vomiting, or diarrhea in the last three months?"

"No, ma'am," answered Jesula. "Only when we arrived yesterday, and she smelled the slaughterhouse. She did vomit a little." The nurse looked up at Jesula but ignored her answer.

"I can see by her vagina and stomach she has not had a baby. Is she a virgin? Her hymen is intact, which usually means there's not been intercourse, but I still must ask these questions. If she has had sex, how long ago, and was it incest?" asked the nurse.

"I think she's a virgin. She's never acted upset, like she was raped or even touched. And her father and brother are away fighting in the rebellion." Jesula knew she should not have said that. "Haven't seen them in a while. We don't even know if they are alive," answered Jesula.

"Momma, I'm a virgin. I swear, Momma," said Etienna. Both Jesula and the nurse smiled at each other. Jesula stroked Etienna's hair as she lay on the cold table.

"She's not had any long-term coughing, coughing up blood, or chest pain? Blood in her urine? Black stool? Has she lost weight lately?"

"No, not at all. The answer is no to all of those," said Jesula.

"Sounds clear of tuberculosis and skin diseases. I see all her limbs are strong and well proportioned, so no polio. All right, young lady, put your clothes back on, and you can both go back out to see Christian. Take this paper from me to clear your health. And young lady, do exactly what they tell you to do in Panama and the treaty will protect you. Stay away from the boys and men when you arrive. If you have a baby over there, they'll take it from you or throw you both out. You'll have time when you're older to play with the boys and have a family. Good luck, precious one, and may God watch over you," said the nurse with an uncharacteristic smile.

As Jesula watched Etienna dress, she wondered if her daughter passing the physical was a good thing or a death warrant. They went to the desk, where Jesula handed over the form from the physical. They waited for the clerk to look up.

"Okay, ladies, be on the dock outside this building. Look for me at Gangplank on Wednesday at eight o'clock. The ship's name is *The Cullen – Panama*. We'll load you girls onto the freighter, and you'll be off to Panama with American military guards protecting you. There will be no more questions. You know all you need to know if you were listening." The clerk turned away, as the next mother and daughter approached his desk.

Jesula and Etienna turned to leave, but suddenly, the clerk called to them. "Wait, wait, I did forget to ask. I assume your daughter is a Christian?" Jesula turned to face him once more. This was her chance to bust this deal. She looked at Etienna, their eyes met. Jesula looked at the clerk and nodded her head. "Yes sir, Lord and Savior." They exited through the colonial doors and joined Nia and Rosa in the street. No one said a word on the walk home, except Jesula. "There, Wednesday, eight o'clock. Ship's name is *The Cullen – Panama*," she said, so choked up she could hardly get those words to the surface.

4

GOODBYE MOMMA, GOODBYE MY LOVE

Jesula and Etienna slept on Nia's floor, holding each other all night long. Tuesday was the shortest and longest day of their lives together. They strolled through the marketplace, holding hands and turning spontaneously every few moments to hug. Even though they both wanted to call the departure off, they were aware it was the only safe choice for Etienna's safety and happiness. If she remained in Haiti, it would be a sad and tragic ending. They knew a different type of emotional desolation was approaching to touch their deepest passions.

Wednesday morning arrived too quickly. All four women awoke before sunrise. No luggage for Etienna, since she had only one dress to wear, and she was wearing it. They ate johnnycakes dipped in goat's milk, made their way down the stairs to the street, then headed toward the harbor; nothing was said. The streets were deserted, but that morning, they felt forsaken and forlorn. Etienna considered running wishfully into nonexistence. Jesula wanted to grab her daughter's hand and find sanctuary where the two of them could hide from the world in peace for the rest of their lives. They continued to walk.

They reached the colonial building where Christian, and the nurse stood with a sign that read *The Cullen – Panama*. A few girls and their families had arrived earlier. All the girls were wearing worn and tattered dresses, the same as Etienna. The clerk held a clipboard with a list of forty names and a series of five check boxes next to each.

As Jesula and Etienna approached the clerk, he asked, "Name."

"Jesula Gabriel and Etienna Gabriel," Jesula answered.

"We don't need yours, Momma, just your daughter's," he said curtly. "Have your daughter step over here and see the nurse. She'll need to check your daughter one more time before she boards the ship. We take no chances with our cargo. Go behind that sheet with the nurse, young lady."

After another quick check-up, mostly for last minute sperm from love making, the two came out. "She's all clear," said the nurse to the clerk. "Honey, you can stand there with your mother until we call your name." Jesula held Etienna in her arms until the dreaded moment arrived. The clerk checked off another box on his clipboard.

When the roll call of girls began, it went rapidly. "Etienna Gabriel, up the gangplank." Etienna and Jesula turned and hugged on last time. "No more goodbyes young lady, I'm sure you and your momma have said more than enough. Go, right now." shouted the clerk.

Etienna detached from Jesula, their hands sliding apart as in slow motion, their eyes holding on as long as possible. She ascended the ramp, looking back every few steps, waving to her mother and sobbing. She was tempted to run back to her momma's arms and take her chances in Haiti. In that moment, Etienna thought it would be better to die in the arms of her momma than never see her again. When she reached the top, a soldier snagged her arm and swiftly moved her away. She let him lead her, but with the hope she would someday be reunited in the loving embrace of her mother. But that would never happen.

Jesula turned to Rosa and fell into her embrace. She totally broke down, wailing desperately, as she collapsed to her knees.

"Do you want to leave now or stay until the ship sails away?" asked Rosa gently.

"I have to wait until the steamer is out of site for the money, remember?" said Jesula just before she turned and vomited on a crate. "That sounds terrible, Rosa. I'm waiting for five dollars. I sold my little love for five dollars, five dollars, Rosa."

"No, honey, you didn't sell your daughter. You gave her a chance at a life you and I will never have in Haiti. That five dollars means nothing to you," said Rosa with a compassionate smile.

"I want to buy something with the money that will always remind me of our love for each other, "replied Jesula. As Rosa looked around, the entire dock was a scene of mourning. And from the dock, all anyone could hear was the faint sobbing and crying of the mothers' daughters in the distance.

A thundering low-pitched horn bellowed from the ship, and the tugs began to launch the freighter from the pier. There was no sign of the girls waving one last goodbye, just men scurrying around the deck, untying ropes, and watching the shore from the rails. After thirty minutes, the ship was out of sight, only steam could barely be seen rising from the horizon.

"Okay, let's get the money and get out of here. I'll never return here for the rest of my life," said Jesula as she got in line with the other forty women waiting for their money.

When she got to the clerk, he asked for her name again.

"Etienna Gabriel," said Jesula. She remembered not to give her own name this time.

"Sorry, you already got your money, Momma. Don't try to con me. I know your Haitian tricks. At least one of your kind tries this every day. Now, get out of here before I call a soldier." Jesula didn't know whether to be confused or furious, or both.

"No, I'm her mother. Look again on your sheet. I never got any money," Jesula said, trying to stay calm.

"She's Etienna's mother, Christian, for sure. I remember her," said the nurse.

"I don't care if she's your mother, Nursie. She's trying to get paid twice. I know these Haitian bitches. They lie and cheat whenever they can. They send someone up early to get the money, saying they are somebody's momma, then they come up near the end and say they never got paid. Or one of the other bitches just listens for a name when we call them out to board and uses it to get somebody else's money. Either way, what do you expect me to do, take it out of my own pocket? Get her out of here before I have her arrested, Nursie," said the clerk.

"You asshole, I know what you're doing. You're keeping our money for yourself," said Jesula, so angry she was ready to kill him. "You're the crook, you goddamn bastard. What else do you have in store for our little girls? God, I hate men."

Suddenly, two soldiers heard the commotion and came over. "Everything okay, Christian?" said one of the guards. Both had fingers on their triggers.

"Just get this crazy wench out of here. She's just angry because she sold her daughter for a measly five dollars and didn't even get that. Life and family mean nothing to those people in Haiti. They disgust me," said the clerk.

But before one of the guards could grab her by the arm, Jesula reached out and yanked a patch of hair from the clerk's head. "I'm not done with you yet," she said. "And you'll never see me again." Jesula stormed off with Rosa and Nia, the bit of hair tucked safely in her white-knuckled grip. Neither the nurse nor the clerk said a word as they departed. The terrible man simply stood there in stunned silence, rubbing his scalp.

The nurse glared at Christian with vicious eyes. She'd seen him pull this scam on every shipment of girls since she started. But she would lose her job if she spoke up. She thought, *how can a man, especially named Christian, cheat these poor mothers out of anything on the saddest day of their lives?* The nurse knew why Jesula had grabbed a patch of his hair. She'd noticed the pentagram on a chain around Jesula's neck, hidden inside her blouse. *Clerkie has some rough times in front of him.*

5

VOYAGE TO THE UNKNOWN

Soldiers herded the girls to the middle of the main deck where a lanky old man carrying a rifle and wearing an American marine uniform instructed them to sit cross-legged inside a red painted circle. They were ordered to be silent and keep their crying to a minimum. They tried to stretch their necks to see their mothers one last time, but they could not see over the gunwale of the ship. The tugboats maneuvered into position as the freighter's horn droned two long, deep blasts. Forty innocent seeds were launched into future generations, crammed like lambs into a cage of uncertainty.

As the ship reached the point where it could navigate from the harbor under its own power, the tugs freed the ship to a life of its own. Nothing but the roofs of buildings and tops of trees were visible from the deck. The lanky marine approached the painted circle to address the girls, as well as the crew. The crew was ordered to keep its distance, well behind the other subordinate marine guards. Other than an occasional involuntary sob or the sound of the bow cutting through the waves, the crew could be heard whispering and chuckling among themselves as they fantasized about the fun they would have with the little girls on their two-day orgy.

The soldier cleared his throat. "Ladies and crew, since most of you speak Spanish, I will say what I have to say in your native language, and I will only say it once. If anyone breaks my rules, you will receive severe punishment. I hope that's understood, ladies and crew." He paused a moment to let it sink in. Silence and disappointment came over the crew, like the moment their rum bottle was empty.

"First, to the crew, these girls are corporate property. They'll be placed in two storage holds, covered, and locked under steel grates. Only I and the captain of this ship have the keys. This cargo of girls is owned by the Pan/Am Canal Zone Trading Company, a partnership owned equally by the American and Panamanian governments, formed as part of the Panama Canal one-hundred-year lease. It is my job to ensure these girls arrive in Panama City untouched, unharmed, and unscathed. They are to be clean and healthy when they stand on the auction block and bring top dollar to the partnership. Any man attempting to get at them, or even approach the holds, will be shot. If not killed, you will be locked in the brig and turned over to the Panamanian authorities when we dock." The news was met with grumbles. "My four armed soldiers will guard the area. Your captain on the bridge is bound to uphold these rules as well, meaning anyone breaking them is committing mutiny and could be hanged. Now you can all get back to your duties."

The crew mumbled as they returned to their stations, securing the sugar cargo for its journey across the Caribbean.

"Now ladies," began the soldier, "my name is Lieutenant Matthews. These four soldiers are my assistants, and their only job is to protect you until we reach the auction house in Panama City. We're now going to take you to the front of the ship, where you will be divided into two groups. When instructed, you will climb down a wooden ladder into one of the two cargo holds. When you reach the bottom of the hold, you will remove all articles of clothing, yes, including underwear, and put them in a basket which we will provide on the floor of the hold."

A few gasps emanated from the circle of girls. They glanced at each other, moving only their eyes. With the thought of total nudity, they wondered if their mommas were tricked, and they were now sex slaves. But the soldier said they would be protected. They hugged themselves and began to shiver in fear, but they continued to listen to the soldier.

"When all of you are naked, we will pull the basket onto the deck and store your clothes until we reach Panama City. We do this because most of you have never been on a ship at sea, which means most of you will be seasick most of the journey. Your being naked makes it easy to hose the vomit, diarrhea, and piss off you and the floors. Your clothes will be unstained and dry when we reach Panama. And your stench will be bearable to the crew."

"You will be fed twice per day, and water will be lowered to you twice per day. And depending on how rough the seas become, we will hose you down when I decide you need it. You'll be hungry and thirsty, but I'm sure most of you are used to that in the poor villages you came from. And do not, I repeat, do not drink any of the sea water, or you will be a very sick little girl."

"As you heard me say, me and my men will protect you from the crew. However, our company has agreed to allow the five of us to visit you pretty little colored girls one at a time down in the hole as long as I'm watching. These men know the rules, and they know I'll report them if they cross a line. They're not allowed to touch you, but you will be required to touch them with your hands or mouth if they request it. It is a thank you to us old soldiers for protecting you."

Etienna had never touched a man like that before. Looking at the soldiers, she pictured them in her mouth. It was a disgusting thought. Touching them with her hand, well, not so bad, she thought. Then she remembered the nurse telling her to do whatever they told her to do. Etienna tried to wipe the picture from her mind, but she was already feeling dirty and defiled.

The lieutenant had the girls stand up, and the guards escorted them to the cargo holds. They climbed down the ladders, took off all their clothing, and placed them in the basket. The baskets were lifted, and the grates were closed and locked. When the ship hit the high sea, the vomiting was instantaneous. Shortly after, diarrhea muddied the holds. The last days with her mother were sad but loving. Now Etienna felt anger. This was horrid. She felt she was being treated like an animal.

How could these men treat us like pigs in a squalid pigpen? I'm still a little girl and now without a momma. This smell of bile is detestable. I thought we weren't allowed to have rashes, but that girl over there has a bloody one. She gets anywhere close to me; I'll kick her into the wall. Then I'm going to have some ugly old man stick his wanker in my mouth. Now I know why momma says she hates men. Going to be a long two days, Etienna thought. She was shocked by a reality unknown to her, and feelings utterly foreign. She didn't like them, but they were now implanted in her soul as if demons invaded from hell. Etienna looked around. No pleasant conversation was being exchanged; no love or sympathy; only tears and sobs. Their sadness was turning to ire with each new stream of vomit and diarrhea.

6

THE RESURRECTION

It was noon when the freighter approached the newly opened harbor at the mouth of the Panama Canal to unload its cargo of sweet sugar and young, but not so sweet girls. The sea was calmed as they came closer to shore. The air was hot and humid. The girls in the holds were nauseated, hungry, and dehydrated. The high seas were angry this time of year. The entire trip, the girls slid back and forth on floors made of metal slats, spaced far enough apart to allow their waste to funnel into the sea. Their buttocks, backs, and elbows were scrapped raw and stung terribly when hosed with salt water. And the girls were exhausted from a lack of sleep. But nothing compared to the emotional suffering from leaving their mommas and the anxiety of the unknown.

"Okay, ladies," the lieutenant yelled to the girls below. "We're approaching the Panama City harbor. We will begin a thorough cleanup process. No more vomiting, pissing, or shitting in the hold. If you're going to do it, get it over with now when the seas are calm. The ocean is behind you forever."

They hadn't fed the girls for the last twelve hours, so they were empty, with an occasional dry heave or expelling of gas. Suddenly, bars of lye soap and rough rags rained down from the grates above.

"We're pulling the big hoses over here this time, the ones used to clean the decks. the stream will be forceful, not like the buckets we've been dropping on you. Between the salt water and the lye soap, protect your eyes, ladies. It will burn, maybe damage them. We don't want anybody appearing to have pink eye or infection. Soap up those rags and wash yourselves off as we hose you down from up here. Clean yourselves well, including your hair and your girly parts. You'll have about five minutes."

Two hoses, one for each hold, started the showering process. The water was warm, and it was the first pleasant thing the little girls had felt since Santo Domingo. When all finished their cleansing, the lieutenant yelled down once again. "Ladies, we must anchor here for another hour until the tugs get us. You should be dry by then. Then we give all of them horny crew members a treat." Etienna frowned at the amusement in his voice. She knew any treat for the crew would be altogether unpleasant and disrespectful for them.

"You will climb up the ladder naked," the lieutenant explained, "three at a time from each hold. The dresses, undies, and shoes you came with will be in one big pile. We washed and rinsed your clothes the best we could to remove the stench of your stinky little bodies. They should be mostly dry. If not, the breeze will finish the job. Find your clothes and sit in the painted circle. The guards will be surrounding you in case one of the crew tries something stupid. And no more crying. Look like you're happy to be here. You'll get a better place to live, the happier you appear. Nobody wants a crybaby working for them. You should be happy being out of your godforsaken Voodoo land. Okay, first three, climb up. I'll help you if you're not smart enough to count."

The girls scaled the ladders naked and dug through the pile to find their clothing. The crew stood on the upper decks watching and whistling, laughing, and pushing each other like schoolboys. Some stood quietly and stared, with one of their hands down their pants. As Etienna emerged into the sunlight, she smelled the fresh aromatic breeze. It reminded her of wash day in Haiti, her momma hanging their laundry on the clothesline. But the funk in the hold was still fresh in her mind, a smell that kept Etienna's throat tight. She forced her mind to dwell on someplace else, any place other than where she had slopped around for two days. As she rummaged through the pile for her shoes and dress, she could feel the eyes of the sailors focused, like hungry wolves, on her petite black body.

She knew she was safe. The old guards would protect her, even though they made her touch them a few times a day. But only once with her mouth. All the time, the lieutenant watched. Why he never came down was a mystery.

At last, all were on deck and clothed, sitting tightly inside the circle. The tugs took their positions, and within an hour, the freighter was docked. Etienna's heart pounded with anxiety, like voodoo drums at a village burial. She could hear that same beat. What now? Many of the girls hugged and rocked themselves, trembling with fear thinking about the world at the end of the gangplank. They remained within the circle while the crew unloaded the cargo and disembarked from the ship. The lieutenant then addressed them.

"Here we go, ladies, your new home. For your protection, the crew has left the ship. We will now take you, five at a time, to wagons and transport you to where you will stay for the two nights before the auction. We took good care of you and protected you to this point. But if I don't deliver all of you to the auction house safely and unharmed, I don't get paid. And I mean all of you, not thirty-nine. So, if any of you try to run, me and my boys don't get paid. I won't be happy, and neither will my boys. And if you do run, you will be scooped up in this city faster than a piece of roadkill by a buzzard. You will be rammed in every hole in your body like a chunk of street meat by every dirty pervert until you finally die of some sex disease. Or they will beat you to death. So, climb into those horse-drawn wagons. Me and the boys will walk on both sides to protect our payday. Got it?" The girls either nodded their heads or just looked down at the ground and followed the girl in front of them. The lieutenant had made his point. Nobody was going to attempt an escape.

The wagons didn't travel far from the dock. The streets were bustling and congested with other wagons, carrying everything from fruits and vegetables to crates of clothing to livestock. Etienna smelled the earthy odor of horse dung and the pungent scent of blood from the slaughterhouses, like Santo Domingo. But unlike her first whiff of Santo Domingo, none of this was as grotesque as their own human stench in the hold of the ship.

As the horses clopped down the dirt streets, they approached a gate guarded by two handsome Panamanian soldiers. The lieutenant handed the soldiers a roster of names, and they went to the back of each wagon and counted the girls. One soldier signed the lieutenant's paperwork and opened the gate. The wagons passed through the black iron bars.

The building was the most colossal, majestic building Etienna had ever seen. She was sure it must be a palace with a king and queen inside; it was three stories high and made of white marble. The entrance to the palace was edged with carved pillars on each side of two tall, rounded doors. A Panamanian flag hung with nobility above the doors. The roof was the most breathtaking shade of green. As the wagons went up the semicircle driveway leading to the entrance, Etienna thought, *oh my goodness, we might be going to work there, and we are going in those big, beautiful doors.* But suddenly, the horses took a quick right turn and journeyed to the rear of the building, where the wagons pulled to a halt. Four women in formal white nurse uniforms exited from a steel door; the windows were barred. The lieutenant handed the paperwork to one of the nurses, a large woman with a serious countenance. She reminded Etienna of the nurse in Santo Domingo. The girls, whose legs were weakened and bruised from the trip, were helped from the wagons. When all were unloaded, the lieutenant was given a handful of balboas for the forty girls, the door was shut, his job done. No good-byes or thank you were warranted by either side.

The girls were convoyed single file straight into a long barracks-type room with a row of narrow beds against opposite walls, made up with perfectly clean white sheets and perfectly spaced equidistance from each other. A bathroom with multiple sinks, tubs, toilets, and a large gang shower could be seen through the archway at the end. Each girl was positioned in front of their assigned bed, facing each other. The big nurse spoke.

"Girls, for the next two days, you will be safer than you have ever been in your lives. Know that only my nurses are permitted in this area. If some brainless man tries to sneak in, the law says he will be hanged, and I promise you, he will be." Etienna noticed the other nurses putting on special attire, as the head nurse b\started her inspection. She continued to speak, looking each girl intensely in the eyes as she passed them. She did not move on until she was convinced the girl acknowledged her power and her seriousness.

"Our job is simple; to sell you to families in need of servants for the highest possible price. The purchasing family will be responsible to clothe, feed, house, protect, and educate you, but only as long as you do precisely what their head servant tells you to do." The nurse came to the end of the aisle, turned, and gazed back. She squinched her nose. "First, everybody takes off those disgusting smelly rags you call clothes and shoes. I swear, those old soldier boys think they impress us by washing you and your clothes before you arrive. They're idiots. We're going to collect them in baskets and burn them all. If you have a pin or a piece of jewelry that is special to you, take it off now. Keep it in your hand until you get your new clothing." Etienna thought *That is the first kind thing anyone has done for any of us since the nurse in Santo Domingo.* She wanted to cry and hug the nurse.

As the head nurse continued, two nurses wearing leather aprons, masks, and rubber gloves pushed wicker baskets down the aisle. The girls threw their peasant apparel into the baskets as they went by. "We take no chances with lice, bedbugs, roach eggs, or anything you poor little creatures may have toted with you from afar. Next, you'll all need to crowd into that glass room over there, and for God's sake, don't touch the beds on the way or we must burn those sheets as well." The girls moved into the center of the room and listened to the nurse.

"My assistant nurses," she pointed to the other end of the room where the baskets were taken for incineration, "will take four at a time from the glass room, immerse you in the tubs behind me, wash your hair, and scrub your skin thoroughly. It may hurt a bit, but you will be clean. Let us know if you're bleeding this time of the month. We'll scrub you in the shower. After your cleansing, you will be sprayed with chemicals that destroy any insects I mentioned along with any other type of pests still living on your bodies. From there, my nurses will check your ears, nose, and private parts for anything dead or still alive and attempting to hide. They will check your mouths for rotting teeth or gum diseases. They'll test your hearing and eyesight. When all is done, you will have a number tattooed on your buttocks to correlate with your health report. It'll be small, so the chance of infection will be slim; however, it will sting for a short period of time." The head nurse, now standing rigid with her hands behind her back, smiled. "When you are cleaner than you ever imagined, probably a shade or two and a pound or two lighter, you will be given soft fresh gowns and slippers. You will be led to the dining area, where we begin the process of improving your health for auction." It was the first time, even before the harbor in Santo Domingo, that cute smiles surfaced on the girls' faces as the thought of real food entered their minds.

The nurse stomped her foot to regain the girls' attention. "In the end, all of this health preparation determines how much the bidders will pay for you. The healthier you appear, the higher the price, and the higher the price, the better the family. We will feed you well, give you medication to kill the parasites inside your guts, and give you plenty of clean water and rest. Okay, girls, let's all get healthy and happy."

In a weak voice, Etienna blurted, "What if nobody bids on me and nobody wants me? My momma's friend says I'm not very pretty." The nurse gave Etienna a warmhearted smile, then looked around the room at all the girls.

"We'll find somewhere for all of you, I promise," answered the nurse. "I want no more questions like that. Let's get started. Everybody's naked, so let's get those nasty varmints off you and down the drain. You're all about to be young ladies." They made their way to the glass room, some walking, some limping on their bruised and wounded legs.

For the next two days, Etienna felt the most comfortable she ever felt in her life, physically, at least. She was well fed, well clothed, clean, and rested. She slept without fear of soldiers, snakes, scorpions, or rats. But the big nurse's words played on "repeat" in her mind, '*We will find somewhere for all of you.*' She could hear the lieutenant's words echo through her head, 'street meat.'

* * * *

The day of the auction arrived quickly, too quickly for most of the girls. They were bathed once more, their hair trimmed and groomed, and their armpits shaved and sprayed. They were given spotless white dresses, along with sandals exposing their feet for inspection of fungus or deformity. They would stand against the wall around the room with their numbers pinned to their dresses, the number that correlated to their health record and their tattoo. The bidders, well-dressed aristocratic woman accompanied by their head female servants or butlers, would walk around the room, inspect the health records, and attempt to carry on a conversation. This would take an hour in total. Then the girls, still standing against the wall, would wait for their number to be called. A nurse behind a curtain would confirm their number with their tattoo. The girls would then stand on the auction block and the bidding would.

Before the inspection began, the big nurse scanned the girls for any obvious flaws. Even from a distance, she detected Etienna was scared. The nurse approached her. "What is it, girl? Not good, not good at all to look scared. If you continue to shake, or worse, faint, it will appear something wrong with you. So, what is your problem, dearie?"

"What if no one wants me. That lieutenant man said we would become 'street meat' if we were on our own. I think I know what that is," said Etienna, trying to hold back her tears.

"Girly, girly, girly," the big nurse said as she shook her head and studied Etienna's physical report. "You are number twelve. You have one tooth that needs pulled, and those scars on your back from only a few beatings. All you girls have those. You appear strong, your smile is kind, and when you speak, you talk politely and respectfully. And, if you think they speak English, tell them so in English. It is important here. And you're not pretty and have no breasts to speak of. Beauty and breasts are not good, especially if there is a husband the wife doesn't trust. You'll be taken, I'm sure of it. Just be sweet and stand up tall. I promise dearie, someone will take you. I think you're the best of the bunch. I can feel it. Your powers are strong, and you exude kindness."

"Thank you," said Etienna. "You're the nicest person, other than my momma, I have ever met."

The big nurse offered Etienna a forced smile. She thought *what a sad life this poor child has had if I'm the nicest person she's ever met.*

The inspection began. Bidders asked Etienna questions, both in Spanish and in English. And although her English was more Haitian Creole than American English, it was acceptable and could be polished.

The bidding started. "Number twelve, come to the stage," said the auctioneer. Etienna, still nervous as any young girl would be, approached the stage. She walked tall and stood up straight like the nurse had instructed, but she did not swing her arms. They stayed right by her side. It was innocently cute.

Etienna went behind the curtain. "Tattoo please," the nurse asked. Etienna lifted her dress high enough to expose the number *12*. "Okay, honey, walk to the stage and stand in the middle. And hey, smile darlin'."

Etienna took the stage, smiled a humble and lovely smile, and like the big nurse suggested, continued to stand straight and tall. She could feel her legs starting to shake.

A bid was placed on her before the auctioneer could say a word. Etienna's eyes widened as she took a happy breath. With that she realized she would not be cast into the street.

The bidding ended. A well-dressed Chinese woman in her mid-twenties approached the cashier. Etienna was sold for twenty-eight balboas. Next to the woman stood a large black Panamanian woman, with huge breasts and buttocks, wearing a maid's uniform and a beautiful purple bandana.

"Welcome," the woman said to Etienna in English with a Chinese accent. "Eda, my head maid, was impressed with you, young lady. She can use a helper who speaks English. My husband works at the Chinese Embassy, and we both had to learn English for him to get the job. Your shoulders look like you have done heavy housework," she observed. "Eda, I think Mr. Chang will be pleased with your selection. And I believe I will as well. Do you speak any Chinese, child? And what is your name?"

"No, ma'am, only Spanish and Creole English. But I would like to learn. My name is Etienna, Etienna Gabriel, ma'am. Thank you so much for giving me a job. I wish I could tell my momma back in Haiti how wonderful you and Eda are," said Etienna, her voice shaking as she held back her tears of relief. "I will work very hard, ma'am, and do whatever you ask."

"Your mother raised you well, sweet child. She would be proud right now. I'm sure she must miss you terribly. We have heard stories about the dangers to the Haitian girls due to the revolution. You're safe here if you do what we ask. I can't imagine giving up my daughter for her own safety.

Let's go home, Eda." With that, the Chinese woman began walking to her carriage, followed by Eda and Etienna.

Approaching the exit door of the auction room, Etienna spotted the big nurse standing against the wall. Taking Eda by surprise, Etienna suddenly veered off and gave the head nurse a devoted hug. Both said farewell with tears in their eyes as they parted ways. The nurse smiled and called to Etienna, "New country, new life, new mother. Bless you, my little angel."

1919-INNOCENCE LOST AND NEW LIFE BEGINS

Etienna was an indentured servant for the Changs approaching four years her seventeenth birthday only a few months away. She was developing into an eminently handsome and mature young woman. Her intelligence placed her in the upper echelon of her class. She voluntarily learned enough Chinese to converse with the Chang family and their guests, something Eda had not conquered. She was invaluable at dinner parties. Mrs. Chang praised Eda often for her excellent choice of servants.

Etienna, although often pondering the safety of her mother, now she had a female family of her own. She shared a dorm room with three co-workers, and now was the oldest of Eda's staff. Two of the girls were let go on their eighteenth birthdays. Where they went no one knew. Etienna was aware of her eighteenth birthday looming, and turning seventeen would be a crucial reminder. Her anxiety was building.

"Etienna, Mr. Chang's brother is in the study. He would like you to bring him a pot of tea and johnnycakes. I will have them ready in a moment," Eda called.

"Eda, can one of the other girls take it to him? I have some studying to do for my algebra exam tomorrow," Etienna asked in a pleading sort of way.

"No, child, he absolutely insists on you. He asserts you are the only one of the girls he can converse with in Chinese and the only one capable of following his directions. He also said he finds your Haitian heritage intriguing," said Eda. "He's an extremely intelligent and powerful man. I guess that is why he spends such time working in Mr. Chang's study."

Etienna's anxiety secretly heightened when she was asked to serve Mr. Chang's brother, but as she was ordered, she grabbed the tray and pressed on to the study. Mr. Chang brought his son with him and insisted he play chess with his cousin at the other end of the mansion, so she knew he arranged to be alone in the study. Etienna knocked on the door, her heart began to pound. Mr. Chang's brother opened the door with a beguiling smile. "Well, come in my child. Place the tea on the desk, please. Do you know when my brother will return home?" he asked Etienna.

"Eda said he and Mrs. Chang would be back in a few hours. They had a business dinner. I think he left a number where he can be reached. I will get it right away, sir. It is in the kitchen," she promptly answered.

"No, just wanted to know when they would return," he said. "Continue to pour my tea and prepare the bread and butter for me on the plate, please."

She finished organizing the refreshments on the desk, but when she turned around, Mr. Chang's brother was behind her. "Did you do what I told you to do whenever you bring me tea, child?" he whispered in a low sinister voice. "Did you take your bra and panties off?"

"Please sir, you promised never again. You said you would leave me alone. You said you were tired of me. Please don't force me to do this again, please sir. You have a wife and children, sir. And you refuse to wear a condom. If I wind up with a problem, I'll be expelled from this house and into the streets. Please, sir, please no."

He pushed her over the desk and threw the skirt of her dress up onto her back. When he saw she still had her panties on, he let out a disappointed sigh and yanked them down to her ankles. Within minutes, it was over; he was finished. Sperm was running down her inner thighs to her ankles, then onto her shoes and socks. Etienna whimpered softly as she pulled her panties back into place, now moistened by this man's vile conduct.

1919-INNOCENCE LOST AND NEW LIFE BEGINS

"Stop your whimpering, child. You know the rules. Don't ever say a word to anyone about this, or you'll never work in this city again, except for the traffickers. And if that happens, I'll never touch you again, you little whore. Do you understand?" Etienna placed a hand over her mouth, muffling her cries as he continued his threats. "And I promise, I' will have you killed before my wife finds out. Now, take the tray and leave the tea and bread. I'll see you next time my brother and his wife are away. I said go." he snapped in a nasty tone as he went to the bathroom to clean himself.

Etienna returned to the kitchen and cleaned the tray. She tried to hide her tears from Eda, but suddenly a loud sob burst from her. "What is it, child? Are you getting worried about approaching eighteen and having to leave us? That's still over a year away. I've been discussing that with Mrs. Chang, and—" Eda stopped suddenly and looked at something white on Etienna's leg, staining her shoes and ankle socks.

"Oh, no." Eda said. "Is that from Mr. Chang's son or nephew? Those boys' hormones will get them and us in such trouble. Panama has a 'close-in-age' law, so they can't be arrested for statutory rape. But they're getting to that teenage time none of us have dealt with. Let me talk to them. But we must keep it from our parents. If Mrs. Chang knew, she might just fire you to avoid a problem. Which one was it? Please don't tell me both?"

"Neither." Etienna buried her face in Eda's breast and continued to cry.

"Oh no, honey, Mr. Chang's brother? It was his brother? That's not good, not good at all. Is this the first time?" asked Eda. Etienna shook her head no. "So that's why he only comes over when Mr. and Mrs. Chang are gone. He thinks you'll say nothing, and he can continue to go up your skirt for another year until you're gone. How long, child? How many times?"

"About six months, a few times a month. As long as it's me," Etienna said quietly, "the other girls are safe. I am the oldest."

"No, it's against the law, plain and simple. It's against everybody's law. You're under eighteen, and even the Canal Zone laws protect you. Not if he was Panamanian, but he's a foreigner. His wife and Mr. and Mrs. Chang will be furious. Let me give this some thought, dear, and I'll talk to Mr. Chang. I will tell him the entire story. He's a good man. In the meantime,

I'll tell his brother, if he touches you again, I'll call the police myself. My job is to protect all of you, and Mr. and Mrs. Chang," said Eda. Etienna hugged Eda even tighter.

"I missed my last period. And I'm getting sick in the morning like my momma told me she was with me and my brother. And my breasts hurt. Eda, I think I'm pregnant." Etienna's voice broke as she choked on her own words.

"Could anyone else be the father, my sweet child?" asked Eda.

"No." Etienna turned away and ran crying to her dorm room.

8

THE FAMILY CHAT

Li Chang summoned his brother Ju-Long by phone and set up a meeting in the study. He told his brother he had an important business venture to discuss, and Ju-Long scampered over right away. As Ju-Long entered the study, Mr. Chang was situated behind his desk in his high-backed leather chair. "Have a seat, my brother." Ju-Long took a seat in the side chair across from Mr. Chang.

"Ju-Long, how are you? Can I get you anything? What if I have Etienna bring you some tea and bread?" Mr. Chang sarcastically suggested, staring into his brother's eyes, getting right to the point. "Then I could leave the two of you alone for a few minutes, so you can talk."

"Excuse me, Li, why would I need to talk to one of your girls?" asked Ju-Long, shrugging his shoulders, and looking as guilty as a young shoplifter.

"Exactly, you stupid idiot, she is one of my girls. Not one of my women, one of my girls. They are all under eighteen. Damn you brother, I would have your balls cut off if it were up to me. What you are doing is not only rape, but also statutory rape. My Panamanian servant wants to call the police and have you put in jail right now. Eda told me the whole story. And you bent her over my desk, you disgusting pervert? There are even stains on my carpet. I should make you get on your knees and clean those stains with your tongue." Li was furious.

"C'mon, Li, really," said Ju-Long. "You telling me you never stuck your penis in one of your little Negro girls? Our wives aren't getting any younger. Don't lie to me, big brother."

"No, brother, no, no, no. We're Buddhist, and you're telling me you don't honor the third of our five precepts. Along with adultery, you did the worst, the most heinous. You have taken sexual advantage of someone unable to defend themselves. A young girl, a servant, whom all cultures living in Panama promised to protect from sexual trafficking and you, one of the privileged, raped a helpless, terror-stricken girl of sixteen. And Ju-Long, are you ready for this? You're going to be a father."

Ju-Long stared over the desk with a stone-cold grimace. "Whoa, that little girl is lying to trap us. It's only been a dozen times over the last six months, what are the chances? I bet she's also fucking delivery boy or two. Let's just call her a liar and kick her to the street. I'm your brother, protect me from this little wench. She's just a little Negro girl. Protect me, brother."

"Protect you? Damn you, Ju-Long, give it up. I don't care if she's orange or green or purple. That's an obscene comment. She's a good girl, and I assure you, she wouldn't lie. She says you're the only man she's ever been with, and you know that. That baby is going to be born looking half-Chinese. What then?" Li was on the palms of his hands, leaning across his desk toward Ju-Long. He glared into his brother's eyes for what seemed an eternity. Finally, Li fell back into his chair.

Li and Ju-Long sat quietly, trying to figure out what to do. As it stood, Ju-Long was going to jail, his wife would divorce him, they would have no money, and his family would return to China. The Chang family in Panama, as well as in China, would be disgraced. Etienna would be on the street, with no way to earn an income other than prostitution while attempting to care for the child. And the Changs, by Canal Zone Treaty, would be forbidden to hire any more servants. Li told his brother to wait in the study while he talked to his wife.

"Li, no. She'll tell my wife, she'll leave me and take my son back to China," pleaded Ju-Long.

"That's too bad, but what else do I do? My wife adores that little girl, and we were going to offer her a paying job next year. But with a baby, it's a whole different thing. I have to tell her," Said Li, "you left me no choice.," He walked out of the room.

When Eda saw Mr. Chang leave the study, she decided to pay his brother a visit. She walked into the study and observed Ju-Long with his face in a linen napkin, crying. "Mr. Chang, here's a fresh linen, sir. Please feel free to wipe your tears and your nose." Ju-Long blew his nose into the linen. "Here sir, let me take that one and leave a few fresh ones on the desk." Ju-Long handed Eda the linen, soiled with his tears and snot. She put the cloth in her apron pocket and made her way to the door. As she reached the door, she turned, "Thank you, sir."

"For what?" asked Ju-Long.

"For being emotional, sir." Eda had plans for that soiled linen. It would be a good opportunity to further Etienna's education with the gods.

Li returned an hour later after talking to his wife and making plans. Ju-Long was on the brink of vomiting.

"Well, what did she say, Li? Am I going to jail? Brother, how could you do this to me? How could you be so cruel?" cried Ju-Long like the sniveling brat that he was.

"Shut up and listen. You got yourself into this. We both are so ashamed of you, we both wanted you taken away in cuffs. But we're going to do something we never thought we'd do to save our family and our country's reputation." Ju-Long sat quietly. "There will be only five people aware of this plan. But you must admit to me you understand Etienna, and her child are the only victims in this. She's a sweet, precious little girl, stripped of the love of her mother because of men like you. We made her feel loved and safe, but now she stands with a terrible future in front of her, as do we, if we don't fix this. Etienna has agreed to seduce your son."

"Pardon me, why would I allow that to happen, and what makes you think he'd do it?" said Ju-Long. "I know what you're up to, and I will warn him."

Li broke into laughter, feeling pity for his brother's stupidity. "No, you won't and yes, he will do it. He's sixteen years old so it won't take much. We'll distract our son and Etienna will make him unable to resist. Since she is only six weeks pregnant, she'll announce she and your son had sex, and he's the father," said Li. "Simple and done."

"Again, why would I agree? His mother will be so upset with him. She will want you to get rid of Etienna right away," said Ju-Long.

"Your wife will get over your son and Etienna's mistake, figuring they could not control their teenage hormones. But she would never get over her husband raping a sixteen-year-old Haitian servant girl on his brother's desk. If you refuse to cooperate, Eda and my wife will expose the truth, and you'll go to jail. We told Etienna we are going to hire her and help her raise her baby, since it will be part of the Chang family. And we will never allow you through the doors of our home again. You are a disgusting pedophile, my brother. How does that sound, Ju-Long? I never thought our family could produce a monster like you. Etienna and Eda will set up your son in the next few days. And if it doesn't happen, we will be forced to have a sit-down chat with your wife. Now, get out of here forever." Li opened his study door. He looked at the floor as Ju-Long walked out of the room.

* * * *

Late that afternoon, Eda called Etienna into her room. After holding and rocking her gently, Etienna's surrogate mother stood up and went to her dresser drawer. She pulled out a soiled linen.

"What is that, Eda?" Etienna asked. "It looks disgusting."

"Since you will be with us forever, I have new lessons to teach you. We'll meet tonight in my room, after the Changs have gone to bed. We're going to make a doll for Ju-Long Chang," said Eda with an austere expression.

"To cast a curse?" asked Etienna, not knowing how she felt about this new twist. "How did you know of my powers and my mother's teachings?"

"We both knew the day of the auction. That is why I picked you. I knew I would need you someday. And that day is here," Eda was ready to resume Etienna's training, especially on Ju-Long.

"The nurse at the auction felt my powers as well. She gave me confidence so you would notice me," Etienna added.

"Yes, I want us to cast a curse on that man and ask the gods for justice. I will help you write it. I want to see how much your momma taught you in Haiti. You will be the last girl that horrible fiend ever touches. See you at 3:00 A.M.," said Eda. Both returned to their chores.

Later that night, the hour approached when the spirit shadows flowed between heaven and hell, between good and evil, listening for someone summoning their powers. Etienna slipped quietly out of her dorm and down the hallway to Eda's room. After a hard day's work, the other girls slept deeply. Eda had seven candles burning on her dresser top, along with a doll, stuffed tightly with Ju-Long's dirty linen. A ceremonial needle lay alongside Ju-Long's effigy.

"Tell me, child. What would your momma suggest you do in your situation? You have been terribly wronged and scandalously molested. Your revenge must be tenacious. Yet I know, and Mr. Chang and his wife know, how sweet and caring you are within your soul." Eda brushed Etienna's long black hair gently with a pearl-handled brush.

From those words of kindness spoken by Eda, Etienna remembered only one time she felt this kind of anger towards another person. It was in the hold of the ship on the way to Panama. Her soul had wanted to destroy all who treated her and the others with the same disrespect they showed rats. But she decided to keep that her secret.

"As High Priestess, Momma would form a coven and arouse the attention of the family of Ghede and request the justice she believed deserving. She allowed the gods to determine what was appropriate, never taking the wrongdoer's punishment into her own mortal hands," said Etienna. "She told me the family would examine the wrongdoer's soul and determine if any other human would be subjected to danger from this person. My momma taught me how to piously petition the Ghedes with prayer for justice or protection, while being humble and respectful. She never let me forget I am an earthly being, not a god, with no power or rights of my own to violently carry out my curses or spells. Only they were capable of that."

"Were you ever part of her covens, or did you witness her cast a spell or curse, my child?" asked Eda.

"Only once, that was a man we encountered on our journey to Santo Domingo from Haiti, just before I came here. He attempted to fondle me at the age of thirteen and attempted to persuade my mother to allow him to sell us all as street whores. That was the first time I saw my mother place a curse on someone. But she told me prior of the Ghede, the family of Loa."

"We are familiar with that family in Panama," Eda said. "Sit still, my love, and meditate. I want you to place this curse on Ju-Long, as well as a protection spell on your fetus." Eda continued to brush Etienna's hair.

"Why on my baby?"

"Because you are putting a curse on the father of your child, and I want to be sure the gods know that."

With eyes shut, Etienna contemplated the seriousness of what she was about to do for the first time. She reviewed what her mother had taught her. She felt confusion within her soul. Her revenge was resolute toward the man by whom she was violated, but her inner peace was derived from her love and deep piety for the people around her. Finally, she heard her mother telling her she may ask the gods for her mortal desires, but the gods would ultimately judge. Her eyes opened slowly. She was calm and in a trance. She stared at Eda's candles. She stared at doll. A chilling voice, never heard before, emanated from her body.

"Eda, my High Priestess, the deed shall be done when you gather what I need. I will make my appeal to Baron Kriminel, the same Ghede my mother approached when the man defiled me on the path to Santo Domingo. He helps families of murder victims and the abused. He uses horses to attack and eat the persecutors. Sometimes the horses reach such a frenzy they eat each other. But we are in the city, with walls, gates, and guarded mansions. I have faith in Baron Kriminel to succeed if he chooses. He must employ a different kind of animal in the city. In preparation, he requires us to sacrifice three black roosters to him, soaked in petrol, and set ablaze. Then we finish it with the needle in the doll's genitals."

"Child, your mother taught you well. She is powerful as well as righteous. I will help you prepare. We must not be caught. These people, especially the Chinese and the Americans, would not understand what we are about to do. I look forward to sharing our teachings."

* * * *

A few days later, while the Changs attended a dinner party at the Chinese Embassy, Eda had three black roosters brought in cages to the mansion. The Panamanian guards at the gate called Eda to inform her a delivery had arrived.

As Eda and Etienna grabbed the cages from the delivery boy, one of the guards caught a glimpse. He had not seen a black rooster. The delivery boy took his tip and scurried off like a scared squirrel. The other guard glanced at the roosters, turned his head, staring at the street as if he had seen nothing. Eda and Etienna carried the cages to the secluded jungle behind the mansion.

"What was that?" asked the curious guard. "I have not seen a black rooster. Are they good to eat?"

"Forget you saw that, my friend," said the other, still staring into the street. "And no matter what happens tonight, we do not leave this gate. Do you understand me?"

"No, but I trust you do." The guards stood silently.

Behind the mansion, the night was deathly still. The crescent moon shone over the jungle in a faint hazy sky. The Changs' mansion covered three acres, two of which were pristine rain forests, the home for parrots, toucans, vultures, and an occasional troop of white-faced monkeys swinging through and raiding garbage bins. The harmony of hundreds of species of insects was seductively deafening. As Eda and Etienna carried the black roosters farther from the house, the jungle got darker and louder. The cages were placed in front of Etienna, who faced the thick brush. Eda placed a white robe over Etienna's shoulders, covered her face with white opaque powder, then painted something above her eyes. Eda placed a black flowered headdress surrounding a dark gray skull on Etienna's head.

"What did you paint on my forehead, High Priestess?" asked Etienna.

"It is a red upside-down cross, my child. Christ's apostle Peter was to be crucified as a martyr, but he insisted he be upside down. He believed he was not equal to Jesus Christ and not worthy to die right-side up like his Lord and Savior. Never forget, our Voodoo has strong ties to Catholicism and all its saints. Like Peter, it is our symbol of humility and unworthiness when we address the saints and gods, especially when we are petitioning their aid and their holy presence. I will hold the candle as you perform your incantation. Let's begin and finish before the Changs return home."

Etienna knelt, lifting her outstretched arms, gazing to the heavens. Eda knelt next to her, bowed her head, and closed her eyes. Then, in the same mysterious voice Etienna manifested in Eda's room, she began:

> *"Oh, Loa, sacred family of Ghede, please hear my humble plea.*
> *I come to you for many a child, not just for me.*
> *Who else will be put in danger by this wicked, demented man?*
> *I pray for you to protect them all from his vile, perverted hand.*
> *A man who comes to us from far, far away.*
> *A man who, within his soul, his abuse cannot be held at bay.*
> *He touches the girls, many far younger than his years.*
> *One now, myself with child, is filled with future fears.*
> *I pray protection for others he still yet plans to maim.*
> *With his sexual acts of violence and with no regret, no shame.*
> *Please give his body to your chilling Baron Kriminel,*
> *Who will torture him with powers so unknown and subliminal.*
> *Remove him, I beg you, from this innocent earthly face.*
> *Let his body and his soul be dispersed with pain into a space*
> *Where this monster's agony and torment will be only his,*
> *While you continue to protect the innocent from him until finally it is*
> *His bitter end.*
> *And please, Baron, protect my unborn fetus*
> *From those unfaithful and selfish who will try to defeat us.*
> *So, accept our prayers upon our knees.*
> *We pray to you, our humility will please.*
> *And accept these burning sacrifices thrown,*
> *To give you the reminder of food and rum.*
> *To the entire Ghede family, we pray you come."*

Eda and Etienna carried the cages deeper into the jungle, doused each of the roosters in a mixture of petrol and rum, then set them ablaze. The roosters went rabid. The women could only hope Baron Kriminel enjoyed this display of passion and attract the attention of the rest of his family to their devotion. As the roosters drew their last breaths and were being reduced to a smolder, Eda held the doll in her hand. Etienna jabbed the needle through its genitals. They dumped the dead roosters into the thick brush to be eaten by the ants, roaches, and vultures. Then threw the cages into the rain forest to be eaten by the termites.

"Come, my child, back into my room before the Changs return. I must clean your face. And we mention nothing of this to the girls. I am proud of you, my child. A child of your age has just gained the respect of the Ghede. And remember, love is still the answer, not hate. You must now move on with no vengeance." Eda put her arm around Etienna, and they walked to the house.

* * * *

Within the next year, Ju-Long Chang would acquire dengue fever three bone-crushing times, each progressively worse. The third time, it would be fatal, and blood would come spewing from his mouth and through his pores as his organs hemorrhaged. Baron Kriminel left his horses at home this time, but he was pleased with his new little mosquito servants.

9

ONE FAMILY GROWS – ONE FAMILY GOES

Li Chang again sat behind his desk, only this time ever so callous. His wife sat in one of the side chairs in front of him, impervious to what was to unfold. On the couch, to the right of the office entry, sat Etienna, now six months pregnant. Eda walked through the doorway, escorting Shu Chang, Ju-Long's wife. She was seated across from Li, next to his wife. Eda took a seat on the couch next to Etienna.

"We requested a meeting with you, Shu, to discuss a political situation," Li began, looking directly at Shu with a cold demeanor.

"And what might this political situation be, my honored brother-in-law?" answered Shu in a tawdry fashion. "I assume my husband was not invited due to his illness?"

"That is correct," said Li. "Let me get to the point. Our servant, behind you on the couch, is six months pregnant. Questions are being asked by my superiors as to who the father might be. Our country, is currently in chaos, clashing in civil war since the death of President Shikai three years ago. The Communist Party is gaining strength, and the Americans and Panamanians are becoming concerned over the safety of the canal. No matter who controls it, the Panama Canal is vital to our country and all other economic powers in the world. The Americans would benefit from our expulsion, then lack of authority in this region," Li explained.

Shu interrupted. "Li, what does this situation have to do with Ju-Long and myself? What do you need us to do?"

"Shu, when all countries wishing to use the canal came together, an agreement was made we would institute restavek, meaning indentured slavery taken from the Caribbean islands, but with restrictions. Only girls age thirteen to fifteen could be purchased, and only until age eighteen were they allowed to go unpaid. All of us agreed to feed, clothe, lodge, and educate any domestic servants who voluntarily remained in our care."

"I don't need a civics lesson. That's for you politicians to sort out. What could your point possibly have to do with me, Li? I have things to do, not to mention taking care of my terribly ill husband."

Li continued. "And one of our bedrock agreements was absolutely no sexual misconduct toward these girls. In other words, these girls brought to Panama, backed by our embassy agreements, would be protected from sexual abuse by all of us. If the girls became sexually promiscuous with anyone outside our control, we could let these employees go, and they would be left to fend for themselves in the streets. But if the sexual misconduct came from inside our homes or offices, from our staff, the staff members would be subject to Panamanian laws and would either be arrested and placed in a Panamanian prison or be deported, with monetary reparations for the servant. And their child if befitting. Are you following me yet, Shu?"

Shu stared at Li and then at his wife. She looked over her shoulder at Etienna and Eda. "No, no, no, Li. I'm not sure exactly what you're saying, but if you're saying my son has something to do with the pregnancy of that little whore back there…no. First, how do you know it wasn't your son? They hang out together a lot, at least until recently." Shu stopped and became silent for a moment. Then began again. "Have you talked to your son, Li? How do you know it wasn't a delivery boy or a guard?"

"Shu, we're positive the child she is carrying is from your family. No doubt. And we're sure your son had intercourse with our servant girl. And we're sure it was only once," Li's wife interjected.

"Okay, let's step back. You're saying that little liar back there says my son raped her, and now she's pregnant? I guess she wants to press charges and get a handful of money from Ju-Long when she turns eighteen. What a scam." Shu stood, shaking her head. She approached Etienna. Eda stood up and came between them.

"Go ahead, you fat Panamanian bitch. Touch me, and your black ass is in jail. You put that little Negro girl up to this, didn't you? You're all liars. We have power in this part of your country. Li, get our attorney and let's have this little tramp deported or cast into the street. I refuse to fall for this. My husband won't stand for it, either. It almost sounds to me like you're protecting her, Li. My son is not going to a Panamanian prison at age seventeen. They'll eat him alive." Shu began to walk out the door.

"Shu, come back and sit down please. You don't want to do this. We have some ideas," said Li.

Shu stopped and turned but did not sit. "No Li, I'm going to the embassy right now since Ju-Long's sick. I'm going to have a hearing on this before this pregnancy thing goes any farther. And don't even think about suggesting I take that Haitian slut and her baby into my home. I'm going right now, and don't try to stop me. Li, you're a traitor to your own family. You're a liar." All eyes turned to Li.

"Shu, we never said it was your son's baby. We just let you know he and Etienna had sex together. All I said was the child comes from your family," said Li. "No one has lied, yet."

"What, you think this is funny? It's your son's, isn't it? And you're trying to pin it on us to save your career, you selfish bastard. You tried to see if we'd take the blame first." screamed Shu. "But I called your bluff. I'm out of here." Shu turned to leave again, but before she took a step, Li blurted.

"It's your husband's baby, Shu. Your husband was sneaking over here when my wife and I were away, and he was raping her over this very desk."

Shu came running at Li, swinging her fists. Li grabbed her by the wrists.

"Liar, liar, liar." She spat in his face. "Now you're blaming my husband? It was probably you, you egotistical bastard. How are you so sure my husband did that? He would never do anything like that. He's a good man and a staunch Buddhist."

"Because Eda saw the sperm running down her leg after Etienna left his presence here in this office. And she was sobbing. Then, when we discovered she was pregnant, I approached him and told him I knew what he had been doing and revealed to him her pregnancy. His solution was to cover it up. But the baby will be half-Chinese at birth, so that could never be an option. I told him how disgusted I was with him, raping a sixteen-year-old servant girl who we have grown. The only solution to keep him out of jail was for Etienna to have intercourse with your son and claim him to be the father."

"Why would you do that?" Shu asked. "Why would she do that?"

"Two reasons. Ju-Long took her virginity and was the only one who could have impregnated her—that's statutory rape. He would go to prison and be fired from his embassy position. Our entire family would be disgraced both here, and in the homeland, a major scandal. But if it was mutual, and the kids were about the same age, that is not against the law in Panama, but it is in our corporate agreement with the international community. We feel the embassy would be more lenient, and the Americans would avoid sex scandal involving us Chinese." Shu looked at Li, still in shock over her husband's perversion.

"So, you want me to take this girl and her baby into my home and support them?" said Shu with a disgusted look on her face.

"According to our contractual agreement with the Panamanians, that is required. But frankly, I find you as selfish and obnoxious as my brother. There is no way I would put that angel with child in a place where your husband could rape her as often as he wished, like every time you go to the market," said Li.

"I want to kill him. If he weren't in such horrible pain from the Dengue, I'd slit his disgusting throat right now." Shu began to cry as she sat back in the chair. "How do I tell my son he's innocent, and his father is a wicked child molester?"

"We already talked to him. He honestly believes he's the father; his guilt is tearing him up."

"And my husband would let him keep believing that. He would lie to him, bold face lie to him." Eda and Etienna held each other's hands. The curse had worked, and the Ghedes had made their judgment.

"Shu," said Li. "We're fond of Etienna and her dedication, we will keep her with us, along with the baby. Someday we will tell the baby your son is the father. He does not need to feel guilty. He can come visit. Just tell him accidents happen. We will all treat your son wonderfully with no hint of vengeance. But none of us want the child to know his father raped his mother. And your son does not want to know what his father is. All of this stays in this room."

Shu was sobbing. She got up from her chair, but this time gently approached Etienna. She knelt at her feet, held both of her hands, and looked her in the eyes. "I am so ashamed of my husband's treatment and disrespect for you. No one deserves that, my child, especially a kind and innocent young girl stripped from her mother in a foreign land. My son may or may not accept his role in this as your child's father, but you are in wonderful hands. You have a loving family here in this house. Bless you and may your God and your Christ love you and keep you in the palm of his hand."

Etienna squeezed Shu's hands and smiled at her. "Thank you, ma'am. And I'm sorry for the pain caused to you by your husband. May your gods embrace and protect you and your son during your husband's time of illness." Shu and Etienna exchanged smiles.

They all hugged each other. Shu left the house. The chores of the day resumed.

10

THE PROGRESSION OF THE GABRIELS

The Ghedes protected the future of the innocent, and in particular, Etienna's fetus. Etienna gave birth to a healthy, delicately exotic daughter a few months before her eighteenth birthday, half-Haitian, half-Chinese; the world was getting smaller. The infant's skin tone was so unique it could not be described, and her skin so soft that to hold the child naked was like holding the light cast from an angel. Her eyes were shaped like teardrops, the outside corners tapering to a point like the thorn of a rose. And her eyelashes, already long, were black, like the color of her mother's skin on a moonless night. The infant was enchanting. They decided to name her Jesula Gabriel Chang, her first and middle names in remembrance of Etienna's mother and her last name to give her more power and respect as she advanced in years. Etienna loved the idea, for without the Changs, Jesula would not have the opportunity of life itself.

The Changs converted an extra room into a bedroom and nursery for Etienna and the baby. The room was decorated with classic Chinese furniture, fresh red and pink lotus flowers floating on the nightstands in beautiful glass vases. Chinese murals were painted on the walls, the prominent two being the Buddha becoming enlightened under the Bodhi tree and the Samsara, or the Buddhist 'Wheel of Life.' It was all on a background of bamboo trees and scenes of temples and monks travelling on their own roads to enlightenment. Etienna would sit quietly in a bamboo rocker and nurse Jesula, dreaming of her mother and the sacrifice she made to place her and her granddaughter in this nirvana.

The child added a warm, loving energy to the entire mansion and was adored by all, except Shu, Ju-Long's wife. She carried a haunting sense of guilt over her husband's debauchery and the need to eternally deceive her son. Ju-Long was now beginning to bleed from his mouth, nose, and pores, wasting away in bone-crushing pain as the last stages of a rare strain of hemorrhagic Dengue fever spread through his body. He was on his deathbed. She knew she and her son would be transported back to China within weeks following Ju-Long's death. They would never be seen in Central America again. Li and his wife prayed Ju-Long would remain silent and leave the family's disgrace at the Buddhist funeral pyre.

Etienna and the Changs came to a fair and equitable arrangement, allowing Etienna to remain in the mansion and continue to work for them, even though her pay would be far less than most other domestic workers. In exchange, she and her baby were well cared for. Mrs. Chang helped Jesula Chang attend the private Chinese schools, since Jesula started her life naturally trilingual. Jesula Chang found herself well respected, being from this prominent family. To show her gratitude, she studied hard. Finally, after her high school graduation, the Changs sponsored her through a two-year RN program in Panama City.

With her RN degree completed, Jesula Chang was immediately offered a position in the Santa Fe International Hospital, treating not only Panamanians but the many nationalities now doing business in the Canal Zone. Her trilingual language skills became invaluable, so much so she received a scholarship to continue her studies and obtained a four-year degree, specializing in surgical nursing and emergency room care.

It was in the OR Jesula met her husband, a brilliant Panamanian surgical resident. They moved into a quaint three-bedroom house and had two children, a son, Anthony, and a daughter, Miriam. But in addition to Jesula's higher education in medicine, languages, and the arts, Eda and Etienna didn't neglect to teach her, as a child, their extracurricular powers in case she would ever need them.

As Jesula's and her husband's careers became quite busy, Jesula offered Etienna a room in their house to take care of the children. Eda was aging and having trouble walking. Etienna explained to her daughter how indebted she was to the Changs for all they had done. Jesula agreed. Etienna took over Eda's duties, and Mrs. Chang was supportive, allowing Etienna to babysit whenever necessary. Tragically, Jesula's son, Anthony, died at the age of three from encephalitis. Miriam was only one year of age. Etienna and Miriam became remarkably close. Etienna shared their family history with her many times and taught her their special powers. Miriam would later find them quite useful when used properly, and dangerous when used improperly.

THE DEPARTURE OF TWO LIFETIMES

After Anthony's death, Eda and Etienna helped Jesula with Miriam. The Changs blessed Etienna by sponsoring Miriam into the embassy school, promoted by the aristocratic Chinese in the Canal Zone. Miriam, like her mother, became trilingual. Miriam's heritage was now a blend of the Panamanian, Chinese, and Haitian cultures. She helped her grandmother with chores and became acquainted with the domestic servants purchased by the Chang from numerous foreign countries. And most were separated from their mothers as was her grandmother. She could carry on discussions with the highly educated friends of her parents in the medical community. And she was exposed to her father's family who worked on the docks of the canal, living a rough and questionable lifestyle. Miriam was a combination of her previous three maternal ancestors, starting with her selfless great-grandmother who endured a broken heart, collapsing on the streets of Santo Domingo as she opened the gates of heaven to her daughter. Miriam was the most educated and socially versatile of the four generations. Her future was at her feet like a red carpet welcoming a Princess.

Miriam was awarded a scholarship out of high school and became a well-respected surgical nurse at Panama City's international hospital. But Miriam, to the confusion of all who knew her, had acquired one flaw as she entered her adulthood, a characteristic not present in Etienna,

Jesula, or the Chang woman; her choice of men was physically driven, not intellectually driven.

As Miriam began her career in the OR, she vigorously studied to obtain her four-year degree. Silently in her heart, she wanted to be a doctor like her father, preferably a pediatric surgeon. Her parents warm-heartedly welcomed her to live with them and their tutoring was invaluable. Miriam's uncle, her father's brother, would stop by unexpectedly from time to time with his friend Raoul, a brawny, dark-haired Panamanian dock worker whose herculean arms were tattooed with sinister symbols of sex and evil. Raoul, kindling a base and unclean aura, exuded a body odor that saturated every room in the house. And visits from Miriam's uncle were not for the purpose of showing his brother's love. His visits were solely to mooch food and alcohol from his obligated sibling. But Raoul came along because he wanted a shot at Miriam for his financial well-being and future inheritance. He knew how to sexually arouse a young woman, especially a naïve little bookworm.

Miriam was still a virgin at the age of twenty, and her relationships with men had been rooted in academics: teachers, tutors, or fellow embassy students. Miriam's mother, father, and grandmother instantly detected her attraction to Raoul and warned her of his intentions. They assumed she would take heed and lose interest quickly when his inane purpose became obvious. Unfortunately, Miriam could not resist the physical strength of his body and the masculine smells of this working man. She was never exposed to a raw, manly specimen like him, and she found him irresistible, her thirst for him insatiable. Consequently, it wasn't long before Miriam was pregnant with Raoul's baby. It was a well-planned working-class ambush.

Miriam was so inflamed by her desires and fearful of eternal damnation by the Catholic church, she agreed to marry Raoul. Maria was born three months later, in 1958, delaying Miriam's education. Two years later, Miriam's second daughter, Andrea, was born, causing a second delay in Miriam's education. Jesula knew Raoul's intentions and found him revolting. A curse was considered by Jesula but decided against by Etienna. She felt this was a voluntary act by an intelligent Miriam, not a rape. However, Jesula refused to allow them to live in their home, so Miriam rented a small flat near the hospital. With no financial or childcare help from Raoul or his family, Miriam was in a jam to continue her education. Eda died of a stroke four years earlier, and Etienna, now age fifty-five, was struck by two boys drag-racing as she shopped at the market. Her hip was shattered, and she was unable to climb the stairs to her bedroom. She moved back into the first-floor dorm with the young servants. What seemed to be a blessed course for all, was sliding in the wrong direction. It was time for Etienna to speak to the gods.

* * * *

One afternoon, Mrs. Chang came into the kitchen, her voice quivering with emotion, and requested Etienna's presence in the parlor. "Have a seat next to me, please," she said, patting the cushion on the sofa. Etienna, with her broken hip, sat straight legged as Mrs. Chang placed her hand on Etienna's knee. "You know what I have to do, do you not?"

"Yes, ma'am. I have been expecting this day would come soon, and I have been trying to figure out what to do as well. With Eda dying, Jesula married and gone, and Miriam not needing a babysitter, the house feels barren, like a palace devoid of life. I find myself lonely and in pain most of the time these days, both emotional and physical. I find myself weeping a lot. I can hardly walk, not to mention climb stairs. I know you're going to fire me. And I do understand why." Etienna began to cry. Mrs. Chang hugged her, and they both cried.

"You and Eda, Jesula, and Miriam, have been part of our family since the day I purchased you at the auction. You have been a godsent to all of us. And please my loved one, I'm not firing you. I would never do that. But your lifestyle will need to change. Mr. Chang and I are going back to China after all these years. He has been replaced due to his age. He will be sixty-five this year, and we would like to go back and spend our last days with our families. Mr. Chang and I considered taking you with us, but I know you, my dear. You're so dedicated to your girls; you could never be happy without them." Mrs. Chang continued to weep through her words.

Etienna responded, "Jesula asked me many years ago if I would move in with her and take care of Miriam. Now Miriam is grown, and she has married a terrible man. Miriam must take care of her daughters by herself, while at the same time, working and continuing her education. That man won't help her, emotionally or monetarily. I think I'll take Jesula up on her offer and move in with her and her husband and help them with housekeeping, while being Maria and Andrea's nanny. I have been praying to the gods recently. They always have a way of working things out for the righteous, Mrs. Chang." Etienna took a deep breath and held it, realizing for the first time, she exposed her Voodoo religion.

"I believe our lives have been enhanced with each other in it. We love you and your family, Etienna. Tell them all we will miss them terribly," said Mrs. Chang. "I believe my heart is breaking as we speak, Etienna."

"Mine also, Mrs. Chang, almost as much as when my mother placed me on that freighter, then the gods placed me into the arms of you and Eda. My whole family loves you and our souls are indebted to you. I am sure my mother and Eda connected before I arrived. But Mrs. Chang, I must tell you something I've kept from you for a long time. And so did Eda." Etienna hesitated for a moment, taking a deep breath. Mrs. Chang stared, waiting patiently for her to continue.

"Eda and I killed Ju-Long. His death was not from natural causes. Eda and I put a curse on him after he raped me. We were both Voodoo priestesses, but only once did we use our powers to hurt anyone, and that was Ju-Long. We did it to protect others young girls he would rape and damage in his future, not for revenge. We also cast protection spells on members of your family when needed, along with the servant girls." said Etienna as she waited anxiously for a response.

Mrs. Chang gave Etienna another hug. "We knew what you did. A few weeks after the discovery of Ju-Long's death, our dog dragged a burnt rooster to the front gate as we were leaving. The guards were funny. They didn't move even an eyeball and they were shaking. The rooster had been eaten almost to the bone by insects. But after a stern inquiry by Mr. Chang, one guard told us he was there when you and Eda had three black roosters delivered, which seemed odd to him, since we had no chickens to impregnate. Mr. Chang asked his Panamanian servant at the embassy about it, and he told him their purpose. When Mr. Chang told me Ju-Long contracted Dengue, we understood. You see, we Buddhists believe in

Karma. Or, as the Americans say, 'What goes around, comes around.' He would have hurt others. Your gods gave justice to the world of the meek and innocent."

"Thank you for your understanding," responded Etienna. "I was young, and Eda made me ponder that decision deeply. It was hard, but I felt an inner peace. You do know Eda picked me that day because she sensed my powers and their loving nature."

"She told me on her deathbed about both of you. She felt our Chang family, being so far from home and our religious homeland, needed the protection of Voodoo within our home. She could feel the vibrations radiating from your soul at the auction. She told me we obtained you as her backup in case anything happened to her. And you have been our protector. I'll love you forever, in this world and the next."

Etienna hobbled to her room and returned with a duplication of the pentagram necklace her mother gave her as a child. "Please keep this with you always and when you meet my mother in the next world, don't be humble. Tell her about the beautiful life you and your husband made for us and the incredible lives my children have earned due to you. She will be so proud. That was the only reason I did not jump off a balcony and end my life the night before I boarded the ship. She told me our separation would bring happiness to our future family. You are divinity, Mrs. Chang, and you fulfilled my mother's prayers."

Mrs. Chang held Etienna's face in her hands. "You and I brought our love together as the world should know it. Bless you, and your family, forever and forever."

"Bless you as well, my Chinese Savior."

12

RAOUL BOWS TO THE DEVIL

Maria was now seventeen, her high school education near completion. She prepared to continue the family tradition of nursing school. She wished to specialize in emergency room medicine, with a subspecialty in pediatric trauma. Andrea, Miriam's second daughter, was fifteen and going in a different direction. She wanted to be a concert pianist, hoping someday to play classical music in the Panama City Symphony, and she was talented enough to have a chance. Her grandfather purchased a beautiful piano for her. It sat crowded in Miriam's small living room. For Maria to concentrate on her studies, Maria and Etienna would spend the afternoons at Jesula's house while Andrea practiced alone at home.er grandmotherhhhhh

Andrea's daddy, Raoul, had little interest in his wife or daughters these days, unless he needed money for drink or heartless sex from Miriam. She was in her mid-thirties, and Raoul was finding younger girls much more fun to play with. But if he did want Miriam and she refused, it was common for her to wear long-sleeved shirts and extra makeup to cover the bruises. The daughters hid from the violence. Only once did Maria try to protect her mother. That was the night her daddy smashed her nose in like a piece of ground beef, blood splattering onto Andrea's piano bench.

One rainy afternoon, thunder rumbling far away, Andrea was practicing hard for her recital the next day. It would be in front of a group of university professors who heard of Andrea's talent and looking for young students worthy of entry into the Panamanian Conservatory of Music. She knew she had only two hours before her mother and Maria came home. After that, she would have trouble concentrating, as she always did with someone, anyone, present in the house.

Andrea heard the back door open, then slam powerfully. "Hello, Mother, Maria, is that you?" Into the living room staggered Raoul. Andrea's heart raced. "Hi, Daddy, how are you? I haven't seen you in a while. Mother's not here, and Maria's at Grandmother's studying. They should be home in a couple of hours if you want to come back. I'm practicing for a recital tomorrow. I might get into the Conservatory of Music if I perform well."

"Fuck, girlie, you still playing that stupid piano? What kind of money are you gonna make for us doing that? Your momma got any extra money around?" Raoul slurred. The odor of whiskey oozed from his pores; his breath was obnoxious. He looked and smelled like he hadn't bathed or shaved in a week.

"No, Daddy. She keeps it in her purse. I'll tell her you stopped by." Andrea tried to ignore him by returning to her piano.

"Don't ignore me, you little bitch. You're just like your mother. Now go into her bedroom and find me some money, or I'll bust that pretty little face of yours like I did Maria's." He grabbed her off the bench and shoved her toward the bedroom with his forearm. "Got any whiskey around here?" he asked, then hesitated, shaking his head in a disgusted fashion. "Fuck, what am I asking? You haughty little sluts don't drink, do you? I bet you and your sister ain't never been screwed yet."

Andrea was panic-stricken. The rain was coming down hard. She considered dashing to her room and locking herself in, but he was tenacious enough to kick her door down. Instead, she hoped, with no money or whiskey in the house, he would become tired of tormenting her and leave.

Raoul continued to drive Andrea into her mother's bedroom. She looked in her mother's dresser and her nightstand. She found a few coins. She smelled her daddy behind her. Then she felt his hands reach around and grab both her breasts. "Why, look what we have here. I noticed them puppies when you turned around on your piano bench. Fifteen years old, and those babies popped up real big in a hurry."

"Daddy, stop. I'm your daughter. That's wrong what you just did," said Andrea as she shuddered in fear.

"Turn around here, little girl, and don't ever talk to me that way. I'm your daddy," demanded Raoul as he spun her toward him and grabbed her bare breasts from the front. Staggering and panting like a street dog, he unbuttoned her blouse. He backed her against the wall, his forearm pressed against her throat, gawking down at her breast. "Look at the nipples on those titties. I need to taste those." Andrea could feel his erect penis pressing against her. Suddenly, he grabbed her arm with one hand and her crotch with the other. He slung her down onto her mother's bed, and before she had a chance to react, he lifted her skirt and pulled her panties off.

Andrea began to struggle. "No, Daddy, don't do this. What will Mother do when she finds out?"

Raoul laughed. "Shit, girl, tell her, she won't do shit. You see what I do to her when she gets smart-ass with me. You shut the fuck up, or I'll beat both you bitches. Then I'll only have one of you left to fuck. But she's a homely little bookworm with no titties at all. She's not even worth my cock gettin' hard. I doubt I could if I wanted to. Now lay still and spread those cute thighs of yours. It will be over in no time."

Andrea lay on her back, still as a corpse, and cried. Her virginity was gone, and it hurt. She grimaced in pain. Her daddy finished quickly and shot his sperm inside of her. He went to the bathroom, washed himself, and left the house.

Andrea clutched her mother's pillow and wept, so ashamed of herself. After a few minutes, she walked gingerly to the bathroom and soaked in the tub. She needed to expunge that repulsive smell of her daddy. But it would never completely go away, ever. There was a small amount of blood in the water. She felt dirty even after the bath. She changed her clothes and went back to her piano, but she couldn't concentrate. As she tried to practice, she found herself starting her piece rather soft and sad, then her teeth began to clench, her lips pressed tightly together, her eyes squinted, and her eyebrows furrowed. She played her piece increasingly violently, until she was pounding ferociously on the keys. She stood up, turned around, and kicked her piano bench across the room. Then she went to the mirror in the bathroom and looked at herself. She looked different. She looked older. She looked ugly.

13

ANDREA'S DECISION FOR ETERNITY

Andrea's recital did not go well. The classical softness of her hands moving so beautifully across the keys tied to her intellectual expression of the piece had turned angry. She double-stroked keys and did not display the cleanliness of her past performances. The professors spoke with Miriam and expressed to her she needed more emotional maturity. They said they would check back in a year. Andrea was devastated, but not surprised. She was the only one who knew what happened to her that stormy afternoon. She was now afraid to be in the house by herself; therefore, her practice time was reduced. And every time she sat on the bench; she could smell the stench of her daddy.

Two months after that gruesome afternoon, shaking and with tears rolling down her face, it was time to tell her mother she missed two periods.

"Andrea Blanco, you're fifteen. How could you do this, child? Are you fooling around with one of your little schoolboys when we aren't here? Is that why your piano playing has declined? You're having sex instead of practicing?" Miriam was getting hot-tempered as she spoke. "Tell me, who is it? I'm not going to pay for this baby on my own. You haven't even finished high school. How could you do this? I never thought you'd turn out to be a little slut." Miriam slapped Andrea across the face. "Who is it, or are you going to tell me there's more than one? Tell me, or I swear, I'll slap you again." Maria stood by in confusion. That did not sound like her little sister, or her mother. Maria always saw Andrea as a little angel. And so had her mother.

"No, Mother, I'll not tell you, ever. I'll take care of this baby myself if I must, but I'll not tell you who the father is. You can ask, you can strike me as many times as you wish, but the answer will always be silent," said Andrea sternly, but sobbing intensely. Her shame turned to anger.

"I'm so disappointed in you, Andrea. We let you follow your dream and stay out of medicine where you can make real money, and you turned on me and your grandparents," Miriam said with tears in her eyes. "We are friends with an obstetrician at the hospital who will help us with some of the costs, but your piano days are over. You'll need to get an after-school job to help pay for this child. Understood?" Andrea ran to her bedroom and slammed the door, locking it behind her.

* * * *

Seven months passed quickly. Andrea was ridiculed inhumanely as she walked pregnant through the halls of her school. Miriam insisted she stay enrolled until her last month of pregnancy. Then, one night at dinner, Andrea's water broke. They rushed her to labor and delivery and stayed by her side. But Miriam had not forgiven Andrea for her apparent promiscuity.

What appeared to be a normal healthy pregnancy from the beginning began to show distress in the early parts of Andrea's labor. "Mrs. Blanco, may I speak to you in the hallway please?" asked the doctor. Then he walked out of the labor room before Miriam could ask a question.

The hallway was dingy with plaster-chipped walls and a worn marble floor. Miriam looked at the doctor. He had a grim look on his face. "Is there a problem, Doctor? She seems to be progressing normally."

"Mrs. Blanco, the heartbeat of the baby is getting weaker. And we are getting some blood spotting from the vagina prematurely. We aren't sure what the problem is yet. I need to ask you and your daughter a few questions right away." The doctor walked back into the room. Miriam followed.

"Andrea, I must ask you a few questions in between your contractions," said the doctor.

"Is there a problem, Doctor?" Andrea asked with a panicked look on her face. The doctor didn't answer. He began his inquiry.

"Have you had any accidents, falls, car wrecks, or anything like that in the last few months?" he asked.

"Not really, but on my last days in school a month ago, two boys got into a fight in the hall. They crashed into me and fell on top of me. That did hurt for a while, but it went away. I never said anything, because this is already costing my mother lots of money and, like I said, it went away. I didn't want to bother my mother by having her drive me here and cost her more money. Why do you ask, Doctor?" said Andrea.

"Have you had any back pain since then, or spotting?" asked the doctor.

"I have had back pain, but I assumed it was from the boys falling on me. And yes, I have had a little bit of spotting, but it's not much. I didn't want to worry anybody, and really, it's not much. I just wore a Tampax and flushed it, so my mother and sister didn't worry. I was less than a month away from the birth." Suddenly, Andrea went into a contraction, and more blood came from her vagina.

"Miriam, may I talk to you in the hall again? And honey," the doctor said to Andrea, "just stay calm. I want to talk to your mother and another doctor. Just be easy. It's almost time for the delivery room. You're about to be a mother." And the doctor gave Andrea and Maria a sweet smile.

They returned to the hallway, and the doctor explained what he believed to be the diagnosis. Another doctor joined them. "Miriam, I believe we have a placental abruption on our hands, probably caused by the trauma of those boys falling on her. The back pain is not muscular. It is a symptom of abruption, as is the spotting. The baby's heart rate is falling due to a lack of oxygen from the placenta."

"What do we do? Are she and the baby going to be all right?"

"Miriam, they are both in danger. If we had known earlier, a premature C-section would have been the answer. But it's too late now. Her labor is within a couple of hours of birth, at most. But depending on how much the placenta is separated from the uterus and on the position of the baby, both could die." Miriam turned pale. "Miriam, you must be strong. Your little girl needs your strength and love right now." The doctor turned to his colleague and asked, "What do you think?"

"Immediate vaginal delivery. It'll be hard with her being so young and her first child. Her muscles are not stretched. Is she far enough dilated to use forceps? And get whole blood ready for the mother. We need to keep her from going into shock," said the second doctor.

"Yes, she's dilated just enough, but it will be dangerous for both. Get the spinal started right away and get her to the delivery room now. Everybody move. Let's go, people." They returned to Andrea's room, and she was quickly moved to the delivery room.

"How is the baby's heartbeat?" the doctor asked the nurse.

"Weak, but still there," the nurse answered quietly. Andrea screamed as she had another contraction, bloodier than the last.

The spinal was administered, and the episiotomy performed, but even with that, the vagina was tight, and Andrea and the baby were going to be damaged badly.

As the doctor struggled to get the baby out as quickly as possible, Andrea cried and screamed, not from pain, but from terror. She still did not know what was happening. Maria knelt in the hallway, her hands folded on a chair and praying to the gods and Jesus Christ for the life of her sister and baby. She then entered the delivery room and snuggled close to her sister's face. The doctor's first attempt with the forceps was unsuccessful, and as he moved the baby, a pool of blood came out. The baby was blocking the separation of the placenta from the uterus, which was why Andrea's spotting seemed minor.

"Doctor, the heartbeat is weakening," said the nurse.

The doctor went in again, squeezed tighter, and the crown of the head appeared.

"Heartbeat is faint," she said.

With one last powerful effort, the doctor pulled on the forceps, and the baby came out. Miriam and Maria told Andrea the baby was out, and they all began to cry; all except the baby.

"Can I hold—"

The doctor stopped Andrea. "It was a boy, but we were too late. The lack of oxygen from the separation caused him to suffocate," said the doctor.

"Mother, I still want to hold him if just for a second. Please, Mother, please." Maria and Miriam were now crying full force. "It's something I never want to forget, or any of us to forget. Just for a second, please," pleaded Andrea.

Miriam and Maria looked at each other with confusion on their faces.

"Andrea, and all of you," said the doctor. "Since the baby died from lack of oxygen, it's a disturbing shade of gray. And because I had to pull as hard as I could, the baby's skull is torn and misshapen. Before you do this, Andrea, I just want you to be aware. It will not be pretty. It will be disturbing. A sight you will never forget."

Andrea looked at the nurse and gave her instructions. "Take my gown down from my neck and expose my bare breast. Then open the blanket so I can see him. Then lay his dead body on me." The nurse looked at the doctors, who in turn looked at Miriam. She nodded and the doctor approved Andrea's request. The nurse placed the naked, bloody baby on the chest of his mother. Andrea held him tightly as blood ran down her sides. But she had stopped crying. With a blank stare on her face, just stared at the dead child. No one ever saw a mother's reaction like this, and no one, especially Miriam and Maria, knew how to interpret it. It lasted until the doctor made the decision, it had been long enough.

The baby was taken to the morgue. Andrea was stitched and taken to intensive care, where she would receive two consecutive blood transfusions. The medical staff observed her closely to be sure she didn't go into shock. As Andrea lay there, attached to machines and an IV tube, As Miriam held one hand and Maria held the other, Andrea screamed, "I hate men." Then, in a demonic tone, she uttered, "I'll always hate them, and there will be many men to suffer and die at my feet. Mother, teach me your skills, the ones you and Grandmother are teaching Maria."

"No, Andrea, your soul is one of an artist. Your passion does not blend with the science of Voodoo. What you do emotionally and physically to break men's hearts is something the gods won't stop unless asked by another coven of witches. You need to be careful as to why you punish certain mortals, and whom you choose to punish. Some will be stronger than you in different ways. And if it is other witches you challenge, they could stop you, even by death, if the gods agree with their curse on you.

The gods will not let you punish all men, and you will be obsessed by your hatred and grief. There are good men in this world, my love, Mr. Chang, and your grandfather, for example. Sometimes, we choose poorly and make mistakes, like I did with your father. I'm sure the young man who is the father of your son, did not intend for this to happen to you and the baby. Perhaps he should know. Perhaps he would care." Miriam kissed Andrea's hand.

"It was Daddy, Mother," blurted Andrea. "Daddy, your husband, raped me when he was drunk, the afternoon before my recital. As my dead son laid on my breast, I knew I wanted to kill that man. I want Daddy to be dead. And I will kill him, and every other man I can get my claws into on this planet. Those bastards killed my son."

Miriam's face lost all color. Maria, shocked to her core, could do nothing but stare coldly at her mother, awaiting her reaction. For more than a moment, no one spoke.

"Maria, my child, we have work to do," Miriam said. "You, Andrea, must stay out of this, or you'll spend the rest of your life in prison. Your help is not needed here. You can trick men, break their hearts, con them, but never kill one. The mortal laws on that are strong. Your sister and I will take care of this. I'll be back in a few minutes." Without another word, Miriam rushed from the room.

"I need the bloody blanket my daughter's dead son was wrapped in," Miriam instructed the nurse when she arrived at the morgue.

"Miriam, I'm not allowed to release that in case there was disease or infection that caused the infant's death. It must be disposed of," answered the nurse.

"You know me from the pediatric ward. I would never ask you to do this if I didn't know why the baby died. And you know it was an abruption, not disease. I won't tell anyone if you won't. I really need it. It's important." Miriam stood firm, determined not to leave without it.

The nurse retrieved the bloody blanket and placed it in a plastic garbage bag. "You didn't get this from me, Miriam. I could lose my job and even do jail time." Miriam gave her a hug; the nurse hugged her back.

"I'm so sorry, Miriam. Take good care of your daughters. They need you and your love, especially now."

Miriam made sure the bag was sealed tightly to keep the blood from drying and ensure the odor was contained. She put the bag in her locker, then returned to Andrea and Maria. They remained with Andrea until late in the evening. When the medical staff assured them Andrea was out of danger, they each kissed her and told her they would return first thing in the morning.

On the way out, Miriam instructed the obstetrician to watch Andrea closely. She also asked that he arrange for psychological help to get Andrea through this mystifying time and keep her safe from herself. She then stopped at her locker and grabbed the garbage bag.

"What's in the bag, Mother?" asked Maria.

"Fresh DNA from your daddy," Miriam answered.

That very night, Miriam formed a coven with Maria and four other women. They were all powerful and experienced. The curse was cast, and within six months, Raoul was eaten internally by exotic parasites never seen in Panama and for which no medication existed. He lost seventy percent of his body weight by the end.

Andrea finished high school, and as a reward, the three girls went to Balboa on vacation, but only two returned home. Andrea wanted nothing to do with Panama City, her failure as a pianist, the lingering smell of her father in their home, or the memory of her dead son covered in blood on her breast. And Balboa was a perfect place to find men, men she could crush in so many ways other than death. She took her mother's advice and concluded she could not hurt men if she were behind bars for murder. But she was concocting creative ways to destroy them.

BALBOA, PANAMA – 1995

14

THE DEMISE OF ANDREA'S HUSBAND

It was a hot night in "The Loop." Antonio and Michael sat at the bar surrounded by a swarm of defeated gringos, drinking cheap local beer, the alcohol content being the same as a bottle of water. They discussed the status of Michael's repairs in progress at his hotel, while being distracted by the local chicas passing by. But Michael abruptly changed subjects. "What the hell happened to Grant? I heard he moved back to the States. Was it health or family issues? Is he coming back? Are he and Andrea still together?"

"Nope, and they won't ever be," Antonio said angrily. "You deal directly with me from here on, Michael. Don't give Andrea another penny. You know Grant and I were close, and I'll tell you the story if you promise to keep it to yourself. Different versions of this story have been flying around town like a colony of bats. No one except me knows the real story. I've been on the phone many times with Grant now that he's back in Texas. I'm trying to keep his business alive long enough to finish his commitments. He told me most of what happened, and you'll no doubt hear others telling their truth."

"Antonio, you know I'm a professional writer, right? Is this a story people would enjoy reading? You mind if I put it to paper when you're done?" asked Michael.

"It's a whale of a story, Michael, but if you do, someone may kill you or deport you. But first, they will torture you to get my name, then kill me. I can't stop you from writing it, but promise me you'll never let anyone read it, unless it's back in the States, and even then, you must change names and places," responded Antonio. Antonio knew the danger but was dying to tell the real story to someone he could trust. "Let's go back to your house, Michael, so no one will overhear. I will grab some beers on the way."

"Deal, my friend," agreed an anxious Michael.

As they sat on the veranda, Antonio began, and Michael listened intently. He scattered single word notes in no logical order on pieces of note paper. The next day, Michael began to write. The story went like this.

THE DEMISE OF ANDREA'S HUSBAND
A Short Story by Michael Harper

Balboa was a small tourist town that seemed like paradise, an archipelago of small to medium sized islands surrounded by mangroves, swarming with breathtaking wildlife, and encircled by vibrant coral reefs and fishes. But when looking behind the curtain of this seemingly peaceful sanctuary, it was more like paradise lost. All was well for centuries until Adam and Eve arrived, not snacking on just one apple from these trees, but downing an entire bushel basket full of them.

A young couple, Grant, and Andrea married two years earlier. Grant had an uncharacteristically small physical stature for a Texan, but he was a decent guy, a hard worker, who had lots of friends. Andrea, on the other hand, was a happy-go-lucky Panamanian party girl with an intense physic and beautiful dark hair and eyes. She was a siren of classic literary proportion. They seemed quite happy but seldom seen in town together.

Grant moved to Balboa to start a construction company but needed a Panamanian citizen to own part of it, since he had not yet qualified for residency or a work permit. As word of his plans hit the streets, Andrea quickly saw an opportunity to get her talons into an unworldly Americano with money.

"Hi, can I get you something to drink, handsome? I don't think I know you," Andrea said from behind the bar. You're not from around here. My name is Andrea, Andrea Blanco." Andrea extended her hand and Grant returned the introduction with a gentle touch and a smile. "What brings you to Balboa?"

Andrea said as she leaned over and smiled, her sensuous eyes locking onto his, her breast resting on the bar, accentuating her long, dark cleavage. Grant tried not to look down to where she was leading his eyes.

"My name is Grant Thomas. I'm looking to start a construction business here in Balboa. Know any good workers? And I need someone Panamanian to hold a couple shares in the company for residency and work permit reasons." Grant had innocently and unknowingly exposed himself to one mean set of claws. In other words, he just 'left his wallet on the nightstand.'

Andrea lured him into her web like a Golden Orb spider lures a naive butterfly. They were married within months. I guess you could say Grant married for love and financial reasons, and Andrea married for, well, financial reasons. She helped him obtain residence and a work permit, not actual legal ones. She was aware, according to Panamanian law, with a simple 'I do' she owned half the stock and therefore half the profits of Grants fledgling company. And with her connections to corruption, his business would grow quickly. She also made it clear her party time with her friends was sacred. She reminded him often, as she would repeat again and again, 'I will never stay home and be some fat Panamanian house bitch with ten kids. She wanted to continue to tend bar a few nights a week while Grant supervised his construction company during the day. Grant rose early and worked hard until sunset in the unbearable heat and humidity of the rainforest. This worked perfectly for Andrea, because he was exhausted at night, and Andrea wasn't. His primary enjoyment came from smoking pot and playing video games after dinner in the A/C. Andrea stayed on the streets partying, bartending, and selling drugs. Andrea's fidelity to Grant was nonexistent, but Grant never seemed to care about that as long as Andrea, from time to time, brought a cute little surfer girl home for them both to enjoy.

Most days, Grant left Andrea supply invoices to be collected from his clients to continue their project. Andrea made her rounds in the afternoon hours. But before her rounds, she would forge a new invoice, twenty percent higher than what Grant gave her. The clients would pay her in cash, she would return the original invoice amounts to Grant each night and put the difference up the nose of her and her friends.

One afternoon, a massive young man approached Antonio in the street. "Your name is Antonio, and you work for Andrea's husband, right?" asked the young man in a half-witted monotone voice.

"Yes, I'm Grant's supervisor. I have seen you around 'The Loop'," answered Antonio. "I know what you do, and I know your boss."

"Well, I'm just a low-level kid for the big guy. My job is to collect outstanding drug debts. And frankly, Antonio, we have a problem."

"Whoa, whoa, you have the wrong guy here, lumpy. I drink beer and sometimes whiskey and only smoke pot when someone passes me a joint. I don't buy and certainly don't owe any of you guys anything."

"No, no, man, don't go there. I'm not putting pressure on you. But I'm supposed to put pressure on Grant this afternoon," he said. "He is your buddy, right?"

"He's my good buddy, but why Grant? He just smokes pot and would never stiff any of you. He doesn't have to. He has money in the bank, plenty of it." Antonio turned to walk into his house.

"No, wait, amigo. I'm here to help your boss, dude. But you mustn't expose me, or they'll snip one of my fingers or some bullshit like that, please promise." The kid was scared. "My brother works for Grant and loves his job. He pays him well and shit man, even on time. It takes good care of his family. One time your boss fronted my bro' money for medicine when his kid, my cute little nephew, had that eye thing. You know, 'conjunction' something?"

"Go on."

"The big guy rotates us collection boys. Today I'm to go see Grant, because I was told his wife is running up a crazy fat cocaine tab. And the big guy says Andrea just tells him to piss off' when he goes after her. She tells him to send one of us 'bumfucks' as she calls us, to get it from her husband. That's where I'm going now. To squeeze Grant for a good chunk of cash."

"I know, my friend, Grant's wife is a digger, and he can't control her. She runs up all kinds of debts on him," Antonio said shaking his head.

"No, amigo, I found out different. It's a scam. I'm telling you, man, this is all a scam. She's got plenty of money. She's a bigtime dealer herself in this town. My boss and Andrea are scammin' him and pullin' me in on it. That's what I'm trying to tell you, man, so maybe you can help Grant." The kid sounded sincere.

"Explain." Antonio paid closer attention.

"Okay, here's how it goes down. The big guy fronts her fifty of those little bags of blow a week, half of which goes for her private use and to share with her male and female sex partners. The other half she sells to the tourist kids and gringos, jacking up the wholesale price that covers the cost of the original fifty bags. Following me, amigo?"

"I've got you so far, but where does Grant come in?"

"The big guy sends us boys around weekly to put a foot up Grant's ass to collect again for Andrea's coke, like it was the first and only payment. We convince Grant that Andrea never paid us at all. I guess because he feels responsible for his bitch or something. So, he pays again. Then the big guy and Andrea split Grant's money two ways. It's a con, dude. They're double dippin' on your buddy. You get it now, man. It's double dippin.' Grant's just another one of her dumbshit ATMs with a penis."

"Well, that bitch. But what is your purpose in telling me?" asked Antonio. "They'll mess you up if they find out you told me. Andrea will snip your nuts off herself."

"I told you why, dude. Your boss is good to my brother and his kid, man. But if she keeps ripping him off, there goes medicine and bonuses and shit for his family. I must collect from him today, or it's my ass. Let me do that just for today so he doesn't suspect me. Whether you tell Grant after I collect is up to you. I just ask you protect me and keep me out of this," concluded the big, but nice, meathead.

"Thank you, I'll tell him to keep you out of it. I'll give you an hour. Grant's home alone. I just left him." Antonio was livid. The kid walked to Grant's.

Antonio waited for an hour, stomped to Grant's, and told him the whole story. Grant was outraged.

Andrea came home at six, bouncing her cute curvaceous bosoms into the room, being sweet to Grant, kissing him, and squeezing his crotch. She proceeded, predictably, to request cash so she could go back out and play. Grant had no reaction. He didn't look up. He just stared angrily at his game screen.

"What the fuck, Grant. I need some cash."

After a long pause, Grant blurted, "I'm wise to your coke scam, bitch."

"What the fuck are you talking about, whack job?"

Grant stood up and faced her. "Andrea, someone in town pulled me aside today and told me all about it, every detail. And don't ask me who she is. I have never seen her before."

"Whoever she is, she's full of shit. No one's conning you, you dickhead. I would never scam you. Why steal money from my own husband? What did she look like? Would you recognize her if you saw her again? Her ass is going to be kicked. Are you fucking this woman when I'm not around, you man-whore?"

"No, I don't remember; she looked Panamanian with bigger tits than yours."

"Well, that narrows it down."

Cut the shit. I know all the details about me paying your fake cocaine tabs. You're splitting the money with your dealer. Look, babe, you want to get high and fuck around, I don't care, your choice. If you OD, I don't care. I would love it. It would save me a lot of money, and things would be more peaceful in my life. I have learned to hate you."

"Cut the crap, drama-queen and give me some cash. It's half mine, Hubby man. My friends are waiting."

Grant continued, "But from here on, you little slut, pay for your own blow, and your boyfriends and bitches can pay for theirs. The Daddy Warbucks days are over." Grant was getting angrier by the second. "I calculate from your squeeze on me, you do three bags a day. Your sales to your junkies are more than enough to cover that. No more on 'Hubby man.' Got it?"

"How about what you snort up that pig snout you call a nose?" said Andrea. She finally pushed the passive Grant Thomas over the edge.

"I never bumped before I met you, bitch, and I quit months ago to stop the nosebleeds. Tell your dealer buddy not one more penny from me, not one." He lifted his middle finger and shoved it into her face. His eyes bulged with rage.

The finger did it. Andrea went manic. "I assure you, Grant, my dealer buddy will nail you to a fucking cross, upside down, and let your money fall out of your pockets that way."

"Andrea, you underestimate the support I have in this town. I have lots of workers and suppliers making money off me. When I tell them you and your drug toad are scamming me and it will affect their pay and bonuses, they will have a talk with him. And I am fully aware you are making money with your tits and bubble ass, fucking the tourist kids of both genders in that apartment you think I don't know about. Con is done, honey. I have half a mind to go to the police or even to the feds. I have no feelings for you." Panting, Grant sat down and went back to his PlayStation.

Andrea exploded into all-out frenzy. She told Grant someone was going to pay. Grant laughed and flew the finger up again. She charged him screaming, calling him a little motherfucker and every other blasphemous slam she knew in English. She picked up their machete. Grant thought she would hack him to bits. But instead of slicing him up, she came straight down on his PlayStation, chopping it to a heap of scrap. Then, turning the machete in her hands like a baseball bat, she smashed his monitor. She went hunting for his passport and wallet. He always hid them in alternating places, to keep them safe from the thieves in town. He never hid them under the mattress where the thieves looked first. Andrea taught him that. She finally flung the machete to the floor and stomped toward the door. As she opened it, she looked back at Grant with a diabolical smile, jiggled her house keys at him and said, "I 'm not done with you yet, asswipe. No one fucks with me. Sleep well, my love." Grant sat down in his chair, quiet and alone, surrounded by his pile of cyber rubble.

* * * *

Antonio sat on the bar stool at "The Loop" having a few beers, thinking about the events of the afternoon, but no way sharing them with anyone. He knew if his friend, the big guy, knew he exposed the scam, he would be tortured to reveal the kid. Antonio was unsure whether Grant confronted Andrea, but question was quickly answered. Andrea thundered into the bar, eyes crazed, huffing like a raging Brahma bull. Antonio knew Andrea was going on the offense.

"That's one pissed off chica," Antonio said under his breath. "Grant confronted her, and the lioness is going hunting. That has deathtrap written all over it. I hope I did the right thing."

Andrea went into the bathroom and did two monstrous bumps of blow, the kind that slams you in the back of the skull like the round end of a ball peen hammer. She came out and sat next to her old and feeble gringo friend, Josh.

"Bernard, bring me a beer and a shot of tequila. And keep them coming, your German kraut. Shit's flying tonight. Put that song 'Heartache Tonight' on the jukebox, cause 'Somebody's gonna hurt somebody before this night is through."

Antonio watched as Andrea chewed Josh's ear off, loud enough for all to hear. She told everyone how cheap her husband is and how mean he talks to her. After a few drinks, a Panamanian man, handsome and well-dressed for Balboa, whispered something in Andrea's ear. It was the big guy. Antonio knew him from school days. She grabbed her cigarettes, and they went outside into the street. She described the confrontation in her own words, of course.

Andrea was animated, arms flailing like a loose sail in a storm, like a tempest incarnate. The boss whispered something in her ear, looked at her face, and smiled. She calmed; her eyes squinted with hate as she beamed deviously. She flicked her cigarette into the street, just missing a mother and her little girl. He walked away. She went back to her bar stool.

As the cocaine and alcohol saturated her brain, Andrea became louder and louder. Finally, Bernard cut her off.

"Kiss my ass, Bernard," Andrea told him loud enough for everyone to hear. "You can't cut me off, you piece of Euro-shit. You know who I am. I'm your best friend." Antonio turned his stool to watch the approaching chaos. The vulture boys with bulging jeans were still hanging around, waiting for Andrea to get drunk enough they could take her back to her apartment and fuck her after she passed out.

"Andrea, its time you go to Dave's down the street. Dave will serve you until you fall off the stool, then help you back on it to drink some more. But you are done here. You're too loud, and your language. I have tourists still eating, even a family with two young children. You can pay me tomorrow, but just leave now, please." Bernard reached for her half-full beer bottle. But before he could clear it, she picked up the bottle in one hand, shot glass in the other, hit the shot, then wailed the empty glass at Bernard, splitting his forehead wide open. Bernard went down on one knee, blood running down his forehead and into his eyes. The owner and his Panamanian bouncer came running. One of the servers got a towel and ice and held it to Bernard's wound.

Andrea ran past Antonio and into the bathroom, purse in one hand, beer bottle in the other. She locked the door behind her. The owner pounded on the door, demanding that she come out, but she didn't. Then the sound of shattering glass was heard.

"Did you break my mirror, you drunk? Open this door right now. No more, you hear me, no more." screamed the owner. They were about to kick the door in when Andrea unlocked it, standing in front of the sink, blood running from her cheekbone onto her shoulder, soaking the top of her white low-cut dress. She made no attempt to stop the bleeding. Andrea had broken the beer bottle on the edge of the sink and sliced her cheek with a shard. She was posing with an evil smirk, punching her fist over and over into the cut, blood splattering, like a boxer in a ring.

The owner lost it. He grabbed her by the wrist to stop her self-destruction. "What in the hell are you doing, Andrea? Is this a suicide attempt? You missed your wrist by a mile, babe."

Andrea left the bathroom and shouted at the owner. The whole room was listening. "No way, asshole. I wouldn't kill myself. I'm too important in this town. But my fucking husband is going to do some jail time for what he did to me tonight. As far as you guys are concerned, my husband jumped me on the way home and did this to me. Get it. That son of a bitch is going to pay for being such a prick. Just keep your fucking mouths shut. That little gringo butt-face of a husband hit me, right?" Then she looked around the room and stared at the patrons eating dinner. They all looked down. The father with the only family in the room had his wife and two daughters standing behind him while he held a long-necked beer bottle in his hand, hoping Andrea would advance. Then, in an evil, raspy voice, she said, "And I mean all of you fucking drunks in here. Keep your fucking mouths shut, or I'll cut your balls off." She looked straight at the two little girls peeking out from behind their father. She pointed at them. "You understand, you little piss-ants? This goes for you, too." And with that, Andrea flung the owner's hand off her wrist and stomped out of the bar, straight to the police station, where she told her fabricated story. But Antonio's cousin, Jose, was the captain in charge that night.

Antonio looked at Bernard," Cover my tab, I must follow her. Pay you tomorrow." Bernard nodded and Antonio trailed Andrea to the station without being seen.

Her face bloody and bruised, Andrea filed a complaint and pressed charges against Grant for assault. Jose immediately sent two officers to Grant's house to arrest him. They banged on his door. Grant was asleep. When he finally woke, he was confused as to why the police were at his door, sticks in hand.

"Are you Grant Thomas and are you Andrea's husband?" they asked. Grant confirmed he was.

"Is she alright?" asked Grant.

One officer slammed Grant against the wall, twisting his arms behind his back. "That's a funny question coming from a man who just smacked his wife in the face with a beer bottle and left her beaten and bloody." The officer pushed Grant through the house to his bedroom. "Get dressed and get your passport and wallet." Grant did what he was told, and when finished, the officer smashed Grant's face into the wall once again. "Mr. Thomas, you are under arrest for assault and domestic violence." They handcuffed him, put him into their SUV, then straight to the police station.

Antonio lurked in the shadows of the police station. It consisted of one community jail for the child-support dodgers, two private cells for the violent and insane, and the open-aired interrogation room near the gate on the street. Antonio listened intently. He heard Andrea's tale about the alleged attack. He heard the officer's orders and watched them leave and return with Grant in cuffs.

As they brought him into the station, Grant saw Andrea waiting at the captain's desk, still covered in blood. He saw those unstable eyes before. He knew when she was emotionally unmanageable, totally whacked out on coke and alcohol. But still, she was coherent enough to put on a great act as she began the scene by charging the defenseless Grant like a wild boar. She was stopped by the officers, stepping in front of Grant.

Andrea commenced screaming profanely in a heavy slur, "You fucking gringo. Everyone, including my mother, warned me about you Americanos, especially you Texans, how violent you are and how you love to beat and rape your women. All those other little slaps and shoves you've given me over the years have been nothing compared to hitting me with a beer bottle in the face. You could've killed me. You're crazy, Grant. I knew you were jealous, but holy shits, never have I seen a man so psycho. You need help."

It all seemed so ridiculous. Everyone knew what a gentle guy Grant was, except the cops, and they didn't care, he was a gringo. Grant looked at the captain. "Captain, ask Andrea what happened earlier today, and what's been happening every day for months with her drug dealing buddy. Who did hit you, somebody's husband, boyfriend, girlfriend?"

Andrea responded with more lies and insults, telling Grant no one believed a gringo over her. She gave Grant the finger and walked out of the police station. Antonio followed her to Dave's, where she would be served no matter how high or loud she became. Grant was behind bars. Antonio took a seat close enough to Andrea to overhear her, telling anybody she didn't know how she got the cut on her cheek from her loco Americano husband. She got lots of sympathy and lots of free drinks and the opportunity to sell lots of cocaine. But she didn't talk to anyone who saw what really happened. By that time, Bernard was off work and at Dave's, holding a towel filled with ice to his forehead and blood on his shirt. All the locals knew what happened and Andrea knew they knew.

As Antonio watched and listened, he realized he could not let this happen. He headed back to the police station and had a heart-to-heart talk with his cousin, both about "The Loop" and the scam. "Bring me two witnesses, and I'll reconsider the charges against Grant," his cousin said, hoping to appease Antonio.

Antonio returned to Dave's and asked if anyone would tell the captain the truth. Bernard and the owner agreed. They walked into the station, Bernard's forehead still bleeding. The owner, a Panamanian, and all the police, knew this wasn't the first problem with Andrea's violence. The captain asked a couple quick questions. The charges were dropped.

Antonio went home. He had to rise early for work and would see Grant then. But Grant was not released by orders of the police chief.

Closing time came at two-thirty. A few tourists were left still trying to get laid or get higher. And a few locals, like Andrea, waited to make money off the needy. It was not a pretty sight. The two officers that arrested Grant were assigned as damage control on Andrea. The game of the night, "The Falsification of her Beating." Andrea emptied many a surfer-kid's wallet with her sob story, but they didn't care about Andrea's problem, they just wanted to get their willies wet. But Andrea was a professional. Getting free drinks, selling cocaine, and stealing wallets was her job. The police watched as she corralled the 'last boy staggering.' The routine would begin. She would lead him down the street to her apartment, put a sleep aid in his last beer, and watch him pass out. She would drain his wallet like a swamp and leave him on the couch. The next morning, he would wake fully clothed, not remembering what happened.

He would call his father and tell him he was robbed at gun point and say 'Daddy, they stole your credit card.'

The officers watched it unfold. "There she goes, Pedro, taking that kid to her love shack. He will be in the station by noon wanting to press charges for theft. Glad we will be off duty and won't have to hear him whine."

"You believe she smacked herself in the face to control her husband? And why is he still in jail?" said one officer.

"Don't ask," said the other.

The police duo took one last stroll around town to be sure the night was finished, then sat on a park bench, did a bump, and smoked a joint.

* * *

Grant's construction company boomed, for Balboa anyway, cashing in on the island's building craze. His employees respected him, and his clients trusted him. He had a backlog of contracts. But Andrea treated the employees like peasants, even though she was one herself. The employees called her "The Queen B." She thought 'B' stood for 'boss'. It did not.

The next morning, the police chief was brought up to date on Grant's situation, but he was already aware. It was seven-thirty. Grant was released from his cell and taken upstairs to the police chief's office. He entered; the door was shut. Grant and the chief were alone.

"Grant, we know you are innocent of assaulting your wife. Antonio saved you last night, along with two others; one with a nasty gash in his forehead."

"So, I can go now? I have to get to a project site, sir. Thank you. I'm sorry this happened." Grant stood up.

"You might want to sit back down, Grant. Letting you go is not what I am saying." Grant was puzzled.

"We are all aware of your wife's temper and dangerous personality. For you, that's not good, but for us, it is. You see, she's a hard-ass and especially important to the drug economy of Balboa. Drug dealing is our backbone here, and she is one of our best. And she is a great con artist. She has something we men don't have if you know what I mean. Sorry to say that about your wife."

"I know, her pussy is just a tool of her trade. She even cons me. But the money from my business is safe. She can't sign checks or withdraw money from my account. I control how much I give her."

"It's not about money, Grant. It's about your life. Let me explain. She's going to kill you someday, and I predict soon." The chief was cold. "As long as our drug economy is getting fat off her sales, we put up with her craziness. Police, politicians, dealers, even the feds in Panama City; we all have a set of rules that work for us. That's why you never see a drug bust in Balboa unless it is a petty one to squeeze a bribe from a smart-mouth yuppie brat."

"I will mind my own business, Chief," responded Grant.

"No, you can't. As you just saw, Andrea does not take 'No' for an answer. And you are telling her no. Our rules are simple, no one dies from violence or a drug overdose. That's why heroin is nonexistent here. The cocaine snorted by the expats and tourists can only be mixed with laundry detergent. It keeps it weak and virtually impossible to overdose. Dealers can only get pure stuff from the Columbians. Crack can be smoked, but only among the dealers. And only native Balboans can be dealers. So, our job as police is to control what is dealt on the streets, and who deals it. The dealers make their money by selling, of course. But we do allow Andrea to play her pseudo-prostitution scams as her private deal."

"I know she hooks. I fell out of love with her a year ago, Chief. I really don't care. Her jealousy accusation last night was bullshit," interrupted Grant.

"Doesn't matter. Let me finish. The final agreement is, nothing gets smuggled into Balboa except for specific Columbian suppliers, and both sides must go through one top dealer. That keeps us all one big happy family, but Grant, you upset the apple cart."

"What? Me? How?"

"Every time Andrea gets involved with a gringo with money, she starts her con. He figures it out, her craziness begins, and the gringo gets hurt or killed. When it comes to money, she's like a shark smelling blood. Then here come the feds from Panama City, the FBI from the States, and the US Embassy, then the press and the victim's family. Our dealers are forced underground for a while, and the streets dry up. You must cooperate before she kills you or you squawk to the US. If you stay here, we must arrest you every time she blows up. We can't let you die. She will never get off your ass until she gets crazy high some night and kills you."

"What do you want me to do?" asked Grant.

"We know Andrea is back at your house and won't be awake until noon. She assumes you are in jail for weeks. But now that you know our rules, you can't stay here. Nobody wants you dead for business reasons." said the chief.

"You should not have told me, Chief. I did not need to know your rules." Grant was angry.

"But you do. You are a threat to all of us; dealers, feds, politicians, Columbians; even me. The US doesn't care about this place, and the Panamanian feds don't care, if no gringo dies. Andrea is just a pest now, but she will kill you someday. And if she doesn't, the others will. You cannot stay here, Grant."

"I won't say a word to anybody. How will they know I know?" asked Grant.

"Because I will leak it to them."

"Why would you do that, unless you told me on purpose." Grant stopped. He now understood.

The chief put the plan in motion. Grant was told two officers would escort him to the ATM and grab the maximum $500. He will take the nine o'clock water taxi to the mainland, then the bus to Panama City. Then take the first flight back to Texas, never to return.

"Grant, let me warn you. If you try to remain in Panama, especially coming back here, let me just say, it is a big ocean, and the boys around here can always use more fish bait."

Grant had one unanswered question. He explained to the chief that if he left, his business had unfinished contracts and Antonio was the only one capable of completing the work. He knew what was needed and he was the only person who could sign checks. After all is completed and all workers paid, he estimated there would be $80,000 left in the account.

"I will talk with Andrea about your unfinished contracts," said the chief. "I doubt she would stiff the local employees and suppliers. That makes enemies. And by finishing the contracts, she would have $80,000."

"Right, a no-brainer for Andrea," said Grant. At that point, he slammed his hand on the chief's desk. "Chief, how do I get my $80,000 wired to me in the States? That is not Andrea's money."

The chief shook his head, "Grant, you were a dumbass for marrying her in the first place. That 'I do' by law, gave her fifty percent ownership in your company. You are the victim of what we call 'Gringo Bingo.' We don't play by the same set of rules as you naïve Americans. Andrea knew what she was doing even before she served you your first beer. It was game on. You were a chump. You played right into her dirty little hands."

"Why can't I stop at the bank on the way out of town and sign a paper authorizing a wire transfer to the States?"

"You might have been able to do that, but you must sign the papers in person. And for some strange reason, the mayor closed the bank today." The chief had a sinister grin on his face.

The final act was set into motion. Andrea set Grant up to be unofficially deported. Grant swore he would get back at her somehow, someday. He wasn't the first man the hateful Andrea and her team would con, and not the last. To the others, it was about money. To Andrea, it was personal; it was vengeful, starting with her father.

A week later, Grant sent Andrea a telegram from Texas telling her he wouldn't be back, and instructing her to finish the contracts, close the bank account and wire half to his bank in the States. She could keep the other half. She sent back calling him an ignorant asshole and telling him he needed psychiatric help. And just to be cute, she told him she was HIV positive.

That was the last communication between Grant and Andrea. Grant and Antonio, however, continued to speak frequently on the phone, putting the pieces together. It started at the top.

The mayor knew exactly what was in Grant's bank account, and he wanted it. He, the police chief, and the big guy cooked up the game. To begin, they needed Grant to have a reason to hurt Andrea. He instructed the big guy to send a goony collector kid, informing Antonio of a con perpetrated on Grant by Andrea. The mayor knew Antonio would tell Grant and he knew Grant was already upset over her increasing drug tabs. The big guy knew Grant was close to a breaking point. Knowing Andrea had plenty of cash and now knowing it was a con, Andrea pushed him, and Grant went off. She made him angry just because she loved watching men in pain. She destroyed the only thing he enjoyed and lived for, his video game. And that gave him a motive to slash her face. It was the big guy outside 'The Loop', sent by the mayor, who whispered in her ear to cut herself up and blame it on Grant to get him into the station. The next morning, the police chief put Grant in the position to leave or become fish bait.

Andrea would wait for the projects to be completed before she withdrew Grant's $80,000. She would then tip everyone involved, the goony kid, the dealer, the police chief, the bank manager, and the judge. But what she did not see coming. The mayor's brother, the bank manager, closed the bank the morning of Grant's departure. Then the mayor's sister, the judge, froze Grant's account for three days, giving them time to complete the paperwork giving only the mayor permission to close the account and confiscate the money, due to 'back taxes.' Andrea was helpless.

In the end, the mayor took $40,000 for himself. He split $30,000 among his sister judge, his banker brother, and his uncle police chief. The remainder went to the kid, the dealer, and finally, to Andrea, who received $2,000. She was furious. She went on a two-week binge. She beat up a few surfer boys. Men had fucked her over once more. Her hatred for them was in the danger zone.

THE END

15

OH WHERE, OH WHERE HAS MY LITTLE BOY GONE?

It was a peaceful night. A gentle ocean breeze drifted onto the veranda, touching the wind chimes ever so tenderly, as though stroking the soft hair of an infant. The gloaming was spiritual in its final hours as the mystical winter solstice advanced. But the pastel sunset passed to nightfall. It was eight o'clock. The sky was dark, and the heat of the day faded slowly away.

Michael and Maria sat quietly, but anxiously, on the veranda that stretched over the ocean. They awaited the return of Andrea with Alejandro, Michael, and Andrea's three-month-old son. Maria, Andrea's older sister by two years, agreed to come to Balboa as the baby's nanny after the child's birth in Panama City. Maria was without employment, without a husband, and without children of her own. Andrea convinced Michael to hire her and live with them, paying her more than an appropriate salary. Maria's presence also appeased Andrea's mother, Miriam, who despised men since the incestuous rape of Andrea by her father. The fact her precious Andrea had now given birth to a child sired by an older gringo, even though wealthy and kind, was offensive to her. But for now, Miriam was satisfied both her daughters, and her grandson were supported. It removed the financial burden off her.

Michael spent the last hour sharing his short story with Maria about her sister and still legal husband, Grant. "Michael, thank you for reading your story to me. I tried, but even though my spoken English is fine, my reading and writing are weak. You're sure that is the gospel truth? But why did you insist I hear it?" Maria asked.

"Maria, the plot, and surrounding circumstances came from Antonio and Grant. I trust them both. And you asked, why did I want you to hear it?" responded Michael.

"Yes, why?" Maria asked in an uneasy tone. "She's my sister, I love her, and she loves me. And we both adore Alejandro. Are you warning me I should fear her? She would never turn on me or her son, Michael. You have been so sweet until now. I also know you two have not been getting along ever since we returned from Panama City. Signs of break-up are floating through this house."

"My dear Maria, I understand your faith in Andrea and how you want me to be wrong. I am not an immature boyfriend." Maria nodded her head. "But humor me for a moment. Promise me, if anything happens to me and you sense you and Alejandro are in danger, you will go to Antonio immediately, no one else. He knows who to call and who can protect you and the child." As Michael answered Maria, he ripped up the pages of his manuscript and began placing them in the charcoal grill on the veranda.

"What are you doing, Michael?" asked Maria.

Michael doused the torn fragments in lighter fluid and set them ablaze. He continued until only ashes remained, then he dumped the incinerated drama into the sea.

"That story exposes powerful and dangerous people in this town, including Andrea. If they know we know what happened to Grant, they will have us killed. Other than Antonio, you are the only person who has heard that story; no one else." responded Michael. "Someday, in the future, I would enjoy changing the names and make a movie of it." They both smiled, but Maria's smile was laced with fear.

"I assume there's another copy somewhere. That can't be the only one," asked Maria. Michael questioned why Maria cared. He decided not to ask. "But I am still confused. Why did you read it to me?"

"No, it is not the only copy. I sent a copy to someone in the States, who will remain nameless. I printed this draft on my printer this afternoon, deleted the file and burnt the rest." Michael sat at the table across from Maria. "Now, the reason I read it to you. I know you don't want to believe it, but I want you to be aware of the deviant society she has been in for the last seventeen years. I want you to watch for yourself and realize no one is safe here." Michael stared coldly at Maria. "But Alejandro is in the most danger."

Maria's love and loyalty were stretched, not between Michael and Andrea, but between Andrea and Alejandro. "Michael, when did Andrea tell you she was returning home with the baby? She told me by dark." Maria was concerned.

"She said the same to me, but I don't trust Andrea these days. She's changed since Alejandro's birth, and not in a safe way. Other than during her pregnancy, I have known her to party harder than I thought possible. Now that she has the baby, I assumed she would cut down on the drugs and alcohol. But since she has you to nanny and me to support everyone financially, she's been stepping on the gas of late. I'm concerned for Alejandro's safety, and hers."

"I hope she's feeding the baby. I helped her pack his diaper bag this afternoon when she left. She didn't take enough formula with her to last this long, nor enough diapers. She should be breastfeeding, you know," Maria added, taking a sip of her wine.

"Yes, she should, but we know that will not work. She doesn't get up until noon, so no feedings in the night and no feedings in the morning. Then, when she gets up, she's a mess, her breakfast is a cigarette and a beer, 'the hair of the dog,' as she says. With alcohol, pot, cigarettes, cocaine, and Xanax, she binges twelve to fourteen hours a day. I won't allow that lactation cocktail to enter my son's body; not that she cares about his health. She loves flashing her tits in public, and that gives her a great excuse to do so."

"You're right, Michael. Then she goes to the mountains Thursday through Sunday without him. I'm sorry, but I must ask. Why did you decide to have a baby with my sister? You knew her history. I am thirty-seven and never knew this, Andrea. Our mother and I have a different perception of her and her life in Balboa, though I can understand why."

"What does that mean, you can understand why?'"

"Oh, living in this environment, which is all I meant." Maria dodged the question, like a matador dodging a clueless bull. "I still question whether some parts of your story about her are, let's say, embellished?"

"Maria, why did I decide to have a baby with Andrea?" Michael laughed. "Decide, Maria? You are smarter than that. I had nothing to do with that decision. I assume she made an independent decision without telling me and stopped taking the pill. Perhaps she planned it so it would give you a job and her child support when we split up."

"But if it weren't for you, Alejandro would become just another Balboa street kid. What man around here would take care of her baby while she's gone most of the time? The jails are packed full of guys dodging child support. Most have multiple kids from multiple mothers. Most don't even know their kids' names. Or, if the father's a foreigner, he hops on a plane and gone forever. Please tell me you won't go back to the States when you sell this Bed and Breakfast, leaving the child alone with my sister. Or worse, taking him from us. Please promise me, Michael," pleaded Maria. "I'm already in love with that little boy."

Michael smiled at Maria. "Andrea was different when I first met her. She was what you are seeing now. I was skeptical, but then we started dating. She seemed to change. We traveled to Mexico, Costa Rica, and Columbia together, had amazing conversations, and the sex was fantastic."

"Michael, leave that last part out. She is my sister," interjected Maria as she looked over Michael's shoulder to see whether Andrea was home yet.

"My apologies, Maria, but she constantly expressed how much she loved me. And though many who knew her warned me and told me stories concerning her violent and scheming behavior toward men, when I confronted her, she told me she had matured and was ready to settle down with someone like me. She said her mother promised her she'd meet a good man someday. But still, she was undecided about having a baby. I just supposed that decision was because of the irresponsible fathers in this culture. Was your father good to you and Andrea?"

Maria didn't answer the question. "We will talk about that later. My focus is on Alejandro right now. Keep going, Michael."

Michael continued. "So, when she got to know me and meet my grown children, she knew I would never abandon our child to this lifestyle." Maria gave Michael a gentle nod and a modest smile.

"She also knew, if we split, I would be unable to take the baby to the States without her permission. Both parents must approve of their child crossing any border, unless one parent dies. She knew I would always support Alejandro. And if she tried to leave me, I must give her full custody to leave Balboa with him, which I would never do. She has reverted to the old Andrea. She has me trapped as her meal ticket, and you as Alejandro's mother."

"Michael, I assure you, if this is one of her traps, I have no knowledge of it. Maybe my mother does, but not me. I'm here to help with Alejandro if you need me. I love my little nephew. He's the child I can never have. Please believe me," Maria said in a loving and convincing tone, her eyes beginning to weep.

"Maria, to answer your question about me leaving? No, not my style. I'm Alejandro's father. I have three grown children back in the States and five young grandchildren. I put them through college and supported them financially and lovingly. I would prefer to raise Alejandro in the States. There are too many drugs here, it's a corrupt society, and it lacks decent education. That worries me. And as Andrea's party life becomes her priority once again, it is not a good motherly image. Andrea will never leave this lifestyle and her nefarious circle of friends. And she is still legally married to Grant, who is in Texas. And he wants to kill her."

"Are you not afraid Andrea and her politicians will con you and you will be gone someday, like Grant?

"I am aware of the danger, but I can take care of myself and Alejandro. My eyes are wide open. She can't sneak up on me. For now, Andrea will not put herself, you, and Alejandro in danger. And where is Andrea? Let me search the bars."

"No, let's stay here for a little longer. Let me call a few of her friends and see if they have seen her," Maria suggested.

Maria called, but with no luck. Suddenly, a sweet female voice from the garden door called out in Spanish, "Hola? Buenos noches. Hola?"

16

THE SECRET HIDING PLACE FOR ALEJANDRO

Michael and Maria rose from the table and glanced curiously at each other. Standing in the doorway, a humble but attractive Panamanian woman in her late twenties appeared, holding Alejandro tightly in her arms.

"Es Senior Harper aqui?" the woman asked.

"Si, I'm Senor Harper. Habla Inglais, senorita?" asked Michael.

"No, senor, solo un poco." With that, Maria took the lead in the conversation as Michael took Alejandro from the woman and into his arms. The woman was shaking. With a sigh of relief, Michael and Maria cuddled the baby in a warm, protective embrace, Maria stroked the crying baby's head with the touch of an angel.

Maria graciously invited the woman into the house and led her to the veranda. She invited her to sit. They spoke intensely in Spanish. Alejandro cried, but Michael sat quietly with him cradled in his arms. With strange and extraordinary patience, he waited to discover who this woman was and how she came to be in possession of his son. However, with Alejandro crying and needing to be changed and fed, Michael lost his patience; he found it frustrating how Panamanians could talk for so long and say so little.

"Maria, enough jabbering. It's time to let me in on what's transpiring."

"She won't tell me her name," Maria said. "And she's exposing very few details, but she has been sent with the baby by someone wishing to remain anonymous. She's been instructed to put the baby safely into your custody, not Andrea's, and when he's been changed and fed, she must call a man. He wants to talk only to you, Michael, to warn you Alejandro is in danger. We must call him before Andrea gets home."

On the brink of panic, Maria took the baby from Michael's arms to change his diaper while Michael went to the kitchen to prepare a bottle. The woman remained silent on the veranda, fear in her eyes. Alejandro, with a nasty rash, was in pain from his saturated diaper, feces noticeably leaking out the bottom, his tummy cramped from hunger.

After Maria cleaned the baby, put ointment and powder on him, she returned and fed him. As the nipple entered his mouth, Alejandro stopped crying, only a sob sporadically emanated from his tiny nostrils. His suffering began to fade, and he appeared content and safe. His eyelids drooped like those of an adorable baby sloth. He finished only half the bottle before his eyes closed ever so gently and he fell asleep, nestled in the warmth of Maria's arms. But even though he was now secure and unharmed, she didn't put him in his crib. Maria continued to rock him. They both felt the devotion. She and the young woman exchanged something in Spanish.

"What now, Maria?" asked Michael.

"She's ready to make the call. Are you ready, Michael? My instincts tell me this could be unpleasant. Promise you will use an adult tone with him. Leave your emotions out of this. Promise me. Consider this a business call." With that, she told the woman to make the call. The woman dialed and handed the phone to Michael.

The phone rang and a man answered, speaking fluent English with a Spanish accent. "Does this call have to do with a baby, yes or no?" the voice asked, making sure he had the correct number.

"Yes, it does. My name is Michael Harper. I'm very concerned. Your woman tells me my son is in serious danger. I must warn you, sir, I have powerful contacts in Panama City and the US Embassy, and if you are threatening or endangering my child." He was interrupted.

"Michael, I assume I can call you Michael, the purpose of this call is quite the opposite. I'm contacting you to make you aware of the danger your son is in due to his mother, Andrea. There are things you must know, and I, too, have powerful contacts. But in this situation, I want to use them to protect your baby, not harm him." The man's voice was rough and raspy, but his tone sounded concerned.

"What is your name? I'm here with Andrea's sister. We need your name."

"You can call me sir, Michael," he responded abruptly.

"Then respectfully, sir, you can call me Mr. Harper and Andrea's sister Ms. Blanco." Michael knew the rules of negotiation and needed to keep the power on equal ground.

"Sir, may I put this on speakerphone, so Ms. Blanco may hear as well?" Michael waited for a response. He heard the man talking to someone in the background, instructing him to get everybody out of the house and let no one in until he finished the call.

The man asked to talk to his woman for a moment. Michael handed her the phone. She spoke with him and relayed to Maria that she and Michael were the only ones able to hear the conversation on speakerphone. Maria nodded. She also told Maria if Andrea came into the house, the call would be disconnected. She placed the phone on speaker, but kept it firmly in her hand, not Michael's.

"Okay, sir, how did you get involved with my baby?"

The man responded quickly. "I'm the top drug dealer in Balboa. Some people call me the big guy. Everybody in this industry works for me, including Andrea. You've been around long enough to realize how important the drug traffic is to this town's economy. And, as you can deduce, my occupation has dangerous moments."

Maria and Michael looked at each other, both wondering whether this was the beginning of a scam, like the one Andrea pulled on her husband. Michael winked at Maria and smiled. They both knew caution was necessary.

"I assume you want to tell me Andrea, working for you and getting high, is not a good motherly image? We know that. But what we don't know is your motive for this call. If you're the top dog of the drug world, why in do you care what happens to my baby?" Michael asked, his voice began to rise in volume. Maria waved and motioned for him to stay calm.

"Michael," the dealer began.

"Mr. Harper," interrupted Michael.

"Mr. Harper," Andrea's has worked for me for years, ever since she moved here in her late teens. She had a chip on her shoulder back then and loved taking advantage of tourists and gringos, mostly boys and older rich men. And for many years, including now, she has been my top dealer. She makes a lot of money, not only for herself, but for the politicians. That's why they protect her. I know it may hurt when I tell you this, but she has some incredible scams going here, and she is inventing new ones every day. She is a diabolical genius."

Michael responded, "Yes, and I am one of them. That's how we first got together. I was leaving her apartment after we'd played music together. When I reached the street, she called to me. I looked back. She stood naked in her doorway, smiling." Maria looked at Michael, her eyes wide in a scolding fashion. "She saw me as a big fish for the future, so she stole nothing from me. Whenever I came into town, we hung out. I bought her food and drinks and clothes. We went on trips. I fooled myself into believing she was in love with me."

"Sorry Mr. Harper, you aren't the first or last. But you know that now. When two of her boyfriends come to Balboa at the same time. She goes to her place in the mountains to play piano." The man paused and cleared his throat. Michael could not figure whether this man was a loose-lipped small-town criminal, or this was a clever con. But the truth was about to be exposed sooner than Michael imagined. When he spoke again, his tone was darker. "Mr. Harper, I have told you way too much, but for a reason. If you report me, you will disappear. You will be dead. I don't want that to happen to that baby's father. Understand, both of you?" The dealer didn't realize Michael and Maria knew who he was from the Andrea and Grant saga.

"I do," said Michael. "What you do is your business. I have no reason to put myself, my baby, or Andrea's sister in danger over money or drugs. I only care about them. Is that understood?"

The dealer understood. Michael again asked the critical question.

"Andrea's unique hooker style, her drug dealing, her conning, I know it goes on, and frankly, I don't care as long as she does it outside my compound. But if you are the big guy in this town, you must frighten and control many with that title. So again, if you are such a badass, why do you care about the safety of my baby? A 'nice guy' image cannot be good for business."

The dealer answered. "I have not heard from Andrea's sister. I don't want to start a family war, but I need for her to know if she repeats what is being said, I don't care whose sister she is, she will be dealt with harshly as well."

Maria was brief in her response. "From what I'm learning about my sister, my only concern is this baby in my arms. If you are protecting him, I am on your side. But if you hurt this baby, all deals are off. You aren't the only one with powerful friends. Do you understand me, sir?"

"Andrea has talked to me about you and your mother, and I believe I know who your powerful friends might be. Ms. Blanco, I certainly don't want them as enemies. You have my respect for being so bold. Before Andrea returns, allow me to get to the reason I called. My reason is not all business." Michael and Maria listened intently.

"Andrea, when not running drugs to the mountains or meeting a boyfriend, she works here. The baby is a prop for her, like a puppy dog in the park. She takes the baby for walks in the streets or on the beach. They get a lot of attention, especially from the young girls who then are followed by a herd of boys with hard-ons. This is her current marketing scheme."

"I get it, go on." Michael was angry and disgusted over Andrea's exploitation of Alejandro.

"She and the surfer kids become acquainted, they start drinking, and by nightfall, she's selling them coke or pot and infers sex in the evening. At that point, your baby becomes a problem. The boys feel uncomfortable partying with a crying baby in the room. To solve the problem, she comes by my house, lays the baby on my sofa, and tells me she'll be back soon. Before I can tell her no, she's out the door. Lately, she's gone longer and longer."

"Unfortunately," Michael said, "I'm not surprised, but I am sickened by the exploitation of my son. Please, sir, get to the point."

"My line of work is not performed in a family-friendly environment. I have a one-year-old baby with my girlfriend, the woman sitting across from you. I never wanted a child, but what a surprise. That little girl has given me love. She brought out a side of me I never thought I had. I do not let my child or my girlfriend near my workplace. I rent a second house to protect them. My workplace is filthy, both the furnishings and the people. I have lowlifes in and out, I have sleazy Columbians making drops. I have substantial amounts of cash on the premise. Then something happens and my army draws their weapons. It is usually a standoff, but not always. Sometimes people fight and fall over things, like sofas."

"You mean where she leaves Alejandro?" Michael was connecting the dots.

"Exactly. Recently, Andrea bolted one afternoon with a young man. She came back near dark a mess, and the baby was crying for hours on my sofa. People got pissed, telling me to shut the kid up or they'd shut him up. That baby would be crushed in a fight, shot in a crossfire, or kidnapped. And Andrea is starving the child. This is child endangerment on her part, and now it's on me as well. It is my house."

"Yes, it is, and Maria and I told you what would happen if this baby were harmed." Michael was stern, his voice diving deeper into his heart.

"Michael, Michael, I mean Mr. Harper, calm down and let me finish. I told you, we're on the same side," said the dealer. Michael backed off and let him talk.

"The police let me deal as much as I want. They don't interfere. It is a corrupt town. But one thing they will not back is child endangerment. The mayor knows his voters. I have instructed my girlfriend, if Andrea's drops the child in my house, she comes and takes your baby to her house for protection, then waits for Andrea to return. Mr. Harper, she refuses to be responsible for your child's safety. And she is scared when she gives him to Andrea."

"I agree, you should not be responsible for my son's safety, and I don't want you to be. I sincerely thank both of you, but you know Andrea. She does not take no for an answer. If I tell her she can't take the baby from the house without her sister or me, she will retaliate."

"I agree and here is the best I can do. I will tell her she cannot leave the baby with me ever again, and if she does, like tonight, I will immediately deliver the baby to you. Secondly, I will tell her if she does not bring the baby home to you by 8:00 P.M., we will all together press child endangerment charges against her."

"Dark, not eight o'clock," Maria interjected.

"Alright, dark, Senorita. If charges are pressed, the judge will enforce custody guidelines in favor of the gringo father. Senorita, you will inform your mother in Panama City. I know Andrea. She does not want her mother involved. She fears her for some reason."

"Yes, she does. My mother would be on the next plane." interjected Maria.

"And any resistance and she will no longer works for me. Child endangerment scares the politicians. The mayor will lose the women votes. Look at the families in the parks, the churches, and the Indian villages on the islands."

"I appreciate you doing this for us, especially Alejandro. I wish I could thank you in person. But you must explain it when she is not crazy high," responded Michael. "You are sure the police will support us?" He locked eyes with Maria, who nodded in agreement.

The drug dealer continued, "You don't know me, though you have seen me many times. But I know who you are." Michael knew who he was and knew his name was Luis. "What I know about you, when your partner spent your profits on coke and your hotel reached the point of bankruptcy, you bought him out, and paid all back wages to your employees from your pocket. One was my auntie. It's a small town, and we respect what you did. We are not friends and never will be, but I will watch out for you and your child. You know Antonio. If you have a problem with Andrea, tell him, and I will know. But promise me, do not do anything to purposely set her off. Light that fuse, and an explosion will occur. I'll talk to the police. They will protect you and the baby from any of her games."

"I'm glad we talked," Michael replied. "Family is important to me. I will raise this child with love, as you are raising yours. She will be forced to change, at least around the baby. Immigration laws won't allow me to take my son out of the country without Andrea's permission, but an arrest for child endangerment might change some minds."

"You are welcome, Mr. Harper." They disconnected.

The woman stood and approached Maria and Alejandro, sound asleep in Maria's arms. She rubbed his soft black hair and kissed him on the forehead. She and Maria clasped hands. She told Maria she would stop by to be sure all is well, then report back to her boyfriend. Then she turned to Michael, said something to him in Spanish, walked through the kitchen and out the door.

"What did she say?" asked Michael.

"She said she'll be one of Alejandro's guardian angels and be in my coven if ever I need her."

"What does that mean? What's a coven?"

"She has powers, and she knows I do. We could sense it right away. My mother has these powers as well," said Maria. "She taught me in my youth."

"That is what the dealer was referring to as your powerful friends, right? How about Andrea? Does she have what you call 'powers'?" Michael was perplexed and unnerved.

"No, Andrea harbors a lot of hatred from something that happened to her as a young woman. Mother felt it dangerous to give her those kinds of powers, for her own sake. Those powers from the gods would eat her up inside, as if she swallowed a nest of baby rats." He looked at her with a combination of curiosity, and surprisingly, respect.

17

ANDREA COMES MARCHING HOME

It was two o'clock in the morning. The dominant roosters were beginning to crow, making their presence known to any ovulating hens. Luis could hear Andrea's cackle from blocks away as she approached his house. She needed a few more grams of coke to sell to her new chumps waiting on the corner. And, of course, to pick up Alejandro.

"Luis, I need three grams of coke in separate bags for the gringo kids. And I will take Alejandro. Where is he? I assume he's asleep?" Andrea asked.

"He's not here. I had Fernanda pick him up. He was crying hard; it was agonizing for all of us. He had not been changed or fed in hours. Don't ever leave that child here again. We will talk about it in the morning when your brain turns back to a solid. How can you do that to your child? When will you realize the child is yours, and his life is your responsibility?"

"Fuck you, Luis, you're not my daddy. I knew he would cry, and you would call Fernanda to take care of him. She always does. I put a lot of money in your pocket tonight, asshole. Be careful how you talk to me. I have a sugar daddy in my panties and could cut back on dealing at any time." Andrea slurred, and she lost her balance falling over the curb. "Can the kid stay with Fernanda tonight? I need to deliver this coke to those little fuckers on the corner. I think I might be too high to carry him home. I might drop him on his head, oops." She giggled.

"What will you tell Michael you did with him, left him with a drug dealer while you got high and dealt coke all night? He will love that. You know he will do whatever he must to protect that baby, if he is the kind of man you tell me he is. He will not be okay with you keeping that baby out all night when you have your sister." Luis wanted to watch Andrea squirm, so he enjoyed watching those drunken wheels slosh in her head.

Andrea was high enough, or shall we say, low enough, to be in a 'kick a man's ass' mode. After hearing Luis's question, she quickly came forward with an idea.

"I know. I will say I went to the store for cigarettes and left Alejandro on my friend's porch while my friend was inside cooking dinner. When I returned, some guy I know was on the porch, and Alejandro was gone. I will say I freaked, but my friend promised Alejandro would be safe, and his buddy had him, and needed $500 just this one time to get himself out of trouble, and he knew the gringo daddy could afford it, and I am to meet him back on the porch at noon for the exchange. But he told me, if the gringo daddy calls the police, he will never see Alejandro alive again. Yeah, I will blame it on Michael for having money. Michael will pay $500, no questions asked, to get the baby back. Shit, that's nothing to Michael. Hell, that's only one trip to the ATM. Michael gives me $500, I pick up the baby off the porch, I can give Fernanda $100, and I will keep $400. What do you think? Then I will settle the ignorant gringo down with a blow job. Although, it has been a while. And for some reason, he won't let me fuck him anymore either."

Andrea didn't realize she was giving Luis ammunition to control her. And if he had not already returned Alejandro to Michael and Maria, he would have challenged Andrea's plan. But Luis was tired of her using and abusing the baby, so he allowed her to swoop in and make a fool of herself. What he did not know, the tail wind from her swoop would start one dangerous landslide.

"Sounds like a good plan."

"Good," she said. "I'll pick him up around noon and give Fernanda $100 of the ransom money." She started laughing. She was convinced she would act out her story and Michael would hand her the money and let it go.

Andrea bounced off, coke in her bandana, to make her final drop. She floundered home, thinking through her act when she walked onto her stage of fabrication.

* * * *

It was three in the morning. Michael heard Andrea at the garden door keyhole, struggling to open it. *I wonder why,* he thought sarcastically. Finally, the door swung open, crashing into the wall, and the Queen B came buzzing in. Next, Michael's bedroom door crashed into the wall exposing a glassy-eyed Andrea, slurring terribly as she wobbled into the room. She stood before him, hands on hips, bent forward and pigeon-toed.

"Michael, someone kidnapped Alejandro." she blurted in hysterics. *Take one—action,* Michael thought.

Andrea began her saga, rambling through without a breath. "I was visiting a friend, and Alejandro was on the porch, and my friend was inside cooking, and I went for cigarettes. When I returned, the baby was gone. Gone, Michael, just gone. A man was sitting on the porch and told me his friend told him to tell you he needed $500, just one time, and he will return Alejandro unharmed tomorrow at noon. But if you go to the police, he'll kill Alejandro. And I'm the only one he'll make the exchange with, not you." She took a shaky breath, letting the tears flow like she believed her own story. "I swear, I was just gone a minute. This was planned, and I was followed. Damn it, Michael, I knew this was going to happen someday when people found out Alejandro had a rich gringo daddy like you. This is all your fault, Michael, all your fault. Why did you get me pregnant, you selfish prick?"

Andrea's theatrical panic might have been convincing. Maria woke when Andrea came crashing in the door. She stood at her bedroom doorway. She could hear Andrea's piercing voice telling Michael her TV script of the prince being kidnapped by a Teutonic horseman demanding treasure for his return. All this while Alejandro lay fast asleep in his crib. Maria let it continue.

"Andrea, keep your voice down," Michael said, making a silencing motion with his hand. "We have neighbors."

"Fuck the neighbors. Do you think I give a shit about the neighbors? My precious little baby has been kidnapped, or worse. If I get him back, it'll be the last time you ever see him. I'm not going to have my little man in danger all of his life just because you are his daddy." Andrea stared at him with a wicked frown. Michael stayed silent. He wanted to see how far Andrea would take her silly farce.

"I have the solution. We move to the States with him, where he'll be safe," said Michael, knowing what reaction was coming. Only then did he remember his promise to the dealer he would not do anything to set her off.

"Right, like that would happen, dickhead." Andrea rolled her eyeballs. "My family, especially my mother, would never let that happen. You'd be a pile of ashes before you left Balboa."

"Okay, let's go to the police and they can set a trap for tomorrow. We'll teach them to mess with our child." Michael swung his feet out of bed and started to get dressed. "I'm sure somebody saw or heard something last night."

"No, no. That'll make it worse. He said only me. If you go with me or go to the police, he said the baby will be killed. Let's go to the ATM and get me $500 in the morning, and I will take care of it. We'll have him back by one o'clock, unharmed," Andrea insisted. Suddenly Maria walked out of the bedroom, took Andrea by the hand, and walked her to the crib where Alejandro was sleeping peacefully.

"Oh my God." Andrea gasped. "You got him back. Has someone already come for the money? Did he need the money right away, so he sent someone early? I searched for him all night." Andrea was believing her own lie, but then she realized she was busted.

"Cut it, Sis." Maria said in a nasty tone. "I've been hearing stories about you ever since I arrived in Balboa, but I didn't want to believe them. Andrea, for God's sake, they are true. You are worse than I imagined. Tonight, I see who you've become in the last twenty years. What an incredible liar you are. Your boss, the drug dealer, had a talk with us earlier tonight on the phone. And just so you don't blurt anything, he did not tell us his name, for our protection. His girlfriend brought the baby from his house, where you left him. Andrea, I don't care if you are my sister, I will bring in the police and lawyers. Don't ever put that baby in danger again. I will make you regret it. I'll tell Mother about your life here and how you treat her grandson. She'll kick your ass, or worse, if you know what I mean," said Maria.

"Maria, you think it will be that easy?" Andrea was smug. "Mom won't believe you. Your life hasn't been so clean either. I will tell her you're jealous of me. I'll tell her you are fucking Michael. You've gone after my boyfriends since we were kids, but you were just too plain and frumpy to have a chance against me. Men don't like sweet chubby girls; they like us bad girls with tits and asses."

That stabbed Maria in the heart. She knew Andrea was a temptress and she could not compete. Even her father, as perverted and disgusting as he was, had no interest in her. In some strange way, that hurt.

"Michael knows I will have people hurt him if he talks to Mother. She hates all men, especially gringos, and especially Michael, and she has not even met him. The police won't do anything because my boss won't let them. They'll take Michael out before they touch me. Neither of you understand the power I wield on the streets here. Now, give me Alejandro. I want to take him out on the porch and play. I missed the little bugger tonight."

Andrea's slurring was getting worse as she went to the fridge for another beer. On the way, she took a swig of rum from the bottle on the counter. When she did, Maria went to her room, then locked, and latched the door, barricading herself and the baby inside. When Andrea realized it was locked, she shouted for Maria to unlock the door and give her Alejandro. She pounded the door with her fist and kicked it with her heel like a mule against the back of its stable. Alejandro woke and started to cry.

"Go to bed, Andrea, we'll talk in the morning. There's no way I'm letting you touch this child tonight." Maria turned off the light and tried to rock the baby back to sleep.

Outside Maria's bedroom, Andrea turned, looked at Michael, and screamed, "You have no idea the war you two just started. I will have that baby taken from you, and you can go fuck yourself, Michael."

"Andrea, sleep in here by yourself. I will sleep in one of the rooms in the hotel tonight. It's vacant." Michael gathered his phone, laptop, passport, and wallet.

Michael crossed over to the hotel, down three steps, two paces across the sidewalk, and up three steps to the hotel's boardwalk. As he unlocked the door to the room, Andrea came to the office window of the house. "Oh, by the way," she screamed, "I'll give you both something to do tomorrow so you don't get bored."

Andrea went to the kitchen, opened the cabinets, and grabbed glasses, dishes, anything she could pulverize. She threw them onto the tile floor. She continued until the cabinets were empty and the entire floor was ankle-deep in broken glass and porcelain. Michael locked himself in the hotel room. Maria held Alejandro tightly, rocking him as he cried. His primal instincts could sense hate and violence. Tears ran down Maria's cheeks from her own fear and from the sadness and disappointment in her sister. She knew it stemming back to the horrific act of their daddy and the stillbirth of Andrea's first child. Suddenly, blue flashing lights poured through the windows, swirling on the walls. When Andrea saw them, she ripped the phone from the wall and smashed it on the floor. Two police officers came to the door, demanding entry.

"The crazy gringo's over there in that room," Andrea responded. "That one right there. He got pissed off at me because I came home too late. He threatened to beat me, and look, he destroyed my kitchen. He broke all my dishes. Look at this mess. My sister's been hiding in the back room, protecting my baby. None of us are safe here in our own home. Arrest him, right now." Andrea began to fake cry, hugging one of the officers as she pressed her large breasts tight to his bulletproof vest. She was convincing. "He was determined to kill us all, even the baby, if you wouldn't have come along. Thank God you did because he smashed the telephone. That's why he ran. He saw you coming and needed to hide. I'm not sure, but I think he has his gun with him."

Drawing their guns, the police proceeded to flush Michael from his supposed hiding place. "Sir, you need to lay your gun on the floor, open the door, step back, and put your hands on top of your head," said one of the officers.

"I don't own a gun, and I'll be happy to come out. You're making a big mistake. She's lying to you. Ask her sister who's locked in her bedroom to keep herself and my baby safe. Don't you think it is odd she's roaming around, and we're locked in our rooms? Don't shoot. I'm unarmed. I'm coming out."

Michael opened the door, put his hands on his head, and took a few steps back. The officers entered; their guns pointed at Michael. "Where's your gun, sir?" They both looked at the backpack.

"I don't own a gun. Check the room and the backpack or check the whole property if you wish. She told you that, hoping you'd shoot me in a panic. But I'll need the backpack if you're taking me into custody," Michael was keeping his cool.

"Your wife said you have a gun." The officer cuffed Michael's hands behind his back.

"She's not my wife," replied Michael, "and she lies continually. I am sure you know her. I suggest you question Andrea's sister, locked in her room, before you arrest me. She knows what happened tonight. She and the baby are in danger."

"Shut up, gringo. We know who she is, and she tells everyone you are her husband." The officer searched Michael's backpack for the weapon. He looked under the beds, under the mattresses, and inside dresser drawers. Michael stood quietly, in pain from the cuffs. They gave up on the weapon but took the backpack with his passport, wallet, phone, and laptop with them. As they led him to the car, Andrea stood at the door smiling. Maria watched from her bedroom window.

Michael turned and twisted the best he could toward Maria in the window. He yelled stay in your room and go where I told you to go first thing in the morning. Have him talk to our friend." He looked at Andrea in the doorway. She smiled again and gave him the finger as a loving parting gesture.

As the car drove off, Andrea yelled, "You can come out Maria. He's gone, and that's the last we will see of him. They will run him out of the country. He will be back in the States in a few days. We will have the baby all to ourselves and a place to live. Mother's going to be so pleased. I guess I don't need her or your kind of power, do I? My kind of power is quite intimidating, would you not say?"

Unfortunately for Andrea, she was too high to understand what Michael's instruction meant to Maria and too drunk to care. But she would soon find out. The rocks and mud had been jostled. The landslide had begun.

18

HIGH TIDE BEGINS TO RECEDE ON ANDREA'S BEACH

Sunrise broke gently over the horizon. The ocean was like a versicolored tinted mirror. Maria nestled the traumatized infant back into his slumber, but she was unable to sleep. The anxiety and adrenaline from the insane events in the primordial hours still pounded in her heart. The contemplation of her and Alejandro's future together would not allow her to close her eyes. In the last twelve hours, Andrea was no longer the sister she knew and loved.

She needed to find a way to the kitchen and obtain fresh water for Alejandro's morning bottle. She cracked the door slightly and listened for any sign of life. After a couple minutes of eerie silence, she stepped out of her room, noticing both the garden and veranda doors were wide open. She crept out the garden door and around the house, to the veranda to see if Andrea was awake. She peeked through the latticework covered in flowering vines. She saw no sign of Andrea at the table, in a hammock, or even on the floor.

As she tiptoed like a frightened kitten across the floorboards, she observed beer cans, an ashtray full of butts, and an empty rum bottle. Andrea knocked over a potted plant, the dirt stretching in front of the doorway. Maria entered the kitchen and saw Andrea, face down on her bed, fully clothed and completely comatose. The light in the bathroom was on, and a bag of cocaine sat on the sink counter. Maria stepped slowly and carefully through the broken glass to the clean water tank, where she filled Alejandro's bottle as well as her own water bottle. She delicately retraced her steps back to the veranda, avoiding the bulk of Andrea's carnage, then back around the house to her room. She packed the baby's bag and prepared his morning bottle.

As the sun rose and the sky continued to brighten, the house remained as quiet as a graveyard. Maria waited until eight o'clock to begin her search for Antonio. It was now seven-thirty. She knew Andrea would be out for hours, but to be sure, she changed the baby and fed him his bottle. He was quiet and content. She put Alejandro in the carrier on her torso and threw his diaper bag over her shoulder. It was time to flee to safety.

The tour boats next door were preparing for their days as well. Some drivers struggled to start their engines, others revving theirs loudly as dark purple smoke and fumes of gasoline and oil drifted through the air. Since it happened every morning, Andrea slept through it. This would be a typical day for the tour boats, but not for Maria. She exited through the gate and walked up the street past the hostel adjacent to them. She saw Joel, one of the owners of the hostel, sitting at his front desk.

"Maria, Maria, hold on, I need to talk to you." Maria stopped as Joel ran to her, although she wanted to avoid what was coming. "What happened at your place last night? My guests were frantic and pounding on my door. I'm sorry, but I had to call the police. I couldn't ignore that kind of violence. It sounded like someone was going to be murdered."

"It's a long story, Joel, but I'll be brief. Michael's in jail, and I must find someone quickly. Andrea came home about three o'clock an absolute mess, and without the baby. She left him with some dealer she works for."

"I know his name and where he lives."

"No, Joel, that's not necessary. He told us he wouldn't tell us his name to keep us out of danger."

"Small town, Maria. Nothing's kept secret for very long. But go on, please," said Joel.

Maria briefly explained the events leading up to Andrea's crazed actions, filling him in on her sister's attempt to scam Michael. "When we exposed her lie, she went berserk. That's when the police came and took Michael to jail. Andrea says they'll deport him, and he'll lose the baby. I locked myself and Alejandro in my room, then laid in bed unable to sleep. That's when I figured out that's what she had planned all along. I need to find someone named Antonio. Can you help me?" Maria voice trembling with anxiety.

"Oh, Maria, you never knew that part of your sister, did you?" said Joel. "He won't be the first man she's forced out of town. She's an important part of the drug thing here. He's going to have to leave his child here forever, I'm afraid."

"Oh my Joel, that can't happen." Maria squeezed Alejandro to her bosom, her eyes moistening the top of his head. "Michael is the only thing keeping this child safe. Her boss, the dealer, even knows that. He explained it all to us last night. That is why he asked me if the baby was ever in danger, to find someone by the name of Antonio. Please tell me you know where I can find this man. I've heard of him but never met him."

"He works for the city. He and Michael are close friends. You have seen him. He works around the hotel for Michael, and I assure you, he doesn't like Andrea at all. She's been a bitch to him, and he was good friends with Grant, Andrea's husband."

"That Antonio. I do know who he is. Where do I find him?"

"You know the little square where the guys play dominoes, right down this street, at the sharp curve? Go there. There's a tiny little building. Tell them you're Michael Harper's nanny and you need to see Antonio right away. He should be there around eight o'clock, depending on how much he drank last night. If not, someone will find him for you. If Michael's in trouble, he'll come running no matter how hung over he might be. And remember, we're all on your side, even those you think are not. Most of us would like to see Andrea gone. She's the wicked witch and a brat, and without a doubt, a psychopath." With that, Joel gave Alejandro a kiss on the forehead and Maria, a sympathetic kiss on the cheek.

"Thank you, Joel, you and Charles are a wonderful couple."

Maria walked up to the little municipal building, found Antonio, and explained what had happened.

"Maria, I know your dealer friend needs to know. But his job, as you have surmised, is a nighttime job. He won't be up yet. I can't expose him, but I'll let him know around noon. In the meantime, I suggest we go to the police station and talk to the night captain, my cousin, before he leaves. We'll tell him what really happened. After that, I will have my girlfriend take you and the baby to my house until Andrea's boss tells me what's going on."

"Antonio, I know the story behind Andrea and Grant, and you can trust me, I will tell no one. But what happened to Grant won't happen to Michael, will it? Will he be on a boat to the mainland by noon? How do we stop that?" Maria was petrified.

"Let me talk to Michael and my cousin right away, and I mean right now, before they do ship him off."

Maria and Antonio went to the police station with Alejandro to tell his cousin the true story and make him aware of the danger Michael, Maria and the baby were in from Andrea. Antonio's cousin listened, but he really didn't care; their lives meant nothing. The police knew the drill, and they had their orders. Michael would be given his walking papers in a couple of hours. But Antonio did manage to convince his cousin to allow him a quick visit with Michael.

As Maria waited with Alejandro, Antonio went to Michael's cell. Michael and Antonio embraced like brothers, then sat on the bunk.

"Antonio, after you leave, call this number right away." Michael gave him a name and number. "Tell them you are calling on my behalf and ask for Vanessa Perez and no getting back to you later or tomorrow. Have Maria talk to her and relay to her what's going on. Tell her she needs to get here as soon as possible. Make sure she emphasizes this is serious child endangerment for my baby, now and in the future. It will mean so much more coming from Andrea's sister. Now go quickly and thank you."

19

THE POLITICS BEGIN

Maria and Antonio went to Antonio's house, where they briefed his girlfriend on the situation. Antonio assured her Andrea had no idea where they lived. Maria picked up the telephone and made the call. The person on the other end of the line answered, "Perez and Perez, Attorneys-at-Law."

"May I speak to Vanessa Perez, please? I'm calling on behalf of one of her clients, Michael Harper. It is of grave importance, ma'am," said Maria.

"Oh, Mr. Harper. Yes, ma'am. I'll pass you right through. Just hold, please, she will be right with you."

In less than a minute, a different voice came on the line. "Hello, this is Vanessa Perez. And with whom am I speaking?" The woman's tone was strong and professional.

"Hello Mrs. Perez, this is Maria Blanco. I'm Mr. Michael Harper's nanny for his three-month-old son, Alejandro. I am also the child's auntie. My sister is Andrea Blanco, the child's mother. We have an emergency here in Balboa involving Mr. Harper and myself, but more importantly, his baby. Mr. Harper is in jail due to a story my sister fabricated in one of her drug-and-alcohol rages last night. I'm hiding with the baby now, so my sister doesn't hurt him."

"First, is Mr. Harper truly innocent of all charges, and are they letting him out on bail?" asked Vanessa.

"Yes, Mrs. Perez, he's completely innocent. I was present the whole time, locked in my room with the baby, protecting us from my sister. But I could hear it all. No bail, ma'am, he's still in jail. They're telling us bail's not possible yet, but the story gets even worse. There are things my sister does here in Balboa that her mother and I never knew she could do. I've only been in Balboa for three months, and there appears to be some a conspiracy here. I'm afraid Mr. Harper is going to be deported or out under the threat of bodily injury, perhaps death. My sister has done this to other men in the past, including her husband, but that was a money scam. This is about a child's present and future life. If Mr. Harper leaves, my sister will gain complete custody of the baby, and the baby will live in constant danger."

"Why would the baby be in danger?"

"Because she is a drug dealer and a con artist. Mr. Harper and I have the baby most of the time, but when my sister has the baby, she is usually too high to care for him, so she leaves him with the head drug dealer in town. Drug deals and prostitution happen as the baby lies on the couch." Maria went on to relay in detail to Vanessa the story of Andrea's actions the night before. The woman listened to everything Maria said without interruption.

"Mrs. Perez," Maria pressed, "Michael wants me to express how desperately important it is he stay in Balboa to protect the child. He says he never needed you more." Antonio's girlfriend wiped Maria's tears from the phone.

"Ms. Blanco, I have worked with Mr. Harper for many years. He is a wonderful man, but oddly enough, his wealth and honesty attract fraud, like his former partner and your sister. But since he feels this strongly about his child's safety, and he only calls me when he truly needs me, I will clear my calendar and be there first thing tomorrow morning. I will inform the police of my visit and set up a meeting. You stay hidden with the baby until I arrange for your protection. I will speak with Mr. Harper when all is set. And Ms. Blanco, Mr. Harper isn't going anywhere. You are in good hands. I want to get right on this, Ms. Blanco, so I am saying a quick goodbye." Click.

THE POLITICS BEGIN

As soon as Vanessa was off the phone, she had her secretary arrange an early morning flight out of Panama City. She then placed a call to police chief of Balboa, Chief Nicolas Nevarez.

"Hello, is this the Balboa police station? I am the attorney representing Mr. Michael Harper, whom you currently have in custody. Please pass me through to Police Chief Nevarez right away. Tell him it is urgent," said Vanessa.

"Oh, I'm sorry counselor, but the chief doesn't take calls from lawyers. You'll have to leave a number, and someone will return your call whenever available," said the young police officer answering the telephone.

"Officer, get a pen and paper and please write this down so you get it right. Tell your chief that Vanessa Perez is on the line. Tell him my husband is Roberto Perez. He is s the assistant attorney general of Panama, and we both, along with the entire Attorney General's Office, find this case involving Michael Harper of great interest to us," Vanessa said in a strong, firm, and unemotional tone.

"Uh, uh, okay. Vanessa Perez, with a 'P', right? And Roberto Perez, and you said he is the Assistant Attorney General's Office. Is that correct?" asked the officer. Vanessa could almost hear his hand quiver.

"Yes, son, now connect me, please," said Vanessa as she rolled her eyes and leaned back in her chair.

"Hold for a moment, Mrs. Perez. Let me see if the chief can take your call. I just saw him walk into his office."

The officer scurried like a little mouse chased by a broom.

"What is it, Carlos?" asked the chubby police chief. He patted his bulging fat belly as he spoke. "Spit it out, boy. You're shaking. Too much coffee this morning or too much rum last night?"

"Sir, I have a call holding from that Michael Harper guy's attorney. You know, the old gringo Andrea put in here last night."

"Fuck Harper and his attorney. We will get that Americano out of here like we do all the others who start trouble for Andrea. Tell him I had to stop a bank robbery or something." The chief continued practicing his Bimini Ring Game, swinging the little metal ring attached to a string and landing it on a hook attached to the wall. Very important police business.

"Chief, this is not a normal lawyer call. I have a feeling we don't have a normal gringo in our cell. First, his attorney is a she, not..."

"Well holy fuck, kid, she's she, even better. Let's have some fun." The chief smiled as he envisioned making Vanessa cry when he bullied the little senora on the phone. "They get as scared as little bunnies by us men. And what kind of pussy hires a chica attorney unless he's fucking her." The chief grinned at the kid and threw his ring again. "Tell her somebody will call her back in a few days. By that time, we'll have Harper's gringo ass back in the States."

"I did that already, but she told me to tell you that her name is..." The young officer looked nervously at his note. "She told me to tell you her name is Vanessa Perez."

"So, what the fuck does that mean? All those asshole attorneys think they're so goddamn important. I'm the Balboan chief of police. Now that's important. I don't have the time nor the desire to talk to some snobby city bitch. Tell her, and don't bother me again. Now scoot. I have work to do." He emphasized his point with another careful toss of the ring.

"Sir, she wanted you to be aware she's the wife of Roberto Perez, you know, the assistant attorney general? She says she and her husband, along with the entire Attorney General's Office, have a great interest in Mr. Harper's case."

Silence came over the chief. He sat down at his desk. His palms begin to sweat. "No shit, Roberto Perez? Why didn't you tell me that in the first place? Okay, pass her through, and hurry. You've made her wait long enough, you incompetent little shit. Go, go, and hope I don't tell your daddy."

The officer went back to his desk and apologized to Vanessa for the wait. He sent the call through.

Back in his office, Nicolas Nevarez cleared his throat. With a nervous quiver in his leg, he picked up the receiver. "Hello, Police Chief Nicolas Nevarez here. I understand this is Mrs. Perez in Panama City and you are the attorney for one of my prisoners? How can I help you, Mrs. Perez?"

"Yes, Chief, this is regarding Mr. Michael Harper. Let's get to the point. Grab a pen and paper, sir. You don't want me in Balboa any more than I want to go to your smelly little dump of a town. Mr. Harper

THE POLITICS BEGIN

doesn't bring me in on routine issues, but he feels there is a serious child endangerment issue for his son by one of your, let us say, associates. This associate happens to be the child's mother, and a prominent drug dealer in your province. I want you to listen carefully."

"I assure you; I'm listening. And I have a piece of paper and a pen that really works." fumbled the chief.

"Good. Your associate, whose name is Andrea Blanco, has a sister, whose name is Maria Blanco. She is the baby's nanny, as well. The nanny is currently in possession of the baby and is hiding in fear of retribution towards her and the child. We are 're not fond of children needing protection from their mothers, are you Chief?"

"Absolutely not, Mrs. Perez. The protection of our children is of utmost importance."

"That is wonderful to hear, Chief. So, Mr. Harper, of course, is in jail because he is trying to protect his child from his irresponsible and violent mother, Andrea. I want you to be sure Mr. Harper, the nanny, and the child remain safe and unharmed. First, I want Mr. Harper out on bail immediately, but you must keep him guarded around the clock."

"Done."

"But Mr. Harper and I are specifically concerned about the nanny, and his baby. That baby must not fall into the hands of his mother for any reason, even if you put them under police protection in separate cells."

"Well, Mrs. Perez, we have a rapist in one cell and Mr. Harper in the other, and we only have two cells. That's not enough for everyone."

"Then put the mother in jail, Chief, since we know she is the real guilty party in so many ways."

"I can't say with certainty, I can…"

"I will be flying over early tomorrow morning from Panama City," she continued, ignoring him completely. "I want to meet with Mr. Harper at 9:00 A.M. along with the two officers who arrested Mr. Harper, the night captain on duty last night and Andrea's sister. They can tell us exactly what happened. Then, at 10:30 A.M., when you and your staff admit Mr. Harper is innocent, I want to meet with you, the mayor, and the judge in a room large enough to hold six people. I believe we can work something out, or else I will bring my husband onto this case. Who knows what else we may uncover in the process of our investigation? Is that understood, Chief?"

"Mrs. Perez, who all ..."

"Oh, and please make sure there are coffee and bagels with cream cheese in the morning for Mr. Harper, Maria, and me. Thank you, Chief. Now, do you have all that? If not, I've recorded this conversation. And before I hang up, can you put Mr. Harper on the phone with me, please? Preferably your phone in your office. I would like to inform him what is going to transpire tomorrow. And if he is cuffed now, get them off immediately. And don't you dare cuff him again. Now hurry, I have a meeting in ten minutes with the deputy chief of staff."

"Mrs. Perez," said the chief, finally able to get a word in. "With all due respect, it's against regulations to have prisoners out of their cells, and certainly not in my office uncuffed."

Vanessa went silent for thirty seconds. And that was all the encouragement Chief Nevarez needed.

The chief ordered the young officer to uncuff Michael and bring him to his office immediately. When Michael got on the phone, Vanessa informed him of the meetings and what she needed from him. She told Michael to tell the chief of their needs and to call her when all was completed. Michael thanked her for Alejandro's sake, and they hung up.

"I believe everything is understood, Mr. Harper. We'll take diligent care of you and the others tonight." The chief changed his tune entirely. "We will get all of this straightened out tomorrow, I assure you. You have powerful friends, sir. Anything else I can do for you?"

"Yes, I need to see Antonio right away. Vanessa would like you to put the three of us up in the Hotel Tortuga, two rooms please. Have someone bring the baby's crib from my house, along with the box of diapers, formula, and the baby's bottles. You are to feed Maria and me well, and it shall all be on the city's tab. You need to assign officers to guard us around the clock. She also told me to tell you, if Andrea or any of the drug dealers threaten us or hassle your officers in any way, arrest Andrea and her accomplices on the spot, then keep them in custody until Vanessa arrives. She said you can decide what to do with them later. That is all for now. Vanessa wants me to call her within two hours to assure her all has been executed." Michael started back to his cell but turned quickly. "Oh, and Chief, did she mention the bagels and cream cheese for tomorrow morning? Sounded important to her."

"Yes, she did, Mr. Harper. I will get right on it, sir," said the chief. Michael strolled back to his cell, escorted by two guards.

When Michael was out of sight, the chief called in two of his reliable officers and began barking specific instructions on what to do with Michael, Maria, and the baby. He called in the captain on duty and said, "Right now, I need Luis the dealer, the mayor, and the judge in my office immediately. Tell them we have a problem, no, a big problem. Tell Luis I need to see him first. And bring in Antonio right away. He knows where the baby is hidden. But have him talk to Harper to get permission."

Oh my God, thought the chief. *What has this loco chica gotten us into this time? Maybe I should arrest her now and put her in the cell with the rapist, but I wouldn't do that to any man.*

20

THE SHOT THAT FALLS ON DEAF EARS

Before the political bandits of Balboa arrived in the chief's office, Luis strolled in, escorted by the two officers ordered to retrieve him. It was eleven o'clock by now, and Luis looked as strung out as any open-all-night illicit drug dealer could look at that hour. It was obvious he could not have cared less about his personal hygiene. His attitude was irritable and arrogant.

"What the fuck are you doing, getting me up this early?" You know I work nights, you old asshole, unlike you bozos, who come and go whenever you please. What is it now? This better be good, chiefy-poo."

"Shut smartass and listen," the chief snapped. "I don't know what went down with your looney-tune bitch Andrea last night, but that big-tittied nutcase flipped out around three last night at Harper's house. Broke all his glasses and dishes, then tried to take their baby to the veranda that sits over the ocean when she was high as a kite."

"Oh my god, Chief, that's terrible. She will kill that kid someday soon. She went over the edge this time, but you guys will fix it. You always do. How can I help?" Luis had a newly found paternal concern.

"Calls came in because of the broken glass and she yelled so loudly she woke the tourists two blocks away. When my guys got there, she made up some story that Harper did all the damage and had a gun as he hides in one of his hotel rooms. She said he was going to kill them all. They arrested Harper and left Andrea alone, as they had been instructed to do.

They cuffed him and brought him in at gunpoint. Shit, man, do you know what would have happened if one of those clowns would have shot him?"

"The streets would go underground for a long time," responded Luis.

"It gets worse. Harper's attorney called me from Panama City an hour ago, and guess what? She's the goddamn wife of the assistant attorney general, Roberto Perez. Now we have the feds on our ass. This isn't good, not good at all." The chief ended his rant, staring hard at Luis.

Luis shook like he was having a convulsion but tried unsuccessfully to appear intelligent. "What's the big deal? You get Harper out of Panama, then it is Andrea's word against her sister's, game over," he said, as he shrugged his shoulders.

"Wake up, bonehead. The problem is this attorney bitch is dropping everything and flying here tomorrow morning. She is claiming child endangerment and says she and her husband are taking great interest in this case. Andrea has the feds involved, dumbass, and that is always bad for us. If Perez didn't think she had enough evidence against us, you think she'd drop what she's doing tomorrow and come here?" The chief's face turned beet red with rage.

Luis finally woke from his late-night stupor. "Chief, this is my fault. I got that crazy bitch riled last night. She left her baby at my house while she went dealing, scamming, and getting wasted. You know if that gringo baby got killed or kidnapped at my place, the feds and the Americans would shut down this town for a long time and put me away forever. So, last night my girlfriend took the baby to Harper's house. I told him none of us want any part of child endangerment charges, especially if the kid gets hurt, and neither did the police. But I set Andrea up before she went home by making her think Fernanda still had the baby. But to keep herself out of trouble with Harper, she tried to con him with some sort of kidnapping ransom scheme. She got caught in her lie, and went crazy, as you say. I filled that insane brain with gunpowder and lit the fuse." Luis sighed. He clasped his hands behind his head and stared at the ceiling. "Oh my god, Chief, what do you want me to do? Can we simply drop the charges on Harper?"

"Shit, boy, you know Andrea. This will only get worse if she thinks she can get away with harassing Harper. And Perez won't forget it if she messes with Harper a second time. Perez already knows the story and she knows you were involved in endangering the child. The feds leave us alone, but they could shut us down any time if we break their rules. This is international politics. We must straighten this out and kiss their asses or we go belly-up. If we don't straighten this out and kiss their asses, they will shut us down."

"Without a doubt, Chief."

"Get that little whore to cooperate any way we need her, or we are finished, including her. Who in the hell is this Harper guy? No, don't answer, Luis, just handle Andrea." The chief stood, "I have to see the mayor." He kicked over his chair in anger as he exited.

Luis left the station and walked down the street, contemplating Andrea's future in the town. Like the top salesperson in a small corporation, she was the single biggest money producer for the little bigwigs, the bar owners, Luis and the Columbians, and kickbacks to the mayor, the judge, and the chief. Last night she was certain she was above the law. But their attitudes would be different in the daylight. She did not realize things would be different when she awoke.

Luis knew the clueless Andrea poked the wrong bear this time. The feds were invading Balboa at daybreak as they are taking a personal interest in some gringo and his baby. With no humility in her soul, she would not react well. And he knew the politicians and police would not stand behind her pompous posturing. A cross might be under construction right now with her name on it outside City Hall.

As Luis reached his house, he summoned James, his number two, James, to go drag Andrea out of bed and bring her to him right away. His assistant departed without hesitation, knowing this was not going to be a pleasant task, but James was looking forward to having physical control over the disrespectful wench.

As James arrived at Harper's house, he walked in through the open garden door. He called out for Andrea. She had risen from her bed sometime in the morning and locked her bedroom door. James waded through the broken glass and dishes. He called her name once again. He heard a feeble, but nasty, "Go away."

He pounded on the door. "Andrea, it's James. Luis sent me. He needs to see you right away." There was no answer. James pounded again, harder, and louder, but still, he found total neglect to his request. "Okay, I'm going to bust your door in and carry you to him over my shoulder, kicking and screaming, you little bitch." With no answer, James took a step back, preparing to attack the door with the heel of his boot.

"Okay, okay." Andrea muttered before he did any damage to the door, but Andrea was more worried about the damage to her hangover than to Michael's door. She opened, her curly dark hair disheveled, and still wearing the dress from the night before. The smell of alcohol exuded from her pores. "What the fuck do you want, James? What time is it? Never mind, that doesn't matter. Tell that fucker I went back to sleep. I'll be over later this afternoon. And tell him his ass is kicked when I get ahold of that little kinkajou. He played me last night, and that wasn't funny. Now get out of here before I kick your balls into your throat, you big fucking meathead."

But as she went to close the door, James pushed it open and grabbed her by the back of her dress, ripping it at the zipper. "You fucked up big time, chica. Your temper and bully-bully bullshit started a war with the feds. I'm not going to say anymore. But you have enemies out there you never knew you had. Get your shit and let's go, right now. If you don't, the police are going to throw you in jail," James said, in a mean tone she'd never heard him use on her.

"What is their charge? They think Michael did all this and threatened us poor girls and the baby. Shit, they always believe anything I tell them, "Said Andrea, but with a hint of doubt in her voice.

"Get your things and please, just shut up. Luis will fill you in." With that, Andrea did two big bumps of cocaine off the sink, got her purse, and emptied it of all drugs and condoms. She went with James, still stumbling and slurring from the night before.

As Andrea pranced down the streets, word got out from Joel as to what really happened. And Andrea, looking an outright mess, still strutted as if she were in charge and untouchable. They approached Luis's house, Luis intercepted James, ignoring Andrea's screaming and squawking. The three walked to Luis's girlfriend's house. They needed to talk in private. He told James to wait across the street.

The moment Andrea saw Fernanda, she started her bullying. "Look momma, I know you're in on this..." Luis quickly interrupted Andrea. He grabbed her arm violently and jerked her into the bedroom as Fernanda left the house with their daughter.

"Don't even think about it, Andrea," Luis snapped. "Don't even come close to Fernanda and my baby. You don't understand what you have done this time. Your actions involve not only a baby, not just a gringo with money and a penis, or a stupid tourist..."

"Right, it involves my baby. Not my sister's and not that gringo's baby. I'll decide how my child is raised. Look at me, I'm doing pretty well. I have more money than all you tree monkeys," said Andrea. "Hell, my son will probably be mayor someday, and he and I will build this ring into a national cartel."

"It will be hard to do that from a jail cell with no income, you stupid arrogant bitch. You need to listen."

"Don't give me that shit, Luis. I make as much drug money for you as the rest of your flunkies combined. And the bartenders, and the police, and the politicians all get a nice cut. Not to mention those boys in the mountains. Don't bluff me. Nobody will let me go down. And nobody will let you fire me. You will all do what you always do, get rid of any gringo problem. Just get him out of here so I can go back to sleep. I need a bump. You got one? C'mon, asshole, where's your blow? I said I need a bump." Andrea pushed Luis out of her way and began searching his house for a little baggie.

"I don't keep any drugs in this house. You know that. What do you know about Harper?" Andrea didn't want to believe him, as she rooted through Fernanda's dresser drawers.

"What do you mean? He's from the States, been around Balboa for about twelve years. Used to come and go because he ran some kind of business up there and had kids and shit." Andrea continued to look for a bag of blow, this time under the cushions.

"What kind of business? Was he the boss? Did he have employees?"

Andrea continued to pace around the house. She couldn't stand still. "I think so. He bores me when he talks, so I don't really listen. Yea, he was the president and CEO, he said, whatever a CEO is, and had, like, 400 employees."

"Andrea, for God's sake, stop. I told you there are no drugs in this house. Stand still and look at me. Does he still have his business?"

"No, he sold it for, I guess, a lot of money. His kids are grown and married, and he has some grandkids. He moved down here, bought out his partner at the hotel to save it from bankruptcy, settled up on taxes with the government and the wages for the employees his partner fucked over down here."

"Then he had some power up in the States. Probably a pretty smart businessman," Luis concluded. Andrea gave up her hunt and was out of breath sitting on the sofa. "How did you two get together and why?"

"I knew him for a while as he came and went, fucked him a few times to set him up if he ever came down here to live. It worked, and he takes me on trips and thinks I'm really poor."

"But you're not. Why do you let him think that?"

"I am poor by his standards. I'm a fun little peasant girl to him. He pays my rent in the mountains, and food and clothes and shit. He's in love with me and he thinks I'm crazy about him. Then I got myself pregnant and decided to make him believe it was his. Now he not only gives me money and a place to stay, but he supports my baby and my sister. She can't have babies, so I decided to have one for her. This pleased both her and my mother. You know what's funny?" Andrea lit a cigarette, crossed her legs, and gave Luis a smug look.

"What might that be, Andrea?" asked Luis, shaking his head, always amazed at how conniving she could be.

"My sweet little sister is so in love with Alejandro, and she's in on this con on Harper. And he still doesn't know." Andrea belly laughed at herself.

"Just one problem, smart one. Who supports your sister and Alejandro when you get rid of Harper?" Luis asked. "You? Your mother?"

"Harper is such a devoted father, it makes me want to vomit. He makes me look at pictures of his grandkids and I go, 'Aww, they're so cute,' like I give a flying fuck."

"And what do you know about his lawyer?" Luis asked.

"Not much. He relies on her a lot, and she helped him pay all the back taxes and debts. Her name is Vanessa something. Seems like some haughty Panama City bitch to me," said Andrea.

"It is Vanessa Perez, not Vanessa Something," said Luis.

"Big fucking deal, whatever her name is, she is a haughty bitch. But I'm telling you, he will take her advice over mine any day, even though she has no idea how this place works."

"Her husband is Roberto Perez, the assistant attorney general of Panama. His office is the one that leaves us alone over here, at least until last night and your temper tantrum."

"What's your point, Luis? You're starting to bore me," Andrea responded with a whine. She wasn't really hearing what he was saying. She was only interested in a bump up her nose. Andrea popped off the couch. "You must keep some in a coffee cup or a sugar bowl. Maybe even under the mattress, but, no, that's too amateur, even for you."

"Andrea, stop rooting through Fernanda's house and look at me. I mean it and listen closely." Luis grabbed her by the face. "My point is, Vanessa Somebody, the wife of the assistant attorney general, dropped everything she was doing and will be here tomorrow morning to meet with the mayor, the chief, and the judge. This isn't like every other gringo we take care of for you. I am afraid you're going to receive no backing from anybody in Balboa, including me. You're in a world of shit, honey."

"We'll see." Andrea pulled her face from Luis's grip and paced around the living room. She needed something foul in her body, and soon.

"I suggest you stay away from Michael, your sister, and the baby until the lawyer leaves, and something is worked out. Go back to your house, clean up the mess, clean up yourself, and don't talk to anyone. Keep as subdued tonight as you can in case you're requested to come to the police station tomorrow morning. And don't, in any way, threaten those three directly or through someone else. If you do, the feds have instructed the police to arrest you and any of your cohorts for longer than you might think."

"Yea, right, they are full of shit."

"They mean it. This isn't a threat. We are all watching you closely. Michael, Maria, and the baby are in protective custody, being guarded by the police somewhere in hiding until the meeting with Perez in the morning. I'm telling you, nobody's happy with your antics this time. This is trouble, big time, Andrea, for all of us."

Luis then poked his head out the front door and called for James. He came into the house, and Luis gave him instructions. "Take her home and hang out there tonight, and I mean all night. Call me if our little girl tries anything cute. She cannot leave her property. Understood?" James smiled and nodded.

James stepped forward and took Andrea by the bicep to lead her home.

"Don't touch me, you fucking gorilla," Andrea barked as she jerked her arm out of his grip. "And you are going to clean up the mess while I go back to sleep. Maybe I can put all the glass in the beds in Michael's hotel. And, yeah, I can blame it on you, Dimwit. Or better yet, let's throw it in the ocean, so that gringo asshole will slice his feet when he snorkels. Would love to see the ocean run red with his blood. And fuck you, Luis," As she was leaving, she turned and, walking backwards away from Fernanda's house, yelled, "Like I should clean up that mess. Michael did it, remember, not me. By the way, anybody around here know a good lawyer?" Andrea asked, her evil giggle haunted the street. She walked off as James followed a few paces behind the Queen B.

Luis knew she still didn't get it.

21

LET'S MAKE A DEAL BALBOA

The sun rose. The streets bustled as the local citizens of Balboa prepared their wares for another day of small-town commerce. The indigenous from the outer islands paddled their fish and vegetables into the docks, loaded in the bottoms of their dugout canoes. It was eight o'clock, hot, and muggy. T-shirts displayed heavy stains of perspiration, and their wearers, subtle expressions of exasperation.

Balboa Police Chief, Nicolas Nevarez, as it read in bold letters on the wall plaque outside his door, arrived early for a change. Pacing in his office window like a caged animal waiting for his civic massacre, he phoned his night officers, the same two who arrested Michael two nights before. Ironically, they were now on the other side of the foxhole, protecting Michael, Maria, and Alejandro from Andrea's potential attack at the Hotel Tortuga.

"Boys, bring our guarded guests back to the station by eight-thirty," he barked on the phone in his melodramatic tough guy voice, "and guard them with your lives. Take a bullet if you have to." He heard that in a movie once.

The officer saluted the air and thought, *"Right, we'll certainly do that, Chief, we will take a bullet."*

The chief continued, "Once you place them safe and guarded by the day cops, proceed to the airport in our new SUV. Two of our motorcycle cops will lead you there to pick up Mrs. Perez and her assistant. Put them and their luggage in the SUV, then the motorcycles will escort you back to the station." The overreacting chief boringly repeated his movie line, "and guard them with your lives, take a bullet if you have to."

"Chief, how will we know who they are? I mean, what do they look like?" asked one of the officers. "A lot of people get off those planes, and most of them look alike."

"You can't miss them, boys. Well, maybe you two idiots could, but the lawyer's secretary called this morning and informed us they will be arriving on a government jet, not one of those Air Panama suicide junkers. I doubt if there will be two of those landing in our skimpy little airport at the same time. Hell, we only have one runway. C'mon, boys, don't screw this up. Get their luggage, and whatever you do, keep them away from the toothless old ladies collecting our trumped-up five-dollar tourist tax. That might start us off on the wrong foot." The chief squeezed his forehead with his hand and closed his eyes, wishing the anxiety would leave his body alone.

"Yes sir, we'll get right on it. I think we may have time to clean the SUV inside and out and put one of those Christmas tree deodorant things on the rearview mirror," said one of the officers. The chief rolled his eyes. He saw a few *Andy Griffith* reruns with subtitles. He told his two "Barneys" to get moving and hung up the phone.

The day was beginning to move into action, like a flash flood after a heavy deluge. Everything was on schedule, with no surprises, yet. Michael, Maria, and Alejandro were brought to the station right on time, were greeted cordially and respectfully by Chief Nicolas Nevarez, then promptly escorted to the ocean deck, usually populated with the day-shift officers eating pastries, drinking coffee, and sharing lewd tourist stories. This morning, however, only Michael, Maria, and Alejandro, guarded by two armed officers with Uzis, were allowed on the deck. One guard secured the deck entry, and one observed the boats passing by in the busy Balboa bay. No one was permitted to dock that morning at the station.

As Maria fed the baby, smiling down at him in her loving arms, his hands loosely grasping the bottle. His feet kicked happily. An elderly Panamanian woman with flour covering her apron appeared at the deck entry. After she was frisked, she had a frightened look remaining on her face. She brought homemade bagels, donuts, cream cheese, and coffee to the honored prisoners. Placing a checkered tablecloth on the picnic table, she artistically arranged her delicious breakfast. Maria and Michael helped themselves, comfortably awaiting Vanessa's arrival. The elderly woman scurried quickly and nervously away and out of the station.

"I believe that was Antonio's mother, Michael," said Maria with a grin. "I saw her in his house yesterday. I bet Vanessa called Antonio after we left to make sure no one prepared our food except him."

"Vanessa is afraid we all could be poisoned. That is a bit extreme?"

"Andrea is not right. And Antonio's mother is probably scared her family will be pressured by Andrea and her thugs. Anyway, we know the food is safe. We have already downed a donut each, and I feel great, how about you?" Michael was almost choking from laughing. He was halfway through his second. Antonio's mother was a great baker and cute as a button. No way she would hurt a fly. A mosquito, yes, a fly, no.

"Michael, I'm frightened. Never in my wildest nightmare did I foresee myself sitting in a jail in the middle of a drug and corruption ring, clutching a baby. I was just going to be a sweet nanny for my little sister and love a baby like the one I prayed to the gods to share with me. Your house is more beautiful than I ever imagined, and you couldn't be sweeter to me."

"Maria, we are all blessed to have been drawn together, except Andrea." Michael reached over the picnic table, smiled, and stroked Maria's delicate black hair. Chill bumps ran up Maria's arms.

"But now, I'm stuck in a moral dilemma. If I protect my sister and cherish her baby, I'm helping her deport you. Mother will love me for that. Or I protect you and rescue her doomed baby, pushing Andrea out of the picture. Then Mother disowns me. How did this go so wrong?" Maria started to cry. Her voice quivered as she spoke. "This was supposed to be paradise, a dream come true."

Michael moved to Maria's side of the picnic table and put his arm around her shoulder, wiping her tears with a napkin. "Maria, all you have to do is tell the truth to Vanessa, like you did on the phone yesterday. We have the dealer and his girlfriend on our side. And the chief is scared out of his wits, like a baby rabbit being chased by a tomcat. Your sister has bullied people for years in Balboa and is irresponsible with the baby, and he's only three months old. I understand your love for Andrea, but the Andrea you love no longer exists."

"She can change, Michael. The good part is in there somewhere." Maria sighed.

"Panama City Andrea and Balboa Andrea are two different people. It is called schizoid. Neither can live without the other. All I ask of you, for the sake of that innocent child in your arms, is to be honest. Tell Vanessa again if she asks. The rest of the politicians and dealers will have no choice but to protect us. This might be a blessing for Andrea if it settles her down. And someday, I want to know what made her so hateful. You are loved, honey."

Their eyes connected. With that one term of endearment, both found themselves wondering whether that was a fatherly statement or love in its infancy.

The moment lingered in awkward silence. Michael wanted to kiss Maria, but this was bad timing. "Maria, you asked me two nights ago to promise not to leave Alejandro and go back to the States. I promised you I would not, and that is what this legal battle right is about. Now I must ask you the same question. I will protect you. Promise me you won't leave us." He spoke with a cherishing look into her eyes.

"I promise, Michael. I'll always be around for him, and you, if you want me."

They were interrupted by the chief, who marched through the entry and onto the deck. He was clean, shoes shined, hair slicked back, and beard trimmed. The aroma of his Balboan cologne permeated the air like a leak in a sewage pipe, despite the ocean breeze. Michael equated it to perfume on a pig.

"I hope your evening was comfortable. Did you have a good dinner and sleep well? Did you take the little tiger into the pool? And my guards were pleasant and attentive?" The chief needed all the brownie points he could, so Vanessa would find him, and his department *civilized*.

"Yes, sir," said Michael. "Thank you for your kindness. We did take the child into the pool, and he loved it. We had no breakfast, but someone brought us this continental, put together in such a heartfelt way." The chief was becoming fond of Michael and Maria. It wasn't often he dealt with prisoners so refined and reasonable. And he knew Michael had power stuck deep in his pocket and no reason to let it loose.

"Have you heard from Mrs. Perez this morning, Chief? Is the Air Panama flight on time for once, or will we be delay?"

"No, Mr. Harper, they are flying on a private jet. They should be right on schedule, ground traffic permitting. There will be two of them. The other, I assume, is her paralegal assistant. Your guards are gathering them at the airport and escorting them here. You will meet with her for an hour and a half, then with me and our town officials." The chief offered a nervous smile. "I must go and complete some paperwork. I will let you know when she arrives."

The police SUV pulled up to the front entrance of the station. Luis made an unusual point to awaken early to witness their arrival. He was anxious to see what they were up against. He sat at the table of a small sidewalk breakfast café across from the station, drinking a Bloody Mary and pretending to read his newspaper, even though he was illiterate. As he poked his eyes overtop his paper. He watched the officers jump out of the SUV and open the back doors. Vanessa quickly pulled her door shut. From the left side, a large, compelling man, clean-cut in a form-fitted black suit and sunglasses, stepped out onto the street. He walked to Vanessa's side of the vehicle, the shape of a shoulder holster obvious under his jacket. When in place, he opened Vanessa's door and took her hand as he helped her exit the vehicle. She wore a dark blue suit, matching heels, a few pieces of conservative, but exquisite jewelry. She showed no expression behind her sunglasses. Luis was already intimidated.

The chief approached the car to introduce himself in as dignified a fashion as he was capable. Vanessa looked at her shoe to see if she had stepped in anything, then realized the smell was the chief's cologne. The chief's mouth turned to cotton, his tongue felt like it weighed fifty pounds, and his hands began to tremble." Mrs. Harper, I'm sorry, I mean Mrs. Perez, welcome to Balboa. I am Police Chief Nicolas Nevarez. We spoke on the phone." He extended his hand. She shook it firmly. He then extended his hand to her bodyguard. He did not respond.

Vanessa scanned the dilapidated buildings surrounding the station, looked at the chief and inquired, "Do you know where I might find the law offices of the attorney, Danny Meeko?"

"Why yes, Mrs. Perez. You can see the building from here. It's two blocks away, the white building on your left. Why, may I ask? Is he somehow involved in this as well? I was unaware of that," said the chief.

"Yes sir, he is," said Vanessa. "We, meaning Mr. Harper, Maria, the baby, and myself need to meet with him in his offices."

"Mrs. Perez, he has only one office, but may I be so bold as to ask, how is Mr. Meeko involved?"

"No, you may not, Chief Nevarez, but I will tell you anyway. First, I don't want to discuss this case in open forum in your station with your people's ears pressed against your walls."

"Oh, that wouldn't happen, Mrs. Perez. I run a tight ship here at the station." The chief smiled proudly.

"Chief, I already see three of your little spies, including your scumbag, Luis. Look at him across the street pretending he can read a newspaper. That is cute." She whispered to her bodyguard, pointed at Luis, and waved to him. He lifted the paper to cover his face. It was a feeble attempt to become invisible. "And if you would, please remind all your other fledgling spies, my friend is touchy about anyone getting close to me. He loves to pull that revolver. It makes him feel important. Secondly, regarding Mr. Meeko, I need a set of eyes and ears in this town to report to me if, after our meetings and agreements, anything is not respected. If it is, I will involve my husband and his office. Now gather Mr. Harper and his family."

Vanessa waited with her bodyguard as the chief barked orders. Michael finally appeared at the front gate with Maria and the baby, armed guards on both sides, ready to take a bullet.

"Vanessa, it's so good to see you," Michael said with a smile. "I can't thank you enough for your quick response. This is Maria, my nanny and the baby's aunt. And this is my beautiful son, Alejandro; the star of the show, you might say." Michael looked down at the grinning baby.

That baby does not appear to have an ounce of Caucasian blood and not one of Michael's features, thought Vanessa.

Michael and Vanessa gave each other a soft, dignified embrace and an amicable kiss on both cheeks. Vanessa took his hands in hers and looked him straight in the eyes. "Michael, you never cease to amaze me. I have never met anyone as honest and caring as you, yet you still get yourself in trouble." Vanessa looked at Maria and the baby. She held Maria's cheek in her hand, smiled, and kissed the child on the forehead.

"Chief, before we leave, are these the two arresting officers involved with Mr. Harper's arrest? I need them for questioning. I also need guards while with Mr. Meeko."

"Mrs. Perez, our mayor does not allow our officers to be questioned outside of court. "And these boys have been up all-night standing guard. They need some rest. I'm sure you understand protocol."

"Chief, my questions are simple. Perhaps you could answer them and save us the time for a full-blown internal affairs investigation involving not just this case but many other cases involving Andrea?" Vanessa stared at the chief until he almost wet himself.

"I'll try, Mrs. Perez, but I'm not supposed to answer either. Vanessa ignored his response, even though that was protocol.

"Did your officers interrogate Andrea's sister, Maria, before arresting Mr. Harper? A simple yes or no will suffice."

"They did not. They arrested him based on Andrea's recollection."

"Did your officers know Andrea's sister and the baby were barricaded in her room the whole time?" asked Vanessa.

Everyone looked at the officers. They nodded their heads yes.

"Thank you for your cooperation, officers. That's all. Chief, and if you have two competent day officers, at least as competent as can be in Balboa, I am fine if you send the night boys home."

The chief grimaced. Vanessa just put his department in a false arrest case. *This woman's dangerous*, he thought.

Two fresh officers were quickly assigned and told to take orders from the bodyguard. Vanessa then turned to her entourage. "Okay, let's get to work and keep this little fella safe. Chief, we will meet you back here at ten-thirty."

"We can walk from here, people, as long as we watch where we step." Vanessa waved goodbye to Luis as he covered his face once again.

As the group walked to Meeko's office, people stared in bewilderment. The town knew a government jet landed at the airport and a police car escorted by a motorcade went to the station. This was big time. Luis paid his tab, walked across the street, and stood next to the chief.

"Oh my God," said the chief. "We're in trouble. That woman is power. I feel like an old security guard at the bank next to her."

Vanessa, Michael, and Maria, with the baby in her arms, reached Danny Meeko's office. The bodyguard drew his gun and went in first. He looked around, frisked the startled Danny Meeko. He gave Vanessa the all-clear. The bodyguard positioned himself in front of the door. He put one officer behind the building in the knee-high brush, probably harboring a snake or two, and one outside the iron gate in front of the building.

Introductions were made. Danny and Michael worked together on the buyout of the hotel, so Danny knew the intelligence and professionalism with which he was dealing. In this situation, he would be a listener, not a talker.

Danny brought extra folding chairs into the room. He gave Vanessa his desk. The office was painted stark white, a framed law degree on the wall, and a Bobble-Head of the President.

Vanessa organized herself at the desk. The room stayed quiet. She pulled out papers from her briefcase, a pen and a notepad. She began. "Danny, I have you here as a watchdog for the moment." Danny listened intently. "You know everyone in this town, including Andrea. First, I want you to keep your eyes and ears open in case the settlement we make today is broken in any way, and I mean even in the slightest. It's imperative they know we're watching. But if an agreement is not made, or if they break it, you will be appointed the judge in Balboa on the spot, supported by us in Panama City, meaning the Attorney General's Office. I know you want that. Do I have your support and loyalty?"

"I don't know what to say," Danny answered. "I would be honored to be judge here someday, notably supported by all of you. Yes, you have my complete support and loyalty, Mrs. Perez."

"Good, Danny. Next, Maria, is the baby hurt physically in any way?"

"No, other than the diaper rash and vomiting after Andrea has him. She mixes his formula with water from the pipe because she is too lazy to walk to the store. But I can't prove that Mrs. Perez," said Maria.

"Then why do you, independent of Mr. Harper's opinion, think the baby is endangered, Maria? Most babies have rashes and vomit."

"Mrs. Perez, I have not spent time with my sister in Balboa over the last twenty years until the last three months. Her mother and I have lived together in Panama City. She was our pride and joy. But she is not the Andrea I knew. Mrs. Perez, I explained the events that transpired two nights ago. Finally, when she wanted to play with him on the veranda at three in the morning, over the ocean, drunk and high, I locked us in my room."

"But she hasn't hurt him, correct?"

"He doesn't feed him for hours. She abandons him. She uses him as a prop. What mother leaves her baby for hours on the couch in a drug den filled with dealers and addicts? Or with sexual perverts and sex junkies coming in and out? Where will that child be when he is ten, if he is still alive? He will be dealing drugs in his grade school and getting high with his mom every day. She's a hooker, a con artist, and a druggy. That boy is doomed from the start without Mr. Harper and me to protect him and raise him in a proper healthy manner."

Meeko stopped taking notes. He looked at Vanessa and then at Alejandro with sad eyes. Alejandro was content. "That's awful, Ms. Blanco. Your evaluation of Andrea is accurate. I have prosecuted many young boys for the city's coffers based on her cons and villainous."

"I think I understand," Vanessa replied. "But tell me again. Why was Michael arrested that night and not Andrea?"

"Because Andrea lied to the police and told them Michael was the one who went crazy, broke all the dishes, and threatened her, me, and her baby with a gun," said Maria.

"So, Andrea lied to the police, falsified a report, destroyed private property, threatened you, Michael, and the baby, and disturbed the peace. Why did they believe her, even though they knew she does things like this quite often? And why did you not speak up on behalf of Mr. Harper when the police were there?"

Alejandro began to reach for Maria's face, along with a cooing noise. He sensed the safety that surrounded him.

"To answer your second question—there was no way I was coming out of that room and giving Andrea any chance to get ahold of Alejandro.

She was in no condition to hold him, and she would have taken him from me by force."

Maria realized what the baby wanted. She handed the baby to Michael and reached into the diaper bag for a bottle and began mixing the formula, all the time continuing to talk. Alejandro sat quietly with wide eyes in Michael's arms, watching his bottle being prepared.

"He was crying hysterically, confused from the noise and violence going on around him. I held him tightly to help him through his panic. The answer to the first question is…" Maria took Alejandro back into her arms, kissed him on the cheek, and started his feeding. The sound of the bubbles from the formula was adorable. Maria resumed.

"Michael and I have been told she's the top drug seller in this town. If she wants someone thrown in jail, kicked out of town, or even killed, that's what the police have been instructed to do, no questions asked. Her stories are considered gospel. She wants Michael gone, and total control over that baby, then that is what will happen. But I can't figure out why she wants him gone."

"You heard she is the top money producer from whom?" asked Vanessa.

"From the head drug dealer. We talked to him on the phone. The one who had his girlfriend bring Alejandro home to us that night. But he wouldn't give us his name. He and his girlfriend did a nice thing for us that night, Mrs. Perez," said Maria.

"His name's Luis, Vanessa," said Michael. "I know who he is, but I pretend I don't. I don't want to hear his silly threats."

"You're right, Michael. We have a file on him six-inches thick, and he isn't the smartest chess player in town." She paused and looked around. The baby was asleep. "I want everyone to give us the room, please. Wait outside behind my man and the officers. They all went outside and waited behind the iron fence, her bodyguard's hand inside his jacket.

Vanessa sat across from Michael and asked the question she had been waiting to ask. "I would be confused if I didn't know you as well as I do, Michael, but I must ask. Why do you care so much about this baby? You could fly back to the States and never come back. You have already closed your hotel to the public. Certainly, you can't love living here enough to put yourself through this insanity. You could return to the luxury you came from and live around your family permanently. Andrea would serve child support papers to you and she and the mayor would try to stick it as a lien on your hotel, but I could get you out of that easily. So why, Michael? You and I both know what I'm asking."

"I'll be succinct, Vanessa," Michael began. "I've known Andrea for ten years. After her husband was run out of town by the crime ring here, she was my sex toy when I visited. Now she's using the same coercion she used on her husband. I am twenty-five years older and single. I figured she was my last tango in Paris, but I didn't see all this coming. She seemed to have matured during her pregnancy, but that was an act. She knows I'll continue to help support that child. Can we just agree that sometimes I can still be a very stupid man, even at my age? Can we just leave it at that, Vanessa?" he said with a silly grin.

Vanessa smiled back. "Yeah, yeah, I get it. You had some candy, and she had a sugar daddy. But what makes you conclude, for sure, you are the baby's father? That baby doesn't have any of your features, and he's not white in the slightest. Andrea's an amateur hooker and a con woman. She's a large component of the corruption ring here in Balboa. But Balboa is still small potatoes compared to what we prosecute on the federal level. However, we do keep files on most everybody in the ring, including you, Michael," said Vanessa, holding him with her stare.

"Me, whoa, why me, Vanessa? You know my past, and you know I'm clean," Michael insisted as he leaned forward in his chair.

"Because you had a business partner we were watching closely. He was ripping off the government and his local employees, and now you've been hanging out with Andrea. But settle down, Michael. We know you're clean, because I checked your file before I came here today for any updates. If you weren't, I would not be helping you. And I'm glad you stopped that coke thing quickly that Andrea was dragging you into." Vanessa smiled as she looked over her glasses. "And never mind how I know."

Michael held his hands up in front of him, palms toward Vanessa. "I'm glad I stopped as well."

"You're fine, Michael, and I'm here to support you. But again, I must ask, what makes you think you're the baby's father? I know you can't be that naïve." Vanessa closed her eyes and shook her head. "I can get you out of this paternal responsibility and keep you safe. One DNA test, and it's over."

Michael again looked at Vanessa with a smile on his face. He stared directly into the eyes. "I'm the baby's father, because it says so on his birth certificate."

"No, Michael, give me a real reason to fight for you," said Vanessa.

"Vanessa, when Andrea told me she was pregnant, I knew it was a con. I have money and a place to live. I played the game, and she assured me I was the only man in her life, blah, blah, blah. That's when I knew I wasn't immune to her cons. No one is. Her love for me was a joke, but I pretended I believed it. What she didn't know was I had a vasectomy fifteen years ago, way before I came to Panama. No way I could be the father. I figured I could get out of it if I wanted. But she was fun to play with." Michael shrugged his shoulders.

"Why didn't you tell her way before her pregnancy?" Vanessa was puzzled.

"Simple. I lied. She was in her thirties and said she wasn't sure whether she wanted to have children. I led her to believe I could still have a baby to keep her from leaving me. I guess we were both conning each other. But as you see, she was going to have a baby with or without me. And she did. This is all attorney-client privilege, correct?"

"Correct, but Michael, why? I still don't have a reason to fight those guys at the police station just so you can be father to a child that isn't yours."

"Vanessa," said Michael, now with a melancholy look on his face. He slumped and sat back in his chair, "I never asked, do you have children?"

"No, Michael, but nieces and nephews."

"And you love them?" asked Michael.

"Like they were my very own," said Vanessa.

"Exactly."

"Okay, Michael, tell it to me in your own words."

"Vanessa, this has nothing to do with me, or Andrea, or the drug ring, or Maria. I thought about doing the DNA test, but then I thought about kids in my neighborhood growing up without fathers in the States. They were always the ones in trouble. I thought, what kind of life will

Andrea's child have if I'm not in it? Andrea for a mother, no father to take responsibility or love him, an education that would be completely discarded? Left with drug dealers while his mother goes off and hooks? The kid will be a junky by the time he's fifteen," said Michael, tears clouding his eyes. "I'm not a formally religious man, but I keep feeling, for some reason, God divinely put that child into my life and into Maria's. I can feel the connection and the tenderness. I know, not exactly a good legal argument, but I do love that child, and oddly enough, I did before he was born."

"Michael, you're sure you want this?" said Vanessa. "If you're sure, I'll protect that baby and scare the hell out of everybody in this town to keep the three of you safe."

"No, Vanessa, first, keep the baby safe. This has to be about the baby," Michael corrected.

"Michael, you're right. But I must keep you and Maria both protected from these people to keep the baby safe. Otherwise, Andrea takes over complete control. They will only care about the money they make from drug deals, never the baby. Are you willing to take full custody?"

"Absolutely, if you can do that," responded Michael. "Vanessa, thank you. You're a saint." He became emotional.

"'That means you will only be able to visit your own family in the States occasionally."

"They can come here as well, not a problem," smiled Michael.

"And you know the rules about taking Alejandro out of the country. She won't allow that. You'll need to live here permanently and get your residency papers. Michael, this is your last chance. I can get you out of this whole mess, and off you go, back to your hassle-free life in the States." Vanessa challenged him one last time.

"Go forward, Vanessa. This is about the child. It feels so right to me to raise and protect him. But we must get his mother out of his life. Otherwise, I may take you up on getting me out of here. Vanessa, please, let's save this child's life," said Michael.

"Michael, I don't know what to say. My husband and I will make sure you and your child will be protected, but we'll not do anything criminal to help you. This is special, and you say God has a reason. I'm mysteriously touched by all this. Like God is involved somehow. Let's go up the street and let me do *my* magic. And Michael, I don't want you in the room when I negotiate. You may not like that part of me."

Vanessa and Michael stood, and uncharacteristically, the serious hardcore attorney, Vanessa Perez, had tears in her eyes as she gave Michael a hug. "Michael, no one, not even my husband, makes me cry. If Alejandro ever needs godparents, let us know. I'll meet you outside. Let me go fix my eyes." It was time for Vanessa to get back into coldhearted mode.

Michael went to the door to wait for her. When she finished in the bathroom, she joined him at the exit door. He turned toward her, smiled, and whispered in her ear, "Vanessa, your heart never fooled me, but I am so glad you are for me, not against me." Vanessa smiled and squeezed Michael's hand.

22

THE RING CATCHES FIRE WITHOUT AN EXTINGUISHER

The church bells indicated ten-thirty. Vanessa was orchestrating the situation artistically, like a sophisticated composer writing a modern-day symphony. She had the officials of Balboa in fear's grasp, moving their temperaments up and down like minor falls and major lifts in the second movement of her concerto. She was on schedule and shrewdly focused, now that she heard what she needed to hear from Michael.

Michael and Vanessa exited Meeko's reception area into the courtyard. Michael donned a smile, a look of peace radiated from his face. Vanessa exuded confidence and determination. It was showtime for her, the very environment and situation the elite attorney embraced.

"Alright, let us take a stroll to the station. I will prepare for the meeting," said Vanessa as they began their short trek in masse. She stopped, "Wait, someone must retrieve the officer behind the building, or he will be there all day."

Walking up the street, the bodyguard kept his hand inside his jacket, finger on the trigger of his Snub-Nose 38. The other officers took notice. Meeko began to speak to Vanessa, but she shushed him with her index finger, giving the strong message to all to remain silent. Meeko handed a sealed envelope to her addressed "Mrs. Perez – Personal and Confidential."

She opened it, read it, then put it into her briefcase. Vanessa was silent and pensive. She walked slowly, reviewing her strategic maneuvers in her head. She was undaunted about where she would lead the meeting. She was informed twenty-four hours ago, allowing her the entire day to research all the players and craft her tactics. She was now sure of Michael's position, convinced he was virtuously committed to the outcome.

Vanessa stood in front of the station with her assemblage. The chief joined them. To take control by intimidation, she began barking orders. "Officers, I want the two of you to escort Mr. Harper, Maria, and the baby back to your bayside deck. Be sure no one can see them by land or sea." The chief felt overthrown from his rank. "Someone find the little old lady from this morning and have her bring Michael and Maria some fresh donuts and coffee, as well as clean fresh water for the baby." Michael nodded to Vanessa in appreciation.

Vanessa turned to Meeko and whispered in his ear, "Mr. Meeko, I want you in the meeting to take notes. I want them returned to me in contract format by four o'clock this afternoon. If there is something you do not understand, save your questions until I address you. Do not break my momentum at any time with a question or addition. I am sure that is understood." She looked at her bodyguard. "And I want you guarding the door of our meeting room from the outside with your shoulder holster and that cute little snub-nose on your fingertip. Everyone understand?"

The group nodded. Vanessa and her bodyguard approached the chief. He greeted them. "Mrs. Perez, I assure you, all your needs will be met, with our priority going to the safety and welfare of Mr. Harper and his people. Are we ready now?"

"I don't know, are we, Chief?" Vanessa responded in an arrogant tone, preparing him for the political confusion she was about to cause inside his head.

"Yes, Mrs. Perez, we are certainly ready. We will meet in the mayor's office in City Hall." He pointed to a large stone building with chipped paint and broken windows. Vanessa thought the two rusted-out eighteenth-century cannons in front were a fascinating touch of history. "The mayor's office is bigger than mine, and he even has A/C. I think we will be more comfortable there. Is that okay with you?"

"That's fine, and very considerate of you, Chief," said Vanessa. "I want only five in the room, with my bodyguard stationed outside the door. I want you, the mayor, the judge, myself, and Mr. Meeko, my assistant here in Balboa. If Andrea or Luis show up at any time, I will have them both arrested on the spot by order of the Attorney General's Office of Panama. Is that understood?"

"Let me make a quick call, Mrs. Perez." The chief hurried to his office to call the mayor and relay the information he just received.

Vanessa, Meeko, and her bodyguard marched with tenacity to City Hall. Meeko scampering to keep up. The chief, delayed by his call, was last in line.

When they arrived, they were escorted to the mayor's office. Vanessa's bodyguard, with gun drawn, explored the meeting room and gave the all-clear. They entered the mayor's office and from there went into a small adjoining conference room. As Vanessa and Meeko entered, the bodyguard positioned himself outside the door. All rose, introductions were made, hands extended, and smiles exchanged—all except for the judge. She did not stand up or smile. She did give Vanessa a limp handshake from her seat. She ignored Meeko.

The mayor spoke first, "How is Panama City these days, Mrs. Perez? And how is your husband?" Vanessa did not look up. She opened her briefcase and removed a number of files.

"He's quite busy with these international money laundering accusations at the moment, but that's not why I'm here, is it?" She finished arranging her files. She looked coldly into the eyes of the mayor. "Let's get to it, Mayor," She sat with perfect posture, her legs crossed at the ankles, her hands folded in front of her. "I assume Luis was here, and he just left. He is an important part of our business today, but I don't want to deal with him in person. He is your ugly little problem to deal with if all goes as agreed upon."

"Luis, you say? I'm sorry, I don't believe I know of whom you are speaking, Mrs. Perez," said the mayor.

Vanessa took a deep breath and gazed down at her files. After a moment of silence, she stared back at the mayor. "Fun time's over, folks. We, and by we, I mean the Attorney General's Office, have a file six inches thick on Luis as well as the rest of you. Be careful if you think this is a minor problem today. And don't insults to my intelligence, or bad things will happen to all of you. Mr. Harper is not only an honored client of mine, but my friend. And he is highly respected by my husband's office and the US Embassy. Yesterday, I was briefed on your Balboa operation. Are you ready to hear my demands? Or will you continue to stick your finger in your cheek and play stupid. What is it, Mayor?"

The mayor was not used to such disrespect, but he also knew he tried to outsmart a legal virtuoso. His face turned red with embarrassment. He now knew what the chief had been going through for the last twenty-four hours. "Oh, Luis, sure, I know who you mean now, Mrs. Perez. I know him as 'L,' a nickname only I call him. My apologies. Please continue." The mayor glanced around the room at his cohorts, but only when Vanessa looked down at her notes.

"I am aware you met earlier Mayor, including Luis, while Mr. Harper and I were meeting down the street. I give you credit for leaving Andrea out. Mayor, we always have people undercover watching you, every week, every day. We want to be sure you are keeping the arrangements between Balboa and our federal government. So, should we, as they say, begin again?"

The group remained silent as they once again exchanged glances. The mayor nodded his head, the others followed suit.

Vanessa continued. "Allow me to start by being blunt. My husband and his department in Panama City don't care about your amateur drug and corruption ring over here. We view you as a high school fraternity party. Nor do we care about the extortion and cons you execute on the non-Panamanian population. It's petty. You sell most of your drugs to the expats who retire here. They make no money, and the country gets no taxes from them. You sell to the kids in the hostels, and again, it generates no tax revenue. So, since we collect a pittance in tax revenue from you, we give you nothing in return. To clarify, we have only one need from you, no gringo or tourist deaths, especially Americans. You sell no heroin, which you have executed well, and we have tracked very few overdoses since you label them heart attacks. We applaud you for that. Prostitution is almost nonexistent here, even though it's legal. The surfers have sex with each other for free, and the old guys are too cheap to pay for the girls, condoms, and Viagra. But we have two problems that have arisen."

"What might those be, Mrs. Perez?

"Luis and Andrea." Vanessa stopped abruptly.

The three politicians remained silent during Vanessa's dissertation until the mayor broke the silence. "Mrs. Perez, since you are obviously well educated as to our operation and arrangements, you must know Andrea and Luis are very important to our tourist trade and economy," he began, trying to be firm and nothing but business. "We're aware there was an incident two nights ago involving them, but we are confused. It seems minor to us. Some dishes were broken, Andrea raising her voice. An allegedly innocent man may have been mistakenly arrested. I am sure if everyone at this table will agree to say, 'Let's just get along,' we can save time and end this now." He looked at his cohorts, smiled, and nodded his head yes. They did as well.

Vanessa chuckled. "Mr. Meeko, did you note the mayor's initial proposal? Be sure you did. My husband and his entire department will find that amusing. Among my husband, myself, Mr. Harper, Andrea's sister, and even your good friend 'L,' no one finds this a minor incident."

"Go on, Mrs. Perez."

Let's start at the top of the pyramid. Top my list with child endangerment. What would happen if Andrea and Luis are involved in the death of an American's infant son when she was high, or the baby was shot in a crossfire inside Luis's drug den? Or what if the baby was kidnapped and held for ransom? What if the baby drowned in the ocean while Andrea left him on the beach to do cocaine in the bathroom?"

The grin was wiped off all their faces. They knew that was more than a possibility.

Vanessa raised her voice, stood up and came across the table at the mayor. "Do you know what would happen, Mayor? I do. My husband's office, the American press, and the US Embassy, along with the FBI, would swarm this place. I am sure you all have considered it."

"I agree, Mrs. Perez. That would be horrible for all of us," said the mayor.

"All of us, Mayor, all of us? What about the baby? What about the life of a baby before it has a chance to start, you selfish piece of crap?"

Vanessa stopped. She was on a roll. "Okay, hold it. Let me settle down for a moment." Vanessa sat, laced her fingers in a prayer-like position on the table and took a deep breath. She knew exactly what she was doing. What a performance.

The mayor, again, had been called out and responded, "Mrs. Perez, we all have families and understand your concern. I assure you, all of us here feel the same way. But first, I talked to Luis yesterday, and he is completely on Mr. Harper's side. He spoke with Andrea yesterday and promised us she will never do that again."

Vanessa started to laugh sarcastically this time. "Mayor, I have a file on this wretched woman, a thick and nasty one. We could make a movie out of her shenanigans. We know she goes to Boquete on the weekends and plays piano in the lounge of the 'El Quetzel Hotel' while the baby stays with Mr. Harper and her sister. She's only with the baby during the week, and only when she needs him to attract surfer kids and sell them drugs. The child is a prop."

"That is true, Mrs. Perez. I hear Andrea is a beautiful piano player. I'm sure she will teach him someday," said the mayor.

"We also know her piano playing is a front. I have heard her play. She is bad. She makes a little money playing piano but makes a lot by sleeping with our government officials, but that is not our concern. We have a different arrangement with them up there. But she smuggles cocaine and THC wax into Boquete for the gringos, splitting your profits with their mayor. She has that red bandana with the zipper pouch where she hides the drugs from us feds. She thinks she is clever. Would you enjoy photo of her doing cocaine with the checkpoint guards and giving them blow jobs behind their stations?"

"Okay, but that seems to fall under our agreement, wouldn't you say? No one gets hurt, and we are selling to tourists and gringos."

"How about the men she assaults and the men she claims beat her? You take a nice bribe from the rich ones to keep them out of jail, confiscate their businesses, and unofficially deport them; like you were about to do to Mr. Harper. Her craziness works for all of you, but you are backing the wrong horse on this one." They continued to sit still, getting more concerned. Finally, the judge, who was the mayor's sister, spoke up.

"Mrs. Perez, what do you want? We obviously took an important man into custody."

"Wrongfully," Vanessa interrupted.

"No, that hasn't been proven in court yet, Mrs. Perez," spouted the judge.

"Wrongfully Judge," interjected the chief powerfully. He knew this might be his only chance to find any mercy for himself from Vanessa.

The judge frowned at the chief, but knew she was stuck. "Okay," agreed the judge, "Mr. Harper was wrongfully taken into custody. And a baby was endangered, but the baby was not injured in any way."

"I know you have a limited knowledge of the law, Judge, along with everything else, but why is it called 'endangerment?'" Vanessa went on before the judge could respond. "If we let it go until the baby is injured or killed, then it is called abuse, assault, or murder. And remember, no one dies over here, especially a gringo baby. Can you imagine, Judge? You would meet the international press core, my dear, and you're not photogenic."

"That was cruel, Mrs. Perez, true but cruel." Vanessa put the judge on her heels. "But still, what can the three of us do for you?" the judge reiterated. "It still sounds like a family matter."

Vanessa ignored the judge's ignorant comment. "You can start by arresting Andrea for child endangerment, prostitution without a health card, falsification of a police report, destruction of private property, sale of illegal drugs, smuggling cocaine across provincial borders which, by the way, does pull us into federal law. Then bribing checkpoint guards and disturbing the peace. Can we think of anymore, Judge? Oh yes, false arrest by your police department. That alone is cause for my husband to send over federal investigators, and your streets dry up, right? Are you getting this down, Mr. Meeko? And if you don't, my tape recorder is running."

"Mrs. Perez," the judge replied. "If we press all these charges against Andrea and send her to a prison on the mainland, will that satisfy you?"

"No," said Vanessa.

They all hushed once again and subtly exchanged glances around the table. Everyone was fearful of Vanessa pulling their files and reading charges against them. Then their whole corrupt little ring goes up in flame. It was smoldering so strongly one could smell it. It smelled like pungent venality.

"What else can we do, Mrs. Perez?" asked the mayor as he took back the floor, his voice quivering.

"Mr. Harper wants no charges pressed against Andrea if she cooperates."

"What?" asked the baffled judge. "We all know she's on the brink, if not over the brink, of crazy. She puts so many drugs and so much alcohol into her body she loses control these days. And she's getting worse. But I beg you, Mrs. Perez, please don't tell me Mr. Harper still loves her and thinks she can change. Please don't tell me that."

"Heavens no. That little twit's ego is so big, she thought he was in love with her all along. He has been playing with her like a baby with its rattle. Her Spanish helped him with his workers at one time." Then, like a stone skipping over a creek, Vanessa added, "And the sex, of course," she continued. "He told her how he loved her and missed her when she was in Boquete, but it gave him wonderful quiet time away from her constant yapping. Then she got pregnant. Mr. Harper had a choice. He could prove he wasn't the father with a DNA test and kick her and the child to the curb or stay and raise the baby. He decided to stay and raise the baby."

"Please, Mrs. Perez, we just want to know what you want," the judge repeated, getting impatient as she attempted to hide her ignorance of the law.

Vanessa knew this far enough. She finally had everyone scared and in their place. She could sense, like a circling shark, it was time to move in for the kill. "Okay, Judge, are you ready? Mr. Meeko, write these demands down in case my tape runs out.

"Number one, Mr. Harper gets full custody of the child and makes all decisions regarding his health, education, and welfare. We will agree Mr. Harper must keep the residence of the child in Balboa."

"Is he the legal father?" asked the judge.

"It says so on the birth certificate, Judge," Vanessa said.

The judge came right back with, "What if Andrea lied, Mrs. Perez?"

Vanessa looked her in the eyes and repeated, "It says so on the birth certificate, Judge. That's a legal document."

The judge interrupted. "But if he is not the father, why would he…"

Venessa spoke over top of the judge. "Number two, Maria, Andrea's sister, at Maria's consent, becomes the nanny for the child and lives in one of Mr. Harper's rooms in his house. She will be provided with a reasonable salary, a room, and meals." They all nodded.

"Number three, Andrea has visitation rights from Sunday noon to Wednesday at 8:00 P.M. only. Even if she stays in Balboa and does not go to Boquete, she still only has visitation rights Sunday through Wednesday.

"Number four, on visitation days, she may not pick up the child prior to 10:00 A.M. and must return the child to Mr. Harper's home by 8:00 P.M. During that time, either Maria or Mr. Harper or both must always be with her and the child. She cannot be alone with him, ever, under any circumstances.

"Number five, at all times, Andrea must act civil to Mr. Harper and her sister, Maria, behaving the way a mature mother and adult would act. And the reverse is true as well.

"Number six, if Andrea wishes to visit with her family for holidays or other family events, it must be in either her residence in Boquete or at her mother's home in Panama City; however, Maria must still be with Andrea and the baby at all times. We will work out acceptable holidays later. Andrea agrees, if the child is not returned on the specified date, she will voluntarily confess to kidnapping, found guilty, and be placed in prison.

"Number seven, Andrea must remove all her belongings from Mr. Harper's house within two days from today. We understand she has a love shack in town, giving her living quarters in Balboa and Boquete already. She should not be inconvenienced.

"And finally, number eight, if anything happens to Mr. Harper, Maria, or the child by anyone in a violent or threatening manner, Andrea will be arrested and held as the first suspect and/or co-conspirator until all facts are gathered. Also, we, the Attorney General's office, will be required to assist you with federal forces and investigators, and I pray we do not stumble across any other unrelated problems if you understand my drift."

The judge responded. "And what if she doesn't agree to these terms, Mrs. Perez?"

"Then all charges I mentioned earlier are brought against her, including the smuggling charge across provincial borders. That charge will also be considered a breach of our agreement with Balboa. I'm sure that will cause Andrea to expose many of you to reduce her prison time. I'll be required to bring people in from Panama City to investigate all of you at that point, and during that period, your business will be on hold. We will need to replace you, Judge, with a person who has a law degree as opposed to an eighth-grade education. Is that clear? Mr. Meeko will be my eyes and ears." Vanessa finished and gathered her files.

With that, the mayor stood up and offered his hand to Vanessa, then to Mr. Meeko. "Done, Mrs. Perez," he said. "We're on the same side. Thank you for helping us protect one of our children from danger. I will make it clear to my electorate their mayor, in cooperation with the federal government, will not tolerate any abuse or endangerment of any child in our town, no matter what nationality it may be." Vanessa rolled her eyes and wanted to stick her finger down her throat.

"Thank you, and you're welcome, Mayor. And one more thing. I would assume Andrea will not going to take this well. I believe we have doubts about her sanity. I need someone, or all of you, to talk to her and make her realize the gravity of this matter to her and the entire town's economy. She is on the edge of a prison term. And if she goes, so do all of you. Mr. Meeko will work on this the rest of the day, with a short draft and bullet points to be explained to Andrea."

Vanessa looked around the table. All three characters were dejected and defeated. The mayor looked at the chief, "Let us meet back here at four o'clock. Bring Andrea and anyone else you feel is important. Mr. Meeko will present these points to Andrea. It will be a legal document signed by me. Luis must make his employees gravely aware they are to protect Mr. Harper and his child, not help Andrea."

Vanessa added, "Mr. Harper is being kind to Andrea, more than I would be. Until you are sure she understands the gravity of this situation and she has vacated Mr. Harper's home, I want the city to pay for two rooms at the Hotel Tortuga and guard Mr. Harper and his family against her wrath." Vanessa completed her demands.

"We all agree to your terms," the mayor assured her. "It has been such a pleasure to meet you, Mrs. Perez. Tell your husband and his colleagues they have our full support here in Balboa. Now, where can we take you?"

"Oh, wait, one more thing," added Vanessa. "We must not forget about this false arrest charge by your police department. I should send my legal invoice to who? You, Mayor?"

The mayor glared at the chief with deep frustration although the chief was just following orders. "Yes, Mrs. Perez, that will be fine. Now, where can we take you? Do you need a room for the night? Hotel Tortuga with Mr. Harper and Ms. Blanco?"

"Mayor, really? Get me to the airport and out of this shithole you call a town. I can't wait to get back and take a cool shower. And Chief, bury that cologne of yours deep in the earth. I wouldn't even suggest the cemetery. And don't dump it in the toilet or the ocean. Who knows what it could kill." With that, Vanessa turned and left the room. The chief looked like he was going to cry.

The chief escorted Vanessa and her bodyguard to the deck at the station. On the way, Vanessa told the chief she needed Andrea's signature on the paper by seven o'clock, or else Andrea was to be arrested on federal drug trafficking charges without bail. She told Meeko to get to work and have the bullet points ready by four o'clock. At the station, the chief instructed the officers to take Michael, Maria, and the baby back to the Hotel Tortuga and stand guard. He would send others to relieve them every eight hours.

Vanessa briefed Michael on what to expect in the next few days. She warned him to watch his back for a while until Andrea's ego subsided and she realized the baby was getting in the way of her fun and addictions.

Michael assumed from the start this was a pride issue for Andrea. But Maria knew it was more than pride. It was Andrea's deep hatred for men, especially fathers and husbands. The memories of the stench of her father's body odor behind her and the sight and cold texture of her stillborn son lying gray and bloody on her chest, would never leave her sister's soul. Michael and Alejandro would never be completely safe, but Maria had some unique and powerful ideas about that.

23

ANDREA BARES HER TEETH AND PREPARES FOR A DOG FIGHT

Vanessa said her goodbyes to Michael, Maria, and Alejandro before leaving for the airport. Prior to departing for his office to prepare the document, Meeko shook hands with Vanessa and Michael and gave Maria and the baby each a kiss on the forehead. Meeko extended his hand to the bodyguard and, surprisingly, the bodyguard reciprocated and gave him an ever-so-faint smile. Meeko left for his office.

"Vanessa, brilliant work. I miss being in those types of negotiations. You were right to keep me out of the room. I would not have been able to keep quiet. I would be on my way to the States without my son if it weren't for your friendship and loyalty. It's a tough world, but you granted that child the best chance possible. Maria and I will raise him to be a blessing to everyone he meets." Michael gave Vanessa a hug and a kiss on each cheek. She responded with a hug of her own.

"Of all the dark and dirty cases I've taken in my life, this one is proving to be the most rewarding. I owe you, Michael. You've given me a renewed faith in humanity. Love and loyalty are still alive. Good luck here in Sodom and Gomorrah."

Vanessa hugged Maria with the baby squeezed in the middle. "Take good care of these two marvelous men and protect them."

"I have my own ideas on how to keep us all safe," Maria blurted. But when everyone waited for her to elaborate, she went quiet and stared down at the baby.

Vanessa smiled. "Whatever it is, I am open to hearing it. I am sure it is of an honorable nature."

As Vanessa turned to leave, her bodyguard said his only word. In a deep baritone voice, he muttered, "Wait." He proceeded to cross the deck, where he kissed Alejandro on the cheek, kissed Maria on top of her head, and shook Michael's hand with a tearful smile on his face. Vanesa smiled at him. She never saw him with any emotion whatsoever. Then, he escorted Vanessa to the car with his hand back inside his coat.

At City Hall, the mayor and judge sat speechless at the table. "Jonas," his sister asked, breaking the silence. "Are we waiting for Nevarez to return to discuss this situation? Do we need him to help us make this decision? He is only a grunt."

Jonas, placing his hands on the table and pushed his chunky body out of his chair. He walked to the side table and poured himself a cup of coffee. He then clumsily plopped back in his chair and peered sadly at his sister. "Bonita, we are trapped like monkeys in a pickle barrel, and Perez and her husband are sitting, on the lid laughing. It's a no-brainer. Andrea's been a crazy bitch ever since I first heard her name. I know, her lunatic behavior makes everyone lots of money, but you, my little sister, and our judge, instructed me to let her go about her business as long as no one dies in one of those black widow webs she weaves." The mayor clasped his hands behind his head and sighed.

"Whoa there, cowboy. I didn't tell you to let her be, Nevarez gave me those orders. He said they came from you. You're the boss, Jonas. I'm just a pawn in this nightmare. It all starts at the top, and that means you." Bonita was outraged by her brother laying the nefarious town's politics on her.

"That son of a bitch," said the mayor. "I sensed Nevarez, Luis, and Andrea had something going on the side. But I never cared if we got our cut. So that's how she gets away with her looney shit."

"Still lands on you, Mayor Jonas. Don't try to blame it on the rest of us."

"You're right, sis. It sounds like something I'd say. But we can survive without her. What she does cannot be the foundation of our drug economy anymore. That is the relationship between Luis and the Columbians, and how he controls his dealers. Those surfers and gringos will never stop buying. Maybe inconvenient for them, but they won't stop. She is like icing on the cake for us, not the cake. And Sis, this is not a bluff from the feds."

"No, Jonas, it certainly isn't. If it were, Perez would not have permission to take a government jet here within twenty-four hours, and with one intense, secret service bodyguard. He was a badass."

"Yes, he was," said Bonita, "and I'd love to pull him and his gun into my bed." She drifted off for a moment, while her brother rolled his eyes.

"And those government files she had on us. I would love to see the one on Nevarez. She pulled them together in a day," said the mayor. "They are convinced, after hearing what really happened that night from Andrea's very own sister, then studying Andrea and Luis's files, that baby will die at his mother's hands. I believe that also. It would be world news."

"It would be worse than the rich American girl strangled here a year ago," responded Bonita. "I've never seen so many feds in choppers, the FBI, and news teams. Perez is one connected woman. She is scary. She and her husband would shut us down in a minute and enjoy prosecuting all of us for something. Who is this Harper guy anyway, CIA?"

"I don't know, but if anything happens to him or his gringo baby, they will squish us like that cockroach over there on the donuts. Don't you agree?"

"Absolutely, Jonas, Perez knows I don't have a High School education and totally unqualified in every way to be a judge. I would need to return to Panama City and be a cocktail waitress again."

"Hooker," said her brother. "You were a hooker."

"Only part-time, Jonas. It is legal, and I had a card," she responded in her own defense.

"This isn't complicated, Sis. We ask Andrea, in a civilized manner, to behave herself around those three. No threats, no violence, no endangerment of the baby when she is, or she isn't high. Harper's demands are more compassionate and reasonable than I expected."

"Perez knew that, Jonas. She's clever. She made it harder for Andrea to oppose him by giving us good reasons to support him. And that makes it easier for us to keep Andrea in check."

"Bonita, send someone to inform Andrea and Luis they must be here at four o'clock sharp. Instruct the chief, if either of them refuses to come, to have his officers haul them here in cuffs. No, better yet, have our paddy wagon stationed outside Andrea's, starting now. And we need a boat off the veranda of Harper's Hotel to be sure she doesn't escape by sea. Can you handle that for me, Sis? I have work to do."

The judge nodded; brother and sister both left the room.

It was slightly past noon. It had been quite a morning. Vanessa was in the air back to Panama City. Luis tried unsuccessfully to stay out of Vanessa's sight, hiding like a scorpion in a worker's boot. He approached the station to learn what had happened, but as he did, an officer summoned him to the judge's chambers. He was debriefed on Harper's demands and instructed to find Andrea and inform her of the mandatory meeting. The judge also told him Michael, Maria, and the baby were staying at a location that would remain unknown and were in protective police custody. He could find Andrea at Michael's house.

Luis went right away since Andrea was probably still asleep this close to noon. His number two watching her was probably disgustingly tired of her abuse and more than ready to be relieved. As he opened the gate, he saw his man sitting at the garden table.

"Everything go okay last night?" asked Luis.

"Yeah," he answered, standing up and stretching his back. "She had a few people over. She stayed kinda straight, for Andrea. I heard her constantly bitching and threatening Harper to her friends."

Luis shook his head in frustration, dismissed the guard, then walked to the veranda. Through the latticework, he saw Andrea sitting at the table, smoking a cigarette, drinking a beer, and talking to someone on the phone in a malicious nature.

"Andrea, it's me Luis," he said through the latticework. "I need to talk to you."

"What the fuck do you want? I had to stay here all night with your gorilla watching over me. He shouldn't have been watching me, I should

ANDREA BARES HER TEETH AND PREPARES FOR A DOG FIGHT

have been watching him in some cage at the zoo, feeding him bananas. So, since Daddy wouldn't let his little girl go out and play last night, she had some friends over. We talked about what all of you are attempting to do to me, and they don't think it's cool. You have a rebellion on your hands, Captain Bly. Michael, and that old maid sister of mine, won't be too happy with what I am going to do to them when I find them. People are combing the streets for them right now. They have no right to take my baby from me. Where is he? I want him back now, and I mean right now." Andrea yelled as she flicked her cigarette into the ocean and took a bump of cocaine off her hairpin.

Luis sat at the table. "Andrea, there were a couple meetings this morning between Michael and his attorney first, then the mayor, the chief, the judge, Harper's attorney, and Danny Meeko."

"Meeko? What's that little fucker doing in all this? They better not think he's going to be my attorney. I'd rather have a two-toed sloth represent me. Anyway, they have nothing on me except I accidentally dropped some glasses on the floor," Andrea gaffed in her smartass tone as she chain-lit another cigarette. "Why weren't you in the meeting? You're the one who needs to tell everyone to drop this shit and go fuck themselves."

"Michael's attorney told the mayor, with the file they have on me in Panama City, she would have me arrested on the spot if she saw me anywhere." Luis stared at Andrea. "And they have a thick file on you as well."

"Where is the haughty bitch now? I want to talk to her and set her straight. This is a bluff. Can't you imbeciles see that? Take me to her. Where the fuck is she right now? I wonder if she's ever been bitch-slapped by a real woman?"

"She left for the airport right after the meeting. You could not have gotten close. She had a secret service bodyguard. I think it best you change your attitude and listen to me."

"Let me get my purse. That Air Panama flight doesn't leave until two. She will be at the airport. Let's hurry. Grab a cab, asshole. Don't just stand there looking stupider than you are. This will be fun. She's never fucked with a real woman." Andrea began to cackle through her undisciplined anger.

"Andrea, she's gone. She came on a government jet with her bodyguard, who was packing a snub-nose 38 in his shoulder holster. The police took her back to the airport, escorted by two police officers on motorcycles. Andrea, are you catching what's happening? All of us are out of our league. Our entire operation could be shut down, and people from the mayor down, including you, will go to prison. Harper's attorney said she could put you, Andrea Blanco, in prison for five to ten for drug smuggling across provincial borders."

Andrea hesitated and looked towards the ocean. She grabbed another beer from the kitchen. As she returned, she looked at Luis. "She really came in a private jet with a bodyguard packing heat? And they let him bring it into the station? And they escorted them with police protection and motorcycles to the airport?"

"Yep," said Luis quickly.

"I still say it's a bluff. She's making you all believe she can do something about us over here. This is a provincial matter, not federal. And the Columbians won't let the feds cut us off."

"No, you're correct. The Columbians will guard their drops in Balboa at any cost. No one wants the streets to dry up. And they won't but only if you behave and do what will be asked of you this afternoon."

"And if I refuse to do what they want, then I take matters into my own hands and get rid of Michael and my sister."

"Then, the feds will shut us down still, and the Columbians will find out you are the one causing the problem over your baby. They will cut you up and use you as fertilizer; problem solved," said Luis. "Andrea, are you starting to comprehend what position your little cokehead brain is putting you in? None of us are behind you on this, nobody. I was told to tell you your options are cooperate and behave, prison, or death."

"Nobody pushes me around, especially somebody with a dick," said Andrea. "I hate all you cocksuckers. I'd rather kill you all than look at any of you." Andrea knew she was in a corner and hated it. It reminded her of another time she was trapped and helpless.

"Andrea, from what I understand, Michael and his lawyer are being very fair with you, and me," said Luis. "Michael simply wants full custody of Alejandro."

"Fuck, no." yelled Andrea. "You mean I don't get to see my baby ever again? Not gonna happen. Shit, Alejandro is not even his."

At that point, the air went silent. Luis and Andrea stared deeply into each other's eyes, as cold as ice.

"Andrea, we made this decision a year ago. My girlfriend would cut off my balls if she knew we fuck each other, and I was that baby's father. Alejandro doesn't look at all like a gringo. This was your idea to get 'the rich stupid gringo,' as you call him, to support our baby, to support your sister, and get him hooked on cocaine."

"Right, and it was going fine until you wigged out and had Fernanda take Alejandro home that night. Then you let me lie and look like a fool with that ransom scam. I would have got away with it, you know."

Luis continued, "You brought your sister here not for her sake. You needed her to take care of the baby while you tramped around."

Andrea became indignant. "Again, asshole, you fucked it all up when you wanted to protect yourself from child endangerment charges. Hell, it was my baby. Why did you care? This is all your fault."

"Andrea, you had Harper hire your sister, the baby's aunt, who now, according to plan, loves the baby like it was her own. She is so sweet; she is now on Michael's side, because she sees what a good father he is and what a good mother you're not."

"I know my sister. She just needs a man. She's not pretty. She's playing him, too."

"I don't think so. But the biggest flaw in your scheme was you thought Harper was just another stupid man that would do anything for your love. Honey, rich powerful men are not stupid. They can read people. That's why they're rich. And they surround themselves with strong people. He has strong political connections in the States, but even more so, here in Panama. His Panamanian lawyer is married, hello, to the assistant attorney general, whose office has incriminating files on all of us. You just made the whole town look like school brats. Now are you starting to get it, you little coke-a-nut?" Luis went to the rail and stared out into the ocean.

"Luis, you coward," Andrea said, shaking her head and smirking. "I had way more faith in you and the mayor. I'm too important and adored in this town to be cast out like a piece of moldy cheese. You will all eventually agree to protect me and my baby before you make me give him up to a gringo. You will see in the meeting."

"Be careful, Andrea. I'm warning you."

"When did you say it was, and where? I'll figure out a way to make this all disappear. I will get rid of Michael, like all the rest of those bullshit chumps. I'll have them licking my pussy by the end of the meeting, you'll see."

"Andrea, you better be ready to accept Michael's terms, or you'll not be working for me anymore. If there's any disruption, either our judge, the feds, or the Columbians will take care of you, I promise."

As he walked through the broken glass to the garden door, he turned to her and yelled, "I suggest you take a shower and sober up. Meeting's at four o'clock in the mayor's office. I'll come by at three forty-five and escort you. And if you think about running, there's a paddy wagon stationed on your street. And do you see the police boat anchored in the bay off your veranda?"

"Luis," Andrea yelled as he walked out the door. "I promise you, I will be sure Alejandro doesn't grow up to be a big pussy like his drug-dealing daddy." She flipped him the bird, then flipped another cigarette butt over the rail and into the ocean. That was the end of their conversation.

24

AND THE WHEELS ON THE BUS GO ROUND AND ROUND

After Luis left, Andrea popped a few more beers along with her newfound love, THC wax drawn from her new stainless-steel vapor pen. She fell back asleep in the hammock. At 3:15, her phone rang.

"Andrea, are you cleaned up and ready for the meeting? We have less than an hour."

"Yeah, right, Luis. C'mon, let us blow off this circus act so I can go back to sleep?" Andrea whined like a child woken by her parents for school on a rainy day. "Nothing is going to happen at this shit show anyway."

"Andrea, get up right now," Luis said sternly.

"C'mon, they will scold me, 'Andrea, you must settle down and behave yourself, blah, blah, blah,' and I'll lie and say, 'Oh, you're so right, Mayor. I'm sorry. I promise, I'll change, I really will.' Then you and I will leave the meeting and figure out some way to get rid of Michael, deport him or kill him, doesn't matter which to me. But if the mayor won't deport him, we *will* need to find a way for one of our guys to kill him. Come on, Luis, please, let me go back to sleep. Just go to the meeting and tell them I'm sorry and it won't happen again. That's all they want to hear."

"Andrea, that paddy wagon's still outside your gate, and they've been instructed to cuff you and bring you in if you don't leave here by four."

"Okay, I'm getting in the shower. We'll leave right at four and let the cop boys give us a ride. Now get over here and bring some blow." Andrea hung up.

Luis sauntered to Andrea's and onto the veranda. He leaned on the doorjamb of Andrea's bedroom door, her bathroom door wide open as well. She stood naked in the mirror, putting on her makeup. Luis noticed her ass had started to sag and cellulite had formed on the backs of her thighs since the birth of Alejandro.

"Like what you see, Luis? Been a while since you had a piece of this." Andrea finished her face and turned around, shaking her bosoms back and forth attempting to be racy, but she wasn't. Her breasts had doubled in size and approaching her midriff. Luis hadn't seen her naked in over a year and wasn't sure if it turned him on. "Want to kiss my titties?" She held them up and pointed them at him like heavy artillery.

"Get dressed and stop fucking around. Wear that nice white dress of yours. It makes you look clean."

"I am, but only because it shows off my cleavage, and the shadows of my nipples."

"Andrea stop, this is a matter of life and death. If you don't cooperate, the feds will arrest you for smuggling and shut us down until you're in prison. Shit, the Columbians will kill you before you get to trial. They won't let you disrupt their flow for even a day. And the feds will look the other way."

"Okay, I took a shower," she whined again, "even though that creepy chief likes my dirty smell. And the judge is a lesbo and would love to get her head under my skirt. Maybe that's how we play this. C'mon Luis, that's what I do best. A few genitals get kissed, and they all leave me alone."

"It's almost four. Are you ready? Leave the blow and wax here. Perez would love to throw another log on your fire."

Andrea slid her dress over her head and down over her expanding body. "Two good bumps and my flip-flops, and I'm ready." Andrea left the drugs behind, locked the doors, and started through the garden. But before reaching the gate, Luis wiped the remaining coke from her nostril.

Andrea rolled her eyes. She entered the street and opened the door to the paddy wagon herself. She and Luis hopped in. "Let's go, boys. I have some important ass-kicking to do, so truck me and my man to the mayor's office."

They quickly reached City Hall. The officers unlocked the door, and Andrea hopped out like a chubby pet bunny. The townspeople watched. Since there was no newspaper or local television, the events around City Hall were the subject of conversation in every sector of Balboa every night. The officers ushered Andrea and Luis to the mayor's conference room, where the mayor, the judge, the chief, and Danny Meeko sat around the table. The two officers took their assigned positions in case Andrea tried to bolt or lost her temper.

Andrea bounced into the room like she owned it, her unbridled bosoms purposely flopping. Her belly and ass stretched her white dress tight in her naval. Every crack on her body was visible. During her pregnancy, she stopped all drugs and alcohol, oddly enough. But she had ate like a sow at a trough. She was not the cute Latina hooker and gold-digger she once was.

No one rose to greet them or looked up except the mayor. He peered at Andrea with an austere and unemotional look on his face. "Luis, Andrea, have a seat please," he said. Andrea sighed and conveyed a demeanor of boredom. She deliberately plopped down hard in her chair. "Andrea, do you know why we summoned you here today?" asked the mayor.

"I think so, but first, Meeko's not here to be my lawyer, is he? My baby's already smarter than he is," Andrea said in her smartass tone, followed by the giggle. They all ignored her question.

"Andrea, I will address that issue right away, so we can avoid your ignorant remarks and finish our business quickly. Mr. Meeko works for Vanessa Perez, Mr. Harper's attorney. He is Mrs. Perez's direct contact in Balboa and has our full support."

"You mean the fancy big-time lawyer bitch with the important husband? The one who has all your shorts bunched up to your balls? Except, of course, your sister and Luis, neither of whom have any balls," Andrea responded again with her annoying giggle.

"Andrea, I'll say this once," said the mayor. "We know what a disrespectful person you are. We are also aware of how valuable you used to be to us, but after reviewing your current daily duties, we found several younger people, especially girls, who could easily fill your shoes. So, if you don't shut up and behave like an adult, these officers will cuff you and put you into a cell until you are ready to cooperate. And frankly, we don't care if it's forever." The mayor glared harshly at Andrea, who then looked at Luis, her expression serious for the first time. Luis returned the look, the glare in his eyes said, are *you starting to get it now, honey pie?*

"On what grounds would you arrest me, Mayor?"

"I will explain, but I want no rebuttals, or you will be on your way to your cell. You're not getting out of this with a mild reprimand. No, let me correct myself, you have a way out of this, but first, you must cut your crap and use whatever part of that burnt-out little brain of yours still functions."

Andrea sat quietly while everyone stared at her. The color was leaving her face.

"Allow me to begin with a few smaller charges we are pressing against you, then end with the one that will probably end your life as you know it. Number one, child endangerment charges for abandoning your baby with Luis where he performs his drug business. Second, letting the baby go unchanged and unfed for hours. Number three, falsification of a police report stating Mr. Harper broke all those dishes and threatened you with a gun. Number four, destruction of Mr. Harper's property. Number five, prostitution without a health card. Number six, sale of illegal drugs..."

"Hold on Mayor," Andrea interrupted. "Sale of..."

"Andrea, no interruptions?" The mayor continued. "Number seven, disturbing the peace at 3:00 A.M. And finally, the one Mrs. Perez has promised us will involve the Attorney General's Office, and the one which we have no control over in Balboa, the smuggling of cocaine to Boquete across provincial borders. That is a federal offense and is not part of our agreement between Balboa and the feds. This one includes Luis, as well. All total, our judge here has calculated somewhere from eight to twelve years for you in a federal prison, probably in Panama City."

"I want a lawyer," screamed Andrea.

"Sure, Andrea, we will take you to your cell and you can make your call. By the way, do you have enough money to go up against the Attorney General's Office? We will be happy to assign a Balboan public defender, Marco Mesa. He can start working on your case when he gets out of drug rehab in six weeks. And I would imagine bail will be set at $50,000, wouldn't you say, Judge?" asked the mayor.

"Sounds on the low side, Mayor, but I could be nice if the feds agree."

"You are all motherfucking bastards. After all I have done for you over the years. All the money I've made for all of you. Do you turn on me because of some gringo and his power whore attorney? There will be hell to pay and a lot of destruction in its trail. Go ahead, try it. Arrest me, and I'll destroy all of you, and your fucking families. None of you will ever get a peaceful night's sleep the rest of your lives. Make sure your doors are locked and your guns cocked." Andrea put her arms out to be cuffed.

The mayor stood up and leaned across the table. "Andrea," he said in a fatherly way. "Sit down and settle down. Your threats are not helping. They're only adding time to your prison sentence and putting your life in danger. This is not our doing, it's yours. All these charges are insisted upon by Vanessa Perez, with the feds backing her. If we go against her, she'll have this town raided and they have files on all of us. We will be out of business and in jail. But believe it.

stinky armpit of Panama, filled with dirty gringos and promiscuous surfer brats. All they care about, and they say it over and over, 'No gringos or tourists die.' Are you ready to settle down and use your brain as I suggested at the commencement of this meeting?"

"Go on, then, what the fuck is this all about? I don't get it," asked Andrea, her brain so warped, she couldn't figure it out if she tried. But by the look on her face, she seemed to realize she would never be in charge of this situation.

Luis jumped in. "I tried to tell you, Andrea, but you wouldn't listen. Not everyone in town kisses your ass anymore. You're past your prime, honey, get over it. There's a new set of young dealers, male and female." Luis said it, knowing it would hurt. "One person, Andrea. This predicament is about one person: Alejandro."

"Alejandro? How is this about my son?"

Luis continued. "We all see what you do to that baby. He's going to die while in your care someday soon, or he'll be a cokehead and dealer by age ten. That's what this is about, Andrea. Harper called Vanessa Perez because he's terrified for the safety of his son, and she agrees, and so does your sister, and all of us around this table agree with Harper, as well. Between your sister's love for her nephew and Harper's money and love for his son, Mr. Meeko is going to make you a proposal we all think is fair."

"Hold on, you all decided what's best for my child? For *my* child? Who in the fuck do you think you are?" Her voice began to rise. "He's not even Harper's kid." The room became silent. Everyone looked at each other. Andrea smirked at their reactions. Luis, however, almost stopped breathing and looked around the room into oblivion. "Right, Alejandro's not his kid. I was in the mountains that whole month when I got pregnant. At least, Harper thought I was. What are you going to do now?"

Meeko spoke up. "Andrea, Mrs. Perez foresaw this play, so she had someone pull a copy of the birth certificate from the public records in Panama City. She faxed me a copy this afternoon. It says right here, the father is Michael Arthur Harper, a citizen of the United States." Meeko shoved the copy across the table to the judge.

"Yes," said the judge. "That's what it says. Mr. Harper is the legal father."

"But he's not." Andrea protested. "He's not the father."

"Then who is?" asked the mayor.

Luis closed his eyes and waited for Andrea's answer. But before she could say anything, the judge spoke up, "Mayor, it doesn't matter. The legal father is whoever is on the birth certificate, period, end of story. Unless he's proven to be unable to have children or we run a DNA test."

"Let's do that," Andrea blurted, "then we will prove my son is not that gringo's baby, and he has no custody rights over him."

Meeko jumped in again. "Mrs. Perez anticipated that idea as well. She spoke to me about it. Mr. Harper must sign a legal consent form for either of those tests or the release of his medical records. She spoke to Mr. Harper about it before she called me this afternoon. He refuses to give his consent. He said Andrea told him it was his child, and he believed her. Mrs. Perez said, if this came up, Mr. Harper wants me to ask Andrea right here and now, and this is a quote from Mr. Harper: 'Andrea, why would you lie to me and have me sign the birth certificate if you knew I wasn't Alejandro's father?'" The room chuckled at Harper's question, all but Andrea and Luis.

"Maybe I can get some of his sperm or cut him and get some of his blood while he's asleep," said Andrea.

The judge shook her head. "Andrea, the key word is 'consent.' Will you forge his consent form as well? Mrs. Perez would have me disbarred, and the bench opens for Mr. Meeko. Then Meeko would convict you of forgery. By the way, Danny," the judge said to Meeko, "bringing you in on Harper's side was brilliant, since we all know you want my bench, and if I don't cooperate, she'll put you on it. Tell her brilliant move, just brilliant and congrats."

"Thank you, Judge," Meeko said with a smile. "She'll appreciate your respect."

"Okay, I'm supposed to either go to prison for ten years and not see my baby," Andrea said, "or give up my baby to this Americano and not see him at all, ever? How do I explain this to my mother? He takes the baby to the States, and I can't go there, since my husband is in Texas waiting to kick my ass. And even if Michael could protect me, why would he want me after all this?"

"Neither you nor Harper can leave the country unless there's an official notarized letter signed by both parents allowing the child to cross the border until Alejandro is twenty-one years old. Or unless, of course, one of you dies," said the judge.

"And if he dies, I get my baby back? Or, if he feels threatened and leaves on his own?" Andrea had a ray of sunshine on her face.

The judge shook her head. "Andrea, that solution in open forum is the dumbest thing I have ever heard you say." Andrea's eyes went wide open. "But to answer your question whether you'd get your baby back, depends on whether I thought you could be a good mother. And frankly, Andrea, I don't ever see you being a good mother. I don't ever see you being a good person. I'd have that child given to foster parents on the other side of the country and put a restraining order on you tighter than that flab flaunting dress. So, I guess you'll have to threaten or kill me too," said the judge, a wicked glare on her face.

Andrea again smiled. "I won't have to kill you. You and your brother won't be in power forever."

Meeko presented Harper's demands. "Let me take over from here, please. I think we have heard enough. Andrea, I have bullet points from Mrs. Perez that, when agreed upon and signed by all in the room, will be turned into formal legal documents to be signed and recorded. Are you now, Andrea, of sound mind and body? Are you under any other influence we should know about?"

"I'm fine. You don't know me that well, do you, Meeko? You'll know when I'm not," Andrea said, feeling tired and defeated. Her only solution remaining was to plan the murder of Michael.

Meeko handed a copy to all in the room. He went through it quickly, allowing no questions until the end. Except for Andrea, all heard the demands and agreed. Meeko stopped before the final bullet point, looked at Andrea, then around the room. "Andrea, this last one is particularly important to you and must also be understood by all in the room, including their successors. Mr. Harper and Mrs. Perez foresaw Andrea's previous question concerning Mr. Harper's health and wellbeing."

"What does that mean, Meeko?"

"Andrea's file with the feds indicates numerous acts of violence, and we have no doubt Andrea is capable of harm or threats to Mr. Harper after this agreement. Andrea, I will be responsible for Mr. Harper's and your sister's safety. If Mr. Harper, your sister, or the child is in any way threatened, injured, or killed, no matter who did it, you will be taken into custody without bail, and Balboa will be invaded by federal investigators and the US Embassy. And while they are in Balboa, they will also investigate any other issues such as drug dealing, smuggling, money laundering, or tax evasion. Arrests will be made."

"My friends," said the mayor, "the Attorney General's Office strongly suggests everyone protects Mr. Harper and family, and they will protect all of you. Andrea, do you understand this last point and its gravity? If yes, are you ready to sign?"

All eyes went to Andrea. She was stunned. She had walked into the room, convinced she could bully everyone because she was top dog in the underworld, only to discover her power was fading and she was a routine peasant when it came to Harper and his circle of power.

The mayor spoke first. "Andrea, agree quickly so we can get back to our lives. If you don't agree, none of us will have a life to go back to. Harper's giving you the same amount of time with your son you have now. You do need your sister's supervision, and you must behave and act like a good mother around your son. Other than that, he doesn't care what you do. The money he spent on you now goes to your sister and his son. He's a good man, and somehow, you picked the best father you could have picked in this town. Sign it, get out of his house, and get back to work, or go to prison. Spread the word to protect Harper and let him raise that child in a proper environment."

"Give me a pen," said Andrea. She signed. It was done.

Luis and Andrea walked out onto the street and found a quiet bar where only Spanish was spoken. They spoke English so no one knew their business. "Thank you for signing the paper and not exposing us," said Luis.

"Fuck you, Luis. You really think I'm past my prime?" Andrea whined. "I know I've put on some pounds since the baby, but…"

"Really Andrea? You are worried about what you look like after almost being thrown in prison and losing total custody of our son?" said Luis. "Or wait a minute, is this about you realizing that Harper was never in love with you, and he danced you around like a puppet to get laid? You were his employee, Andrea. You were a sex toy to him."

"I was not. He loved me. He told me every day. 'I love you, Michael. I love you too, honey.' We said it a few times a day. And he took me on trips, and I translated for him, and I bought him any kind of drug…, shit, Luis, I was his employee, wasn't I?" Tears escaped from Andrea's eyes.

"You're really in love with him, aren't you? But your addictions ruin everything good that comes into your life, little girl." Luis threw those harsh words at Andrea's feet.

"Oh, Luis, I am in love with him, and I do ruin everything. I had it all right there in the palm of my hand. He's a wonderful man. He's the kind of man my mother said I would meet someday." Andrea broke down completely.

"But now, it is your sister who has the family you always wanted." Andrea buried her face in her hands. "Not only is it too late to work it out with him, but it was also never meant to be. He always knew who and what you were. This started off as another one of your cons on a rich gringo, but he twisted you good, because his conscience would not let that little baby have a mother like you, a mother without a conscience. Let me ask, Andrea, why do you hate men so much?"

Andrea's eyes, red and swollen, emerged from her palms. Her tone changed instantly. "First of all, Luis, why I hate men is none of your fucking business, and if you ever ask that again, I'll split your head wide open with a machete. I was in love with Harper for a while, but no, you're right, it wasn't going to last. He was too healthy and too old to party with me. But the only way I could keep him here and continue to have him support me was to tell him it was his baby, or he would have gone back to the States, for sure."

Luis thought, "*She's about to tell me she was in control the whole time.*"

"But what I'm really upset about, I lost to that son of a bitch, and he conned me big-time. He made me look like one of those stupid island girls around here. In the end, I wanted to end it, not him. I was planning to have him killed or deported, and then my sister would take care of the baby until I found another sugar daddy. That baby's father could be any one of a half-dozen men, maybe even Harper, so don't get all emotional about the kid, Luis. And I never wanted to take care of a baby in the first place."

"Wait, you told me Alejandro was mine. You were going to con me too? Nobody can trust you." Luis felt duped. He was in the club.

Andrea paused, reflecting on that awful day twenty years ago. "I just wanted to please my mother. With Maria as the nanny and Harper dead, my mother would be so happy with a grandchild. But now that I am not allowed to hurt him, my mother must not know about the custody thing. And I assure you, that kid will only leave Balboa and Panama over my dead body."

With that, Andrea and Luis began to down beers and hit shots of tequila. The balance of power had changed. Andrea's wheels needed to point in a different direction, but she was not done hurting people, and one in particular.

25

A NEW DAY BUT NOT A FRESH ONE

Andrea took her sweet leisurely time vacating Michael's home with the help of her sleazy companions. Michael, Maria, and the baby resided comfortably at the well-appointed Hotel Tortuga; their stay involuntarily subsidized by the generous town of Balboa. Maria expressed to Michael she felt on a vacation and how she loved how tranquil it was without Andrea popping in and out with her loud-mouthed friends. The two rooms adjoined, both clean and spacious, meals were deliciously prepared and artistically presented, and Alejandro never tired of floating in the crystal-clear pool. The officers ran errands for them anytime they required anything, no matter how small.

Maria and Michael relished this time they so rightfully earned. It gave them time to become familiar with each other's present and past, to a point. Maria drank sparsely, only a glass of wine at sunset and occasionally over dinner. Michael enjoyed a good glass of Scotch, and the quality of the Tortuga's was unparalleled by any bar in town. They found themselves discussing needs and remodeling plans for the house when they returned on Thursday. Michael revealed to Maria the deal struck among all parties in Balboa, as well as the feds in Panama City. He particularly made Andrea's visitation rights clear as they pertained to Maria. Then he emphatically emphasized the consequences to Andrea if she breached any legal agreements. It would mean a long prison stint, but more likely, she would be assassinated in her cell before she reached the courtroom. Maria didn't trust her sister's temperament, making her concerned for everyone's safety. But loved and always would love Andrea, so the mental picture of her little sister lying dead in a jail cell was too grisly an image for her to bear. But more gut-wrenching would be the sight of a lifeless Alejandro.

Andrea and her associates stole whatever they could carry from Michael's house. They carted what Andrea wanted to her apartment in town, then the rest distributed around Balboa. She finished just in time to climb into the water taxi, then onto the mainland shuttle on its way to Boquete for the weekend. If she stayed with her routine, she would return Sunday or Monday. Next week would begin the true test to see if Andrea would or could honor her contract.

"Boys, Andrea's out of here for the weekend. Return Harper back to his house. Tell him the coast is clear," the chief told his officers.

Escorted by the officers, Michael, Maria, and Alejandro left the hotel, free of charge, and headed home with the crib and all the baby supplies in the police SUV. Reaching Michael's house, the officers carried the crib to the garden porch. The door was wide open.

One of the officers stopped Michael and Maria. "Mr. Harper, let me go in and look around, just to be sure Andrea or any of her friends are not hiding and ready to do something stupid." He went inside. A strong pungent odor floated on the breeze coming out the door.

"Everything okay, Officer?" asked Michael. The officer had a strange look on his face.

"Andrea's gone, but everything is not okay. You are safe to go in."

As the two young officers began to depart, Maria thanked them by giving them a nurturing and appreciative hug. Michael tipped them generously for their duty and kindness, asking them to split the tip among the other officers who protected them. Those gestures of gratitude would go a long way with the relationships between Michael, Maria, and the city, but not much for Andrea and Luis.

"Oh dear," said Maria, her eyes and mouth wide open as she carried Alejandro into the house. She stopped in the middle of the kitchen as Michael slipped into the bedroom. She called to him, "Michael, she left all the doors unlocked. Do you see the keys anywhere?"

"Really Maria? She's probably had a hundred keys made. Every little thief in town has one by now. We'll change locks this afternoon." Maria heard Michael chuckle at her request.

"It appears she had company, Michael. There must be over a hundred empty beer and rum bottles everywhere. The broken glasses and dishes are still on the kitchen floor. Ashtrays are filled to the brim with cigarette butts and roaches. And Michael, the railing of the veranda is covered in vomit. And, whoa, all your plants are gone."

Maria looked in the fridge and in the cabinets. "The fridge door was left open and empty, except for three dead roaches, some stale French fries, and half a lemon thrown in the bottom. There's nothing in the cabinets, no plates, bowls, cookware, silverware, not even a plastic cup. She stripped the place."

Michael came out of the bedroom. "She and her friends, you mean. They took all the toiletries, and they took most of my clothes, probably yours too. And someone left us with a pile of rancid shit on the bathroom floor, not in the toilet, on the floor. And they pissed all over my sheets and pillows. The mattress is completely soaked, and the urine smell will sting your nostrils. I'd imagine your room is the same." Michael walked onto the veranda. As he waded through the cans, bottles, carryout wrappers, and pizza boxes, he called to Maria. "She did leave one of the hammocks, though. She probably had to sleep in it since the beds are grotesque. Looks like it's filled with something." Michael stopped. "Hey," he called. "Hey, who are you?" he asked as he approached a dirty young man in the hammock. He attempted to shake him out of his chemically induced coma.

"It's me, man, Luis. What do you mean, who am I?" Luis looked up and was finally able to focus. "Oh shit, Mr. Harper, you're not supposed to know who I am. Well, fuck it now. That was a great party these last couple days, maybe best ever in Balboa, thanks." Luis got up to leave.

"Luis, stop. Are you coherent enough to understand what I'm saying?" asked Michael.

"Yes sir," replied Luis.

"Good." Michael grabbed Luis by the throat and got right in his face. "First of all, boy, I expected someone in your position to look cleaner and smarter. And you really stink. This is the last time I'm going to say this." Luis didn't look as tough as he sounded on the phone the night of Michael's arrest. He was scared shitless face to face.

"Luis, your bitch went up against me once, and look what happened. Next time, I won't play nice. I did give her two days to get out of here, so will let this go as a technicality, but if anything like this ever happens again to my home, or if any of us are threatened or harassed from this point on, I will call in Vanessa Perez and her troops, and you'll all be gone. Get it, kid? Make sure you tell her that. And tell her I am bringing the mayor, the chief, the judge, and Meeko here this afternoon to take pictures. I will show Mrs. Perez and her husband what scuzz bags you are. I will tell them 'Luis the dealer' with the huge file, was here when I got home, and we had a conversation. I'm sure the mayor and Meeko will have a talk with you about. And I'll tell Meeko he'll need to add an addendum to cover property damage."

"Mr. Harper, I promise, this will never happen again. My boys are on the alert to protect you. And if she starts up, I will personally take her to the chief. I don't want to mess with you and your powerful people ever again. You guys are scary." Luis looked like a browbeaten puppy.

He turned to walk off the veranda. "Luis," Michael called, "take off the shirt and leave it, please. It's mine and provided I can get your stench out of it; I might want to wear it again. Otherwise, I need fifty bucks." Luis took off the shirt which had a half-naked biker chick on the back and threw it at Michael. He ran for the street bare-chested, like a roach when the kitchen lights come on.

After Maria's investigation of the house, her room included, she turned to Michael. "Michael, who is this little girl I loved so much growing up? I'm afraid. Remember when she said she wasn't done with you yet? When will this end?"

"Maria, I'll call Meeko and have him bring the mayor, chief, and judge right away, so they see what she and her friends are capable of doing. Meeko can send pictures to Vanessa. When Andrea gets back from Boquete, I will make sure they talk with her and Luis."

"Will that do any good, Michael? She will either calm down this weekend or get more fired up. I can't tell."

"Contractually, I gave her two days to vacate, which she did. And she didn't threaten us. She knew how far she could push. She is not allowed to come inside anymore except to gather you and Alejandro. The sooner we get Meeko and the others here, the sooner we start cleaning up. Damn, this place reeks like the bathroom at Dave's bar."

"Michael, maybe you take the pictures and send copies to Meeko and Mrs. Perez. Then none of us brings this up. Like it didn't happen, for now anyway. That way, she won't feel scolded and lose her temper." Maria raised an eyebrow.

"You're right. Why poke the loco mono? I'll tell Meeko to keep the pictures as a reminder and leave her be. Antonio and his girlfriend will help us clean up, and Antonio can change the locks. I will pay them well for their help. Let's see, we need new mattresses, linens, and pillows delivered by bedtime tonight. And then, guess what happens tomorrow?" Michael said with a smile like the Cheshire Cat.

"What, Michael? What's the smile all about? This is disgusting. It's barbaric. Aren't you angry?" Maria said. "I'm not only irate but so embarrassed by the actions of my sister."

"Turn it around, my sweet friend. I'm smiling because we get to do some shopping tomorrow. I mean big-time shopping: groceries, plates, silverware, cookware. Shoot, let's get somebody to paint the inside of the house, paint the outside, paint the veranda. Let's get some new curtains. It will be fun."

"Oh, Michael, that will be fun." Maria returned his smile with a bigger grin as she snuggled Alejandro. "Almost like we just got married and bought our first house." With that, she stopped smiling. "Michael, I didn't mean that the way it sounded. I am your nanny for your son and my nephew. I was out of line. I promise you I am not after your money like my sister. I'm just your employee. It's just, I've never had the chance to do anything like this with someone, and I got excited."

Michael came over and gave Maria a hug while she still cradled Alejandro in her arms. He was still smiling, his hands reaching for her face. "Easy, Maria. You've become one of my favorite people. Because of the power I possess in my lifetime, I do not have many close friends. Now I have you. I was skeptical when Andrea wanted you to be Alejandro's nanny. I figured you were just another weapon in Andrea's attack on my bank account."

"Michael, no, I..."

"Let me continue, Maria. I fully expected you to ignore the baby and become another drunk in Balboa. Then I would be forced to fire you and do what I just did to your sister. But in the last few days, I'm convinced you are the flawless inverse of your sister." Maria bowed her head with humility over the compliment. "I must ask you something, and I need an unconditional answer. I understand and respect you if you wish to return to your mother in Panama City and not put yourself in danger. Do you want out?" Michael held his breath, waiting for the answer. His feelings were becoming confused.

Maria's cheeks moistened as she rocked the baby in her arms. "Michael, I want to stay more than ever. I love this child, and I can't have a child of my own. I have a condition called endometriosis. It started when I was a teen. This is my only chance to raise a child. And you and I enjoy each other's company, it seems."

"Then you will stay and help me raise and protect Alejandro?"

"I will do more than that, however I cannot explain it to you yet. There are things you don't know about me. They are good things. I will let you know how I will help in a few days." She told Michael to sit in the one remaining chair on the veranda. She placed the baby on his lap. She knelt on one knee at Michael's feet, kissed Alejandro on the hand, then squeezed Michael by the forearm. Tears, this time, streamed down her face. "Give me a moment to myself, Michael, then make your calls." She walked to the garden.

Michael sat amid the rubble, the stench of human waste and alcohol radiating engulfed the house. He was confident, but not totally convinced, Vanessa's plan would work. The wild card was whether Andrea was truly insane. He would contact Vanessa to inquire into gun laws, with no one knowing but him.

26

MICHAEL ROWS THE BOAT ASHORE

After Michael took pictures of the primal destruction and sent them to Vanessa to be placed in criminal files. Then Michael and Maria took Alejandro to accomplish first things first. They visited a miniature Chinese version of K-Mart. They bought new locks, mattresses, linens, and heavy-duty cleaning and disinfectant supplies. They picked out cookware, flatware (Maria had never heard it called flatware and thought it a strange name for curved forks and spoons), plates, bowls, glassware, you name it, they needed it. As they shopped, Alejandro soaked it all in with his big dark eyes, while Maria was entwined on Michael's arm. They laughed as they ran across comical artwork choices, hopefully designed by the grade schoolers down the street or the retirement home inmates.

Michael jutted his hip into a rather feminine posture. "Lovey, do you prefer the plates with the out of proportion monkey heads and butts, or the ones with the bloody pirate faces?" he asked, displaying these choices on his right forearm, pointing at them with his pinky finger.

Maria laughed, then held up a glass in each hand, posing as a used car model. "And Michael, would you prefer the glasses with bearded Moses parting the Red Sea, or Adam and Eve each eating a juicy apple wearing only cute little fig leaves? Please note the serpent hidden in the tree behind them, stunning." The fun had begun.

As they progressed, they moved to the paint department, where they discussed and agreed on the color scheme for the entire house, more of a

Caribbean colonial feel, in keeping historically with the original Balboa architecture. From there, they purchased new mattresses and pillows along with linens, bedspreads, then curtain material to pull it all together. They were having a blast. Michael was overwhelmed with a warm fuzzy feeling as he watched the happiness exuding from Maria's heart.

"Oh, Michael, what roller coaster did I get on?" Maria looked him in the face with a childlike grin. "From danger and destruction to safety and reconstruction. And Alejandro is spellbound."

The store assigned two young Chinese boys to follow them, taking their selections to the front counter, where the prices were recorded by hand in a notebook instead of at the cash register. This, of course, avoided sales tax for the store and allowed the ability to launder drug money for the Columbians. This was Balboa. The total came to over two thousand dollars. The store enthusiastically agreed to deliver the items after eight-thirty that night, giving Michael and his cleaning crew time to clear out the domestic wreckage and disgusting human waste.

It was approaching four o'clock, and Michael knew Antonio would be at The Loop for a few beers. They stopped. Especially Maria and Alejandro, were greeted warmly with hugs and kisses by some coherent gringos. Balboa, being the small town that it was, was aware of most details of what happened. And they were relieved the town officials were protecting them, especially Alejandro, from his mother.

Michael saw Antonio and his girlfriend, Karen, across the room at the Loop. He spoke loudly so all could hear, "Thank you, Antonio, and Karen, for taking care of Maria and the baby a few days ago. The call to Vanessa did the trick. We've been hidden away and guarded by Balboan police at The Hotel Tortuga for the last two days, so I didn't have a chance to thank you in person. If it weren't for you, I'd be on my way to the States and never see my son again." Michael walked over and hugged both. Maria gave them both a kiss on the cheek. The room whistled and applauded, then quickly went back to drinking.

Antonio lowered the volume. "Michael, really? Everybody knew where you were, including Andrea. I lost my good friend, Grant, to the Queen B. I wasn't going to lose another. We had our eyes on her. I heard you're one badass son of a bitch, mi amigo. Nobody saw that coming from you." Antonio pretended to shadowbox with Michael's body. "Knowing Andrea, though, she doesn't think she's lost this battle at all. But nobody messes with the Attorney General's Office in this town, nobody. And you threw them all in that shark tank, you slick bastard. You have smarts and connections I never knew you had. Rumor in town is you were a secret agent for the CIA at one time, like James Bond." Antonio hugged Michael again and punched him in the arm.

"No one endangers my kid and Maria, not even his mother." The five of them sat around a wobbly round table and waited on by Bernard the bartender, still sporting an ugly scare on his forehead. Maria was in a festive mood. She ordered a glass of wine. Alejandro was getting fussy, so Maria and Karen took him to the porch, changed him, and prepared a bottle. He had big day.

"Can I feed him?" Karen asked with a "please, please, please" look on her face. "He has the most beautiful eyelashes," she said as Maria placed him in her arms. She gazed into Alejandro's slowly drooping eyes. It wasn't long before Alejandro was peacefully in dreamland.

"Are you busy tonight, Antonio? Will you and Karen help us clean my house? I'm not asking you for a favor and if you're tired from work today, I understand. But I need help, and quick. I'll pay you well, and I know your rent is due soon. Andrea and her gang stole everything, broke the rest, literally shit on the floor, and pissed on our mattresses and pillows."

"I know. I work with some boys that hung at your house. Half the city staff called in sick those days. Sounds like ground zero."

"I need to clean up the bottles and broken dishes and mop the floors before the store delivers the mattresses and kitchen supplies at eighty-thirty. The cleaning supplies should be on my porch now. Can you help for a few hours? And I need good painters to paint the inside of the house and the veranda next week?" Michael looked at Antonio. "And what the hell, let's paint the outside too."

"We will be over at four. They clinked their beer bottles together and smiled. "Welcome back, Michael. We can get pizza and beer when we're done."

Michael and Maria hurried back to the house with Alejandro. On their way home, Michael saw a young man wearing one of his stolen T-shirts, but he didn't have time for the hassle. He just pointed it out to Maria, who could not keep from laughing.

Antonio brought two boys with him to help. The boys took the violated bedding to the garbage bin, scraped the drying feces from the bathroom floor. Alejandro continued his afternoon nap in his crib on the veranda due to the noise, dust, and stench in the house. As Michael shoveled the mess on the kitchen floor into bags, he stopped and looked at Maria. "Maria, your sister, and her friends stripped this house nearly bare. But you know what they didn't take?" Maria shook her head in curiosity. "They left all my artwork and artifacts from around the world. They're worth thousands of dollars. But they stole my corkscrew and bottle openers? Some real aptitude in that group." They both belly laughed.

By eight-thirty, the house was cleared, and floors mopped. Michael tipped the boys well, plenty to get dinner and lots of drinks. The painter came earlier and gave a quote, slightly more than expected, but he said he could finish by Sunday night. Michael offered him a substantial bonus if he could get finished by Sunday noon. Michael also hired an electrician to install multi-colored spotlights in the garden, casting shadows off the trees and onto the walls of the house and hotel.

By nine o'clock, beds were made, and the house smelled bearable. Maria and Karen went to get pizza, beer, and wine. When they returned, all exhausted, sweaty, and dirty, sat on the veranda. Michael and Maria were proud of their vast accomplishments since their return at noon. They were a team. Maria could not stop talking about how much fun the day was with Michael and Alejandro, as well as the pleasure of working with Antonio and Karen.

"I have not spent that much money ever," gleamed Maria. "I felt like a princess." Michael was happy for her to be rewarded for her life of kindness. "The day after tomorrow, after the kitchen walls and cabinets are painted, I can unpack the new kitchenware. We can go to the grocery, stock up on food, and have a brand new, totally functional, immaculate cookery in my house." Maria looked at Michael humbly. "I'm sorry, Michael, I mean in your house."

"No, Maria, it's our house, including Alejandro." Michael gave her a soft grin. "I would call us a family at this point. Antonio and Karen, you will be our first dinner guests." They all smiled and toasted to a job well done.

As they ate pizza and drank, Antonio looked at Michael. "You know, when Andrea sees how you made this place look gorgeous in just three days, she may not take it well."

They all looked at Michael. He smiled like the cat that ate the canary. He swallowed a mouthful of pizza, and with sauce on his cheek, he took a big swig of beer. Maria wiped his face tenderly with her napkin. "I know. It would be so sad if we hurt that little girl's feelings." They all glanced at each other's eyes, unsure how to take that until Michael broke out into laughter. The rest followed. But even though Maria laughed, she was worried. Her sister's disrespect for both Michael and the law was still in in play.

The next day, Maria fed Alejandro his morning bottle on the garden porch. Michael was meeting the electrician. The phone rang. "Maria, this is Andrea. How's everything in Balboa?" Maria got up and moved to her room and closed the door.

"Everything's great, Sis, just feeding Alejandro," Maria responded in a lively tone. "What can I do for you on this beautiful morning?" If Andrea were hoping for some sort of nasty response from Maria about the mess she left, she would be disappointed.

"I'll be back in town Sunday, and I want to hang out with my little buddy for the day. I'll pick him up at noon when I get back from Boquete," said Andrea.

"Where are we going, Andrea, so I know what to pack and what to wear?"

"Oh, just pack the diaper bag. You don't need anything, Sis, you're not going with us. And certainly not that ass-breath, Michael." Maria sensed what was coming from Andrea's tone, like a speargun shot directly into a barracuda. "Alejandro's my son, not his, and I want to spend one-on-one time with my little tiger." And don't think you and your little army can stop me, you traitor."

"Andrea, I'm sorry, but you legally agreed that either I or Michael or both, must be with you whenever you had the baby. I'm sure you remember. I hear you signed it in front of witnesses, Meeko, and Luis," said Maria as her voice began to quiver with anger or fear, or both. She wasn't quite sure.

"All that agreement stuff was bullshit, and you know it. It's Balboa, honey. It's the Wild West. How do you think the two of you are going to stop me? The law can't take a child away from his mother. Shit, the mothers in town won't accept that. They would never vote for that mayor again and he knows it. So, tell me how you're going to stop me, big bad sister?" Andrea growled in a vengeful tone. Her slur was getting more obvious, and the background noise was, no question, an all-night bar early in the morning.

"Andrea, I must tell Michael what you're planning. There's still time for him to call Mr. Meeko. I strongly suggest you reconsider this plan of yours."

"What's that skinny little bastard going to do, stand in my way? Have me arrested? I doubt it. I'd say boo, and he'd run and hide in the jungle," Andrea barked in her haughty tone, then laughed at herself.

"No, he can't arrest you, but he can have you arrested. That's what will happen, I promise you," Maria said confidently. "There's no way you'll ever hurt this baby, Sis. I want to see you pry Alejandro out of Michael's arms." Maria's voice was on the rise. "You ever threaten us like this again, Meeko will call Michael's attorney and the mayor. They'll be waiting at the dock for your ass, and you'll have Sunday brunch in a scuzzy jail cell."

"Watch me. What are you going to do when they do nothing? Put one of your witchy woman spells on me, Mother's little fake sorceress?"

Maria gained control of herself with that statement and remembered who she was. "Really, Andrea, you are being drunk and stubborn. Been up all night getting high, I assume? Obviously, you didn't get laid, or you'd be calmer."

"Fuck you, bitch. Don't take me on. You know better. I'll put a second scare across that homely little face of yours."

"Okay, let's settle down, both of us. C'mon, Sis, really, it's in your best interest and the safety of your son for me to be with you. Think about it, with me along, you can still party with your friends as much as you want, get as high as you want, and only hang with Alejandro when you want to show him off."

"Show him off? I love that little rascal more than life itself. You think I just want to show him off?"

Maria rolled her eyes. "Bullshit, this is me you're talking to, not some bar-rat tourist. Come on, it's no different than it was before, except Michael won't be around, and you won't ever be accused of endangering that child again. That responsibility is on me. You would prefer that, right? And your agreement is you treat Michael in a civil manner."

"My nails will be dug so deep into his cheeks next time I see him, his teeth will show, that motherfucker." Andrea screamed into the phone. "He's far from in the clear, and he doesn't even know it."

"Sunday, call me and I'll meet you in front of the house on the street. That way you'll keep out of trouble and still get what you want, agreed?" Maria finished.

"You're right for now, but I have ways to get my baby back without threatening or killing Michael, at least not yet. Maybe Mom will put a curse on him for me. We must get her some hair or blood or something. Yeah, blood. Then we can test his DNA at the same time. We need the baby's DNA, too."

"It's up to the gods, not Mom, whether Michael is killed or hurt. You know that. I'd be careful messing with things you know nothing about, Andrea. And anyway, a DNA test needs consent."

"I'm an extremely popular person in Balboa, Sis. After I'm done, Michael won't have one friend, not one stinking friend. No one will talk to him, serve him dinner, or even a drink. There are other ways to make him miserable and get around this agreement. Hopefully, he'll become so lonely and depressed he'll ram an ice pick through his chest and kill himself, or at least it'll appear that way. See you Sunday. I'll call you when I get close to the house." Andrea hung up before Maria could say another word.

"Who was that, Maria?" asked Michael as he entered the door from the garden.

"Andrea. She wants to spend the day with Alejandro and me Sunday when she returns on the shuttle, somewhere around noon." Maria looked down at Alejandro, avoiding eye contact with Michael.

"Good. She's cooperating and all is well? That's a relief. She's moving on quickly. I must say, I'm surprised. Just keep me posted as to where you are, so I can avoid you. I don't want to take any chances of her seeing me and backsliding."

"Okay, Michael, I'll keep in touch the whole day," said Maria. She didn't tell him Andrea was not moving on and continuing to contemplate new ways to get rid of him. She could wait no longer. She realized she must summon the omnipotent powers to protect the two loves of her life.

Sunday afternoon came and went. Andrea was on her best behavior, which, to many, was not a stellar image of anybody's mother. Michael enjoyed some alone time after a crazy week. He took a boat to The Blue Dolphin, an alluring deck built next to an ocean reef and a delicate mangrove island. The water was so clear reef fishes, eagle rays, and a family of nurse sharks could be seen from the platform. Gulls swooped along the tables, searching for scraps left; the water temperature was perfect. The place was owned by a British couple, Michael's long-time friends. He enjoyed the day eating, drinking, snorkeling, and viewing exotic women from all around the world in his own solidarity.

It was closing in on seven o'clock. The sunset was a pale shade of orange and gray. Michael entered the garden door, his backpack over his shoulder, fins in his hand. He had made a quick stop at The Deck, where he routinely gathered with his literary buddies. They met nightly, bouncing innovative ideas off each other regarding their manuscripts. The unofficial leader was a smiling eighty-something Jewish gentlemen with a full white beard. He authored a poem every day authored at the crack of "God's new creation,' as he put it.

As Michael walked into the kitchen, the veranda door to the sea was open. A refreshing breeze swept through the house, their home smelling almost pure again from the humid salt aroma of the ocean. He went onto the veranda, and there was Maria, rocking the baby.

"Hey, Maria, give me my little man." He scooped up Alejandro and gave him a nuzzle to the neck. Alejandro smiled as he wiggled his arms and kicked his legs with happiness. "Well, how did it go? Did you have a fun time with your sister? Make any new friends? Are you hungry?" asked Michael, rapid fire. "I'm starved."

"Michael, I don't think Andrea's learned anything at all." Michael's enthusiasm came to a standstill.

Oh no, what now? he thought. *Andrea's in jail.*

"We got home about six o'clock. She was hammered by three, doing blow in the bathroom, beers, shots of tequila, all paid for by her old gringo men. The one unhealthy-looking guy, Josh I think was his name, bought us brunch. He was a mess but seemed to be nice."

"That's Balboa Sundays. Were you at The Crabby Cockroach?"

"Yes, the food was great, and it allowed me to witness firsthand how the baby would be in danger if I weren't around. It was obvious how the gringos in that circle could not care less about Alejandro or anybody but themselves."

"That's because they're burnt out and high all day, every day," said Michael nonchalantly.

"Think what would have happened if you hadn't done anything until he started crawling or walking." Maria said with fear in her voice. "He would have fallen off the edge of that restaurant's deck and drowned, and nobody would have noticed." Maria stared breathlessly out at the ocean.

"I had a couple drinks at The Deck and ran into people who saw at brunch," Michael started to respond.

"Oh no, were they mean to you?" Maria was worried.

"Not at all," Michael chuckled. "They told me Andrea was running her mouth about how I stole her baby using a fake lawyer pretending to be from the Attorney General's Office, and how all the dumbass politicians in town fell for it. Everybody but her, of course."

"Yes, that's what she was telling everyone," said Maria.

"She said I bribed them all to take my side. I heard she told everyone not to talk to me or wait on me. And if she found out they did, she wouldn't be their friend anymore and there would be hell to pay, blah, blah, blah." Michael had a grin on his face.

"Michael, what are you smiling about? She told me she had plans to make you so miserable here you would either leave or commit suicide. Or, as she puts it, it would *look* like you committed suicide. That's not funny."

"That's not what I'm smiling about," said Michael. "I'm smiling because it sounds like a childish grade school silent treatment, telling people she won't be their friend if they talk to me."

"That's going to hurt you, Michael." Maria looked at him again with pity.

"The general opinion relayed to me by my friends was that none of them cared if she was their friend or not. They never liked her and certainly never trusted her. She's strictly their coke source, but they did say it was always a pleasure looking down her top."

"Oh, Michael."

"Well, that's what they said. One woman told me she's tired of getting drenched in beer when Andrea throws her drink on some guy that pisses her off. She'd be glad if she never talked to her again. And everyone is quite aware of Andrea's irresponsible behavior with Alejandro. The whole town supports what we did and agrees the child would not have survived a year. I think we'll see less and less of her as she realizes she lost most of her power last week."

"You think so? I hope it goes that way," said Maria. "Or she changes." Maria lifted her eyebrows.

"Or Balboa becomes a high-class tourist town again, and we reopen the hotel." Michael smirked. "Absolutely, she'll start over and be a dealer for the rich mountain gringos. Rumor has it, she has had a boyfriend in the wings for quite a while. He's a rich, middle-aged trust fund baby who blows in here every few months. He's a Brit with a sailboat, and he promises to take her all over the world with him. I wonder who's conning who?"

"Michael, don't laugh this off. Listen to me. You're aware I didn't know my sister until now, but from what you've told me, what others have told me, and what I'm seeing for myself, I'm deeply frightened for you, which makes me terror-stricken for Alejandro. The way she talks about you and constantly conspires for her revenge, it's aggressive and sinister. She's planning something, Michael, I know she is, and you need my help in a way you never thought possible. I'm in you and Alejandro's lives for a reason, as you are in mine. Will you please allow me to help you both, no questions asked?"

Maria spoke in an eerie voice; one Michael had never heard until now. She even looked different. "Maria, I need more information. I can't promise 'no questions asked.' Talk to me," he said, this time not smiling.

"You're right. You need to know." Maria breathed deeply. "My mother, and the mothers before her, have studied Haitian Voodoo for generations, even before the first woman from our family, my great-great grandmother, Etienna Gabriel, was trafficked to Panama in 1916 at the age of thirteen from Haiti to escape her assured rape and death in the rebellion. She was sold by her mother and became a domestic servant in the Canal Zone for a prominent Chinese ambassador. She possessed those Voodoo powers taught to her as a young girl by her mother, and then her skills were sharpened by a Panamanian woman, her boss, and head servant to the Chinese family. You Americans are way too busy with business and sports and all that material nonsense to get close enough to the spirits. And most of you consider it silliness, like a campfire story. But it's real, Michael."

"Go on." Michael gave her his full attention.

"This Friday night, Andrea will be in Boquete. I want you and Alejandro to accompany me and four friends to a place where we will pray for your protection. Many call it a spell because it's supreme. Its purpose is not to injure anyone, it is for protection, like a suit of armor. Agree to let me do this for you and Alejandro." Maria yearned to call him our baby, but he wasn't, although she prayed every day that someday they would be a real family.

Michael held Alejandro tightly in his arms. He felt unnerved. "You're correct, Maria. My culture views witches as women who are fakes and frauds. I've heard of black magic, but not Voodoo existing in Balboa. I have heard of spirits and ghosts. I consider it folklore. I see no evidence of its use, although I want to. From the moment I met you, you have found ways to keep us safe. I have no reason to believe your spell would not be intended to secure our defenses. But what keeps Andrea from casting a counter spell on me in return?"

"First of all, Andrea would cast a curse, not a spell. Curses are meant to hurt and maim, even kill. But that is not possible. Something happened early in Andrea's life, which my mother and I promised never to share with anyone. It caused an irreparable breach at the core of her soul. My mother could sense it radiating from the primal abyss of her inner being, growing worse by the day. And in Andrea's defense, it was truly horrifying."

"I want to know but afraid to ask, but continue," interrupted Michael.

"After those morbid events in her newly pubescent teens, Andrea began abusing drugs, alcohol, but avoided sex. Her language became profane and insulting. She got into fights. My mother made the decision to leave her untrained in the ways of Voodoo for the safety of the innocent. She cast a spell to block any satanic powers Andrea might try to obtain. There are few 'bad witches,' as you call them, but there are some who have been damaged by demons, leaving them open to possession by Satan, like Andrea was at an early age. Now it's obvious her power comes from her human hatred, not her spiritual power. Then, it is intensified by her drug and alcohol addictions. I would never have been strong enough to protect the two of you from her if she had learned our mother's powers. But I can protect you both from her physical human actions. That's why my mother kept her untrained in our art."

"Maria, my spiritual beliefs will not allow anything to cause Andrea harm or death," said Michael. "That would make me as evil as she."

"Michael, she's my sister, my mother's daughter, my nephew's mother. What I want to do is called a binding protection spell. However, I cannot guarantee Andrea's safety if she chooses to override my spiritual blockades and place herself in the direct path of the protectors. In other words, if she decides to hurt either of you, regardless of the spell, you and Alejandro will be given the mental and ethereal capacity to recognize danger when it's approaching. The gods will surround you and remove the attacker. Will you agree to Friday night, Michael? I plead with you to do so." Maria came over and knelt at Michael's feet, bowing her head in prayer, and placing her hand on the crown of Alejandro's head.

"Yes Maria, you have my conviction to your powers. What do I need to do?" asked Michael.

"You just did it. You gave me your conviction to my powers," Maria said, her tears streaming again down her face. Suddenly Alejandro giggled for the first time in his life as he waved his hand back at himself. Then the stronghearted Michael began to sob, rubbing his tears into Alejandro's hair and kissing the devoted Maria on top of her pure head.

27

GENERATIONS UPON GENERATIONS

The first week of the visitation schedule quickly became a humdrum part of Andrea's lifestyle. She tried vehemently to persuade the town what Michael forced on her and her son was wrong. Stripping a mother of her right to be with her child was against God's will, she claimed. It was a cute attempt to regain her power and popularity among her gringo customers and bar tab benefactors. But her anxiety was growing as she spent every day with Maria and Alejandro. It cut into her hangover nap time and then into her late-afternoon buzz. Her addictions were calling.

Michael and Maria stayed close-lipped concerning any legal arrangements with Andrea when approached by the Balboan gossip hounds. There was no reason to jab her; Michael was mature enough to realize that. Andrea, however, continued to degrade Michael and all involved. But her blabbering was getting old, and it didn't take much for news to get old to the gringos.

As the week unfolded, the only people who treated Michael and Maria with neglect, other than Andrea, were Luis and his dealers. Andrea assumed they hated Michael for taking the baby away and for the danger he had put them in with the feds. But their indifference toward Michael had nothing to do with any sort of loyalty to Andrea. They surmised, if Andrea were out of the picture, their pockets would bulge. Michael bought nothing from them, so Luis told them to stay away. But the real reason they ignored him was deeper. Luis had told them if anything happened to Michael, Maria, or the baby, and they were involved, the feds would lock them up with Andrea across the aisle bitching, and that would be real torture.

In the morning hours, before Andrea's visitation started at noon, Michael observed Maria sitting at their garden table meeting with one local woman at a time. One was Luis's girlfriend. After an hour, Maria might give the interviewee a hemp necklace with a small hand-carved pendant. After two days of this, Michael's curiosity could not be contained. "What's been going on in the garden the last two mornings? Who are those women you?"

"I am putting together a coven, Michael. A coven is a gathering of witches, between three and thirteen in number, but we need five, including me. We planned the ceremony for a week from this Friday night, when Andrea's in Boquete. I am sincerely impressed with all of them, their knowledge, and their powers. With our specific spell, they understand and accept I will be the High Priestess. I'm surprised they are immediately reverent toward my powers and accepting of my leadership, even though I'm not from here."

"That's wonderful. You emit positive, loving energy, my dear. They will learn much from you and your ancestors." Michael never knew a Voodoo High Priestess, and he never fathomed he'd use the words positive and love to describe one.

Maria loved when Michael addressed her in affectionate terms. Michael was doing it more these days. But Maria was cautious to return the affection, but it created an unfulfilled yearning. "You're right; they are impressed with my Haitian Voodoo beginnings and training. They are passionate toward our purpose of protecting you and Alejandro. It struck a beloved chord in their hearts. Being a small town, many have heard of Andrea's behavior and reputation. They unanimously agree you two are in danger. But I also needed to be assured there is no one involved who would be vengeful toward my sister. This is purely about love and protection. I needed them to grasp the strong conviction needed to protect you and the baby from Andrea's hatred and harm. I did turn down Luis's girlfriend. She was honest. After witnessing Andrea's behavior toward Alejandro, she admitted she could not be unbiased towards her. Her quote was 'I prefer a death curse. That bitch needs to go.'"

"Whoa, let's not piss her off," Michael grimaced.

"That showed me she is not well trained. Those that cast death curses usually wind up killed by the gods early in their lives. You don't want those families of gods hanging around. They get bored easy and then you have trouble you didn't expect." Maria smiled but not in a funny way.

"And what about the necklaces with the crosses?"

"They're not crosses, Michael. They're called pentacles or pentagrams. It's the main symbol of our craft. In this case, it shows the Archangel Michael we are together as a special coven, and we stand united in his service forever."

"The Archangel Michael? I thought he was mythical."

"We'll talk more about that after Friday, Michael. But if you want to read history about him, you could walk to the Internet Café and rent a PC for a while," said Maria. "He's God's number one protector."

"I will do that. Do you need help with the baby tomorrow? I will go during his naptime." Michael wanted to learn all he could before he and his son were to be surrounded by five witches. After all, he was still a gringo and was nervous about the ritual.

"Please do, Michael. I'm proud you have the desire and openness to learn about my powers and where they originated. Start with Haitian Voodoo as well as the archangel. Most Americans are fearful and lack education about us. You'll find we are based in Catholicism, primarily the saints. We are caring people with powerful friends not of this world, like you and your Archangel Vanessa in this world." Michael and Maria laughed and embraced. "All will be well, my love." Maria promised, then moved on quickly into the house without wanting to see Michael's reaction to her affection. But it was good.

28

ANDREA NEEDS WHAT SHE NEEDS WHEN SHE NEEDS IT

Andrea didn't return until Monday, telling Maria she was hired to perform at a private party in the Hotel Mariposa on Sunday afternoon. That was possible, but not likely. Michael had joined her on a few excursions to the mountains and witnessed her Saturday-night drunken drug fests with her clientele. He knew Andrea could and would party all night. The cocaine picked her up and slammed her down like a big-time wrestler. That was the reason she missed the shuttle. The seven-thirty A.M. departure to Balboa was impossible for someone who just crashed face-first into her pillow at six.

There was quite a price difference between the four-hour shuttle and a private taxi, covering both land and water. From Boquete to Balboa, the shuttle and water taxi were forty dollars, round trip. Michael paid that weekly without hesitation. But a land taxi ran over a hundred one way.

A year prior to Alejandro's birth, Andrea began to miss the shuttle on a regular basis. She took the private taxi and arrived late afternoon on Sunday. She gave Michael a big hug, pressing her breasts tightly to his chest, then a sloppy kiss. Then, without hesitation, she would say, "Michael, honey, you need to reimburse me for the taxi," in her little whiny-poo voice that was slap-worthy.

The first few months, Michael begrudgingly shelled out the hundred. But soon it became irritating and expensive. Michael knew Andrea figured out a way to retain her party time and rip a hundred from his pocket. (He found out later she hitched a ride with a girlfriend costing her nothing.) She had no guilt stealing his money. She always found new and creative ways to steal which somehow impressed Michael, for a while anyway.

"Andrea, why can't you get to the shuttle office on Sunday mornings? You can sleep on the shuttle for four hours. I'll give you Xanax. Or from here on, just wait until Monday. I'm fine with that."

"Oh, Michael, I can't wait that long to be with you. I love you and miss you so much. I can't wait to be in your arms. I have never had such cravings for a man, my love. I get wet just thinking about you. You are delicious." She would take him by the hand, lead him to the bedroom, and all would be well. But one afternoon, Michael lost his patience. This game was boring, not to mention four hundred dollars a month. Michael put his foot down, as they lay naked on their clean sheets.

"By the way, honey, no more Sunday taxis and I don't know what you're doing with those unused shuttle tickets." (She was selling them). Michael was calm and sweet, although that was not how he felt inside.

In typical Andrea fashion, she responded, "No one tells me no, especially a fucking man. Give me the hundred you owe me." She grabbed Michael's phone from the bed and waved it in his face. "Here boy, here boy, go fetch." She flung it against the wall like a Frisbee. It shattered into pieces.

"There you go, you cheap son of a bitch. I come here because I love you," she screamed, standing over him while he was still naked in bed. It was at that moment, Michael was sure she stayed with him and made love to him for $100 a week, plus free room and board, no other reason. But in Andrea's defense, Michael tracked his expenses closely. Andrea was still less expensive than a girlfriend in the States.

As Andrea stood over him dishing out her insults, Michael quickly grabbed his phone from his nightstand and pounced on top of it. It resembled an NFL player recovering a fumble. He didn't say a word.

"What are you doing? I saw that. Are you lying on my phone, and now you're going to destroy it to get back at me? How childish. Grow up, little boy," yelled Andrea. Michael continued his silence. Suddenly it dawned on her. "Shit, that was my phone I just threw against the wall, you fucking asshole. Why did you let me do that? You're going to be sorry. You owe me a new phone if you ever want to talk to me again." Michael was smiling, but Andrea couldn't see it. He stayed quiet and let her temper run its course. When Andrea visited the fridge for another beer, he bolted naked to the guest room where he stored his music and computer equipment. He locked himself in to protect it. He could hear her scuffling around the house but didn't know what she was doing. After an hour, he heard the garden door slam, almost shattering the windows. He peeked from the room like a groundhog from its den. Andrea was gone with her clothes and some of his. All the house and hotel keys were taken off their rings and scattered across the floor. The room labels were removed. Only a note was left on his desk; *Have fun, you asshole.*

Michael didn't see or hear from Andrea for two months. He had no feelings of loneliness or heartbreak. But then, one peaceful afternoon, Andrea walked onto Michael's porch, crying. She dropped to her knees in front of him, begging his forgiveness.

"Oh, my love, I thought I could live without you, but I can't. I cry myself to sleep every night. I promise you, my love, I'll never mistreat you again. You're the man my mother told me I would meet. Please forgive me, my love." Tears streamed down her face. (And the award for Best Foreign Actress goes to…) She immediately took Michael by the hand and into the bedroom, stripped him down, and made love to him for hours. It was carnal bliss. Those unchaste *jam sessions* went on for three days, until it was again Boquete time. When she returned, the three-day binge resumed. This went on for the next month. Michael sensed something was up. This was too planned. She needed something, like more money, or she was pregnant and needed a father? Then again, Michael needed something as well after eight weeks of celibacy. But now the weekends of rest were, should we say, sorely needed.

* * * *

It was Monday noon when Andrea called Maria, telling her she had a friend in town and could not see Alejandro until Wednesday. She told

Maria to meet her at five o'clock at the Surfing Banana, a quaint and clean little taco joint run by an adorable surfer girl from California. Maria agreed since it was legally within Andrea's visitation time, and Andrea wouldn't have a chance to visit her son for another four days. Andrea had not seen him in a week. Maria was beginning to believe Michael's "Theory of Lost Interest." She was quickly losing interest in being a mother. Her party time rebounded as her top priority. At five o'clock, they convened at a table in the garden, made from a cracked long board.

"Maria, gimme, gimme, gimme. Let me hold my little man." Andrea was still relatively sober. Maria handed Alejandro to her cautiously. "I've missed him so much. I wish I didn't have to go to the mountains on weekends and I could spend time here with him. That's what good mothers do, Maria. He must miss me terribly." Alejandro looked into Andrea's eyes but recognized this person more by her beer and cigarette breath than her looks. She kissed him. "But Michael, that greedy son of a bitch, cut off my support, so now I must work up there more than ever. Do you think Michael would consider child support so I could spend more time with him here?"

Maria looked down and reached into her bag for a new diaper. Besides those of the kitchen, there were a couple other smells hanging in the air, one from son and one from mother. "That's a question only Michael can answer, Sis. Ask him," Maria said abruptly, without hesitation. She sensed another shakedown attempt to squeeze cash from Michael. But Maria knew it wasn't going to happen. Andrea's credibility was shot. Plus, her illicit business income was solid and growing. Her smuggling and scamming monies were plentiful according to Fernanda, Luis's girlfriend.

"Do you think, after dinner, Michael would be so kind as to allow the three of us to go back to our house, relax, and talk on the veranda?"

Our house? Maria thought. *Where does she get off with "our house?"*

Andrea continued. "I know he hits Happy Hour at The Deck and talks book shit with his archaic gringo cronies every night. I promise to be gone by eight. There's such a nice breeze, and all of us, especially my baby, would be much more comfortable. If he says no, I promise I won't get mad. I really do."

"Andrea, if you're sure it's just the breeze and comfort you want, I'm sure he'd say yes. But you must leave by eight. Any craziness whatsoever, and he'll call Meeko on the spot, I swear he will." Maria responded in a stern voice. She had an uncomfortable feeling. Her intuition said Andrea wanted something, but surely not a renewed relationship with Michael, she prayed.

"No craziness. I just want to ask about some rumors I've heard around town. I want us to get along, Maria. I promise you; I have no desire to be friends with Michael or be enemies with him either. I must admit, I'm still pissed off over that tricky legal bullshit he pulled to steal my poor baby from me. But even though I want to see him dead and cut up into little pieces, as long as he leaves me alone, I'll leave him alone. That's as much as I can promise."

Maria still wondered what Andrea was up to. It wasn't like her to be cooperative. Maria surmised Andrea realized she didn't have the power she thought she had in Balboa. Her attempt to plunge Michael into social exile and to convince her dealer buddies to help kill him caused the opposite results. They were beginning to avoid her, not him. It had become dangerous for anyone to join forces with her. In Boquete, however, no one knew about the incident, and wisely enough, she was staying quiet about it.

"Andrea, I'll call and ask him. He certainly doesn't trust you after the damage you and your friends caused in his house. That was grotesque. I'm embarrassed for you. Wow, if Mother ever discovers what you did."

"You won't tell her, right?"

"You're lucky Michael let you off the hook with the chief and the mayor. I think you know, between Meeko and Vanessa, any breaking of your agreement, which now includes property damage, will drop you in prison, not jail, and your drug dealing days will be over."

"I know, some of my friends thought they were doing me a favor by destroying Michael's house." Andrea would not take any responsibility for her actions. And she wanted to see the beat-up, stinky house inside.

Maria rolled her eyes. "I thought you said it was *our house* a minute ago. Never mind. Let me call and ask if we can hang out from six to eight." Maria could see Andrea was restraining her anger.

After incredible tacos, salsa, chips, and even a few laughs, the three, with Michael's permission, went to the veranda. Entering the house, Andrea's mouth dropped to the floor as she entered the kitchen. She wanted to cry. "Wow Sis, the place looks great. Can I look around?"

"Sure, please do," said Maria. She'd been waiting for this moment for over a week. She wanted Andrea to feel envious but not indignant. She also wanted to tell Andrea none of this would have been possible without her, but that would be smug.

"You bought new plates and cookware and linens and had custom curtains made? You even painted the veranda and the kitchen. No, you painted the whole indoors."

"And the outdoors along with accent lights in the garden," bragged Maria. (Andrea will tell some kids to steal all the spotlights from the garden within the next week.)

"Things look so clean." Andrea said with more of a sad tone than complimentary. "Michael never did this for me when we were together." Maria didn't like where her sister was going with this. Maria was unsure what event or situation would finally take place in Andrea's future that would make her emotional dam break, but Maria didn't care if it didn't happen before Friday night.

"Michael had to buy new mattresses. You should lie on his. It is so comfortable," Maria said, hoping to spark Andrea's guilt for ruining their mattresses, while letting Andrea's imagination and envy dig deeper into that hole of jealousy. "Andrea, what can I get you? I believe Michael has a few beers in the fridge, but please, no smoking around Alejandro. Help yourself while I change his diaper and fix him a bottle. I'm sorry, would you like to change and feed him?"

"No, you do that, Maria, and I'll run to the store and grab some beers. I don't want to drink his. He got upset when we came home, and he found I drank all his beers that afternoon." Andrea wanted Maria to know she slept with him first.

Andrea returned from the store and the two sisters and Alejandro were comfortable on the new veranda chairs, the baby pleasantly snuggled to Maria's bosom, nursing his bottle in a fresh, soft diaper. The sunset was nonexistent, as a storm moved in from the North. The breeze was picking up, and the wind chimes were becoming annoying. "Andrea, you said you wanted to talk to me about something? You said you heard rumors?" said Maria." Oh, Andrea, I'm sorry, would you like to feed the baby while we talk? I'm sorry I didn't offer right away."

"No, continue, Maria. I just opened a beer. "Can I smoke over by the rail?" Maria didn't respond and Andrea didn't light up. She came and sat back down.

"I heard rumors you talked to some of our black magic ladies, and you're want to form a coven," Andrea said directly, her tone of voice changing suddenly. "And you'll be the High Priestess. Does Michael know about your powers? Gringos get scared around witches."

"Yes, he knows, and he approves. He is respectful of my powers and is studying to learn more."

"I'm fine with both you and Mother practicing Voodoo, but is he concerned about how you and the other witches might hurt someone, especially him or his son?" asked Andrea. Maria smiled.

"It's not Alejandro you're concerned about, is it Andrea? You're scared I'm going to put a curse on you. The answer is no, my coven will not put a curse on you or anybody. You're my sister. But I am sure you have attracted curses over the years by certain behaviors and the pain you inflicted on people, especially men in your past."

"What does that mean? None of those men were shamans or warlocks."

"Hold on, before you respond. I know why your actions go in that hateful direction. I am so, so sorry. That is still the worst day of my life, and I can't discern in any way how you must feel. I held your hand and was by your side that entire night." Maria began to weep, holding out her hand for a grasp from Andrea. It never came. "I have never recovered from it, and still feel the revulsion and terror as if it were yesterday."

"But I hate them all. I love hurting them. They all deserve it, and I will continue to hurt them."

"It's the gods, not the men you hurt. Mother tried to impress upon you, prove to the spirits you understand Daddy was an evil man, a demon, a cut-throat animal, and they made him pay his price for breaching and contaminating your innocent youthful soul. Like a black balloon filled tight with your hate for that wicked man, you need to let go of the string and watch it float away. But hold on to the white balloon filled with the souls of pure men and loving hearts. Allow the spirits to heal you and protect you." Maria spoke boldly and caringly to her little sister.

"Okay, Sis. I will try. But my addictions that help blot the terror of those times eventually take over my behavior and brew uncontrollable hate storms from the depth of my spirit. I can't control them. I hate them and hate myself when I look in the mirror. That's why I want to inform you, I'm going to spend more time in the mountains and try to change."

"That's a good idea, because Michael was going to say no to your earlier requests," Maria blurted.

"I know he was. That was how I could have people everywhere, especially Mother, to blame Michael for me not being able to see my son. Balboa is toxic for me, my history too long and too predictable. It is effortless for me to be wicked. But Maria, if you're not placing a curse on me, who are you cursing?" Andrea was terrified of the answer.

"Andrea, you will not be cursed, but you must be extremely careful after Friday night. Your name will be mentioned, but so will all mortals and gods at large. It is not a curse, my beloved sister, it's a protection spell. A banishing spell, to be precise. It will cause anyone attempting to hurt Michael or Alejandro or me, here or anywhere in our human sphere, to place themselves in mortal danger. It could be against you, but that will be by your own choosing. It is not a binding spell, which keeps you from your son forever. We want you to know your son. But if you, or anyone, attempts to endanger Michael or Alejandro, or even me, the spirits will protect, even by death, if they must." Maria stared at Andrea, stood up, and laid Alejandro in her arms, then sat back down.

"I don't know what to say," said Andrea, "in one way, I am overwhelmed you will use your powers to protect my child. But on the other side, your spell is to protect you all from me, the child's mother, your sister. And the saddest part, I know you are right to do so. But why protect Michael? You know there's a good chance he's not the father, but he doesn't know that."

"Andrea, he is not a stupid man. He knows that's not only a possibility, but a probability. I know you pushed the judge to prove Michael was not the father and get him off the birth certificate, but Michael refused consent for lab work. Andrea, Andrea?" Maria said as she shook her head.

"I did, Sis, I want him gone and never see Alejandro again. I was ready to kill him to make that happen." The approaching spell changed Andrea's attitude.

"Andrea, why he has taken this child into his heart, I do not understand, but he has. I might say someone put a binding love spell on him for that child. And he is so kind and caring to me, whether you like it or not. He must be protected. The gods chose him to be the worldly protector of Alejandro, and I am to protect both. The gods need something special from that child, and you, or whoever his real father is, cannot provide it, only Michael."

Andrea began to cry. She pulled her chair up, so she and Maria were knee to knee, face to face. "I believe you, my beloved sister. That baby does not have a speck of Michael or Americano in him. Michael is devoted to him for a reason I cannot comprehend. I must accept that, or the gods will take me." They both stared at the smiling face of Alejandro playing with his feet.

"Now Andrea, hold your baby and love him with all your heart. Pray for his safety and a life his mother and our mother will be proud of. Let Michael and me raise and protect him. And pray to the gods they will turn your life around. Who knows what might happen someday?" Andrea continued to sob, and the tears flowed down upon Alejandro's hair, as if a fallen angel were baptizing him.

"I think it's time for you to go, Andrea. Michael will be home soon." The two sisters hugged and wept together, with the baby snuggled between them. "Call me as often as you wish, Andrea. I'll always be here for you if you're doing good things for yourself. But remember, the gods will be watching you. If you, or anyone, puts us in danger, they will be stopped."

Andrea grabbed her purse and left the house, crying profusely and feeling so unloved. She went the long way to town so she didn't run into Michael. She stopped and knelt on the steps of the Catholic Church of the Immaculata. As she cried, she thought of and prayed for her son, her sister, and herself. She still could not reach deep enough to accept Michael, and she never would. He was a man and a father, a good man, and a good father, but still, a man and a father, nevertheless.

29

GAZE INTO MY EYES, SWEET CHILD

It was eleven o'clock on Friday night, one of the calmest nights Balboa experienced in months. A placid ocean lapped gently onto the small patch of beach under the house. Although the breeze was nonexistent, the warmth and humidity of the atmosphere was passive. The moon radiated to the coven the gods were present and ready to descend upon them with their blessings.

Three middle-aged Caribbean women sat around the table on the veranda with Michael, Maria, Alejandro, and a Native American shaman who was beautifully powerful and a skilled boat driver. Dinner was prepared a couple of hours earlier by everyone involved, except Alejandro, of course. He watched with big dark eyes. A pristine, white-feathered chicken was sacrificed to attract the angels of protection and light. The blood from its slit throat drained into the ocean over the rail. Each member of the coven, with two fingers, ceremoniously gathered blood from the stream and wiped it on their forehead. The High Priestess, Maria, finished the ritual by anointing Michael and Alejandro's brows. It was an unction never experienced by Michael, but no feeling of fear entered his being, it was quite the opposite; he was engulfed with feelings of love and peace. All sat silent, reviewing their parts in the upcoming rite. And as they did, they devotedly passed Alejandro from one to the other, passing through to him their spiritual virtues. With Maria's experience, this coven was chosen from the most highly respected occultist in the land, with powers beyond anyone in the province. And Maria, as the High Priestess, was held in lofty esteem for recognizing the group's training and discipline. All were honored to be in each other's presence.

The shaman rose from the table. It was time to depart. Michael and the shaman helped the women into the boat. He started his engine. Quietly they set out for their destination, no wake being created. The seas were flat. A jagged strip of moonlight glistened on the surface. The boat transported the coven to a remote bay on the far side of the island thirty minutes away. The small bay was where few boats wandered this time of night. The jungle was too dense to be approached by humans, even in the daylight. The shaman was familiar with the bay, its reef, and its beach, having been a tour boat driver all his life. He lowered his engine to an idle and raised the propeller out of the water. The boat glided serenely, like a baby caiman in a dark lagoon. As he approached the shore, the surf was flat, and the tide was high. He was cognizant of where the reef started and ended, having studied it at the same tide level twelve hours earlier.

The shaman ran his craft gently onto the beach, jumped out, and pulled the boat farther onto land. He planted a wooden box in the sand to help the others climb safely from his panga. Illuminating his kerosene lantern, he said something in Spanish. Since Michael only spoke English, Maria translated. "He wants us to follow exactly in his footsteps. This is a nesting site where loggerhead turtles lay their eggs this time of year. We are here to respect life, not harm it." The shaman observed the turtle tracks and mounds and made sure all were avoided.

Michael whispered to Maria, "What happens if we're caught here and someone thinks we're stealing the eggs, like the Smithsonian? They're intensely protective of these beaches. I heard they will arrest us."

Maria kissed Michael on the cheek, avoiding the sacred blood on his forehead, and laughed. "Michael, this is a tiny beach. Only indigenous people might stumble upon us, not scientists. And if they do, they will realize what we are doing. Some will hide and watch with curiosity, but most will run in fear. They will all be worried about their safety. Remember, people here know we are powerful, and many believe we can be dangerous."

The beach was flat. The sand was hard and able to be drawn upon. Maria took a machete and drew five straight lines, forming a precise pentagram, six feet in diameter. She then drew a perfect circle around it. She took Michael aside, who was holding Alejandro, and explained to him what was about to happen. Michael was calm, and Alejandro was peaceful, looking so pure and so innocent.

"Michael," Maria began. "We will speak in Spanish, so don't attempt to understand. Just *feel* the spirits surrounding us and the protective globe we will summon. I will explain it to you in detail later tonight. Each point of the pentagram represents the five parts of life: fire, water, air, earth, and spirit. The circle around the pentagram has been covered with sea salt, a metaphysical symbol for protection. Each one of us will stand outside the circle at one of the points, holding a white candle. You and Alejandro will be disrobed. You will lie inside the pentagram, positioning your head at one point, your arms stretched out to the upper two points, and your feet outstretched on the bottom two points. We will lay Alejandro's back on your chest, so you both face the heavens. You will both be naked. It's okay if Alejandro moves and squiggles and you must rearrange him on your chest. I gave him a bottle on the way, and it is past his bedtime. I think he will be still, maybe even fall asleep. But even if he is not, our gods of protection love infants. Then, each one of our earthly protectors will place their candles in the salt and sand at each point of the pentagram. They will light them. I will begin casting the spell. When I am finished, we will chant three more times, you will rise from the pentagram, and our protection is complete. We are about to start. Are you ready, Michael?"

"Yes, Maria," he said, nodding, "but why do I want to cry?"

"You sense the gods swirling through the air, and you know they are here for you and Alejandro. You feel their love and protection. It is okay to weep. It lets them know you accept them with intense piety." The High Priestess again kissed Michael and Alejandro on the cheek as the gods watched and accepted the love with warm hearts.

"Coven, let us begin. Protectors, take your places."

Michael was disrobed. He positioned himself carefully on the pentagram. Maria removed Alejandro's T-shirt and diaper. She laid him on Michael's chest, both facing the star lighted universe. Alejandro's eyes were wide open. He seemed to sense exactly what was happening. The High Priestess began the ceremony of protection. The kerosene lantern was extinguished. The white candles were lit to summon the angels of protection and their saintly light. They spoke together as Maria began in Spanish:

> *"Angels of protection, sacred forces of light,*
> *We call upon your might.*
> *Defend us with your wings,*
> *Love and light always wins."*

The protectors stuck their lit candles in the sand in front of them. When everyone was in position, Maria summoned the gods.

"Let us hold hands and chant three times what our Archangel Michael has taught us when we need his mighty and merciful defense. Let our chant surround us in the globe of his cobalt blue shield."

Together they repeated the chant three times:

> *"Michael to the left of me, Michael before me, Michael behind me,*
> *Michael above me, Michael below me, Michael*
> *within me, Michael all around me.*
> *Michael, with your flaming sword of cobalt blue,*
> *please protect us all as we address you now and in the future."*

"Michael," Maria continued, "our beloved archangel, help us here in your presence. Bless and protect these two within our circle of salt and sand at the edge of your majestic and gentle sea, with the bright light of your heavenly moon beaming upon all of us. Protect this infant child and his earthly protector, who now perches his mortal being, freshly delivered from his mother's womb, on the strong chest of this man who has dedicated his love and very life to this child, as he has dedicated his love and life to all of his children placed under his protection before him. Keep this protector and his infant safe from harm and abuse by his mother, my sister, flesh, and blood, who worships money, deviant sexual pleasure, and her chemical addictions more than she does the child which came from her very womb. Also, protect them from any of her soulmates of Satan who could be persuaded by the reward of sin to cause death and destruction to them. And protect me, so that I may come to you when they are in need. I, as well, will make a solemn covenant to you, along with these other four holding hands with me around this innocent family, to safeguard with our bodies and souls, both this child and this man for as long as you allow us to serve you. Let us bow our heads and again repeat three times…"

> *"Michael to the left of me, Michael before me, Michael behind me, Michael above me, Michael below me, Michael within me, Michael all around me. Michael, with your flaming sword of cobalt blue, please protect us all as we address you now and in the future."*

At the end of the third repetition, the candles were extinguished, and only the moonlight illuminated the beach. Michael handed Alejandro to Maria from his chest. The piety of the night overwhelmed him. Still naked, he stood, took Alejandro from Maria, and raised him over his head to the sky, looking up in silence. He then approached each of the protectors and handed them Alejandro. They each held the infant to the sky, then lowered the child to their embrace. Michael hugged each of them, Alejandro nestled reverently between them. And finally, he and Maria embraced and wept in love, with Alejandro pulled tightly to Maria's loving breast.

The shaman relit the lantern. All returned to the boat. After all were seated, the lantern was extinguished, and the High Priestess spoke. "With the gods in our presence, may you each take all the time you need to pray for the safety of your own families, friends and loved ones."

They bowed their heads and prayed silently in the luminescence of the moon and the gentle lapping of the sea on the beach. When the last protector's head arose from prayer, the shaman started the engine. As they returned to the dock, they resumed the chant to the Archangel Michael. They all, including Michael, recognized a cobalt tint on the water, surrounding their boat and all those in it.

30

THE QUESTION IS REVIVED – WHY AT AGE THIRTY-FIVE?

Six months passed since Andrea's tempest of destruction, an evening that changed so much in so many lives and would continue to do so forever. Andrea found sanctuary in Boquete, causing her to spend less and less time on the streets of Balboa. When she did blow into town, like the cyclone from hell, she wasted only a minimal number of afternoon hours dumping her guilt by visiting Maria and Alejandro. And she was fully aware of the spell floating in the air, so she didn't get anywhere near Michael. So, most of her hours in Balboa were consumed getting crazy high with her girlfriends, and snorting coke on her new boyfriend's sailboat. And occasionally, just for fun, she would score a petty tourist drug deal. Then she would return to the mountains with her red bandana packed tight.

Sitting on the veranda one late afternoon, the baby peacefully napping, Maria sat up in her chair and turned to Michael. "You were right, Michael. Andrea is spending less time in Balboa and even less time with Alejandro. I thought after you and Vanessa put the clamps on her, she might develop into a good mother. She and I had a conversation the week before we cast the spell. She assumed her life would be cursed. She left the house ashamed and concerned about her lack of discipline. She was crying profusely from the realization her baby needed protection from his own mother. She is scared to be around us, Michael, especially you. If she misbehaves, she knows the gods will rain down upon her."

"Or maybe she never cared about the baby. He was her meal ticket. She only stops by now to appease the gods, maybe a little bit of guilt." Michael peered over the ocean.

"Will I ever be able to accept the truth about my sister? Why are you always right about her?" Maria slouched back in her chair with a sigh.

"Because I have known this Andrea longer than you. Secondly, you must have figured out by now I am always right." Michael grinned. "I have not asked, but you alluded to something that changed her in her youth. It is not that I don't care, it is that I respect you and your family's secrets. We all have family secrets, except me, of course, since I am perfect. They named an archangel after me, and I was permitted to hug witches and a shaman when I was naked." Michael laughed with an ear-to-ear grin.

"You're terrible." said Maria as she smiled and threw her empty cup at Michael. "Go talk to your bookworms, funny guy. I'll join you when the baby wakes up."

Coincidently, Andrea called Maria the next day and asked if she could come over to discuss something with her and Michael together. It was the first time Andrea wanted to be anywhere near Michael since the custody battle. Maria cautiously asked Michael, and he agreed to meet her before happy hour.

"What do you think she wants, Michael? Maybe she wants to take me and the baby to Boquete every so often. Maybe she is changing because Boquete is drying her out?"

"Didn't we just discuss this yesterday? Do you still believe she's going to change? But let me ask, do you want time away from me?"

"Oh, Michael, no. The time you spend visiting your family in the States is already too much. But that is what I love about you...or...I'm sorry, I mean respect about you. It feels empty when you're not around. And Alejandro is starting to notice when you're gone," Maria's response made Michael feel appreciated. They both feared any change in their relationship. It was so natural.

"You could not have answered my question any better," he said, making Maria's yearnings rise. "I don't want you to go because I don't want you hurt. When I see Andrea in town, she's high as a kite. She is usually with a guy, the same guy. Has she said anything about him, Maria?"

"Are you jealous, Michael?" Maria knew she should not have asked.

"Maria, really?" Michael responded. "I know, she is always with a guy. They buy her drinks, and now that she has given up her apartment, she needs a place to stay. But this is the same guy all the time. Does she have a knew Michael?"

"Let's listen to what she wants from us this afternoon. She knows better than to ask for more time with Alejandro or threaten you in any way."

Michael and Maria went about their afternoon, cleaning, and gardening, picking almonds from their tree and passion fruit from their vines. They finished, and an hour late, at five o'clock, bounced braless Andrea, a six-pack under one arm, her purse over her shoulder. She popped one open and put the rest in the fridge. She took a seat like she still lived there. She was hyper, speaking way faster than usual.

"My little man around, Maria? Can I see him? Is he around?" Andrea asked, not saying a word to Michael.

"Oh, I'm sorry, Sis. I tried to keep him awake, but you are an hour late. He couldn't keep his little eyes open any longer. I just put him down for a nap so we could talk. I'll take you in to see him if you wish."

"No, I don't have a lot of time. I am meeting someone soon. Let me get straight to the point?" Andrea looked at Maria, then, for the first time, acknowledged Michael was on the veranda.

"Let's do it, Andrea," said Michael with no emotion.

"Well, I have met someone," Andrea said with a smile, waiting for a response from Michael or Maria that never came. She continued. "He's a sailor and has his boat docked offshore. That is it over there, the white one with the blue line down the side. It is so cool. That is where I stay when I visit Balboa these days." She was talking a mile a minute, so fast she stumbled over her words like a stutter.

Michael responded quickly, but in a fatherly tone. "Andrea, stop and please slow down. To save you time, I will be firm. I will not allow you to take Alejandro and Maria onto that sailboat with you and a man I don't know." Maria held her breath. He just told Andrea 'No' even before she asked. And this was a gray area.

"No, Michael, settle down, take it easy. You haven't changed a bit. You're still an asshole." Michael's face was blank. "That's not what I'm asking," said Andrea in a happy tone. "I have the opportunity to sail with him and live on his boat for, I guess, who knows how long, maybe forever. He will offset my expenses as we work together on his boat."

"Work together? What do you know about sailboats except how to get high on the deck and flash your titties?" asked Michael in a sarcastic tone. He was envious since a touch of feelings remained for Andrea.

"Michael, stop, that was uncalled for. Let her finish. Go on, honey. We are excited for you." Maria frowned at Michael and patted Andrea on the hand. Michael wanted to warn the sailor of the trap he was entering with Balboa's own Bathsheba. Like he told Vanessa, he could be a very stupid man sometimes. Andrea gave him a childish smirk, sensing some feelings coming from deep inside him. But she knew he knew what she was truly up to.

"He bases his business out of Cartagena, where locals and foreigners dock their sailboats. Most people are afraid to sail transatlantic, so they pay him to sail their boats to Barcelona." Maria and Michael sat quietly, waiting for a shoe to drop. "I will help Edward, that's his name, cook and clean, and he will teach me to sail." Michael wanted to leave this bullshit story on the porch. There was something missing. "The owners meet us at the docks in Barcelona, then sail themselves around the Mediterranean, staying close to shore and only sailing in calm weather. Then, when they are done, they have us meet them wherever they wish, and we sail their boat back across the Atlantic to Columbia. Cool, huh. We get along perfectly and have the same type of lifestyle. I am excited."

Maria and Andrea stood up and shared a hug. "I am so happy for you, Andrea. What a wonderful opportunity. It's like a dream, like a fairy tale, like a love story. When do you leave, and what do you need from us?" asked Maria. Michael was still leery and held his hands in a prayer position near his mouth.

"I'll only come back here twice a year, maybe. Michael, I want your promise you will remain here in Balboa with Alejandro. It is part of our agreement, and that part was your idea. If I am on a boat, I want to visit my sister and son here, not in Panama City or somewhere inland. We know immigration won't allow him to leave the country without permission from both of us. Do I have your promise, Michael?" Andrea asked.

"You already do, Andrea. Our agreement is Alejandro stays in Balboa. I would like your permission, however, for Maria and me to take short trips within the country or even to Costa Rica," asked Michael. "Deal?"

"But Alejandro and Maria must be present in Balboa when I am. I don't give a shit about you, agreed?"

"No, all three of us must be here when you're here. Andrea, you know I have zero trust in you around that baby, and I need to be here to be sure he's safe. Give me two months' notice of your arrival and departure dates in case I have a trip to the States planned. And it can't be between Thanksgiving and New Year's."

"I want you to go fuck yourself right now, Michael. You're the only man who has ever been able to boss me around, you're a dickhead. And frankly, I could get an attorney and fight you on this one."

"But you don't have enough money to fight me, do you? Will your new boyfriend give you money to fight for your motherhood?" Michael remembered his promise to Luis to not set her off. And he wasn't sure how the gods would see this.

Andrea looked at Maria. She looked very worried. Andrea knew what danger she might be putting herself in with the law and the gods if she lost her temper. She looked at Michael and somehow became rational. "You won't let me visit during the holidays, which is not a problem. People vacation on their boats at that time. And two months so you can make airline reservations and return by the time I arrive?" Andrea again looked at Maria. "I hate you, Michael, but I will agree before I get myself in trouble."

"I will have Meeko draw it up, and I want you to swear to your sister you will sign it. You won't blow her off. Me, in a minute, but not her."

"You're right, Michael, I was going to blow you off, but I see my sister thinks it's fair. She still has concerns over my behavior around Alejandro, or there would not be a damn spell with a harpoon aimed at my soul. I promise Sis, but I leave in a week." Andrea hugged Maria. She turned to leave.

"Andrea?" Michael called. "Your visitations have dwindled and sailing off, you will see him even less per year. Why were you going to make a big deal about this period?"

"Because I hate to lose to you, you bastard," Andrea said with a smile to keep the gods and mortals at bay. "You're the only man or woman I have been unable to control or bully in my life. I never said this before, Michael, but even though I wanted to kill you that week, the way you played me and the whole town was a work of art. I met my match. You could be a great con artist. We could have made an effective team if you weren't so fucking honest. But you would have made a shitty hooker, I'm sorry to say."

"I will take that as a compliment, but all of you had your heads in so many nooses, it was not that difficult. Like the rainforest, one tree falls, and ten get pulled down with it. But I think it's all working out," Michael said kindly as Maria and Andrea gazed at him. They both wanted him more than ever now; Andrea never lost feelings for him. "I'm heading to The Deck to meet the guys." Michael walked out the door and up the street, no goodbye, no congrats, only choking on the hollow hole in his heart for Andrea, the one he thought was plugged by Maria and Alejandro.

Andrea went back inside with Maria and took a quick peek at Alejandro. She kissed him on his forehead. As she stared at his cute little face, looking more like her every day, she said "Sometimes I miss him, but then I get high and forget I even have a son. Nobody can figure out why I had a baby at age thirty-five. They all call it that biological clock shit. But I must tell you, and only you why, because I may never see you again."

"Let's sit on the veranda and you tell me why. And we will see each other again, don't be silly." They took a seat at the table. Maria waited anxiously.

"Well, ask me Sis, go ahead, ask me. Why did a woman with a lifestyle like mine have a baby at age thirty-five?'" Andrea popped another beer.

"Okay, I'll play along. Why did my little party girl have a baby at age thirty-five?" Maria said with a shrug.

"You, my love. I had that baby solely for you. It was your face when my stillborn lay gray and bloody on my bosom. The site has never left my heart."

"Andrea, you're being serious, I mean dead serious, aren't you?" Maria felt short of breath. She grabbed her chest. It was a terrible choice of words. Andrea continued.

"Due to your inability to have a child from the start, I knew it hurt you even more. When I met Michael, I observed him and knew he was the only man that could be a loving and financially responsible father around here. He'd already shown that with his three in the States, and they all love each other. And I knew you would love a niece or nephew as if it were your own."

"And you were right, I love that child with all my heart. But how did you get away with cheating on Michael? Did he catch you? He's smart and it's a small town."

"I stopped taking the pill, then produced a minor scuffle. I left him long enough to have a sexual binge in Boquete. I already hand-picked them. I had a few strong healthy men, fertile men with multiple children already. And they had to be light skinned to fool Michael." Maria was silent. "It was worth a try, and it worked. I became pregnant. I returned to Balboa, begged his forgiveness, and had a deluge of sex with Michael. I performed another pregnancy test and, of course, it came back positive. I told him it was his and he believed me. There is still a long shot it is. I also knew you were struggling living with Mother and had no boyfriends, because you couldn't give them babies. I assumed you would be Alejandro's nanny in a minute. Mother loved the idea except for the gringo daddy. That, my love, is why I had a baby at age thirty-five."

"Oh, Andrea." Maria didn't know what to think or feel. "Mother knows all this?"

"Yes, she does. Maria. I was terrified during the birth of Alejandro, but he left my womb crying beautifully at the top of his lungs. I love you, Sis. Take loving care of both of the boys. My feuding days may be over with Michael. I am not sure. I still think he's a bossy prick. But never tell him what I did and why." With that, Andrea and Maria went inside and sat on the bed, held each other, rocked, and cried. Then Andrea abruptly arose and bounced like Pooh-Bear out the door.

Maria wiped her eyes and washed her face. She pulled herself together. She'd decided not to tell Michael another of their family secrets. She was so in love with Michael, but to tell him would make him feel obligated to keep her around. She wanted him to fall in love with her, not the obligation. She did not know what she would do if he fell in love with someone else. That was a situation she tried to ignore.

Maria sat on the veranda and cried harder. What an awakening. Andrea was a loving and caring sister. But her teenage nightmare still haunted her, and Alejandro would never make it go away, only drugs, sex, and alcohol.

* * * *

Michael strolled onto the veranda as the sky was growing dark. Maria was cooking dinner, and Alejandro was in his walker skating around the kitchen ramming into the cabinets like a pro hockey player into the boards. "Is she gone?" asked Michael.

Maria turned around and leaned her buttocks on the counter, spatula in one hand, the skillet in the other, burgers and onions sizzling. "I will miss her more than I ever thought in one way, but it will make things a lot easier around here. We had an interesting talk after you left, and we will leave it at that."

"Sure, family secrets."

"You say you have seen the sailor? Does he look like a nice man?"

Michael looked out the door at the ocean. He scratched his head. "He is about my age, maybe a little younger, and a Brit. He looks like a sailor, not real clean. He stands quietly but jittery whenever I see them together. Have you noticed hyper Andrea is lately and always wearing long-sleeved T-shirts or blouses?"

"Maybe she doesn't want to get bitten by mosquitoes. What are you saying?"

"We are nine degrees from the equator, and even during the day, they both wear long-sleeved shirts. They are both jittery, and they will be basing out of Columbia. No, forget I said anything. I'm sure it's just my distrust of her." Michael kissed Maria on the top of the head and popped a beer. *What was I thinking*, he thought? Then, sitting on the veranda and turning his chair towards the kitchen, he adored Maria as she prepared dinner and watched Alejandro zoom and boom in his walker.

31

GONE BUT NOT FORGOTTEN

Andrea and her new man set sail the following week for Columbia. Andrea nursed her bon voyage hangover with plenty of Xanax, which kept her out from dawn to dusk on her first day at sea. If a drug existed she had not ingested, smoked, drank, snorted, or run, she was on a mission to find it somewhere in the world. She had now escaped the dangers in which she positioned herself in Balboa, the spells, the law, Michael, and her finances. She was entering a new life with only herself to enjoy or satisfy, not even Edward. She had him pinned tightly under her thumb. He was in love with her unhealthy behavior. And on this altered pathway, no one knew the real Andrea hidden in the shadows.

The supply of cocaine and heroin in Columbia was inexhaustible and dangerously affordable. The fees Edward charged his wealthy yacht owners were exorbitant. The ports they visited in Europe were romantic, exotic, and sexually twisted. No social cocktail could be more perilous for an addictive personality like Andrea's. But what was about to happen in the story "Richie Rich Meets the Devil" was an explosion at close range into Edward's face, something beyond his imagination. Andrea would become intimate with her new best friend fondly referred to as Mr. Smack, aka heroin.

Andrea and Edward were on the move for over a year when Andrea decided to return to Balboa for a short visit. She sent weekly emails to Maria and her mother, relaying embellished yarns involving ports they visited and glamorous people they met, all mostly false and totally self-gratifying. Alejandro was approaching two years. He was walking, beginning to talk in two languages, and enjoying the beaches. He already had friends from all over the world. But Andrea asked nothing about her son in her emails.

Maria and Miriam spoke on the telephone how Andrea was lucky to have found Edward. Miriam asked Maria frequently, if Andrea and Edward get married, they could take Alejandro away from Michael. And no matter how well Maria described Michael as a good father, Miriam believed Michael defrauded Andrea and forced her to involuntarily relinquish custody of her child. Miriam was convinced Michael broke Andrea's heart and spirit, leaving her no choice but to vacate Panama. But Maria was sure Miriam would not put a curse on Michael, not now anyway. Without him, Miriam would need to take care of her daughter and grandson in Panama City, not to mention Andrea, when she dumped the sailor.

Maria came running to the garden one morning. Michael was harvesting the almond tree. "Michael, I just received an email from Andrea. She is returning next week with her boyfriend and wants to visit Alejandro as soon as she arrives. She sounds so excited. She will be surprised how much he has grown. I can't wait." said Maria, almost in tears.

"Wonderful. She's lucky I have no plans to be away next week. Remember our two-month notice in writing? Doesn't sound like she has changed, does it? Email her back and tell her we will be in Costa Rica next week with Alejandro, just to piss her off."

"Michael, be nice, please." Maria responded with a smile and slapped his shoulder.

"I'm betting she needs a break from her boyfriend. Next time, give her our schedules so she knows well in advance."

Maria responded apologetically. "I know, she promised me and signed the agreement, but that is Andrea. And from her emails, I doubt there's a problem in paradise. Sounds like they're having the life people only dream about."

"Will she be devastated when Alejandro doesn't recognize her? You know her ego."

Maria stopped. "She will be fine. She must understand. I will be very protective of Alejandro during their time together. You know she will be off-the-charts partying with her friends both day and night. I expect to be babysitting them both."

"Good, I hope you enjoy each other. I mean it, my sweet. But don't be surprised if she is, uh, different." Michael recalled Andrea and Edward's hyperactivity and the long-sleeved shirts they wore when they left.

"I bet you, she is different in a good way, Michael. She has a dedicated boyfriend, she visited new parts of the world, met intelligent and interesting people. She will have many intriguing stories about her adventures." Maria took her unrealistic expectations back inside to finish cleaning up breakfast. Michael finished gathering almonds along with two ripe passion fruits and two coconuts.

32

THE RETURN OF ROYALTY TO BALBOA

"Edward," Andrea said as she sat on the deck behind him, hugging her knees, her feet touching her buttocks. She wore a Caribbean wraparound, the wind blowing sensually through her hair. "I emailed my friends in Balboa, and when we arrive tomorrow night, they will all be there to throw a party for us at The Deck. It will be such a blast coming home after a year. Edward, I can't wait. I really can't. I think we plan our entrance around six o'clock. What do you think?" Andrea envisioned people cheering and clapping, holding 'Welcome Home Andrea' banners as she walked a red carpet.

"Andrea, you go alone. I have repairs to make on the boat. You'll have more fun without me. They are your friends, not mine," Edward held tight to the wheel, keeping them on course in a strong northern wind. Edward was a sailor because he was a loner. Large crowds, especially drunk ones, were not the Brit's 'cup of tea.' Small talk should be banned by the world court, as far as he was concerned.

"Fuck you, Edward. You're a ten on the scale of lifeless. That is why we are visiting, asshole. I'm so goddamn bored stuck on this piece of junk with you. We used to dock and party, but not anymore, not since your ignorance sunk the old Floridian couple's yacht." Andrea was disgusted with Edward.

"I tell you again, bitch, it wasn't my fault. That GPS was older than they were, and it shorted out. That reef was not on the screen in that storm."

"Doesn't much matter now since you are blackballed by the yacht owners. I am bored. I have no friends anywhere in the world except here. And hanging with you, well, you're about as talkative as a fucking fig tree. Come on, Edward, go with me," Andrea whined. "We'll have fun. We need it. I love you, my little sailor man." Edward made no acknowledgment of Andrea's bullshit claim to love him. He only heard it when she wanted something. Those days were left in the wake of Columbia.

Andrea went below, took a hit off her pipe, and popped a beer. As she came back up, she stepped on her wraparound and tripped. When she finished moaning like a child, Edward answered her insult. "Andrea, you talk enough for both of us. Hell, you make more noise than a troop of howler monkeys, and you make less sense. Maybe I can't talk because you never shut the fuck up. I have heard all your stories a million times. Go to shore by yourself tomorrow night and stay with one of your friends in town. I assume you want to see your baby at some point, and please don't try to drag me along. I hate kids. Maybe you stay in town the whole time we are here. The break will do us good." Edward continued to pay attention to the high winds and the horizon.

"That might be a decent idea. And remember, we must keep the heroin on the boat, it is the only reason Balboa will bust. We have plenty, right?" Andrea asked. "We can't buy it here."

"Damn, Andrea, you told me you would cut back slowly, but…"

"Don't give me your bullshit, Edward. This time is special, and I will do whatever I fucking please. Nobody tells me what to do, and I have listened to enough of your shit for a lifetime. Leave it where we always do so I can come back every so often to run one. I will do mostly coke in town anyway; I want to talk without stuttering." Andrea hit her pipe once more.

They sailed into Balboa the next day in late afternoon. From the beers, pot, and heroin all day, Andrea was almost too high to get excited. Edward dropped anchor in the bay. Andrea jumped overboard attempting to clear her head. She showered and put on the lowest-cut dress she owned. The long sleeves fell off her shoulders, and a slit ran up the side of her skirt. She finished her makeup. She was ready.

As she debuted "clean Andrea" on the deck, Edward looked her up and down. "Honey, you haven't looked like that since Barcelona, when you had the cute little Spanish girl. Do you think you will run into Michael tonight?" Andrea said nothing; she gave Edward the finger. "When will you see your son and your sister?"

"I told her we were coming in tonight and I would party with friends. We are planning the beach tomorrow with Alejandro. I know, you don't want to meet my son, you selfish prick." Edward said nothing. "Will you drive me into shore on the dinghy? Then you can come back and do whatever it is you do to the boat that gives you a boner. Let me run a good one that will last a while." As Andrea was starting to get her wits about her, she ran the needle with precision in between her toes.

"Michael?" she slurred.

"Edward, my name is Edward," he responded with closed eyes and the shaking of his head.

"Yeah, Edward, right. Give me about a thirty-minute nap, then wake me up. That hit me hard, and I don't know why," said Andrea.

"Probably has nothing to do with how big that was, the dozen beers already today, the pot, the Xanax, and the third needle since noon." Andrea was out.

When she finally woke up from her nap, she looked around and stuttered, "Alright, Ed, Ed, Edward, are you rrrready? Party starts at six o'clock. I don't want to be too lllate."

"Okay, honey, but it's almost nine o'clock. I'll run you in anytime you want."

"No shit? Why didn't you wake me, you dumb-fuck? Goddammit. Can't you do anything right, you incompetent Brit? You know how badly I wanted to see my friends. Shit, they threw a party for me, just for me. You did that on purpose, didn't you, you cocksucker?" Andrea raised her mumbling louder and louder.

"Sure, Andrea, my fault, sorry. You drink all day, you smoke all day, you take a couple of Xanax to help you sleep off yesterday's hangover. Then you ram a syringe of heroin into your big clown toes. I was worried at one point you were dead. I even put the mirror under your nose a few times to see if you were still breathing. I tried to wake you every thirty minutes. It was impossible. You still want to go to shore this late?"

"Get the dinghy ready. It is early for Balboa." Andrea did two bumps of coke to wake herself, and off they went.

The night went as expected. She arrived late. The gathering dispersed into the town. Her friends realized nothing much had changed with Andrea. They drank and danced and did a boulder of blow. All night she outran her yearning to go back to the boat. At four in the morning, she went home with her friend, Katrina. They stayed up two more hours, talking and drinking and popping Xanax to help them sleep.

The morning came, and Andrea awoke, her bed soaked with sweat. She looked at the clock. It wasn't morning. It was half past two in the afternoon.

"Oh, shit, Katrina. I was supposed to take my son and my sister to the beach today. I must go. Can you call me a boat? I need to clean up and change into something motherly. I don't want Michael, I mean, my sister, to see me like this. Or my son to see me strung out." Andrea staggered around the room and took a bump to wake herself. Waiting for the water taxi, she felt she would vomit in the breezeless heat. She called Maria.

"Maria, hi, it's me. I got talking to old friends and got to bed late. I will be over as soon as I can, and we can go to the beach, okay?"

"Sure Andrea, but I am disappointed. I was excited to spend all day with you, just the three of us. What time do you think you will be here? Or do we wait until tomorrow?" responded Maria.

"No, I just need to go back to the boat for a few minutes and get my swimsuit. I'll be right there. See you soon. Can't wait. Love, love." and Andrea hung up, went outside, and bent over with her hands on her knees.

As the boat arrived, Andrea stepped into the water taxi. She slipped and hit hard on her tailbone. The driver stared blankly at her. She looked like a dead manatee. He didn't help her. He knew who she was. She stiffed him several times in the past. He drove her to Edward's boat to get her "motherly." She had some nasty black bags under her eyes and could not climb onto the deck without Edward's help.

"I thought you were hanging with your sister and the kid at the beach today?" asked Edward, somewhat confused, but somehow not.

"Just shut up and pay the driver, then get me some cocaine, so I can at least talk to my sister. We have a few hours before sunset, and the kid won't know me anyway. Hell, he couldn't even walk when I left." *Thank God,* Edward thought.

As Andrea went below to change, she continued to bark orders. "Edward, get the dinghy and drive me to Michael's, then make yourself useful and drive us to the beach restaurant across from his house." Andrea's diction was pleasant, but her tone sardonic. Edward was glad she was below deck, so he didn't have to endure her leer.

Andrea rinsed the stench of beer and pot from her pores, put on her swimsuit, and slipped on a cover-up. She took a bump of blow and climbed into the dinghy. "No, no, Mr. Smack, you must wait until I'm finished with Maria and my little boy," she said apologetically to her syringe, her lower lip pushed forward.

Maria stopped at The Deck to call Maria. "Maria, Edward, and I will pick you and Alejandro up at your place in about ten minutes. He will drop us off at Pirate Beach, right across the bay from you. Sound okay?"

"Sure, Andrea, is the dinghy safe, and is Edward safe? I mean, that's a good idea to pick us up, but Michael is here. He assumed we would take a cab, but now, Michael will insist on coming to the dock. He will be pleasant, but I assure you, if he thinks Edward is buzzed in the slightest, he won't let us get in the dinghy with you. We will take a cab. He assumes the two of you have been partying all morning. He wants to be positive Alejandro and I are safe."

"Really, Maria, really? Do you think I would endanger my own child and my sister? You know that's not me."

Andrea has a short and convenient memory, thought Maria. *Guess who hasn't changed.*

"I love the two of you more than anybody in the world. Edward is totally sober; he has been working on his boat all day. But be sure you tell that dipshit Michael, if he starts anything with me or Edward, I'll kick his ass right there on his own dock," Andrea snapped back harshly.

"See you soon, Andrea." Maria hung up and rolled her eyes. It looked like Andrea's feuding days with Michael had not disappeared. She was worried Andrea could wind up in jail if she started any trouble.

Edward and Andrea came alongside the dock in front of Michael's house. Edward tied the dinghy. Maria, carrying Alejandro, came down to the pier to greet them. Michael walked close behind. "Oh, Maria, I have so missed you and my son. He's so big. Did you say he can walk? Gimme, gimme, gimme," blurted Andrea.

"Andrea, let me get his life jacket on him. Then you can hold him in the dinghy."

"Bullshit, Maria, we're only going half a mile. You can see it from here. He doesn't need a life jacket. That is a gringo thing. C'mon Maria, give him to me," Andrea insisted.

Michael intervened as Maria ignored Andrea. He looked at Andrea. He wanted to tell her out wired she looked and how much older and fatter she appeared. He also wanted to point out how careless she was with Alejandro already. But instead, he said in a fatherly tone, "Andrea, welcome back. And this is your friend, Edward, I assume. Edward, it's a pleasure to finally meet you."

Michael extended his hand. Edward shook it and nodded with a weak smile. "I'm sorry Edward to have to ask you this, but are you capable of driving Maria and my son safely in your dinghy? In other words, have you and Andrea been getting high already today? Are you placing Maria and my son in any danger? Be honest with me. Andrea knows any endangerment of Alejandro can carry serious consequences to her and the entire town. A cab will only take a few more minutes, and money's not an issue."

Edward responded, surprised, and intimidated by the forcefulness and paternal strength of Michael's question, but he found it responsible and quite reasonable. Michael knew Andrea's party habits as well as he did. "No sir," said Edward respectfully, even though Michael was not much older than him. "I have been working on my engine all day, and Andrea just came back to the boat about thirty minutes ago. I can tell you; I am totally straight."

"Sir?" Andrea boomed at Edward. "What is that sir shit? You sound like his kid. Michael doesn't deserve sir. He is as big a pussy as you are, Edward. Jesus Christ, Michael, Maria said you'd be nice. Are you ready to go, Maria? I'm so sorry I stuck you here in this little piss-ant town with this old freakazoid. Now, is my son ready for me to hold him yet?"

Michael and Edward glanced at each other. Maria kept her attention on Alejandro and the handoff to Andrea in the dinghy. It was then Michael and Maria were convinced Andrea had not changed, and all but Edward, for the moment, were relieved she was out of their lives.

"Shit, Maria, I can't hug my little man with this fucking life jacket on him. Take it off, now."

"Andrea, Alejandro is starting to talk and turning into a little parrot. He is repeating everything anybody says. Can you please watch your language when you are around him?" Andrea rolled her eyes as if she saw nothing inappropriate in teaching her child a real man's English.

"C'mon Edward, let's get over there where I can squeeze his soft little body to death." A terrible feeling struck Maria deep inside. Michael helped Maria into the dinghy. Alejandro, sitting in Andrea's lap face-to-face, stretched his neck to find Maria. He looked at Michael, not making a sound. He avoided looking at the woman holding him. Usually, he was excited in a boat, knowing it was playtime. But he sensed something anomalous. The scent of this woman and her breath were vaguely familiar from deep inside his short memory. The feeling was fear, but he was too young and innocent to recognize it. It was his first warning of danger from the archangel and his spirits. They were present.

"Wave bye to Daddy, Sweetie," said Maria, and with that, Alejandro twisted his body and reached for Maria with both arms outstretched. He began to sob. Andrea was hurt. "Give him some time, Sis, he will be fine with you by the end of the day. He gets funny around people he doesn't know. Let me take him until we get to the beach." Since Alejandro was loving to everyone, Maria also sensed the presence of the protectors. It was unnerving. Maria was on high alert.

"What do you mean, people he doesn't know? Edward, yes, but I'm his fucking mother, and he must get used to me quick. He might be seeing me a lot more than you think. Okay, here, take him. But when we get to the beach, he and I are going to have some serious fun." She handed Alejandro to Maria in disgust. As Andrea looked out the front of the dinghy, Edward and Maria made eye contact, then looked away. It dawned on both with that last statement, she might be planning one of her famous escape plans, and none of the one's prior were pleasant.

The boat sped across the bay, bouncing on the shallow waves. Alejandro laughed, causing all in the dinghy to laugh as well. They hit bigger waves caused by passing tourist boats, and the 'WEEEEs' came out. As they approached the shore lined with palm and coconut trees, all were wet from the spray, and all had smiles on their faces.

At the landing, Andrea hopped from the dinghy and onto the dock. She wasn't as spry as Maria remembered, and she put on weight; she appeared bloated. Maria handed the child to her. Without hesitation, she took off for the bar. She said nothing to Edward. Maria gathered the diaper bag, her purse, Andrea's purse, and the backpack filled with beach toys. She exchanged pleasantries with Edward. He nodded, turned the dinghy around, and returned to his engine.

Loaded down like a Nepalese Sherpa, Maria approached the bar down a sandy path. She heard the fuss being made over Alejandro. Andrea loved the attention, as if he were a beautiful piece of art she created.

"Oh, he's so beautiful, Andrea."

"Oh, he's walking."

"How old is he these days?"

"You must have missed him terribly."

It was small talk, since people in town saw him often. The whole time, Alejandro kept his eyes on Maria, and Maria kept her eyes on him. He attempted to squiggle from Andrea's grasp, reaching for her with outstretched arms. Finally, Maria said, "Give him to me, Sis. I will get him ready for the water so you two can play. He can build a sandcastle for his mother." Maria and Andrea smiled and embraced.

Andrea took her son to the waterline carrying his buckets, shovels, and his squirt gun. The surf broke on a jagged reef ten yards offshore, causing the waves to lap gently onto the beach. But occasionally, a rogue wave invaded, or the wake of a tourist boat would knock Alejandro down and the undertow would tug at his tiny body. But Andrea removed his life jacket.

"No Andrea, he can't swim yet, and waves come over the reef and knock him down. He needs to where it all the time."

"Maria, I told you, life jackets are for gringoes. He will be fine and how can I hug him with that thing on? He is so soft."

"Andrea, then you must watch him all the time. Never let him out of your site. Let me know when you want me to take over." The danger made Maria feel a presence in the air once again.

Andrea played with him, helping him shovel sand into his buckets to make their castle. He was feeling more comfortable with this woman, but Maria stayed close. And Alejandro glanced over to be sure she was within his reach.

After thirty minutes, Maria saw Andrea was getting bored, but Alejandro would play in the water forever. As Andrea sat in the sand, people came to ask her how she was, where she had been, and where was her boyfriend. Andrea asked Maria to watch him while she went to the bathroom.

"No problem, I have him." Maria got a chair and sat next to Alejandro, who was building his own version of a sandcastle. He beamed knowing Maria was back.

Andrea returned via the long way. She stopped to talk to friends. Maria saw her clinking glasses and doing shots of tequila in between beers. It was thirty minutes before Andrea found her way back, a shot of tequila in both hands. "For you, big sister."

"No, Andrea, I don't drink around him. You have no idea how quickly he can get himself in trouble, sort of like his mother, I'd say." Maria giggled.

"Whatever. Shit, Maria, you and I used to have a blast together. You bought alcohol for me when I was underage, remember? Now you act like a grown-up. What happened to you?"

"Funny question, Andrea. What happened to me is I grew up, had a child, and I must raise him."

"I had the child. You are just the nanny. You can't have a baby, remember. And don't forget, I'm still his mother, not you. I'm getting tired of you driving a wedge between me and my son." Andrea downed both shots of tequila. Maria was convinced Andrea's brain was burnt; paranoia and schizophrenia were setting in. And she was fearful Andrea forgot the protection spell cast on Michael and the child.

"True, Andrea, you did have a baby, but you never grew up." Maria, for the first time, was reaching a tipping point. But they were in public. She was indebted to Andrea for involving her in Alejandro life, but Andrea's attitude and disrespect were wearing thin. "Andrea, calm down. Sit and play with him for a little longer. Sunset is almost here, and we don't allow him in the water after dark. Go ahead, sit."

"Okay, but go get me another beer and a tequila? No wait, I will have the young kid with the tight ass behind the bar bring them to me. He can give me what I need if you know what I mean. I will be back." Andrea bounced her big boobies to the bar.

When she returned, she halfheartedly played in the sand with Alejandro at the water's edge. Her focus turned to conversation with friends. She proceeded to become drunker with each visit from "little bartender buns" as she referred to him.

"Andrea, I must use the bathroom," said Maria. "I'll take Alejandro with me and be right back."

"No, he's fine right here. I'll pay close attention. You can be insulting when you want to be, you little bitch." Andrea was getting mean.

"Maria," she responded in a shaky voice. "Okay, but let's sit him farther back from the water. I feel safer that way. You may become distracted."

"Fuck you, Maria," Andrea said with a slur. "I'm capable of watching my son for five minutes. He's fine where he is. I'll not take my eyes off him for a second. Now go. He's safe with Mommy."

"Okay but watch him close. I'm telling you, he's as quick as a bunny rabbit and has a way of finding trouble. He doesn't play defense." Maria scurried to the bathroom as fast as she could.

While Maria was away, little bartender buns came over with another round of drinks. She began her obnoxious flirty routine with him, laughing and rubbing his hairless brown chest. He was going for a big tip at the end of the night, and so was Andrea.

When Maria came back between a walk and a run, she saw Andrea playing with the bartender, but she didn't see Alejandro. "Andrea, where is he? Where is Alejandro?" Andrea turned around and was terrified. He was gone.

"I don't know. I was watching him, he was right here," she said with a beer in one hand and a shot glass in the other.

It was dusk and difficult to see into the ocean. Andrea suddenly saw one of Alejandro's buckets floating five yards from shore. "There's his bucket, but where is he?" Her voice was panicked. Then she shrieked, "There he is, Maria. I see his feet sticking out of the water by the reef. Get him, Maria, hurry, somebody get him," yelled Andrea, motionless in the sand. The entire bar wheeled around to see what was happening.

Maria sprinted through the surf to the edge of the reef. The undertow had dragged him out on his back, feet first. A devilish rogue wave had swooped in, and although the riptide it created was small, it was strong enough to pull his petite body under and out. His head and torso were submerged. The coral was slashing his heels and the backs of his legs. Maria knelt and felt him under the water. She pulled him up by his armpits, then cradled his body in her arms as she brought him to shore; blood ran down the backs of his legs. Maria's feet were badly sliced by the coral. But Alejandro was not crying because he was not breathing, his body limp. Maria laid him on his back in the sand and started mouth to mouth. His face was turning blue, his body gray. The crowd surrounded them. They were silent; they were helpless.

Andrea became hysterical. "Is he okay? What can I do, Maria? What can I do? Is he going to be okay?" She was freaking out, experiencing the flashback of her first baby's stillbirth. Same color skin, blood on his body, dead perhaps. *Oh, please God, don't let this be the second son that dies because of me*, she thought. She began crying profusely.

A young woman forced her way through the crowd and dropped to her knees next to Maria. "I'm a doctor, I can help. You're doing great. Let me turn him on his side after you breathe in but be gentle and shallow. His lungs are tiny. He still has a pulse, but it is weak. We don't need to press on his little chest yet."

Maria wet her finger and placed it under Alejandro's nose. "He is still not breathing. Stay with me, c'mon little buddy, get it out, get it out." Maria was calm and focused. She was an RN in an emergency room in Panama City, but this was different. After two more breaths, a roaring belch came from Alejandro, along with a projection of seawater through his mouth and nose. Maria picked him up and held him over her forearm. As he continued to cough, more water came gushing out.

Alejandro began crying uncontrollably. He was terrified, but the crying was like the singing of angels to everyone. The combination of coral cuts and salt water was stinging him terribly. People in the crowd were crying and hugging each other, some clapping. Many came up to Andrea, hugging her, so glad her son was alive. Selfishly, Andrea's main thought was thankfulness she didn't have to live with the sadness and guilt of losing another child.

The doctor screamed above the crowd. "I need clean water, clean towels, hydrogen peroxide, and bandages. These coral cuts are bad on both these people. Neosporin if anyone has it, and two blankets. This child could go into shock at any minute, he must stay warm."

Maria and the doctor discussed a treatment plan. Maria refused to go to the Balboa hospital. She said she wouldn't let them touch her dog if she had one. The doctor was from the Floating Doctors, an NGO anchored in the bay. They agreed to an initial cleaning of the wounds, then go to her hospital ship for antibiotics. After the cleaning of the wounds, the woman called her ship to bring a boat around for them. Andrea kept her distance until the doctor left.

Maria sat in a beach chair, Alejandro bandaged and wrapped in a blanket. The bleeding had subsided, and his crying was down to whimpers and sobs. Maria held him tight, her feet stinging like an attack of fire ants. Andrea came over. "I guess one of those rogue waves caught him. I mean, I just turned for a second, Maria. It was one of those freak things. What can I do to help?"

Contrary to Maria's outward calm, she stood up from her chair with Alejandro in her arms, raising her voice like a horse rearing its hooves to kill a snake. Then, with the full force of the archangel, she attacked. The bar got quiet. "You were drinking shots and flirting with the bartender when I came back. You weren't watching him, you hopeless bitch? Don't give me that freak accident, it was 'just a second' shit. Five minutes, not even that. You couldn't stop your bullshit for five fucking minutes, you slut. You ask me what you can do. You can get out of our lives and never come back. You can sink and drown, trapped on your sailboat. I'm so upset with you; I want you dead. I might kill you myself with my bare hands to save this child's life. The spirits were here during the entire ordeal, protecting him from your death squad." People glanced subtly at each other, attempting to ignore what they just heard.

Andrea was stunned. The adrenaline sobered her for a moment. She heard every word. "You may have given birth to this child, but I'm his mother. You almost drowned *my* child, not yours. Just get the fuck away from me and go put more poison in your body. And I know why you wear long-sleeved shirts, you fucking junkie." Maria started to pick up the buckets and shovels with one hand while holding Alejandro in the other. The bartender kid came over and told her to sit. He gathered her things. Andrea walked away without saying a word.

After everything was packed, Maria waited. Alejandro was asleep on her shoulder wrapped in a blanket; he gave spasmodic whimpers into her neck in a natural rhythm. She heard wheezing in his lungs, and a periodic cough, drained saltwater from his nose. The crowd went back to drinking, doing blow, and whatever else they did every night. But concern was not one of them. The excitement was over. In the distance, Maria could hear Andrea running her mouth, trying to convince them she had done nothing wrong, and accidents happen. But she knew she was irresponsible. She knew she put her child's life in peril once again. And so did all of Balboa. And so did the gods.

The bartender asked, "Anything more I can do for you and the boy, Ms. Blanco?"

"Yes, find the doctor and ask her when we are leaving." But just then, the doctor and her boat driver came to the beach.

"Boat is here, Ms. Blanco. Let us help you and your son to the dock." The doctor was an angel.

The doctor helped Maria from her chair. The boat driver took Alejandro's backpack and diaper bag to the boat. Maria grimaced with pain from the lacerated soles of her feet and then felt the pain in her heart, imagining the fear Alejandro endured.

As they reached the path to the dock, the bartender kid came running. "Ms. Blanco, you need to pay your tab. That woman over there said you were all on one tab."

Maria gave out with a wicked laugh. She considered a spell for a moment, but he was just an innocent kid himself. But she did blurt, "you are kidding, little boy? I had one diet coke. Andrea's on her own. But put another coke on her tab, then jam the can up her fat ass. She has no money, but maybe she will pay you with a blow job." Maria's patience was gone, and Andrea knew it. Even their mother would not accept this. Maria could hear her drunken giggle all the way to the dock. She thought, *If the gods don't take care of her, I'll kick that door down myself.*

* * * *

After boarding the hospital ship, the doctor cleaned their wounds once more. Even though she was gentle, Maria held Alejandro down, as the stinging was brutal. She administered injections of antibiotics both to prevent infection from the coral and any post-drowning infection in Alejandro's lungs. She applied fresh bandages and insisted on painkillers. She promised Maria she would check on them every day. She arranged for them to be escorted home. But before they left, the doctor closed the exam room door. "Ms. Blanco, may I have a word with you?"

"Certainly, Doctor."

"Ms. Blanco, I must ask something before you leave, and this will sound silly coming from a doctor. As we were resuscitating the child on the beach, his lungs were filled with water and, frankly, I didn't think he was going to live, I heard something. And I, I saw something." The doctor's demeanor changed, as she was pulled into the mystic.

"I know what you saw, and I am overwhelmingly pleased you experienced it with me. You were not supposed to be there tonight, were you doctor? There is something special about you, something you have not yet realized. You were summoned to that beach tonight because you must learn something of value to mankind."

"Summoned? Summoned by whom?" asked the doctor, puzzled by the use of that particular word.

"Summoned by the gods."

The doctor rolled her eyes at the very thought but stopped herself. She looked at Maria with her brows raised. "You are correct, I was not supposed to be there. I was to leave a half hour earlier, but my ride didn't show. The boat was delayed returning from one of the outer islands. And, at the time you were pulling your boy from the reef, I was getting in a cab. But four drunk kids pushed me aside and stole my cab. That is when saw the commotion and someone yelled, 'We need a doctor.' I ran to your side and dropped to my knees to help you." The doctor's face had a confused look, but it was slowly moving towards 'maybe.'

The doctor paused for a moment, thinking about the coincidences and what happened on the beach. As a scientist, what she experienced caused her to quiver now that her attention was diverted from her carbon-based medical duties.

"Tell me what you saw. It's unusual for an intellectual to be blessed with spiritual awareness and be summoned. Go ahead doctor, what did you observe?" Maria was excited someone shared with her this supernatural experience.

"I remember, at one point, when you were resuscitating your son, I looked up for a split second, but it seemed timeless. We were inside a globe filled with a blue haze. That is the best way I can describe it."

"Would you say the color was cobalt?"

"Yes, that is a perfect description for it. The crowd was outside looking in, and I could not hear them or the ocean, only the clashing of what sounded like giant, unyielding swords in the air all around us. It was when the clashing of the swords ended your child emptied his lungs and started breathing. Then I felt a *warm fuzzy feeling* like I never felt before. It streamed through my body. Did you see and hear any of that, Ms. Blanco?" Maria smiled. "I assumed it was my imagination from the adrenaline. The human body can react strangely when releasing chemicals in times of stress. I will need to research that." The doctor attempted to use logic to escape her fear. "But why do I know you saw it as well?"

"Did you feel the earth tremble beneath us?" Maria asked with a smile.

"I did. It trembled like an earthquake."

Alejandro remained on his stomach on the examination table, the backs of his legs bleeding lightly through the bandages. Maria embraced the doctor. "That was the Archangel Michael protecting my child's life in a battle with the same mighty forces he defeated at the beginning of time, Satan. Death was trying to get to my child, because they know how important to mankind he will become. The demons were attacking from every direction, even from the depths of the earth, to destroy him. The swords stopped when the archangel and his soldiers defeated Lucifer and his demons once again. And they needed your help to do so. You have my respect."

"Why me?" The doctor's jaw dropped, but she seemed unable to articulate any more of a response than that, so Maria went on. The doctor listened in disbelief.

"There's a protection spell on this boy, on me, and on his father. I am a Voodoo Priestess, as is my mother, and as were my grandmothers before me. I and my coven of witches cast the spell a year ago. It protects us from his mother, the drunk woman who neglected Alejandro on the beach tonight and from anyone else intending to harm us. She is my sister, and both the gods and the city have restraining orders on her. Her soul was tragically breached and invaded by Satan at age fifteen. I filled with gratitude to the spirits for summoning you tonight."

"That is an interesting story, Ms. Blanco, but I don't believe in witchcraft or even religion." The doctor shrugged her shoulders. "Your son was saved because you are an ER nurse, and I'm a doctor." Maria smiled again at her naïve response.

"You still think you being there was pure coincidence, and the blue globe and the swords clashing were not real? My dear young woman, if you wish to be a true blessing on life, like manna falling from the heavens, you must accept that you are endowed with powers beyond your formal medical training. If I can help you in any way, Doctor, or you are curious about my powers and those who transcend our worldly existence, I am here for you. The gods are appreciative of your response to save a life while we all fought together. They flowed through your body to thank you."

"Was that the warm fuzzy feeling?"

Maria stroked the doctor's hair. "You are now blessed by the Archangel, my child. And you will be blessed by my coven. We will pray for your protection." The doctor softened; her eyes brimmed with emotion.

"My colleagues and I heard Balboa is a center of Black Magic. We have discussed maladies and cures which have no scientific explanation. I cannot ignore what happened tonight, the globe, the haze, the clashing of swords. It was real. If you would allow me to visit and let me learn more, I would be honored." The doctor rubbed Alejandro's sleepy head as the narcotics took effect.

When Maria got home, Michael was still at The Deck. She wanted to call him, but she needed time alone for a special project. She was shaking badly from the adrenaline, anger, and lack of food. She and Alejandro had not eaten.

Michael burst into the kitchen from Happy Hour, earlier than usual. "I just heard a rumor of what happened at Pirate Beach. Is it true and how are you and Alejandro?" Michael was upset.

"Let me tell you what happened rather than rumors." As she told him the story in detail. He became furious. By the end, he wanted to kill Andrea. He held a chair over his head, ready to smash it against the wall. But Maria convinced him to put it down and sit in it. She sat on his lap and held him until he calmed. He did not know; she felt the same.

"I'm proud of you, Maria, the way you saved our child, not only with the spell, but with your medical skills. You finally stood up to your sister in public. Those people needed to hear that. She has a way of leaving destruction in her path, and now it is her own. I must say thank you to you and your coven. The spell worked. Our boy could have drowned, but he didn't."

"Michael, I'm scared. She is what she is. Like Andrea said to you, 'I'm not done with you yet.' She never gives up. She is a fiend."

"I am afraid it will never end, but the gods will win, right Maria? She will sail out to sea again, won't she?" asked Michael with questioning eyes.

"In the dinghy today, I picked up that she and Edward are not getting along. I am afraid she is moving back. I can't deal with her. I can't stand to look at her. We must make her go away, Michael, before we do something stupid."

"I'll talk to Vanessa tomorrow and explore our options. After this, we may be able to take away visitation. And remember, if we are correct about the heroin issue, she can't bring that into Balboa. Boquete would be her only answer. And, if Edward goes away, she won't be able to afford it until she finds a new man. Let's give it time. But we must keep her away from Alejandro. I will call Vanessa." He went to the kitchen for a beer.

Maria followed him and when he turned around, she threw her arms around his waist and placed her forehead on his chest. "Michael, I don't know what Alejandro and I would do without you. I love you, Michael." She held on even tighter. Michael lifted her chin and looked into her eyes.

"I love you too, Maria."

No Michael, I mean it, I really love you." With that, she moved her arms around his neck. She kissed him passionately.

Michael took her cheeks into the palms of his hands and stared rapturously into her eyes. "I love you too, Maria, and I really mean it as well." He took her by the hand. They made a quick check on Alejandro to be sure his pain medication was allowing him to sleep comfortably. Michael then locked the outside doors, turned out the lights, and led Maria to his bed. There, the two consummated the final detail of their ardent relationship, the one they had both been dreaming about since the birth of Alejandro. And, with a peculiar twist, on the day of Alejandro's near-death.

33

I MUST GET THIS BABY OFF MY CHEST

It was past eleven o'clock at Pirate Beach. Maria and Alejandro were treated by the Floating Doctors and returned home. Alejandro was asleep, his legs bandaged, the wounds still slightly bleeding through the gauze. The sedative stopped his pain, so he was able to sleep peacefully. Maria and Michael were in bed, their bodies intertwined, her head resting serenely on his chest. Maria's emotions were spun like a roulette wheel in the last eight hours, landing on the number she yearned for in the last two years. She could hear Michael's heart beat strongly. She felt safe in his powerful embrace.

Andrea was the opposite. She was drunk and fired up on grams of complimentary cocaine donated to her sinuses by her friends, though she considered her friends to be pure plebeians. And from the time she reached Balboa to party over twenty-four hours ago, she completely lacked an appetite. Starting with the needle between her toes, Andrea maintained a fierce pace of three beers, three shots of tequila, and a double-nostril nose bump an hour. She physically balanced chemicals in her bloodstream like a tightrope walker in a circus. But emotionally, that was a different story.

As the night progressed, she became more boisterous and insulting, calling Maria and Michael "goody-goody fruitcakes." She labeled Michael a spoiled rich gringo pussy, and Maria she termed as a traitor to her own family and an overprotective mother (yes, she called Maria a mother). "The kid will be wearing a fucking dress within a year, probably a pink one. You watch." The rant persisted for an hour. Everyone, except the bartender kid, either had enough and left or moved to the other side of the bar. Several people asked the bartender to turn the music up to drown her out. When she finally realized no one was paying attention to her, she decided to call Edward at The Deck so he could listen and kiss her ass.

"Hey, Edward, it's me, Baby," Andrea slurred, to the point of unintelligibility. On the other end, Edward closed his eyes and leaned his head back at the sound of her voice. "Come out here and get high with me, Baby, c'mon. And bring a syringe. Nobody will notice this far out of town, and only a few people are still around." Her whining was depressing, and her rational judgement had completely vanished.

Edward responded, "Andrea, I'm pretty comfy here at The Deck, and it's a peaceful night. I got the engine purring about eight o'clock. I'm sitting here nice and stoned, drinking a cold one. Just keep partying with your friends, then take a water taxi back to the boat. I will see you in the morning."

"You're a fucking, asshole. You never stop amazing me with how fun you are not," she snapped. "Anyway, I had a problem with the baby and Maria this afternoon at the beach. My sister was so mean to me for no reason. She said terrible things to me. She made me cry. How can somebody be so mean to me? It's that fucking Michael that turned her against me. She has turned into such a bitch since Alejandro was born. I need to get that baby away from her. Let's kidnap him and take off. Everyone will understand. They all saw what happened and agreed with me that Maria was cruel to me."

"Or maybe she was mean because you were flirting with some little bartender kid and your son almost drowned because you were watching the kid's ass instead of your son. What do you think, Queen B? Could that have anything to do with it?" Edward was disgusted with her.

Andrea was silent for a moment, "You heard?" she said. "It wasn't like that. It really wasn't. Ask anybody, Edward. It was a freak accident."

"The whole town knows what happened, so cut the shit. Admit it, you neglected the baby. Thank God your sister has the child and not you. You would have killed it by now. Have you killed any other babies about whom I don't know?" Edward knew nothing about the still birth. "You are such a liar, Andrea. You are the hot topic in Gossipville tonight. They are all singing 'The Bitch is Back.'"

"Bullshit, Edward, they love me here." Andrea screamed into her phone, and the remaining bar patrons called for their checks. "I make them laugh and get them high. Everybody's so glad to see me, and you won't even play with me. Aww, c'mon, please? And bring a needle," she sniveled again. Edward knew that was what she really wanted from him.

"No Andrea, and now that the engine is fixed…"

"Fuck you, then. Go back to the boat and play with your little engine. Maybe you can make love to it and cum all over its pistons. God, I hate men, especially you. You guys are all the same. You want us bad girls until we get really bad, then you don't want us anymore," Andrea was screaming into the phone.

"Andrea, just be back on deck by noon tomorrow. We're getting out of here before they throw you in prison. You probably need to be removed from the planet. Stay away from that baby, or I will call the police myself."

"First, asshole, I'm not ready to leave yet. I'm not done visiting. We'll leave when I say we're going to leave. And secondly, meet me on the boat in half an hour and I'll give you a great blow job. I'm feeling horny."

The fantasy of a blow job from Andrea had now turned into a nightmare of nausea. Edward thought he would prefer a jungle rash between his legs than her face. "Andrea, on second thought, I'll pack your clothes and all your toys in the morning and leave them here at The Deck," he responded. "I'm taking off without you at daybreak."

Edward lit the wick attached to a keg of dynamite, the one many a man before him put a match to. Hell was unleashed, and Edward had no spiritual protection, only his wits. But Andrea threatened to kidnap Alejandro just a few minutes earlier, on top of almost killing him a few hours before that. She was being watched closely by the most unrestricted supernatural beings ever assembled by Divinity himself; a force of energy she and could never defeat. Her radical rancor aroused God and the Archangel's full attention.

"Are you stupid, Edward? You've heard what I do to men who don't give me what I want. You are fucked, you stupid Brit. You and my sister, and Michael; you are all fucked." Andrea shook her fist at the heavens and disconnected her call.

Andrea told the kid to bring her one more beer, then call a water taxi. She watched him bend over the cooler. She then squatted by a palm tree, hiked her skirt, and took a piss in front of him. She shared her last bump on the bar.

He placed the tab next to the cocaine. "What the fuck is this, kid?" she asked, wadding up the tab and bouncing it off his chest. "My sister was supposed to pay for this, or my boyfriend who was supposed to pick me up. I guess they both just fucked you over. I have my purse, but no money. How about a bag of coke?"

"Shit, ma'am, your tab is way bigger than a gram of that cocaine. And what you just gave me is half laundry detergent. If you're not going to pay me or tip me, then I don't have to be nice to you anymore, you old whore. You can blow me for the tip, but somebody has to cover this tab, or it comes out of my pocket."

"I'm good for it. You don't know who I am, do you, you little pissant? I used to own this town, and just might again, so be careful." Andrea was slurring and staggering so bad it was scary. She was the definition of repulsive. "I'll pay you tomorrow. Or go to my sister's house, and she'll pay you. That little cunt always forgives me and bails me out. And always will. She's just a dumb little witch wanna-be."

The bartender accompanied Andrea down the dark and sandy path to the dock, not because he cared about her safety or wanted a repulsive blow job. It was because, if she fell on the rocks and cracked her skull or fell in the water and drowned, he must stick around and wait for the police and an ambulance to arrive. He wanted to meet his girlfriend in town, that's all.

As they walked down the darkened path, she held his arm. She continued to yak about how important she was and all the places she had been. The kid tuned her out. The moon was full, so the dock was visible. While they waited for the boat, he dropped his jeans to his ankles. Andrea fell onto her knees and presented him with his tip. The boat arrived just as Andrea's task was completed. She told the driver to take her to her sailboat in the bay across from The Deck. "See you soon, cutie."

"I hope not, you fat old drunk," he said. And although Andrea did not respond, somewhere inside, a sword rammed straight into the heart of her ego.

Andrea was driven back to Edward's sailboat. Not remembering everything that happened after wading waist deep through pot, cocaine, alcohol, and nicotine, she somehow recalled the high points: Alejandro's near-drowning, her fight with Maria, Edward telling her he was leaving her, and the kid calling her a fat old drunk. She had to get back to the boat quickly. She desperately needed something to keep her subconscious pain cornered; that pain that burned inside of her from her youth.

As they approached the boat, the sky flashed and long deep roars of thunder steadily approached Balboa, like a fleet of battleships beginning their attack. She told the driver to return for her in thirty minutes. She would pay him then.

Lumbering onto the deck, she proceeded to slip on the top step, bouncing on her butt into the galley. She fumbled behind the electric box and pulled out her hidden stash of heroin. As high as she was, she still prepared herself a fully loaded syringe of her favorite tormentor. Somehow, she managed to stay steady enough to run the needle into her vein with Andrea precision and no hesitation into her elbow. She finished with two nasty bumps of pure coke. Then she called Edward.

"Hey, you still at The Deck? I'm on your boat. I have some surprises for you, my love. Can you see me from there?"

"No, why, you naked?" asked Edward.

Andrea was going down quickly. She could hardly talk. "No, buddy, those days are over for you. But I must say, even though you suck playing it, I always loved the beautiful wood on that violin of yours. I love it so much I'm taking a big shit on it right now." Andrea laughed into the phone as she grunted. "Well not exactly a big shit. It's mostly diarrhea, but a hell of a lot of piss."

"You wouldn't. You're kidding, right?" Edward yelled into his phone.

"Done deal, babe. And you must put this thing right in your face to play it. That will always remind you of me." Andrea again laughed into the phone.

"Honey, let's talk about this in the morning. Don't do that, stop," pleaded Edward.

"And since you are leaving me in the morning, I am sending your clothes ahead via Andrea's Aqua Express. They're going into the deep right now." Andrea gathered his clothes and threw them overboard. She emptied the spare gasoline tank on the galley floor and flung it overboard. Now that she wasn't squatting over his violin, he could see her actions on the deck.

"Here comes my water taxi to take me to town." Her words were unintelligible between the slurring and her dropping the phone every few seconds. "Are you ready, asshole? Here comes the big one. Watch this." Andrea gathered all of Edward's cash and drugs from their hiding places and stuffed it all into her purse.

"Edward," she suddenly said in all seriousness. "I have to get rid of this baby on my chest. It must get it off me. I'm throwing its gray and bloody body into this dark ocean. Let the fishes devour it until there's nothing left to haunt me. It must leave me alone. I must absolve myself of its torture. His birth and his death weren't my fault, Edward." Andrea said as clear as day, no slur, no anger, her tone was grave.

Edward was in shock. She kidnapped Alejandro and was going to kill him. "Andrea, no, no don't do that. Don't kill your little boy, no. You're mad at me so kill me, but please, not him," yelled Edward, but Andrea had hung up. The rain started to come down heavily, the wind blew in like a typhoon, and the flash of lightning bolts and the claps of thunder were getting closer and closer together. The sea was enraged.

As the taxi driver slowly and innocently approached the boat, Andrea made her way down the steps of the gasoline-soaked galley. She lit a towel with her lighter and tossed it on the floor. POOF, flames blasted from the galley into the night storm. With her purse over her shoulder, she bolted up the steps, but not fast enough. The back of her dress caught fire and engulfed her in flames. She screamed from the blistering agony, but as the heroin was kicking in, her breathing became shallow. Her lips turned blue as she fell, gashing her temple on the corner of Edward's toolbox. She was unconscious, lying on her stomach, the back of her dress and her hair in flames, blood gushing from her head profusely into a dark puddle.

The approaching boat driver saw the explosion and the flames. He could now see Andrea on fire. His propeller became entangled in Edward's clothing. He feared another bigger explosion if he went any closer. He called the fire department right away and backed off.

In the meantime, Edward saw the fiery explosion from the rail of The Deck. He grabbed the fire extinguisher from the wall, hopped into his dinghy, and headed for his boat. By the time he arrived, the galley fire had calmed down, and so had Andrea's dress. He used the extinguisher on both his boat and Andrea. Everything was charred, including Andrea's back and legs, and her face from her hair. The police and fire boats quickly converged on the scene. The storm moved on as quickly as it arrived. Edward's clothes floated all around the area, his violin was a mess and Andrea's head and burnt scalp lay in a pool of blood. Edward swiftly searched her purse as the police got closer. He hurled only the drugs overboard, scattering them as far away as possible. He stuffed his cash in his pocket. He then lifted Andrea's head, but she was limp, her eyes in the back of her head, and those parts of her not scorched were cold as ice. She had no pulse.

The fire department attempted CPR on Andrea, but to no avail. The police boarded the boat and took Edward into custody for murder. They raised the anchor and towed Edward's boat to the police station. They also took the water taxi driver to the station to get his statement. He told the police he saw the boat catch fire as he approached, and Andrea was already on the deck inflamed when he arrived. He also stated Edward arrived in the dinghy with an extinguisher after the fire started, and he saw no one leave the boat before or after he arrived.

All the way back to the station, Edward screamed at the officers to go back and look for a baby. They ignored him. One smacked him on the head with his club.

When Edward was put in a cell, he began shouting in a bloodcurdling scream, "Does anyone know Michael Harper? Andrea just drowned Michael Harper's son. Michael Harper, Michael Harper." Finally, the night captain, Jose, came over to the cell.

"What's this about Michael Harper and his son? His son is fine. That accident happened this afternoon, and he's fine, so settle down," said Jose.

"No, you don't understand. Less than an hour ago, Andrea told me on the phone she had had enough of Michael and her sister and was going to kidnap the child," said Edward in a panic.

"Go on," said Jose.

"Then Andrea called me at The Deck from my boat and told me everything she was going to do to my possessions, which she did, but at the end, right before she set my boat on fire, she said the baby must die, and she was throwing it into the ocean. She couldn't take it anymore. I'm telling you, she said she was throwing the baby in the ocean. That's when she started the fire." Edward looked at the captain who turned pale.

"I'll be right back. I have to make a call," said Jose.

The captain called Antonio and obtained Michael's telephone number. He called it, and finally, Michael answered the telephone. "Hello," Michael said in a soft, sleepy voice.

"Michael, this is Jose from the police department. I have a strange request, sir. Can you check on your son and tell me if he's okay, please?" asked the captain.

"Sure, but why?" asked Michael.

"Just do it, please," responded the captain. Michael went to Alejandro's bedroom and returned quickly.

"He's fine, Captain. He had a rough day at the beach, but he's sleeping nicely. Again, why the call?" asked Michael.

"Oh, just Balboa rumors, you know. Just had to check. Someone said your son drowned."

"No, no, almost, though. But that was around sunset. Thanks for checking on us and for your concern. Goodnight, Captain."

The captain returned to Edward and assured him Michael's son was unharmed asleep in his bed. Edward was so relieved, but still insisted Andrea said she was throwing a baby overboard.

Edward proceeded to tell the captain he had watched the whole thing from The Deck while Andrea narrated exactly what she was doing, step by step, slurring heavily and getting worse by the minute. And when Andrea told him she was throwing a baby overboard, that is when the explosion happened. He explained the extinguisher, and that Andrea was dead when he arrived. But they kept Edward in the cell.

"Captain, sir, I think you need to see something," said one of the officers. The captain followed him to the boat, where the galley was still smoldering, and Andrea was lying dead on the deck.

The officer said, "I know at first, we thought Andrea was struck with a blunt object, and that's what killed her. Would made sense her boyfriend became angry when she set his boat on fire, and he hit her with something, knocking her into the flames. But there's a small piece of her scalp gouged from her temple on the corner of a toolbox next to her body. That seems to be how her head wound happened."

"So, you think she caught her dress on fire…"

"A fire I believe she set herself, due to the empty gas can we found floating around the boat. And, Captain, the sailor's violin was on the bow of the boat covered in, what I assume, is Andrea's waste."

"Oh my God, we have dealt with her doing these crazy things in the past to men, but she outdid herself this time," said the captain. "He was breaking up with her, wasn't he?"

"And something we never dealt with in the past." He took the captain down into the head. On the floor in the corner was a syringe. "It could be for insulin, sir."

"I never knew her to have a diabetic issue. I will ask the guy in the cell. Check their garbage and cabinets for insulin vials."

"We did. We found nothing."

"I think it's time to reconsider the cause of death. Let's start by doing one simple thing. Roll her over and let's look at Andrea's forearms and between her toes," ordered the captain. The officer turned her over onto her back. The way she fell only the tops of her forearms were charred and blistered. "Oh my, look at those track marks and bruises. There is a fresh blood clot in the crease of her elbow. This girl became a major junkie while she was away. She overdosed. I didn't think the head wound was enough to kill her. And she was burnt, but not enough to kill her."

"You want me to call the ambulance and take her body to the morgue? The coroner can perform the autopsy tomorrow. How soon will he be able to confirm your theory?"

"Yes, but our coroner's not a real pathologist. He's not even a doctor. He's the mayor's cousin. He just signs papers. We don't have a pathologist in Balboa. But in this case, all we need is routine lab testing and our emergency room doc can read those. Get the lab tech out of bed and take him to the hospital right now. Call the doctor to come to the hospital. All right, here we go. Take the body to the emergency room for the blood work and have them do a thorough drug screening. Search the boat inside and out, including Andrea's purse, for drugs of any kind, especially heroin. And for God's sake, put that stinking violin in a plastic evidence bag and seal it tight. It is stinking up the whole station. Move it. I want answers by morning, so I can inform her sister what happened." After the captain's orders, all scrambled. It was now one o'clock in the morning.

* * * *

Three hours passed. The ER doctor phoned the captain with the results. "Sir, the blood shows an extremely high alcohol content, a high agave content, probably from tequila, nicotine, and traces of alprazolam, known as Xanax. There were moderate THC levels from some form of marijuana, elevated levels of cocaine, which blocked her sinuses like a rock quarry, and sir, an extremely high level of heroin. And from the heroin level, I would say it was introduced into her bloodstream within twenty minutes of her death. And finally, her adrenaline levels were off the charts, and her stomach and bowels completely empty, meaning she probably had not eaten in well over a day. I deduce she was emotional and filled with rage over someone or something. And before you ask, sir, we only did an X-ray. No one here, including me, has the stomach to cut anyone open. We're kind of wimpy about that sort of thing."

"Doctor, can you say that you and any other physician, in your medical opinion, would declare the cause of death to be an illicit drug overdose?" asked the captain.

"Sir, the alcohol level on an empty stomach alone could kill a person, but mixed with all the other chemicals, and the freshness of the clot and tracks on her arms, then combine that with the adrenaline levels, her heart simply gave out. The answer is, yes, she overdosed," concluded the doctor.

"Move her corpse to the morgue and have the coroner prepare a death certificate as soon as possible. Have him deliver it to me by eight o'clock this morning," ordered the captain.

The captain hung up and went straight to see Edward. "You will not be charged with first-degree murder. Andrea overdosed, but I assume you knew that. And I'm assuming you came here, not to visit, but to drop her off, and the two of you were going to end your relationship, correct?"

Edward nodded yes and confused about what was coming next.

"I will be blunt," the captain said. "We found a needle on your boat and high levels of heroin in Andrea's bloodstream. We're searching your boat for any unused heroin. I assume Andrea told you heroin is the only drug we do not tolerate, and this is the reason. You are lucky she was Panamanian and not a gringo, or the feds would be here by noon, and you would go to prison. And if you came here to sell it, we will bust your ass, and send you to prison."

Edward leaned forward and took a deep breath. "And I'll be blunt as well, sir. What we had on the boat was for Andrea's use only. If you want to run a blood test on me, you will find alcohol, pot, and a low level of Xanax to help me sleep. But frankly, Captain, I couldn't afford the girl anymore. She was expensive enough, but when we dropped anchor in Cartagena and started hanging out in the night life, she was introduced to smack, for free at first by the cartel boys. They know what they were doing. They developed a new customer. I warned her, but you know Andrea probably better than I do."

"Fortunately for you, I do," said the captain.

"She increased her use every day, and I was falling behind on the payments to her new Columbian friends. When I pleaded with her to stop, she would agree, then buy it behind my back. A few weeks ago, she got nasty. She insisted we come back here, and we had to leave immediately in the middle of the night. I thought she decided to rehab here, but with the amount she brought on the trip, I realized she was stiffing those boys and we had to run."

"Those boys don't forget. They are looking for you."

"She was bad. She knows your rules about heroine. But she insisted. I have not seen her as fucked-up as she has been the last forty-eight hours. Rumor has it, her baby almost drowned today because of her neglect when her sister went to the bathroom. Then her sister got so angry she wished her dead. Andrea told me she comes from a family of Voodoo High Priestesses, but I don't believe in that black magic crap. Andrea was full of shit most of the time."

The captain found Edward's story completely plausible.

An officer entered the room and whispered in the captain's ear. "Edward, I sort of know Maria, and there's no way she's a witch. And there is no way she could have made Andrea drink, smoke, snort, and shoot up all that, so I'm going to forget you made any accusations toward Maria. I was just informed my squad found no drugs on your boat, except for pot and some needles. We have confiscated those."

"I understand."

"We checked the engine. It works fine. And the sails are unharmed. Hop on your boat and leave Balboa before the town wakes up, and never come back. Not ever, or I will let the Columbians know you are here. I suggest you get out of this part of the world. You are not the first man she's hated and done this to, but you will be the last. She was not someone you could tell no. Your penis almost got you killed. Now set sail."

Edward boarded his charred sailboat, filled up his gas tanks, and stocked up some food from an outer island. After weeks of attempting to clean his violin, he threw it overboard, polluting the entire southern Caribbean, like an oil spill.

* * * *

It was almost seven o'clock and time for the shift change. Jose informed the day captain and the chief about the insanity caused by Andrea. The captain requested permission to visit Harper's house and tell Maria of her sister's death. The chief agreed and insisted he go also. He had become fond and respectful of Michael and Maria during the custody battle. The coroner delivered the death certificate by eight o'clock. The two headed to Harper's before the news, or more accurately, the rumors spread through the streets.

As they arrived at Harper's, the sun was rising above the rainforest across the bay, the backdrop of Pirate Beach. The house was serene, and all were still asleep. They woke to a knock at the door. Michael and Maria looked at each other with concern. Michael whispered, "Could that be Andrea?"

He slipped on a pair of shorts, pulled a sleeveless shirt over his head, and put on a baseball cap. He peered out the window to see who was there. "Captain? Chief? I must say, this is a surprise at sunrise. Why, that rhymes, doesn't it?" Michael smiled, and the captain and chief gave him a weak, obligatory grin in return.

"Michael, good morning. Can we come in? We must talk to you and Maria. We brought you coffee and donuts. They are your favorites made by Antonio's mother."

"Why, thank you. Come in, but be quiet, please. The baby's still asleep, I think. He is in a lot of pain from the coral cuts yesterday. I will tell Maria you are here. Please, have a seat on the veranda." Michael went to his bedroom to tell her she was needed and by whom. Then he checked to see if Alejandro was awake. He was, so while Maria dressed, Michael changed Alejandro and prepared for him a bowl of oatmeal and a cup of juice. The captain and chief waited graciously. He perched the baby in his chair at the end of the table, sneaking some crushed-up pain medication into Alejandro's first bite of oatmeal and playing the "airplane spoon" game to get him to swallow it. On the second bite, Alejandro took it from there.

Maria limped out of the bedroom and onto the veranda, her bandages spotted with blood. She shook hands with the captain and the chief and joined everyone around the table, giving Alejandro a kiss on the check and one on his bandaged legs. "How's my little pumpkin?" she said, and all smiled as he kept eating. "Captain, you brought us coffee and donuts. What could this be about? No, let me guess, my sister is in jail for hitting someone? Or she fell into a drunken stupor and broke something? Or she is threating to burn our house down and kidnap Alejandro again?" Maria's guilt from her words to Andrea the night before had turned to anger at having to deal with her again.

The captain stared coldly at Maria. "Ms. Blanco, your sister is dead." Total silence came over the morning sunrise. Michael popped up quickly and stood behind Maria's chair, placing his hands on her shoulders and his lips on the top of her head.

Maria exclaimed, "You are sure, Captain? I mean, this isn't some stupid Balboa rumor, is it? Like somebody told somebody, who told somebody who told you they saw her drowned, or she passed out somewhere and she just looked dead. Impossible Captain, there's no way. Why are you lying to me without any proof? I told her I wished her dead yesterday, and you just want to teach me a lesson, so I watch my mouth, right? That is mean, Captain." Maria was buried deep in denial.

"She OD'd on her boyfriend's boat."

"You are sure it was a drug overdose? He could have hit her and killed her or poisoned her. They were fighting yesterday. Neither seemed very happy with each other," she argued.

"With all due respect, Ms. Blanco, you, and Andrea were fighting last night also, and in public. You not only wished her dead, but you also threatened to kill your sister yourself," the captain expressed factually.

"You're right, I did. But I didn't kill her. I was here the rest of the night." Maria curbed her accusations, thinking about what she said and what she and the coven had done. She turned ashen.

"We considered murder by her boyfriend, due to the head wound and blood pool, but a witness saw her boyfriend arrive after the fire," said the captain.

"The fire?" said Maria. "She died in a fire? Now I'm totally confused. You said an overdose?"

"Let me sum it up. "Andrea became a heroin addict while she was in Columbia. They got behind on drug payments to the cartel. That is why they came back here. We think she made a deal with Luis to work here again and raise enough to pay the Columbians. But her boyfriend tolerated her above and beyond, and she couldn't stop. He could not afford her anymore. He gave her the choice, go through rehab, or end the relationship."

"We picked up on the heroin issue a year ago," Michael interjected. "They were both getting high on his boat well before they left. That's probably what they had in common."

The captain continued. He told Maria the details of the night. In conclusion he said, "We are so sorry, Ms. Blanco, for the loss of your sister. We know you had nothing to do with it. And we know how much you cared about her. We did not perform an autopsy since the doctor felt the lab tests made the overdose obvious. To go further, we would need to send her body to Panama City."

"But Captain, you called me last night checking on Alejandro to see if he was all right. What was that all about?" asked Michael.

"Andrea told her boyfriend they should kidnap your son and sail away from Balboa forever. As we took him to the station, he was in hysterics. He said the last thing Andrea said to him on the phone before she set fire to his boat, and herself, was something about how she had to get this 'bloody baby off her chest.' We assumed she was talking about Alejandro on the beach yesterday and the guilt was eating her up inside. She told her boyfriend she threw the baby overboard during the storm to be eaten by the fishes. We assumed she somehow kidnapped the little tiger, and he was the bloody baby she was referring to. That is why we called. Michael, I was terrified to call you. I thought I would hear the worst. Thank God it wasn't him. And so far, we have no missing children reported."

"Wait a minute, what storm? You mentioned a storm? Did you say around eleven o'clock, Captain? We could see his boat from here and we didn't have a storm," asked Michael. "It was calm as can be here."

"I know, Michael. It didn't storm at the station either, and we are closer to that boat than you. But it was storming terribly as we approached, but it abruptly ended as soon as we arrived. Even the water taxi boat was dry. We thought, at first, the boat was hit by lightning and set afire. But Andrea had vengefully doused the galley with gasoline. How could that storm just disappear?"

"Oh, Michael," said Maria as she broke out in near hysterics. She buried her face in Michael's chest and began to sob. "This is all my fault."

The captain looked at Michael with a puzzled stare; Maria had his back to him. Alejandro just sat and watched, having no clue why the woman he believed to be his mother was crying. "Do you still have any other questions about what happened?" the captain asked. "Her body is at the morgue, and here is the legal death certificate from the coroner. You will need to identify the body for the coroner before it's released, along with her ID, which might be in her purse at the morgue. You will need to make the arrangements for services and her burial or cremation. Ms.

Blanco, again, I'm deeply sorry. If you need me or have any more questions, just call. Here's my number."

"Thank you, Captain, and Chief. "We appreciate you coming to our house instead of calling," Michael shook their hands and showed them to the door. Maria said nothing. When Michael returned to the veranda, Maria was sitting with Alejandro in her arms, holding his head to her breast and sobbing loudly. Alejandro looked at Michael. Somehow, even at an early age, he knew he needed to be still.

"No, Maria, the episode at the beach could not cause such a dire reaction from Andrea. "Your scolding wasn't why she died. Nobody can do what she did to her body. No heroine in Balboa prolonged her life. Her brain fried and her heart gave out. Her hatred of men finally destroyed her."

"Michael, we need to talk," Maria said with a look and a voice he had not seen or heard since the night of the spell.

34

WHICH WITCH WAY WAS WHICH?

For an hour, Maria fixated without speech or movement on Pirate Beach. There was a gentle, steady rain with no breeze. The rain was so fine it created no signs of droplets on the water. The wind chimes were silent. Even the birds were silent. Michael took Alejandro from her arms to his playroom; his virtuous activity was the only sound in the house. Maria cried periodically over the loss of her sister, in direct contrast to the warmth in her heart hearing Alejandro alive. She thought *it could have be different yesterday.* When Michael finally came out onto the veranda, she didn't look at him. She continued her haunting focus across the bay, as still as the weather around her.

As Michael positioned himself next to her at the table, she broke the muted aura. "I killed her, Michael. I was the one who killed her. I killed my sister." She took Alejandro into her arms and stared into his eyes. "I murdered your mother, my precious child."

"No Maria, you just think you did in this moment." Michael stood behind them and hugged them. "Andrea died of an overdose, which has been coming for years. She finally found something strong enough to kill her. It was a suicide."

"But she overdosed for a reason, Michael. She had no choice. Has it dawned on you, shortly after my coven placed the spell of protection on you, me, and Alejandro, she left town with the sailor, and we were all safe and harmonious, including her? Then she returns, and the first time

Alejandro is around her, within hours, she neglects him and almost causes him to drown? And he would have, if not for me and the reef blocking him from being pulled to the bottom of the sea. Any other beach, he would be dead. Andrea came back because she was bored and wanted to be a somebody again."

"You cannot say she was safe on that sailboat. The captain said she stiffed some Columbians when she became a heroin junky. And that last injection was too much, on top of the rest."

"You are right. Even if she stayed and got clean, she would have wanted the same visitation rights. And now Alejandro can walk and scamper; it is way more dangerous than when he left. What happened at the beach would happen again, or in the street hit by a car, or off a dock. But the first night she's with him, she dies during a mysterious storm that only she experienced?" Maria glared into Michael's eyes.

"Okay, but you, Maria Blanco, never forced her to ingest those chemicals in her body. She was doing that before the spell, and she went downhill while she was gone. It was the precise reason for the spell; it was her history of endangerment. Don't underestimate the archangel's decision in all this." Michael held her hand.

"No, that's not all of it. I screamed at her on the beach in front of the world to get out of our lives for good and never come back. Then I told her I was so upset I wanted to kill her myself."

"Maria, people say those things all the time in family feuds. It's just a saying. Family members fight all over the world. And she did seriously endanger his life again, like she did with Luis."

"I have never said that to anyone, Michael." She covered her face with her hands.

"Maria, not in that tone of voice, but you did cast a spell in that unearthly voice you use. What you said yesterday was truly natural and justified. I was going to call Vanessa today and ask if we could take all visitation rights away. But she wouldn't have lasted long here because there's no heroin, and the Columbians are on both their trails to be paid. She was a hardcore addict in so many ways, and she was not the rehabbing kind. She would have found it somewhere, Maria, she was running it into her veins before she left. Rules and agreements meant nothing to her,"

Michael reminded her. "It's almost like she wanted to get busted or die. And what was the baby thing thrown into the ocean? I pray we don't discover she really did murder a child."

"No, Michael, she meant something completely different. I assure you, she didn't murder a child." Michael looked puzzled at Maria's certainty. "But you still don't get it. The spell made her a junky, so if she ever returned, she would be busted or OD. But when we were living here together and she was your girlfriend, purposely clipped her ear cutting her hair and got her blood on a cotton ball. I kept her blood and hair in an envelope and made a doll. I was going to use it to protect her from harm. But last night, I pulled the doll out."

Michael interrupted. "You mean a Voodoo doll? Am I catching the drift now?"

"Yes, Michael, a genuine Haitian Voodoo doll, to be precise. My mother taught me how to make them when I was young and how to cast curses and spells through the spiritual family of Ghede. But we will talk about that later." Michael was enthralled and a bit scared.

"I was so angry when I got home, and you were not here. I sat in my room with Alejandro resting comfortably, his bloody bandages staring at me, the doll in my hands. Over and over in my head, I saw Alejandro under the water, except for his feet, being ripped out by the tide and smashed into the reef. I saw Andrea, a beer in one hand, a shot in the other, yelling at me to go get him so she didn't have to put down her drinks in the sand. Then I felt terror as he was not breathing, losing color, blood running down the backs of his precious legs. It was in that split second, I realized she was incapable of loving anyone, even her own son, enough to sacrifice even a beer. She had such hatred and guilt deep inside; she could only dumb them with her addictions. Finally, when I held Alejandro while a stranger bandaged us and cared for us, I heard her laughing at the bar, defending herself by denying her neglect. I snapped and went after her in public. I came home and put a curse on her last night, via the doll. The needle went straight through her heart. And that is how she died, her heart gave out, my needle through her heart." Maria hung her head.

"What was it? What was the curse, Maria?" asked Michael.

"I asked the family of Ghede, specifically Papa Ghede, to protect Alejandro from his mother. He is the Haitian god that protects children from dying before their time. I asked him to strengthen Andrea's addictions until they took over her mind and killed her body. Michael, I killed Andrea. I killed my little sister." And Maria put her face in her hands and wept with sadness, but still no signs of remorse.

"Wasn't the protection spell to the archangel strong enough?"

"It is. Alejandro was saved by the reef being in the way, and I sprinted back from the bathroom, sensing he was in trouble. There was still enough light to see him. As I revived Alejandro, the doctor and I were surrounded by the blue globe, and we both heard the clashing of swords as the archangel protected him from death. Then the doctor was there to help us with pain and infection. I had faith and patience in the archangel, but I called Papa Ghede out of anger, Michael, not out of love. I watched my mother put curses on people, like my father, out of hate. I swore..."

Michael interrupted. "What do you mean, your father? Why did she put a curse on your father? Is he why Andrea hated men?"

"Please, Michael, not now, but sometime soon. Now that Andrea's gone, I will tell you. Until Alejandro, Andrea never hurt anyone physically; she just took their things and money and broke their hearts. After I saw the hate in my mother toward my father, and after watching her put curses on others, witnessing their pain, suffering, and sometimes death, I swore my witchcraft and Voodoo would only be for protection and love. I broke that promise last night. I murdered my sister, Michael. I murdered Alejandro's mother." Maria broke down in Michael's arms. "How could you, or anybody, ever love me after this? Or trust me? I promise you, Michael, as I pray to the Archangel Michael, I will never use my powers for hate on anyone ever again."

At that moment, Alejandro left Maria's lap. He limped to Michael and hugged him. He limped back to Maria and hugged her. Then he went to his playroom. Michael looked at Maria, his forehead wrinkled with curiosity. "He has the power, Michael. It is unusual for a male. He can feel when love is needed and knows how to give it. That is the direction he is heading and why he is being protected." And they both cried, this time in gratefulness.

After minutes of silence, Michael returned to the topic still unfinished. "Maria, stop your guilt. You didn't start Andrea down her path, but something did, and you're going to tell me soon. She was escalating before she returned with the sailor. She was escalating before she left. Heroin is deadly. She was on a path to hurt someone, and the gods knew it. You pointed it out. Alejandro was in danger. I was in danger. You were in danger. She used to tell me how she was straight in Boquete over the weekend, except for the pot and beers and a line here and there. You did what you did out of love."

"Michael, I loved you last night, and I love you even more today. I must call my mother. She isn't going to believe Andrea OD'd and will want to blame someone else. She always believed in her little angel Andrea. But I don't think it was belief in her daughter; I think it was guilt because of her decision to bring our father into our lives." Michael didn't ask. The time would come.

"I think I will wait until I sign the death certificate with the official cause of death before I call. That way, she might have a harder time getting a second opinion. If she insists, she can fly a doctor in or wait until the body arrives in Panama City."

Holding hands, Maria and Michael left the veranda and peeked into the playroom just to watch Alejandro play. He had no idea his mother had died, and he would not know for a very long time. He also would not know Michael was not his father for an equally long time. But now, they were becoming a real family, something they all, as well as many others, would come to cherish.

35

MOTHER, THE TIME HAS COME AND GONE

It was approaching late morning. Michael crushed another tablet of pain medication and antibiotic for Alejandro, burying it inside a delectable chocolate brownie of Marie's baking. Within twenty minutes, he was ready for a nap free from pain; the drugs made him drowsy. His eyes resembled his stuffed Koala bear. Maria put him in his bed, took Michael by the hand, and led him into his bedroom. They laid comfortably on the bed together. As Maria cuddled under Michael's shoulder, her hand lying gently on his chest, she spoke.

"I must call my mother soon and make her aware of Andrea's death."

"I think that's wise. It's not going to be easy. The loss of a child at any age is the most unnatural grief in life. What can I do?"

"First, I need to go to the morgue and give them a positive identification of Andrea's body. Oh Michael, I am going to be sick just imagining it."

"It is a legal formality. Oh, my love, can you get through it on your own?" Michael hugged her tightly. Maria went on.

"Then I need to consult with the ER doctor and be prepared to argue with Mother over the cause of death. She will not be accepting. The denial trait runs deep in our family. I will warn the chief Hurricane Miriam is about to hit Balboa."

"You don't think she will accept it was an overdose?"

"Mother will blame you no matter what I tell her?"

"Me? Why me?"

"She still thinks you broke her precious little girl's heart, then you stole her child from our family. She tells me that every phone call. She will blame you for the overdose somehow. She will insist you be arrested immediately for murder. You might want to call Vanessa and have her warn the police in Panama City as well. She will try to bring them in, maybe even the embassy. You will need alibis." Maria hopped up onto her knees and gazed sternly into Michael's eyes.

"And I don't want you and Alejandro to go with me to the morgue. Stay here while he naps and, in case the doctor stops by to change his bandages. It should only take an hour."

"Are you sure? I think you need us for emotional support. I'm worried about you." Michael leaned up and kissed Maria.

"Alejandro witnessed me going crazy, crying, and flipping out many times in the last twenty-four hours. The morgue is not what he needs to experience on top of the rest of the trauma and confusion. It is eleven o'clock. I am sure multiple versions of Andrea's death are engulfing Balboa's breakfast bars by now, like a tsunami coming from all directions. They will blame me for her death and speculate how I killed her, but no one, other than my coven, will guess it was a Voodoo effigy. Only you and I know that for sure. Michael, assure me again, the gods, and especially you, forgive me."

Michael pulled her down into his embrace. "Someday you'll accept the fact you didn't kill her. You always told me the gods make those decisions, not us mortals. We just ask and pray to them. That was between the Archangel and Papa Ghede, and they must have agreed. You have not shared with me why Andrea turned evil and hateful, but they know. The result was out of your hands. It seems the gods understood."

"Michael, I know you will love me and forgive me, but what about the town? I don't want to be known as a murderer. They all heard me say I wanted her dead."

"By noon, the story will look like a pot of alphabet soup. The gringoes live for gossip and they know it all. I want out of this viper pit." Maria became short of breath over that statement. "But, in the end, they all saw Andrea in rare form at Pirate Beach. No one will conclude you killed your sister violently. And the gringos would never imagine you did it with a doll and a pin. "Michael raised his eyebrows, "But it would make a great scene in one of my screenplays." Michael laughed, and Maria rolled her eyes. The "viper pit" statement still distracted her. "The gods supported you and are protecting the three of us. Andrea earned her fate. "Go to the morgue and get it over with. I will be here in case the doctor stops by to check on Alejandro's wounds. Are your feet okay to walk?"

"They hurt but don't look infected. Very soon, I will tell you about Andrea's past. You might feel differently about her." Maria continued her blank and pensive stare. They kissed each other's cheeks at the same time.

"I love you, mi amor, for being strong." She showered, preparing for the second-worst experience of her life.

Maria hobbled down the steps and into the garden. She turned. Michael was in the doorway. "Michael?"

"Yes?" he answered, ready to help her with whatever she needed.

"Never mind. We can talk later." She continued to the street to catch a taxi; her feet too painful to walk any distance.

Maria set off on her dreaded journey to the hospital and the morgue. Her mind was spinning, not with concern over the morbid duty needing to be performed, but over the comment Michael made about wanting to get out of this "viper pit." *Is he going back to the States now that Andrea is dead? Will he take Alejandro with him and away from me? Am I going to wind up a lonely old spinster like my mother, crammed into an apartment with her bitter soul for the rest of my years?* For the first time in her life, Maria loved and felt loved by a man and a child. She wondered if the previous night's lovemaking was real or just out of sympathy for her. *But he did call me "mi amor."*

The hospital was four blocks away, but too far to walk. Her feet were bruised and burning. She entered the lobby and announced her name and purpose. She was escorted to the morgue. As the nurse unlocked the heavy steel door, they entered a windowless, airless room. The odor was pungent coming from those not yet embalmed. It was a smell Maria never wanted to encounter ever again. She held back from vomiting. The nurse pulled out a drawer containing Andrea's corpse, her hair burnt from her scalp. Her face and arms blistered and charred. Her body was that shade of lifeless gray she so vehemently remembered from twenty years ago.

"Ms. Blanco, can you identify the corpse?" asked the nurse.

"That is Andrea Blanco, my sister," Maria said as she sobbed, and tears raced down her cheeks. The nurse was callous, having watched this scene many times before. She attached a name tag to Andrea's toe and rolled her coarsely back into the wall like a rusty file cabinet drawer. They left. The nurse locked the metal door to contain the smell of death and to avoid any grave robbing.

"Sign here, please," said the nurse. Maria signed four documents. "And here is the jewelry we found on her body. One necklace, one bracelet, two nipple piercings and one wedding band." Maria was shocked over the last item, but whether this modest wedding band was legitimate would never be proven.

"May I speak to the doctor who read the lab testing last night? I need information to relay to our mother."

The nurse took her into a small office and told her it would be a while. He was stitching a boy beaten severely by his drunken father last night. "Somebody needs to kill that son-of-a-bitch. That little boy's a mess and it's not the first time," said the nurse with outrage in her eyes.

As Maria waited, her thoughts and feelings scattered as she contemplated the bludgeoned young child. She completed more forms needed by the government to release her sister's body to her within three days. She obtained copies of the bloodwork and X-rays. Just as she finished, the doctor entered the room.

"Ms. Blanco, my sympathies to you and your family over the death of your sister. She was so young. I understand the captain and the chief explained a lot to you this morning."

"Yes, they did. And I can interpret these levels on the lab report, and I think I understand the X-ray, but I must ask. You are absolutely positive death came from a mixture of drugs and alcohol, not burns, head wound, blood loss, or anything unexplainable?" asked Maria.

"I am positive, Ms. Blanco. No human body can endure what your sister ingested on an empty stomach in such a brief time yesterday. And only you or her friends can speculate why she would do that to herself. Personally, I would define it, in my own terms, as an 'Illicit drug, self-inflicted overdose.' I assume your family is Catholic, so let us avoid the term suicide. But anyone doing that to themselves wanted to die for some reason."

"Thank you, but my mother won't take this lightly. She will try to blame someone. May I allow her to call you today? She is an OR nurse in Panama City and will be able to talk as a reasonably educated person to you," Maria said. "But I have a few quick questions left. Did you test for HIV or any STDs? She was using needles on a regular basis and has been sexually active with multiple partners over the years." Maria was worried for Michael, and now for herself, after last night in his bed.

"We did, Ms. Blanco. She was not HIV positive, and she was clear of hepatitis or any needle-related infections. She also had no STDs. Her heart simply gave out from the current mixture and long-term build-up caused by the variety and volume of drugs and alcohol she consumed. The hit on the head was minor. She lost very little blood and showed no sign of concussion or internal head bleeds. The burns would have been painful for her today, but they were not life threatening. However, Ms. Blanco, she was pregnant, which I did not tell the police. I thought that to be a family matter, and one that had nothing to do with her death."

"Pregnant," Maria said, startled, as she stood up. "Did you attempt to save the baby?"

"Ms. Blanco, it was six hours after her death we discovered her pregnancy from the X-ray, way too late to save the fetus. And from the size of the fetus, it was less than two months old. I doubt your sister was aware she was carrying a child, and I will be blunt. The negative effects on the fetus with that kind of drug use would have been traumatic. I am sadly confident the child would have been mentally and physically deformed at birth, and an addict of some sort. Does she have any other children?" asked the doctor.

"She does, but she doesn't have custody," Maria responded. "The father told me she stayed relatively drug-free during that pregnancy. But other than that brief period of time, her drug use was always excessive, and it accelerated over the last year. Her son appears healthy and is approaching two years."

"If he appears fine and is doing the things a two-year old should be doing, it sounds like he is good. But if you want to be sure, I will be glad to have our pediatrician give him a complete physical."

Maria thought about her attitude towards Balboa doctors, *'I wouldn't let those doctors touch my dog, if I had one."*

"Thank you, Doctor, but he's okay. But before I finish, I must ask something of you."

"Yes, what is it?"

"This town lives for stories. I ask you to only expose the cause of death on the Death Certificate, 'Illicit drug, self-inflicted overdose.' Nothing more, especially the pregnancy. My family would be forced to take action if you did."

"No, Ms. Blanco, however, the Death Certificate will be of public record. Everything else is confidential. If exposed, I could lose my license. I will even take her file home with me until people lose interest, which won't be long. I assure you, only cause of death."

"Thank you Where do I go from here with my sister's body?"

Maria took the doctor's name and phone number for her mother. She thanked him for his kindness. The doctor walked Maria to the clerk's office who explained her options. Notarized instructions must be presented within three days for release. If Andrea was to be buried in Balboa, embalming was not necessary. But if she were buried outside of Balboa, and transported by bus or domestic airline, the body must be embalmed due to the odor. The amount quoted was reasonable. Maria told the clerk she would have the money and paperwork by the end of tomorrow. She took a cab home. Emotionally drained, she discerned how difficult this call with her mother would be.

It was past noon. The phone started to ring with questions about what happened. Some were calls of genuine sympathy. Maria limped in the door.

"How did it go, mi amor?" asked Michael with Alejandro in his arms and compassion on his face.

"Frightening and deeply disturbing." Maria hugged Michael and took Alejandro from his embrace. "Do you know how lucky you are, little guy? You came so close to not having a life." She sobbed again.

"Yes, it was close yesterday. The doctor came by. She said his lungs sound fine, and his legs are healing nicely."

"No, I mean Alejandro could have been born damaged."

"Explain."

"The X-Ray showed Andrea was two months pregnant. The doctor is convinced, had Andrea continued her lifestyle, the baby would have died or been deformed. But she didn't know she was pregnant like when she was pregnant with Alejandro." Maria realized if she continued, she might jeopardize the new family life beginning to grow. She decided to continue. "Andrea's pregnancy with Alejandro was planned with a purpose. Remember how healthy she became in Boquete after she broke up with you? She had that breakup planned. She purposely provoked you. She went to Boquete to find healthy unsuspecting 'sperm donors' to impregnate her. She needed your money so Alejandro and I would be supported. Then she would take him from you. Oh Michael, I am sorry you must hear it like this. I don't want you to feel differently towards Alejandro, but he is probably not your son. Please tell me you don't feel differently towards him. It's not his fault. He loves you so much. And so do I, more and more each moment."

"I knew what she was doing, Maria. I had a vasectomy fifteen years ago. It's not improbable, it's impossible for him to be my son. That is why Vanessa and I blocked the DNA test. My feelings towards you and Alejandro have not changed."

"But the dead fetus, let us keep that between us." Maria broke out in tears yet again, with Alejandro now in her arms. "I must call Mother. Please sit in the garden and tell any visitors we need to talk to family today and make funeral arrangements? Let the gossip go wild for a few hours. I am sure the police and the hospital are being pumped for information. No one is of any concern to me right now, except you two and Mother."

"Are you sad, Michael? Did you love my sister? She was wonderful."

"I did at one time, when I met the Andrea you knew as a young girl. But it was difficult when I got to know Balboa Andrea. We had fond memories of fun and lust, and I believe she wanted it to work for a while, but something kept pushing her away. That made me sad. But now, no, I am not feeling sadness and grief. I feel relief because you and Alejandro are safer on the earth, and I love you both. Andrea's death isn't a surprise. I knew her death would come early. I am grateful to you and the gods she went alone. I am sad for you and your mother."

"I understand." Maria kissed Michael. Alejandro smiled and hugged them both.

Michael and Alejandro went to the garden to greet visitors. Maria dialed the call. "Hello, Mother, it's Maria. You have time to talk?" she asked.

"I do, honey. I'm working night shift this week at the hospital. What is it? Your voice is quivering. Are you sick? Is Alejandro okay?" Miriam questioned.

"Mother, Andrea's dead." Maria said it quickly, trying not to break down.

"Maria, whoa, back up. Our Andrea is dead? Are you sure she's not just missing? Did that stupid gringo's boat sink? Maybe she's still…"

"Mother, stop. Andrea overdosed last night on her boyfriend's boat."

The pause on the phone felt like an eternity. Maria could hear Miriam sobbing, then it broke into an all-out wail. "Maria, I…I can't talk. I can't breathe. Tell me I'm dreaming. Tell me I'm going to wake up." Miriam let out another almost violent wail of grief.

"No, Mother, this is real. Our Andrea is gone from us. It happened late last night."

Maria just let Miriam cry as long as she needed, not disturbing her more by describing details. The crying went on for minutes, then silence. "Mother, are you still there?"

"I'm here." Miriam began in a dark voice that continued to rise in intensity with every new word she uttered. "I'll kill him, fucking Michael. He put something in her drink or made her try some new drug, didn't he? Those damn worthless gringos. They're killers," yelled Miriam into the phone.

"Mother, please, let me talk. This is hard enough without you jumping to conclusions." Miriam went silent. Maria proceeded to tell her the whole story from the beach to the morgue. Then Miriam started her interrogation, pocked with denial.

"Maria, our little Andrea would never do drugs like that. She was having such an enjoyable time with that man on the boat. She told me so in postcards and phone calls from all over the world. She was excited about seeing her baby, and we talked about how we could get him back. We had a plan, I mean, a real plan. That gringo Michael has schemed and brainwashed you, dear. He did this, didn't he? He's the one that slipped drugs into her drink to make it look like an overdose. He was still in love with her, and he lost it, didn't he? That fucker's dead. Get me something for his doll."

"Mother, stop, stop. No, no." Maria yelled into the phone. "Open your eyes, Mother. I watched her behavior firsthand. She was a mess. She was a drug addict, a drug dealer, a drug smuggler, a whore, and a scammer."

"How can you say such things about your little sister, Maria? She was loved and respected by everyone she met. Except that evil gringo, Michael. She told me all about the things he did to her. Even pulled a gun on all of you one night, even the baby."

"Mother, you are completely wrong. She was a habitual liar. Andrea had so much pain and anger inside from the stillbirth. We were there when it happened. She never got over it. Drugs, sex, and alcohol were the only things she had to drown out that horrendous pain. Mother, Michael was never around her at any time yesterday, other than to make sure her boyfriend was sober enough to take us to the beach in his boat. When you see the lab reports, then decide whether Michael had anything to do with it. I have the doctor's phone number. Call him yourself, please. I insist. You must. And Mother, she and the sailor were splitting up. I heard them bicker. And in the morgue, I saw the multitude of track marks on her arms and between her toes from the needles. Those weren't involuntary."

"No, I still don't trust Michael. He had something to do with this so he could take our baby to the States. I bet he was trying to break them up."

"Mother, at the beach yesterday, Alejandro almost drowned. Andrea was supposed to watch him while I went to the bathroom. But when I returned, she was drinking and flirting with a teenage boy. When I pulled him from the ocean, he was blue, his lungs filled with seawater. Andrea was so high she didn't care. I was angry. I told her I wanted to kill her, and you know my powers. If anybody killed her, I did, I killed my sister." Maria did not have the courage to tell her about the doll; she couldn't be sure whether her coven's protection spell had taken Andrea out of the picture, or it was her curse. Or maybe it wasn't either; or maybe it was everything combined. Marie cried hysterically.

Miriam realized her daughter was in as much of a grieving state as she was, then topped off with guilt. Miriam collected herself from the Blanco trait of denial. "Honey, honey, stop. Let me call the doctor and get more information so we are sure what happened. It sounds like the heroin started with the sailor. Then her return to Balboa pushed her over the edge. But I still blame Michael. He started all this when he took her baby from her. I will get him for this. He killed your sister. Had he accepted her the way she was..."

"Mother, stop. You know the evil and hate she had in her heart from Daddy and the stillborn. Daddy did this to her. That is why you never taught her witchcraft or gave her powers. Mother, I love you. And I love Alejandro. And Michael is a good father and protects me and our little boy. And, Mother, Michael, and I, I think, we have fallen in love," Maria concluded.

Miriam was silent for a long time. Maria asked if she was still on the line.

"Yes, I'm here. Maria, no matter what you say, that gringo is going to take a child belonging to our family to the States. That boy is the only thing we have left of Andrea. I will not let that happen. I will put a nasty curse on him if he tries. He will die, and the baby will be given to me as the closest relative. Then you can come home, and we'll raise him together. My grandson is Panamanian, not American. Be ready."

"Mother, let me talk to him. But remember, Andrea died less than twelve hours ago. And Mother, you underestimate my powers." With those words, Maria confronted her mother's powers for the first time.

"Are you challenging me, my child?" Miriam let out a dry, mirthless chuckle. "I would be careful if I were you, little one. I'm your mother, and a High Priestess. You challenge me, my dear, and you challenge the gods." Miriam went silent.

"Mother, I love you with all my heart, but the gods may not find your cause worthy on this, because you're wrong, you're tainted. You'll have to go past the blue cobalt sword of the Archangel Michael to get at him, or the baby, or me. Along with three other powerful witches and a shaman, united in a coven with me as the High Priestess, we positioned Michael and Alejandro on a pentagram, naked to the full moon on the sand, and placed a protection spell on them a year ago, after Andrea threatened both of them by her words and deeds." Maria waited for her mother's response.

"I don't know whether to be angry with you or proud of you. I have taught you well from generations of your grandmothers, and if you thought your sister was placing my grandson in that much danger, then I respect your spell. But why the gringo, why protect him?" Miriam asked. "Andrea would have disposed of him for us."

"Because our family's not wealthy, Mother. I'm so proud of you and how you raised us and provided for us. Your grandson has a chance to be fostered in a protected and healthy environment. Michael can give him opportunities beyond our wildest dreams. That's why we must keep him safe, so he can keep his son, your grandson, and your remaining daughter safe." Maria stopped and the reality of Andrea's death arose from that statement.

Miriam finally broke the mourning. "Not even I can go through that cobalt orb, because I know you, my love. I'm sure you performed that ceremony with intense allegiance to God's most powerful protector. But if Michael takes my grandson out of this country, whether you go with him or not, I assure you, the gods will permit me to, at least, influence him, if I can't harm him." She laughed, a laugh reminding Maria so much of Andrea.

"Mother, I implore you, promise to leave him alone, at least until Alejandro is an adult. You will feel differently when you witness Alejandro's life and Michael's influence on it. Don't do anything that will hurt Alejandro's future in any way. I love that child and always will. And I love Michael." Maria waited for her answer.

"I promise, my child, for the sake of my grandson and out of respect for your judgement, I will wait until Alejandro is self-sufficient. Maria, I wish I could be there right now so we could hold each other. I love you, my child," said Miriam.

The rest of the conversation focused on Andrea's burial. Miriam insisted on a Catholic mass and funeral in Panama City, where her family could gather to mourn her loss. Andrea did have a cut on her head, a burnt scalp, and a charred face and body, so they decided on a closed casket. The story would be there was a storm at sea, she slipped and hit her head, and then the mast fell and crushed her skull. But if it hit the papers, then the truth was the truth. Miriam insisted Maria's "gringo" did not attend the funeral. She did not even want him in the same city as her family. It was obvious, Miriam hated men as much as Andrea, and like Andrea, she was unwilling to take responsibility for her actions. Her decision to follow her lust instead of her brain and marry that wicked bastard and child rapist, Raoul, was what ultimately killed Andrea and rotted Miriam's heart.

Maria would make plans to fly her departed sister to Panama City. Miriam would organize the funeral. They told each other once again, they loved each other, choking up so much they could hardly say goodbye. Miriam and Maria disconnected.

* * * *

The next two days were physically and emotionally arduous. Maria shared the plans with Michael and why he was not invited. He understood. But Miriam wanted Alejandro to attend. He was the only male she would ever love. Michael was suspicious of Miriam's motives, so he put Vanessa and the attorney general's office in Panama City on high alert.

By Happy Hour, the town bustled with the most dramatic rumors to ever hit the streets in Balboa. Some of the more popular rumors included, Andrea was murdered by Michael or her sister, or both, because of the near-drowning of Alejandro at Pirate Beach; Andrea was murdered by her sailor boyfriend, because she set fire to his boat, and Interpol is scanning the seas; Michael murdered her because she was getting custody of Alejandro; Andrea committed suicide, because she couldn't get her son back; or the sailor murdered her, because Andrea and Michael were getting back together. Everybody had a theory, or two, or three, and with no newspapers or TV stations in Balboa, they were all plausible. Antonio informed Michael of the rumors.

As Michael entered The Deck at Happy Hour, thirty-six hours after Andrea's death, the place went silent. A scant few approached him to give Maria their sympathies, most waited to ask questions. Michael spotted Leo, a twenty something bearded gringo who taught Spanish and wrote a monthly bilingual newsletter containing the gossip in Balboa. In Michael's opinion, Leo always attempted to report the truth, as hard as that was in Balboa. He waved to Leo to join him.

"Leo, do you have a moment?" asked Michael.

"I do for you. What's up, Michael?" Leo knew Andrea was dead, but like everyone else, no details. And for a young kid with a newsletter, mostly about missing cats and cabs routinely running into statues, poles, or an occasional street dog, this was colossal.

"Leo, I will give you exclusive rights to this story. I want you to print a special edition of your newsletter, for which I will pay. I don't want it to be 'Michael said this,' and 'Michael said that.' I will tell you what happened according to official sources, eyewitnesses, the police, and the hospital. I will give you a list of people I insist you interview to confirm or change the details. I am skipping Happy Hour tonight to avoid being hounded and misquoted. I want you to come to my veranda with me and I will give you details. I must approve the story before you publish it. I will pay you $500 if it can be ready for distribution by tomorrow night at six. Are you ready to start?"

"Let's go, Michael." He was excited. He felt like a real reporter, and the money was great.

Michael stood to leave with Leo by his side. "Excuse me, uh, excuse me." Leo clinked a glass with a knife. The room went silent immediately when they saw it was Michael about to speak. "Leo has agreed to write the official story behind what happened early yesterday morning. Since neither Maria nor I were there, I can only tell him what I know from the police and the hospital. Leo will talk to people involved to confirm the facts, just as any good reporter, like Leo, would do. I will not answer any questions to avoid confusion. Please be patient. Leo will publish the story tomorrow."

Leo smiled, feeling proud of himself that Michael called him a good reporter. As Michael and Leo walked out, nobody said a word until they were gone. Then the gossip resumed in full force.

By Happy Hour the next day, Leo's story hit. He also gave the funeral arrangements. The next morning, Maria prepared to go to Panama City. She and Alejandro would be gone for a week. As they sat on the veranda, Alejandro ate his oatmeal, most of it being on his face. Michael looked at his son, then at Maria, "Assure me there is no way your mother can arrange to abduct him in Panama City and hide him somewhere. Promise me, Maria, or I will not let him go with you. If she does, I know you will not have the courage to return and face me, so I will lose you both. Promise me that can't happen."

Maria's voice began to quiver. "Michael, I must return the question. Now that Andrea's dead and you are Alejandro's only parent, you can take him out of this town or even return to the States. I know you hate it here, and I can't force you to stay. If my mother kidnaps him, you and Vanessa would have her in jail so fast."

"All of that is true, Maria. Vanessa is already on alert if your mother tries anything ridiculous. You must let me know if she is plotting something. And yes, I am permitted to legally take Alejandro to the States, and I think that's what I am going to do."

Maria's face went flush as she fought back the tears. Two days ago, her dreams came true. Now she was going to lose the two men she loved most in the world, in addition to her sister.

"Vanessa also told me," Michael continued, "for a single Panamanian woman with no legal children, and no land or home ownership, it would be impossible for the US to grant a visa." Maria looked down at the floor. She placed her finger under her nose to hold back her tears. She closed her eyes, but when she did that squeezed out her tears. They streamed down her face. Michael continued, knowing she was near heartbreak. "Vanessa also told me the only legal strategy left was for us to be married and for you to legally adopt Alejandro before we leave Panama, with my permission, of course."

Maria opened her eyes. Michael was on one knee. He grasped her hand. With a two-dollar ring from the souvenir shop, he proposed. "Maria, will you be my wife and the mother of Alejandro?" Tears were running down Michael's face. Maria lifted him from his knees as she ascended. Maria threw her arms around his neck and said yes without hesitation. They kissed. Alejandro, clueless as to what was happening, but getting used to people crying a lot lately, continued to eat his oatmeal, a raisin stuck on his chin.

"Oh Michael," said Maria. "I thought I loved you when we first met, but I was sure of it when I watched you orchestrate the protection of Alejandro from inside a Balboa jail cell, removing him from the danger of his mother. I didn't think you had a chance to beat Andrea and the politicians. But when you did, I thought, *And I thought I had powers.*

"Maria, I loved you the first day I met you, but I was terrified you were like Andrea. After I saw you protect him the night Andrea was flinging plates and glasses, then we spent those nights at Hotel Tortuga, I wanted you in my life forever. But it felt inappropriate, and I knew the problems it would cause between you and your sister." Michael and Maria kissed again.

"Let me show you what I remember doing with my parents." Michael picked up Alejandro. The three of them put their lips together in a triad and kissed. They all smiled, all except Alejandro, who laughed and said, "Again." It was time for Alejandro to call Maria 'Mommy.'

* * * *

Ready to catch the last Air Panama flight of the day at 4:00 P.M., Alejandro in his stroller, Michael, and Maria arm in arm, made their way to the morgue. The hospital placed Andrea's wooden casket in the back of one of the city's large pickup trucks, driven by Antonio and his girlfriend. Maria signed the release forms, and the three of them followed the casket to the airport. As they approached, they were shocked. There was a huge crowd around the entrance. People lined the fences of the airfield, as well as down the street. Six men came to the truck and carried the casket to the cargo hold of the small prop plane. As Maria, Michael, and Alejandro made their way to the entrance, the crowd parted with royal respect. Some people stepped into the farewell tunnel and embraced the family, giving them their love and sympathies. People gave Maria and Michael bouquets of flowers. Some gave single roses of black, purple, and maroon. Some laid flowers in the stroller on Alejandro's lap. All were bereaved, most were crying. People kissed Alejandro on the forehead and made the sign of the cross as they blessed the child. One of Andrea's oldest and dearest friends approached and placed the palm of her hand on Maria's cheek. With deep emotion, she said, "Maria, Michael, I'm so sorry this happened. It is tragic."

Maria replied, "Thank you, I am sorry as well. But the true tragedy is she was loved by so many, and she did this to herself. We will all miss her."

The woman hesitated. "Maria, many of us knew Andrea for years, and this didn't catch any of us by surprise." She choked up, then finished, "Andrea was always Andrea, and she will always be our Andrea." They both hugged and wept.

The local airline, whose employees knew Andrea well, escorted Maria, Alejandro, and Michael to the front of the security line. Maria's tickets were made ready for her in advance.

"Ms. Blanco," said the employee escort. "We have reversed the charge for you, her son, and your sister. This is our gift to you and your family. We all knew her, and though she could be a handful, she made us laugh, and we loved her for it. You can wait in this private room, and we will help you board before the others."

"Thank you so much for helping us with your kindness," said Maria.

When it was time to board, Maria and Michael expressed their love once again. As they walked to the plane, people stood at the fence, some waving, some praying, some on their knees with a rosary. Flowers and bouquets were thrown over the fence and onto the airfield. Several people held hand-made signs with 'We love you, Andrea.'

The plane took off. The pilot circled back and over the airport. Maria could see the crowd was larger than she thought. It reached down the two entry streets and filled the cross street at the end of the runway. Flowers lay beautifully strewn along the fences; some still being thrown as people waved to the plane.

Maria sat quietly with Alejandro on her lap. There was nothing she could do to hold back her grief and her appreciation. But the people and flowers and the love displayed below perplexed her. Why was Andrea so loved in Balboa? Most people experienced or heard of the corrupt and hateful side of her. She recalled her little sister, so happy and sweet as a child, playing beautiful piano pieces and already having that silly giggle. All was happiness until the incident that doomed her soul, the incident that only she and her mother shared with Andrea. The incident only two of them now have buried deeply in their hearts, the other having it buried deeply in the earth.

Maria recalled it was two years after the hurt, her mother took her precious daughters to Balboa for a vacation and Andrea refused to return with them to Panama City. Perhaps Andrea sensed the essence of Balboa, the powerful emanation of its aura. It somehow understood the irreparable damage and the internal pain she suffered, and it accepted the extreme measures she needed to cover it over. Maybe those people who visited and remained in Balboa did so because they needed a place to hide, a place where they would be accepted unconditionally. It was a town filled with broken souls, bound together by their inability to cope in the world of painful memories and lost loves. Like her friend said, "Andrea was always Andrea, but she was our Andrea."

36

LET'S WRAP THE PACKAGE WITH A BOW ON TOP

A week passed since Maria and Alejandro flew to Panama City. It was good for Maria to see her mother and her family, especially in the wake of Andrea's heartbreaking death. Maria and her mother, when asked, stuck to the story of the shipwreck in a storm off the coast of Balboa. But all of Balboa knew what really happened. The truth would be uncovered someday. But besides all that, without a doubt, Alejandro was the star of the show at the funeral. And the constant question to Maria was, "Why does the boy have no gringo features?"

Michael waited anxiously at the airport for the return of his son and soon-to-be wife. He wanted to greet them warmly and help them home. He was laying odds Maria had done some shopping while in the city. He gave her a wad of cash and told her to spend it all. He was the only one in the terminal to welcome them back, but in fairness, no one knew when they were returning. Andrea's death was already old news in Balboa. However, she would remain a barroom legend for years, her life story embellished increasingly with each new generation.

When Maria and Alejandro paraded through the exit gate, there stood Michael against a faint yellow concrete wall. "There's Daddy," Maria said and let go of Alejandro's hand. He ran full speed to Michael, both with their outstretched arms reaching for each other, and both with monstrous grins. Michael picked up his son and spun him around. Alejandro hugged his father around the neck as tight as love itself. Maria came over and gave Michael a passionate kiss, and then another. The smiles would not disappear from any of their faces, especially Alejandro's.

"How are his legs and your feet?" was Michael's first question.

"Healed, we have some scars, but the pain and bleeding are gone. Mother had a doctor come to the house to check on us daily. She really is a caring woman, just not for you," Maria said with a sarcastic smirk. "I did some shopping. We will need things delivered." This time, Michael was the one who smiled. It felt different for Maria to spend his money, rather than Andrea. Maria did it out of love for others, like Michael, Alejandro, her mother, Antonio, and his girlfriend. But she did buy things for herself.

They gathered the luggage, then a few boxes needing to be shipped via cargo. They were placed in a pile by the exit door. A young boy appeared.

"I will watch those for you, Ms. Blanco, and have them delivered to your house. I am so sorry about your sister," said the teenage boy with compassion and respect.

"Oh, son, that is sweet of you. Don't start me crying again," Maria responded with a hug and a loving smile. Michael attempted to give the boy ten dollars for his help, but he refused.

The three of them pushed through the crowd. It was chaos: porters barking, tourists being jammed into small shuttle buses with their luggage thrown on top. It was fun watching tourists in a state of confusion and panic. Michael found one empty seat on a dirty Volkswagen bus, helped Maria into the shuttle, and gave her the house keys. He then placed Alejandro on her lap.

"Daddy," said Alejandro as he reached out his arms, thinking he was leaving his father behind again.

"No honey, Daddy will meet us at home." Alejandro looked scared. He wasn't old enough to form sentences or understand completely what was said. "My feet are still too sore to walk all that way, Michael. You take Alejandro home with you."

"It's raining a bit. I will walk or jog alongside the bus so he can see me. He'll understand. But if you must drop off tourists somewhere else, I will veer off and meet you at home."

The walk was four blocks, and Michael would arrive before her. The light mist saturated the air. It felt refreshing on Michael's face, in contrast to the perspiration on his brow during those hot, dusty Balboa afternoons. It was like a cleansing. Life felt harmonious and peaceful, as if a new life were born.

As he approached the house, he saw Maria stepping over suitcases and parcels on the garden porch. The kid did a wonderful job. She dropped Alejandro's backpack in his room, and for the first time, put her backpack in Michael's room. When Michael walked in the door, and before he could bring any of the shopping spree in, Alejandro again charged his father with outstretched arms. Michael scooped him up. Alejandro would not let go. It was pure love and devotion from each to each.

Then Alejandro remembered something in Maria's backpack. He squirmed for Michael to put him down. He grabbed Maria by the finger, leading her to her backpack. Maria knew what he wanted right away, no doubt whatsoever. She gave it to him, and he dashed for his playroom to dribble the new mini basketball his grandmother purchased for him in the big city. The hoop was in one of the boxes.

As he did, Maria slid under Michael's arm to watch. She hugged him, kissed him, told him she loved him, and started to cry again.

"Is everything okay, Maria?" Michael said in a concerned tone. "Are you having second thoughts about marrying me and leaving your family here in Panama? You just spent a week with them. I hope not, but I would understand."

"Oh, no, just the opposite," replied Maria. "I realized how lucky and how blessed I am to have the two of you and escaping Balboa is the answer to that little boy's success and happiness."

"Yes, it is, Maria. He doesn't belong here. Balboa would eventually bring him down," responded Michael.

"I agree, but Michael when I left, people were so loving toward Andrea and me. I wish you could have seen the crowd from the air. This town does have its place in the sun. I have had a lot of time to ponder the direction we are heading. What about your children and grandchildren? What will they think of me and Alejandro? Will they see us coming between them and their father's love?"

"Okay stop," Michael answered quickly. "First, we will have lunch, then Alejandro goes down for a nap, and we do too, sort of. I want to kiss you for a while and make love to you. Then we talk. All is fine. Is that okay with you? I missed you more than I ever imagined I would. Love hurts sometimes, in a good way."

"Sounds perfect. Do we have anything in the fridge since you were a bachelor this week?" Maria smiled and went to the kitchen to prepare lunch, needing to be creative with what Michael had left her. They ate, Alejandro conked in a hurry from his already long travel day, and Maria led Michael by the hand to the bedroom with a tender smile on her face.

* * * *

As the weeks passed, Michael and Maria talked about their move to the States, and Maria informed Michael she would not reveal Andrea's secret until the plane was in the air to their new home. Vanessa completed the necessary paperwork for their marriage and Alejandro's adoption. It would be three months before all was in place. Michael's hotel had closed three years before. For the small profits it generated, it was not worth the hassle from the municipality, immigration, tax departments, and the local labor authorities. In the end, it was always the land it sat on that was the profit. Michael put the property up for sale.

All fell into place except for one thing. Would Alejandro, as he grew, continue to believe Maria to be his mother? Should they keep him from the truth about Andrea? And how did they keep him from discovering Michael was not his biological father? They could never bring him back to Balboa, not even to Panama City to meet his grandmother. But he would be curious and would seek the truth.

Michael thought about the problem. He explored several scenarios. When would Alejandro be old enough to understand, not be confused or devastated? As he and Maria had breakfast, an idea entered his head.

"Maria, I have it, but it needs Vanessa's cooperation. My life has always been ethical, but not always, let's say, 'by the book.' I will call her later today." Michael was excited, but they both agreed someday their son would need to know the truth.

Michael called Vanessa. "Vanessa, it's Michael Harper. All going well? Any hitches with immigration?"

"Not a one, Michael, but as I am working on this, I realize how much I will miss you. Your escapades break my monotony. I still laugh when I think of the mayor's face when I took him down in front of his staff. I thought he was going to cry like a scolded child." They both laughed.

"Vanessa, I have something I want to run by you. Is there a way we can remove Andrea's name from Alejandro's birth certificate and change it to Maria's?" Michael waited for her answer.

"Michael, it's a recorded document in Panama City, and cannot possibly be changed. And part of the packet I will give you will contain his birth certificate in order to obtain his dual citizenship. I assume you do not want Alejandro to know Maria is not his biological mother, even though she will be his legally adopted mother. That will be confusing to him someday when he finds out," said Vanessa. "But he will never remember Andrea, thank goodness."

"That is true. Would you want to know if someone like Andrea was your mother? That is why I am asking. What if, when I get to the States, I have a replica made with Maria as his mother?"

"I assume you mean a forgery. Michael, though I understand your purpose, and it is a good purpose, but it is a bad idea. If he ever finds out, say from a DNA test, you are not his biological father, that means his mother, Maria, cheated on you. That is not fair to either of them. Besides, the US will verify his Panamanian birth certificate with us to be recorded in your jurisdiction, along with Andrea's death certificate, Maria's birth certificate, your marriage license, and his adoption papers. She will need those documents to obtain her US citizenship."

"No, that is not what I am asking. I can have one replicated in the States by a forgery artist I know. I have no intention of recording the forgery. I just want one to give to Alejandro if he needs it for minor things, like sports teams or unimportant events. For school and college registrations, driver's licenses, passports, and such, we will prepare his paperwork for him in legal fashion. He won't review it."

"Well, I don't know…"

"Vanessa, I promise not to break the law. I want to spare him the confusion until the time is right. The kid needs a break, for a while anyway." Michael waited for her response.

"Michael, for minor events, fine. But anything important, slip in the real one. He could lose his citizenship."

"Okay, Vanessa, that will work until the time comes, but I want to run one more thing past you. What if we Americanize his name legally to Alexander? Is that easy?"

"It's amazingly easy if you and Maria both agree. But why would you do that? Maybe I'm being too proud of my heritage, but Alejandro Harper sounds more distinguished and unique than Alexander Harper. It is melodic, it flows. They are both good names, but the girls will love the Latin name. And we both know he will look Latin as he matures."

"You are right. I should not strip him of his heritage. Are we still on for November first? I would love to have Alejandro and Maria home with my family for the holidays."

"All is set, Michael. Plan your transportation and reserve your airline tickets. I should complete everything by the end of September, and you can sign the paperwork in the last week of October. I wish you and Maria the best and give you my love. You both saved that child's life. Keep me informed of his progress. I will miss you."

"You were part of that, Vanessa. We all saved his life, but we couldn't save his mother's life, could we?" said Michael.

"No, but we saved the woman God wanted as his mother. She is safe and with him now. And the father God wanted is with him as well. As you pointed out to the town, 'it says so on the birth certificate'." Michael smiled, thanked Vanessa, and they hung up.

Since Andrea's death, Balboa held the family in high esteem, accepting them into their clan. But Michael and Maria knew, from the day of Alejandro's conception, all events that unfolded were about him and what he would become for the lives of many. Divinity had picked Michael and Maria as his mentors and protectors.

37

HISTORY IS SCATTERED ON THE TABLE

Michael, Maria, and Alejandro left Balboa unceremoniously, no parties, few good-byes. It was a cloudless day. A fresh ocean breeze streamed through the house. Antonio and his girlfriend helped them to the airport with their luggage. It wasn't much. No furniture, no pots and pans, no linens, and no big toys. Only a few pieces of clothing along with Michael's guitar and Alejandro's traveling needs, especially his stuffed monkey. They hugged Antonio and his girlfriend. Maria gave her a special prayer only she would understand.

The plane took off and circled Balboa. It seemed ghostly silent. As they peered over that beautiful blue part of the Caribbean, they caught their last glimpse of the home where life and death inhabited side by side. Mixed emotions streamed through their hearts. Maria held Alejandro on her lap as he looked quietly out the window, fascinated by the view and completely unaware he was moving to a new life, a new world. Maria held tight to Michael's arm. No tears, just a hollow feeling, like standing over the casket of an old dear friend.

In Panama City, the airport employees and taxi drivers were all business. Michael and Maria dragged their luggage awkwardly to the exit door, where a cab driver, with an air of aggravation, helped them with their possessions. The cabby knew, with all that luggage, he could only carry one unprofitable fare in his van.

They went straight to their five-star hotel, checked in, and stored their luggage in the Bell Captain's closet. They immediately taxied to Vanessa's office where she had the paperwork ready and organized, but first things first. Unknown to anyone except Michael's family in the States, Vanessa introduced them to her judge who married them, plainly and simply, with Alejandro in Maria's arms. Then they signed adoption papers as well as Alejandro and Maria's passports and visas. They were given a copy of Andrea's death certificate and Alejandro and Maria's birth certificates.

"There you go, Michael. I congratulate the three of you and, Ms. Blanco, my deepest sympathies for the loss of your sister. I am sorry I was rough on her, but I was doing my job. Your boy looks healthy and happy. And he is beautiful," said Vanessa as she gave them hugs. "I wish you happiness and success in your new life."

"Mrs. Harper," Michael said with a smile. "Her name is Maria Harper." Maria smiled as she pulled Alejandro's head into her shoulder.

Michael, Maria, and Alejandro, officially a legal family, spent the next two days playing in the hotel pool and having wonderful meals. They visited the Canal Zone, where Alejandro saw the big freighters and cruise ships. They rode in a small duck boat up the tributaries of the canal where they saw monkeys, toucans, caiman, and capybaras. Alejandro loved it.

On the ride back to the hotel, they passed the Chinese Embassy. Maria wondered in what house her great-grandmother, Etienne, was a Hattian servant. She would tell Michael the story later, for this area of the canal zone is where it all started early in the century. It was where her ancestor's story started and now, for her in Panama, was ending. It was another empty feeling knowing this might be the last time she would see her family and her mother.

Michael stayed in touch with his youngest daughter, Sadie, who worked closely with Vanessa on the paperwork for tickets and immigration protocol, plus she worked with Michael coordinating their arrival plans. Maria asked a million questions about Michael's whole family, the new city she was moving to, how they would make money, and on and on. Michael assured her all was under control.

"Maria, are you sure you don't want to visit your mother before we leave? It is breaking my heart for both of you to not say good-bye."

"I made my decision. I never imagined I would feel this happy and have a husband and child I love so much. Mother will tell me I am making a mistake. I love her because she is my mother, but I don't like her as a person, even though I understand her hatred. I pity her. But once on the plane, I will begin to share with you our family history and secrets, as promised."

The following morning, they went to the airport. Alejandro was in awe of the big jets and the abundance of people. He never saw so many people who all looked so different. And even though travel complications occur frequently, especially in this situation, Vanessa and Sadie did their jobs perfectly, both for departure from Panama and Atlanta immigration. Sadie even arranged for a Delta representative to meet them as they deplaned in case of any confusion or issues.

The plane took off. Michael, Maria, and Alejandro peered out the window at the sprawling buildings of Panama City. She held her men's hands and closed her eyes as they flew farther and farther from her former home.

Within thirty minutes, Alejandro was asleep from the Dramamine hidden in his chocolate chip cookie. Maria propped his head on the pillow on her lap and covered him with his Big Bird blanket. He looked so soft and innocent with no idea of his future. He hugged his stuffed monkey which was almost as cute as him.

"Michael, it is time to tell you some family history, but it will never be discussed again once we land in the States," said Maria. "And this is not a request. This is a demand."

"Oh no," said Michael. "Married three days, heading for the States, and you have already become a demanding American woman." Maria rammed her shoulder into his and they both laughed playfully. "But can I write about it someday?"

"You will need to change the location and the names, and if asked, I will say you made it up."

"I am a writer. I always make things up. It's a deal," agreed Michael, "and the profits will go towards our children's educations."

"Our children? "Asked Maria. "We only have one and neither of us can have another."

"Not anymore, you now have nine, Grandma Maria." Maria grabbed Michael's face and kissed him. "Oh my, do you think they will like me?"

"No, they will love you. Now, start your story, mi amor. I want to hear it all."

"In 1916, my great-grandmother, Etienna Gabriel, was thirteen and in danger due to a rebellion in Haiti, so her mother, Jesula, saved her by trafficking her from Haiti to the Canal Zone as an indentured slave. She was trained in Voodoo at an early age by her mother. She was then purchased by one of China's ambassadors, then raped by his brother, which resulted in the birth of my grandmother. She then married my grandfather, a Panamanian doctor, and obtained her degree in nursing. She was also, of course, trained in Voodoo."

"So that's where the line of health care providers started in your family."

"Correct, and my great-grandmother was so proud since she came to Panama as a slave from Haiti only one generation prior. My grandmother was named Jesula, after my great-grandmother back in Haiti."

"Did your great-grandmother ever see her mother in Haiti again?"

"No, Etienna never heard a word, but she sent word through the spirits. Jesula had two children, but her son died in early childhood, leaving only her daughter, Miriam, my mother, who became a nurse and studied Voodoo. Miriam fell in love with a handsome, but nasty dock worker for purely sexual reasons. He was our father, Raoul. He was a drunk and a ruffian who stayed away from us most of the time. He would beat my mother, but only hit Andrea and me if we tried to intervene."

"So that was why Andrea was so hateful?"

"No, there's more." Maria went on with her story, telling Michael details about Andrea's virtuoso musical talent at age fifteen and her chance at the Panamanian Conservatory of Music and the Junior Symphony.

"But one day," Maria started, with old feelings rising quickly, "when Mother was working and I was studying at my grandmother's house, Andrea was home alone, practicing for a piano recital to get her into the

Conservatory. Our father came into the house, drunk, looking for money. Then he forcefully raped Andrea in our mother's bedroom. Andrea was so mentally tormented, she failed the recital the next day and never played well again. Every time she touched the keys, it triggered that blasphemous memory. But even worse, she became pregnant, but refused to tell Mother who the father was. Mother thought it was some random boy from school and called Andrea a little slut, over and over."

"That's terrible, Maria," said Michael. He was getting angry. "She was only fifteen? So, where's the baby now?"

"The baby died in childbirth. It was stillborn from a placenta abruption. Andrea insisted vehemently the nurse place the naked baby on her bare chest. Mother and I were on each side of her. The dead baby was gray and bloody. It was the worst day of my life. Andrea stared at the baby with no emotion and said nothing for a long time. Then she screamed 'I hate men.' That was when she told Mother our daddy was the father."

"And that was what she meant when she told Edward she had to get the baby off her chest, and he thought she meant Alejandro. Was the stillborn a boy or girl?"

"That's exactly what she meant, because it was a boy," said Maria, staring Michael directly in his eyes. Now things were coming together.

"Andrea went to intensive care for a couple days, and when she came home, she was never the same, and neither was Mother. Andrea, a virgin before Daddy and no drugs or alcohol, became the drunken slut of her high school class. Mother never dated a man again. Daddy died within six months of a ghastly curse she put on him, filling him with exotic parasites untreatable in Panama. His body had to be burned. Two years later, after Andrea's graduation from High School, Mother took us to Balboa on vacation, but Andrea refused to return with us to Panama City. She had been accepted at the same nursing school I was attending and where her grandmother taught. Mother was crushed, but Andrea told her what a fine career she had in Balboa, selling real estate and playing piano."

"So, the hatred stemmed from your father?" Michael was torn up, feeling guilty about the way he treated Andrea and Miriam.

"Michael, when that baby was dead on her chest, her gown soaked in blood, it was as if a red-hot poker was rammed into the depths of her soul, a wound that never healed. My mother was deeply wounded as well, but different from Andrea. Mother was eaten up with guilt for marrying such a demonic man for her own sexual pleasures, a man who destroyed her daughter's hopes and dreams of becoming highly respected in Panamanian society. Her guilt is why she was in denial, always attempting to justify Andrea's cruel behavior."

"How did you become so loving and caring?"

"I spent a lot of time with my grandmother and great-grandmother. They were both adoring and intelligent, as well as gracious witches. I became close to my grandfather and watched him use his health care skills with a compassionate heart. Other than striking me from time to time, my father never raped me. However, he told me many times how ugly I was, and I wasn't worth the bother. But the irony, if I were cute, he would have raped me."

Michael clasped his hands behind his head, "Now it makes sense why you and your mother defended Andrea. And why she tried to cover her unyielding pain with drugs and alcohol, and hurting men any way she could felt right. It was pure rage. She was a beautiful temptress and an evil, but funny, clown."

"Her hate worked for her. It made her a somebody. It gave her power. But all that time alone at sea must have haunted her terribly. She needed to get that child off her chest. After Alejandro almost drowned, she doubled her guilt. The only way she could get both boys off her chest was to kill herself."

"So, you all decided a new baby might heal the pain of the dead one?" asked Michael.

"No, it was Mother's idea and Andrea agreed to cooperate. Mother wanted a grandchild. I was just asked to be Alejandro's nanny. Since I can't have children, they gave me one. The plan was to get rid of you through deportation, confiscate your hotel, and receive child support from you. Then I would move back to Panama City with Alejandro and live with Mother. But all I knew from the start was Andrea had a baby and I was to help take care of it. But you ruined their plan."

"How?" asked Michael.

"You accepted the baby as your own. Then you accepted me graciously and caringly, no questions asked."

"I'm confused. Wasn't that what I was supposed to do?"

"No, you were supposed to reject and ignore the child, and you would find me just another burden. When Luis, who thought he was the father, exposed her kidnapping con, and you tried to control her, it was time for you to go. She had you arrested. You were to be gone by noon. But you brought in Wonder Woman from Panama City and took custody away from her and Mother. Then you refused the DNA testing." Maria had a proud smile on her face.

"So that is why your mother hates me so much. I spoiled her plan. I'm sorry." Michael was grinning ear to ear.

"Michael, I promise you, I had no idea of the plan until Andrea left with the sailor. I learned the rest from Mother at the funeral. Then I remembered the short story you wrote about her coning her first husband of his business and having him deported."

"I understand. You were a tool to them, and nothing more." Michael gave her a kiss on the cheek.

"There you are, no more talk, no more questions. I love you. If you would not have met the Archangel and my coven, you and Alejandro would probably be dead."

He squeezed Maria's hand. "I'm sorry for the loss of your sister, but you lost her years ago. And I am sorry you must leave your family behind. But, after all that has happened, one thing guided us on the path of God's will, and he is lying there with his stuffed monkey."

"Yes he is, Michael."

"God's will is anything done out of love. Andrea gave birth to him out of love for you and your mother. Had she been a good mother, we could all have shared his love. I feel for her. Someday, Alejandro will love his history. But for now, he must grow up feeling he is loved. You both have a new family." Maria had escaped a pack of plotting wolves. She and Alejandro were rescued.

The flight attendant informed the cabin they were landing in Atlanta in twenty minutes. "That was the shortest three-hour flight ever recorded," said Michael. "And to answer the question you asked earlier. I had a business I sold. We're financially sound. I write novels and will resume producing movies. And you are a nurse and can work if you wish. You know, we won't need to tell Alejandro his family history, he can watch the movie someday." They both laughed. Michael and Maria woke their son and tightened his seatbelt. Alejandro was about to be an American with aunts, uncles, brothers, sisters, and cousins, and some pets.

* * * *

Atlanta and immigration went as smoothly as the flight itself, thanks to Vanessa and Sadie. Their connector set down at Greater Cincinnati International, they deplaned with patience, although that was not how they felt inside. Alejandro was wide-eyed, watching the people bustling around him, riding the moving sidewalks and escalators, and especially riding the tram to baggage claim. On the way to Atlanta, Michael realized Maria and Alejandro would have trouble with the weather. It would be a pleasant sixty degrees in Cincinnati, but that would be chilly for them. This was tee-shirt and light jacket weather, but in Panama, it was heavy jackets, scarves, and sometimes gloves. Michael chuckled. He knew they were going to see the changing of the seasons. And soon, very soon, they would experience snowflakes for the first time in their lives.

Michael took them shopping for long pants and jackets in the Atlanta airport during their layover. It was the first time Alejandro wore shoes, not sandals or barefoot. He liked the bright colors of his new tennies but had trouble walking. Maria and Michael howled at his strut. He reminded them of Dr. Frankenstein's big green monster.

As they approached the escalator to the baggage claim, there was a crowd of people gathered at the top. They held a sign that read, *Welcome to the family, Maria, and Alejandro.* There were nine of them, all with, as cute as it was, name tags clipped on their coats. Before they reached the top, everyone was crying, even Michael's eleven-year-old granddaughters. Their grandfather was coming home for good.

When they reached the top, the family hugged Maria, Michael, and Alejandro, but they all wanted to squeeze Alejandro the most.

"Thank you for the name tags. It will take some time to get to know you all," Maria said with a sweet but nervous smile.

"It was my idea, Grandma Maria," said Grace, Michael's oldest granddaughter. She was proud of herself. Maria was not sure, since she was approaching forty, how she felt about the "Grandma" title. But she accepted it, not wanting to take the wind from Grace's sails.

"And you are not 'The Grandpa with no grandma anymore.'" chimed William, Michael's eight-year-old grandson, with a cute, quirky smile.

"No, I'm not, kid." Michael picked him up and hugged him. "I can't do this much longer, big guy. You have grown." William was proud his grandpa noticed.

"I feel I know you all from how much Michael brags about his family. I want to put faces to names," said Maria. She was experiencing a pleasant confusion, with them calling him Dad and Grandpa. It was different from Balboa, and they were not out of the airport. But Alejandro was overwhelmed. Maria picked him up and he hid his face on her shoulder.

"I'm sorry, everyone. He really isn't shy. He is just overwhelmed and confused."

"Maria, we understand, but he is so cute, like Cantor, we all want to hold and love him," Sadie was referring to Michael's two-year-old grandson.

"So, you are Sadie? Thank you for your help. You are marvelous. We will talk later, for sure." Sadie nodded. Maria was quickly feeling accepted, but she knew questions awaited soon, tough questions.

Michael finished his hugs. As they moved to the baggage carousel, Alejandro showed his little face, slightly. Then he became fixated on Cantor. *A playmate* was his first thought. *Does he have a basketball? I brought mine.*

By the time they reached Sadie's house, it was seven-thirty, and the newly merged families were hungry. Sadie and her sister, Alice, and sister-in law, Tara, had dinner prepared. The meal was plentiful and delicious, a combination for all ages. They talked as Alejandro found his way into Cantor's playroom. Alejandro was excited, especially with the train table and the basketball hoop. Alejandro wanted to show Cantor his playroom, but he did not realize he would never see it again. Michael went to the car and pulled Alejandro's basketball from his backpack. He handed it to Alejandro, who immediately shared it with Cantor. Both boys smiled at each other.

Michael observed Maria. She looked concerned. She knew they had heard horrible stories about Andrea. She thought *Were they asking themselves what kind of woman is her sister? Was she the same? Was she going to stick around, or would she try to take their father's money and run? What were her real intentions toward their father?*

Suddenly, Charles, Michael's oldest son, spoke. He was never subtle, so he took the role of interrogator. And many times, it made Michael upset. The family held their breath.

"Maria, we have some blunt questions to ask. I am sorry, Dad, but we have been talking, and we all need to know, actually, we deserve to know." Charles turned to Maria, "Are you aware Alejandro, and I hope I pronounced his name properly, cannot possibly be my father's son?"

The grandkids were all over the house playing, so Michael responded quickly for Maria. "Charles, you said his name perfectly. But feel free to call him Allie. It's a nickname we decided on for him here in the States since most people cannot roll their 'r's." Michael looked at Maria with a smile, then back to all of them. "I am his father because it says so on his birth certificate. And unless I wish to consent to a DNA test and challenge that, I have been and will be his legal father forever."

"But Dad, you know he is not yours. Your girlfriend, sorry Maria, cheated on you, and you knew it," said Charles. Michael gave Charles a warm smile, and the room went silent. Michael's children looked at Maria. "Maria," Charles continued, "our father had a vasectomy fifteen years ago. There is no possibility he is that boy's father. He is physically incapable of having children. He lied to you and your sister. I pray you don't want more children, Maria. I would be extremely disappointed in my father if he gave you false hope."

Maria cleared her throat and responded. "My sister was emphatic she never wanted a baby, so your father never told her of his vasectomy. Charles, my sister was raped as a..."

"Maria no, they don't need to know this. It is your family's secret."

'Yes, they do, Michael. They are suspicious of me and Alejandro. They must know the entire truth." Michael nodded for her to continue. "She was raped by our father at fifteen and became pregnant, but the baby died in childbirth. My mother and I were by her side. It was the worst day of our lives."

Charles interrupted. "Maria, you don't have to continue, but why are you telling us this?"

"I am telling you because, as you said, we are now family, and you deserve to know." They stayed silent, shocked by Maria's honesty about her family's past. "My sister changed that day and was emotionally damaged. She and my mother hated men from then on for what my father did. But we never shared the story with your father or anyone else until today. I was not affected the same way. I yearned to be married and have children, but due to endometriosis as a young teenager, that ability was taken from me. Your father knew of my infertility and gave me a child, my nephew, Alejandro."

Maria continued with a condensed version of the story, including her sister's plot to put Michael on the birth certificate then have him deported. She told them the undetailed version of how he saved the child, knowing all along it was not his. She did not reveal her powers." My sister never knew he had a vasectomy. She attempted to con your father, have him deported without Alejandro, confiscate his hotel, and demand child support. My sister was a tragically damaged soul."

It was obvious Maria was holding back her tears. Michael's oldest daughter, Alice, came and held her. "I want you all to know," Maria went on, "I love your father for a number of reasons, but he could have walked away from that child with a simple DNA test. That makes me love him more every day Alejandro is on this earth. Most gringos, as we call you, would have taken the test and walked away."

Michael stepped in. "Because of the vasectomy, I knew I was being conned from the start. I also knew during the pregnancy; I must get Andrea out of Balboa and to Panama City to live with her mother and Maria. Andrea's heavy drug and alcohol lifestyle would have damaged the fetus. I didn't care who the father was, it was about the fetus. And from Alejandro's birth, Maria assumed the role of his mother. She was so good to him. Maria and I didn't profess our love to each other for two years after Allie's birth, although we felt it. It was the day Andrea almost let him drown, and Maria saved him, we realized, God put that child into our hands, and I mean all of us in this room. He will have a wonderful, happy, and successful life due to all of us. His mother OD'd three months ago, the day Alejandro was almost drown by her," Michael finished.

Charles approached his father and hugged him. "I am proud of you, Dad. Every time I think you are a stupid old man; you do something like this. I love you. We all do. You are a great father, welcome home." Then he knelt in front of Maria. "And we will all love you as well. We know when someone is sincere and really cares about our father. Welcome to the family, Maria." One by one, Michael's grown children hugged her warmly.

"Okay," said Michael. "One more thing. Alejandro is too young to remember what happened so far in his life. He is unscathed physically and mentally. He won't remember his mother's death or even living in Panama. He doesn't know we are not his biological parents. I assume you did not share anything with the grandkids."

Charles spoke, "Until you hit Atlanta, they only knew we were picking you up from the airport, just in case Maria and Alejandro didn't join you."

"Thank you, I think."

"Hey, hold on everybody, listen," said Charles. From the playroom came the sound of laughter and giggles from Cantor and Alejandro. They were shooting baskets together.

"Yes." said Cantor as his ball went through the hoop.

"Olé," said Alejandro as his ball followed.

"They are going to be fun cousins together," said Charles. "And Allie will be a great little nephew."

Michael smiled, "Charles, he is not your nephew, he is your half-brother. And like the rest of the grandkids, he is Cantor's Uncle Allie, so teach Cantor to show his uncle some respect." With that, the family accepted the two new members, and love swept the room via laughter, and it would continue for their lifetimes.

2017

TWENTY YEARS AFTER ANDREA'S DEATH AND THE FAMILY'S RELOCATION TO THE US

1

SOMETHING HAS ARISEN FROM THE PIT

It was a delightful Sunday afternoon in late autumn following a heartwarming Thanksgiving dinner three days prior. It not only included Maria, Michael, Alejandro, and Cantor, but was open to Allie and Cantor's college friends from foreign countries. Thanksgiving was a holiday celebrated by all, regardless of religion or nationality.

Remaining leaves hung precariously from the most barren of trees, their hues remained bright against the deep blue sky. Maria, having grown up in the tropics, loved the approaching winter with its fashion and fireplaces, but the snow and ice, not so much.

She cruised up the street in her SUV, exuding the faint smell of a new car. With a smile on her face, she tapped the steering wheel with her index fingers as she listened to her favorite Venezuelan CD. As she approached her house, she waited for the fire hydrant to push the button above her rearview mirror. The first jerk of the garage door was seen, followed by the humming motor and the rattling of the multipaneled entrance. Maria liked to play games she invented, and this was one of them. She would not slow down at all. Then, as she entered the garage, she would hit the button again. She would turn the car off and roll to a stop, just as the door hit the floor. She was proud of her little stunt, even though Michael scolded her every time she did it.

The day was routine as she returned from the grocery. She punched in the code numbers to turn off the alarm and unlocked the deadbolt and the door handle with her keys. She grabbed her groceries from the back seat and entered the house. She felt good. Sunday was her and Michael's favorite night together. It was fondly known to them as 'Date Night.'

Michael and Maria would prepare a delicious authentic Latin meal of enchiladas, tamales, homemade guacamole, and refried beans. After cooking, eating, and cleaning up together, Maria would stroll into the TV room, curl up by the fireplace in her oversized chair, and put a respectful dent in her latest romance novel. This novel happened to be Michael's recent release, and he was in the process of transforming it into a screenplay. It would be his eleventh movie. Although Michael could be a hard-ass and a bit grumpy at times, he was still helplessly romantic. Maria was always anxious to start one of her husband's new novels because she knew she would be falling in love with his latest self-resembling lead character. And Michael loved falling in love with the new 'Maria Blanco' character he brought to life. As she read, he glanced over to see what her face revealed. He could tell where she was by her reaction. And, as he sat in his recliner watching football, she could tell whether his team was winning or losing by the quantity of profanity he exuded. But this night would be different.

"Hola, mi amor, I'm home," Maria called to Michael. "I don't need help with the groceries. Todo está bien. I have it under control."

"Maria, do exactly as I say," Michael grunted frantically and weakly from the kitchen. "Drop the bags right now, loudly, on the floor, not on the washer, on the floor, so something breaks. Then go straight into the hall bathroom. And take your phone with you, but only if it's in your coat pocket. If you must look for it, leave it. Don't waste a second, go. But make sure nothing is in the bathroom before you enter. Then shut the door and lock it."

Maria panicked. In a cracking voice, she called, "Why Michael? Why should I..."

"Just do it, muy rápido. Drop the bags and run," he yelled as loud as he could through his pain.

Maria did as she was told. Michael heard the groceries slam and heard Maria run down the hallway.

"Maria," he yelled, "if there's anyone…or anything…in that bathroom, run to the garage and lock yourself in the car, then call the police."

"Michael, what is going on?"

"I'll tell you when you are locked in the bathroom."

"What's going on, Michael?" she asked again. "I'm scared. You sound in pain."

"What do you see?" Michael asked.

"I don't see anything. I am in the bathroom."

"Call 911 and get the police and an ambulance out here as soon as possible," Michael was calmer now that Maria was safely locked in the bathroom.

"Mi amor, I left my phone in the car. I was charging it on the way home. I can run out quickly and grab it. Michael, I'm worried about you. What is going on? Tell me right now," she demanded. "Why do you need an ambulance? Are you bleeding? I don't know what to do." Maria started to cry.

"Okay, my love, here is what I need you to do. Be silent for five minutes. Not a peep. I am hurt, but not critically. No bleeding, just a lot of pain and having a tough time breathing. I think I broke my shoulder and maybe cracked a rib or two. And I hit my head."

"No, Michael, you need help now. I won't stay in here. I'm coming out."

"No," he yelled, "you must be perfectly quiet and do as I say. No more questions for five minutes, total silence. I need to listen for something before you come out of the bathroom. But tell me if you hear something inside the house other than me slapping the floor, or me growling like a dog." They both went mute. Maria thought Michael may have hit his head and was a bit unhinged.

Michael lay motionless on the cold kitchen tiles. He could catch a glimpse of the groceries scattered in the hallway. He slapped the floor with his hand and made a growling sound. After five stressful minutes, he called to Maria. "Okay, honey, peek out the door. If you don't see a dog, go to the garage, get your phone, and grab our machete from the wall. Then, moving slowly and quietly, come to me in the kitchen. If you hear or see anything other than me, hurry and lock yourself in the bathroom, or better yet, in the car."

Maria opened the door a crack. She peeked out. "What is going on, Michael? What am I looking for, a dog, or should I ask, what is looking for me?"

"Be quiet and do as I say, Maria. This isn't playtime," Michael said calmly. "I think we are safe now. If we were not, something would have happened in the last five minutes. Now go, but if you hear me yell, don't come back into the house. Just lock yourself in the car, pull out to the street, and call the police."

Maria's heart was pounding. "Should I phone the police or 911 from the car?"

"Not yet. Get our machete first and come back. Then we call. I need your protection with the machete as soon as possible."

As Maria entered the garage, she could see the still pernicious machete hanging on the wall. She could still do damage with it. She stretched for the weapon, then slowly entered the house, and peeked around the corner. "Is it safe, Michael?"

"I think so. Now come over here with the machete and if you see something, you must chop it up violently like you used to do to the rats in Panama. I can't because I believe my shoulder is broken. Now, come to the kitchen and look around. Keep watching and listening."

Maria tip-toed into the kitchen. Michael was lying motionless. He supported his left forearm with his right hand. He was grimacing in pain. His breathing was shallow. His pants in his lap area were soaked and he was lying in a puddle of hazy tainted fluid. Maria thought, *'What could cause Michael to be so frightened he would wet his pants?'*

"Maria, now call 911. Tell them we had a break-in, and I have broken my shoulder and maybe a rib or two. Then stay with me until the police arrive. I need your protection, the machete kind, not one of your spells, unless you can cast a quick one on us, my adorable Voodoo Priestess? He left when he heard the garage door."

"Who left Michael, the dog? But where did he go? Are you sure you didn't hit your head on the tile? Let me walk around the house to make sure the doors and windows are locked in case he comes back."

"No, Maria," Michael said staunchly, "I hit my head, but not hard. I know my own name. It's Michael Muckerhiede."

"Come on Michael, no funny stuff now?" Maria said with a serious frown.

"Stay with me, Maria. Don't leave my side. I have faith in the way you wield a machete." Ever since she met Michael, he knew what to do in tough situations. She trusted his judgement and his problem-solving from the days of their son's custody battle. There wasn't anything he could not defeat. And he still had her protection spell and the Archangel hanging around.

"Michael, what happened? Talk to me." Maria caressed his soft, newly shaved cheek with the back of her hand. She was regaining her composure, and her mind was getting less cloudy by the minute, but not less curious. She moved to the far side of the kitchen with her back to the counter where she could see all three entrances to the kitchen. She called 911 and put the call on speaker, laying her cell on the counter. She then stood over Michael, holding the machete in both hands, like a ninja warrior.

"911, what is your emergency?"

"Hello, this is Maria Harper, 1614 Clineview Avenue in Westerville. We had a break-in less than an hour ago, and my husband was attacked. He has a broken shoulder and ribs. Send the police and an ambulance right away." Maria spoke calmly but firmly, her words flowed in rapid succession. "And he may have a head injury," she added.

"Is the intruder still in the house, and is your husband bleeding or unconscious?"

"We don't know if the intruder is still here. My husband is on the kitchen floor, and all I have is my machete to protect us. I do not want to move him. I am an ED nurse and know what to do. He is conscious and coherent, and there is no bleeding, not externally, anyway."

"People are on their way. It will be less than ten minutes. Let me confirm, 1614 Clineview, and your telephone is the one we are on, 513-852-6937? Is this a single-family house, or is there an apartment number?"

"It's a single-family house, and all the information is correct."

"The police are on Park Avenue and the ambulance is on Race Street. If we lose connection, call us back right away and give us your name and address. This is important in cases of break-ins. And be sure not to touch anything until the police arrive. Don't open any doors until they arrive. And be sure to verify they are Westerville police from their cars and badges. Can you see them when they come to your front door? Window, peephole, anything?"

"Yes, yes," Maria said impatiently.

"Is there anything else I can do to help? I will stay on the line with you until they arrive.

Tell me if you are feeling danger at any time. I have an open line to the police as we speak," said the operator.

"Yes, that would be…" Suddenly another call came on Maria's phone. It read: 'Westerville Police, 513-900-1007'. "Can I put you on hold? The police are on my other line. If I don't come back to you within the next minute, all is okay. Thank you for your help."

"No, Mrs. Harper, you must tell me yourself you are okay, then the police will confirm it before I end our call. Is that clear?" said the operator in a soothing manner.

"Yes, thank you."

Maria answered the incoming call, but before she could say hello, a voice said, "Is this Mrs. Harper of 1614 Clineview who placed a 911 call?"

"Yes, this is her."

"This is Officer Caine of the Westerville Police. Can you give me the last four digits of your social security number, please?

"Why do you…"

"Mrs. Harper, we must be sure you are not the intruder. We have you and your husband on our computer from the DMV," said the officer.

"Nine-eight-six-three," answered Maria.

"Good, we are on our way. Be there within five minutes. Is the intruder still there?"

"We are not sure," replied Maria.

"Listen closely. Don't move your husband. Let the paramedics do that. And don't move or touch anything inside or outside your house. And especially, don't let anyone enter your house until we arrive, not even the paramedics, unless your husband is in critical condition. We understand he is stable. Keep us on the line until we arrive. Does all of that make sense, Mrs. Harper?" The officer spoke in a strong yet caring tone.

"Yes, Officer, I understand. I will be standing in the kitchen, guarding myself and my husband until you arrive."

"Do you have a weapon we need to know about, ma'am? Is it a firearm?" asked the officer.

"Oh, no sir, and this may sound silly, but it's a machete we use to cut open the fresh coconuts we buy at the store. We both lived in Panama for a while and never gave up our love of fresh coconut," said Maria with the first lightness she felt in thirty minutes.

"Okay, we can handle that as long as you don't swing it at us. If you do, we get fresh coconut, right?" Maria let out a chuckle. "It sounds like you're feeling a little more relieved than a minute ago. We will be there shortly. And let me repeat, don't touch, or move anything, absolutely nothing. And let no one in except us," said Officer Caine, knowing she was safe as long as she was talking.

"I understand, sir. We will see you soon." And without thinking, Maria hung up. "Oh my, Michael, I was to stay on the line with the officer until he arrived. I wonder if I call this number back…"

Before Maria could redial, the doorbell rang. She looked out the window and saw a Westerville police cruiser in front of the house, its lights spinning red and blue on the neighbor's houses. There was a paramedic unit backing into the driveway. Maria went to the front door, looked out the peephole, and unlocked the front door. She left the chain on and peaked out the crack.

"Are you Mrs. Harper? I'm Officer Caine, and this is Officer Daniels. Are we in the right place?" They both flashed their badges.

"Yes, and we are so glad you came quickly," Maria said as her eyes unleashed her emotions and tears rolled down her cheeks. "Come in, please. My husband is on the floor in the kitchen."

"Thank you, Mrs. Harper. Has he remained stable? Has he lost consciousness at any point?" asked Officer Caine.

"No sir, he's alert, but he is in a lot of pain. His shoulder and ribs mostly, and he has a headache from hitting his head on the floor. He can talk, just not move."

I MURDERED YOUR MOTHER, I THINK?

"Confirm you are okay with the 911 operator, and I will also?" stated Officer Caine.

"I will. She was wonderful."

Officer Caine turned to Maria. "Mrs. Harper, I will wait here with you and your husband while Officer Daniels looks around your house to be sure no one is still here. It will only take a few minutes. Then we can bring in the paramedics. In the case of a break-in, we must keep the paramedics safe as well."

"I work in an ED, and every so often, we have a paramedic with a knife or gunshot wound. Michael, my lazy husband taking a nap on the floor, will be fine. We've been through rougher situations than this." Maria put her hand on her upper chest and exhaled a long sigh of relief. Michael heard what she said, but laughing would hurt.

Officer Daniels scanned the small house with his revolver drawn, then returned to the kitchen. Maria still had the machete locked-and-loaded in her hands. "All is clear. I assume you do not have a basement. I found no one in the house except us, so it is safe to let the paramedics do their job," said Officer Daniels. "And Mrs. Harper, you might want to put the machete down, so the paramedics don't get the wrong idea."

Maria said with a rebounding smile. "We always kept one nearby in Panama for all kinds of reasons. I think I may keep one close again."

"She could really wield one of those babies in the old days, Officers. We both could. We killed many a snake and rat, even a scorpion or ten," said Michael, proud of his wife.

At the go ahead, the paramedics moved in. They carted their medical kits, supplies, and gurney into the kitchen. They directed questions to Michael as to his condition, his medical history, and his demographics. They then asked Maria if she knew of any medical issues he may have forgotten.

"Not in the twenty-three years we have been together."

"You look familiar, Mrs. Harper. Aren't you an RN at St. James emergency department?" asked the paramedic.

"Yes, I am, and your name is Howie, if I am correct." The paramedic nodded. He was proud to be recognized. "Thank you for your quick response time, but can we begin work on my husband?" With that, the paramedics prepared Michael for his trip to the ED.

"Mr. Harper," Officer Caine began, "I need to ask some questions while we are here on-site. In the meantime, Officer Daniels will look around again, and this time for clues or prints or anything that may give us ideas about who might have done this."

"Please do," said Michael looking up at Officer Daniels. "But look for paw prints, dog hair, and dog slobber. We don't have a dog or cat so that makes it easier. I'll explain why to your partner." The officers exchanged a quick glance. The paramedics kept working.

"Okay, Mr. Harper, are you up to telling me what happened before you go? We want to be sure your wife is safe while you are in the hospital and when you return. I know you are in a lot of pain, but we must hold off on pain medication so you can talk with a clear head."

With a grimace, Michael responded, knowing he had an opportunity to be his story-telling self. "No, no, that's fine if it won't take too long. I have been lying here for an hour already. Let me start, so we can stop this pain." Michael began his recount.

"As you can see, it is a beautiful day in Westerville..." Michael began, but Maria interrupted.

"Michael, this isn't the first chapter in a new book of yours. The more details you give, the longer it is before the pain goes away. Focus, mi amor," said Maria, shaking her head as she pleasantly scolded her husband.

"Okay, you are right. Stop me when I start to ramble, Maria."

"Are you Michael Harper, the writer and producer? I loved that movie about...," Officer Caine was interrupted as he put his clipboard to his side to converse with Michael.

"Officer don't get him started. Both of you, stay focused." Maria pounced like a mother on her two ADD sons.

Michael told the officer about Maria going to the grocery. "After she left, I went to take a hot shower, getting ready for her to return as I always do on Sundays. As you can see, I am seventy-nine, and she is twenty years younger. We married in Panama when I was fifty-seven. My point is, she is still as beautiful as the day we met, and well, I haven't gotten any prettier. So, I try to look my best for her." Michael chuckled for the first time, but it hurt.

Maria leaned down and kissed him on the forehead, staring into his eyes with her piercing dark pupils. "I so love you, mi amor. But as Vanessa used to say, 'How does such a nice man like you get himself into so much trouble?' But he has made my life exciting, officer."

"Okay, honey, enough of our love scene. Focus, and that means all of us." Michael looked at Officer Caine. "I hopped out of the shower and put on some nice clothes, getting ready for my angel to return. As I was sitting on the bed tying my shoes, I heard a strange clicking on the floor in the kitchen. When I glanced out the bedroom doorway, I saw the head of a dog peering at me around the corner, the rest of its body positioned in the corridor. As it crept closer, it came completely in view. It was a pit bull with an ashen gray coat. It had numerous scars on its face and torso, along with an unhealed chunk of flesh gouged out of one side of its head. One of its ears was shredded, and it wore a spiked metal collar around its neck. It was obviously a well-trained and experienced fighting dog. I was petrified."

Officer Caine interrupted. "Do you know anyone involved in dogfighting, Mr. Harper?"

"No one at all, sir, not here anyway. We knew people in Panama on the outer islands twenty years ago, but we never witnessed an organized fight. It was a different crowd that followed that sport if you want to call it a sport. Maria and I stayed away from her sister's…, I mean those people." Michael glanced at Maria with an apologetic smirk. "As I was saying, when the dog saw me, it stared at me with its deep gray eyes and slowly crept toward me. You talk about scaring the piss out of someone. I stayed still and stared back into its eyes. It began to growl, bearing its fangs, white foam frothing from its jowls. It began to circle like a vicious shark, not taking its eyes off me for a moment. When it reached the far side of the room, it realized it couldn't get behind me to attack. It could have jumped on the bed, but for some reason it would not. It was then I realized I had only that moment when the animal was not between me and the door. I had both shoes on, but one shoe untied.

"So, you ran?"

"Yes, I bolted for the door, faster than I have moved in years, and in that instant, I thought I could lock him in the bedroom. I grabbed the door and pulled it shut, but I managed to wedge his head between the door and the frame. It had to hurt, but it didn't faze it any more than a harpoon stuck in Moby Dick. And, at that time, I was unsure if its master was in the house ready to attack me as well. My original plan was to dart into the bathroom, but that would leave Maria in danger. I decided to go to the kitchen and grab a butcher knife.

"Then what happened, Mr. Harper?"

I stepped on my shoestring and fell on my back and shoulder where I am now. I dropped the knife, and it skidded over there. The dog came charging at me viciously, jumping over me from one side to the other. But it would stop before it could get its fangs into my neck, like it was hitting an invisible wall."

Something sounded strangely familiar to Maria. It was hitting its head on a shield, her protection spell.

"It straddled me and looked me in the eyes with terrible hatred. I didn't make a sound, although my shoulder and my head were killing me. I was having trouble breathing and my heart was pounding like a jackhammer. I knew that dog could rip me wide open. It could tear my throat out. But it didn't. It couldn't."

"So, it just disappeared, Mr. Harper? It just left. How did it leave the house?"

"Not yet. As I laid motionless on the floor, it sniffed me from head to toe. Then it straddled me and pissed all over my crotch. That is when I realized it was a female, by the way it pissed. As its face hovered over mine, it gave me a look that seemed familiar, a smirk I have seen somewhere in the past. And its breath smelled like cigar smoke. Then, when I heard my wife pull into the garage, it got off me and bounced playfully down the hallway, not like a dog at all, and disappeared." Caine was scribbling notes. Maria looked concerned. She walked down the hallway to find the door to her prayer room unlocked and open. She did not leave it open. She never left it open.

"How could you tell it was Mrs. Harper in the garage? It could have been the dog's master?" asked Caine.

"Impossible. You see, Maria plays this silly garage door game where she opens and closes it back-to-back, getting in with the car before the door hits her roof. She's going to be asphyxiated someday. You paramedic boys will be retrieving her body. I tell her every time, but she doesn't listen," ranted Michael. Maria smiled, rolling her eyes. She loved how that bothered him in a playful way.

"Mr. Harper, sorry I asked," said Caine. He turned to the paramedics. "Gentlemen, you may administer pain medication. My questioning will be done by the time it takes effect. "Any questions from you, Officer Daniels?"

"Mrs. Harper, you didn't touch or move anything in the house. Is that correct?" inquired Officer Daniels. "And Mr. Harper, you didn't move from where you are right now. Is that correct?"

Maria responded, "That is correct." Michael confirmed.

"Okay team, put Mr. Harper in the ambulance," said Officer Caine, "and Mrs. Harper will follow you. Give her a few minutes to gather some personal items. I will give you permission when she is ready." Howie did a thumbs-up and the others wheeled the gurney to the driveway.

Maria went to the bedroom to gather some toiletries for Michael, Michael's novel she was reading, and Michael's wallet.

"Bill?" Officer Daniels asked.

"What is it, Juan?" Caine replied.

"May I ask Mrs. Harper a couple more questions?"

"Sure, we have a few minutes while they get him strapped in," said Caine.

Maria came out of the bedroom with a backpack. "Mrs. Harper, I know this is a stress-filled moment for both of you, but this is important for your future safety and that of your husband."

"Sure, if it's quick. We need to get Michael to the ED," Maria responded coldly. "I fear one of those rib fractures might puncture a lung or his heart. I've seen it happen."

"Your husband told us you came in from the garage through that laundry room door, then went straight to the bathroom to hide. Then you went from the bathroom back to the garage to grab your cell phone and the machete. Then, upon your return, you locked the laundry room doors, reset the alarm, and stayed by your husband's side until we arrived, correct?"

"Yes," Maria answered with an attitude of frustration.

"So, the next time the house was unlocked and disarmed was when you let us in the front door. Your husband did not unlock any doors while you were at the store."

"He said he was getting cleaned-up."

"Did he take out the garbage, maybe?"

"Officer, I know my husband. He never takes out the garbage unless I make him." Maria checked the kitchen can just to be sure. It was full. She smiled.

Officer Daniels began to read his notes. "Well, I have searched the house thoroughly. All your windows and doors are locked."

"You are being repetitive, Officers. Can we end this, please? I have an injured husband in the ambulance.

"Just have one unrelated but important question, Mrs. Harper." Maria rolled her eyes. "This is a quaint neighborhood. Break-ins are rare, especially on a Sunday afternoon. Why do you have all the locks and a sophisticated alarm system?"

"My husband says he hears noises at night. I have not. I tell him it is the house settling. When we met, our town in Panama had a significant drug scene, many break-ins. We had innocent friends shot by mistake in their homes. Memories linger on. Find the dog and whoever did this. I'm going to the hospital."

But Maria stopped and turned. "Officer Daniels, how did you check the room down the hall? Was it not locked?"

"You mean the one with the altar? No, Mrs. Harper, it wasn't locked. The door was wide open. I just walked in. I dusted the knob for prints. And I left the door open." Maria's eyes widened and a mystical question entered her mind. She went back to the room. It was undisturbed. She locked it.

She showed the officers out and went to her car. The garage door opened. Maria followed the ambulance out of the driveway. She watched carefully as she backed out to see if anyone or anything was sneaking into or out of the garage. Nothing appeared.

HE IS A WRITER -
HE MAKES STUFF UP

The ambulance drove off with Maria following close behind. Caine and Daniels stood in the driveway. Juan turned the police flashers off so the neighbors could go back to whatever they were doing half an hour ago, just like Balboa.

Bill looked at Juan, "Juan, talk to me. This is a strange one. A lone fighting pit bull attacked an elderly gentleman in a suburban neighborhood, with no trace of the dog or its owner. No trace of forced entry into an extremely well-fortified house. Dog urine all over the victim. He was consistent with his facts."

"Well, Bill, they both were. But we are not sure it is dog urine. Let us take a walk around the outside of the house. I want to see if I missed something like paw prints, feces, shoe marks, anything," Juan stated.

"Let's do it." They pulled out their flashlights. "You know, Juan, the inside is hot and downright humid for this weather outside. Is it because of his age? And a strange smell, like fragrant oil or candle wax, not marijuana or tobacco. They have fascinating, but creepy, masks and statues on the walls and shelves. Let's take a walk," said Bill.

As Bill began to walk, Juan grabbed him by the arm and gently spun him around. Bill was surprised, as well as puzzled, when he saw Juan's serious expression. "No Bill, this way," Juan said. "Always walk around a temple or a religious shrine clockwise. In the Northern Hemisphere, the energy is clockwise. Like the way your sink drains. It's the same for all energy, but imperative for temples and religious shrines. And if you want even greater energy, wet your hair and clothes as you walk around them."

"Where did you hear that bullshit? One of those zombie movies you watched late night?" said Bill with a chuckle. "Next thing you're going to tell me is I should dance naked in the moonlight." Bill laughed sarcastically.

"Actually Bill, naked and wet is best, but I didn't think you would take me seriously if I threw in the naked part," Juan said with a smile. "But I am dead serious."

"So again, where did you hear that bullshit?" asked Bill.

"Mi madre. Does that work for you? And watch your answer," Juan said with an edge. "You gringos can be so ignorant. You just realized what this place is, and you don't even know you did. Those aren't just knickknacks in the house, those are religious effigies of Voodoo gods. And the smell is not from cheap Walmart candles. She made those candles from scratch, from exotic herbs. The room with the altar is her prayer room. It is beautifully exquisite. Those candles and incense are on an intensely ethereal altar. That room has a powerful, but peaceful aura. She and this place are spiritual. Let's continue to look around, and who are you calling a whacko, gringo?"

Bill smiled and patted Juan on the shoulder. "Good work. I'm following you on this one. Teach me more. I wish we could get back inside."

"I took some pictures, Bill. We can look at them later, and I'll explain. And the heat and humidity emanate solely from the prayer room. It is the climate of a rainforest."

As they walked around the house and scoured the yard, Juan continued to talk. "Bill, Maria mentioned she is Panamanian and lived there until they got married twenty years ago. Her skin and accent gave it away also. But, if I were to guess, her deeper skin color and facial features suggest her family is from a slave descent. Not Spanish, probably Haitian, Dominican, or Jamaican. And a hint of Asian, probably Chinese. Chinese have resided in Panama for over a century now, due to the canal. And she also has an aristocratic ambience to her personality."

The two walked around the house, clockwise, and checked the yard for dog feces, paw or footprints, and any damage to pry doors or windows. They looked across at the neighbors' yards to see if any stray dogs were roaming about, but it was getting dark and chilly. They returned to their cruiser and began to compare notes.

"Juan, last question. Were there any outside skylights?"

"None," Juan responded.

"Fireplace?"

"Yes, but there was a fire in the fireplace, and if it entered before, I saw no ash stains on the carpet."

"Air ducts?"

"Too small."

"Correct, so the dog could not have come in the house after she left," said Juan.

The two officers attempted to put the puzzle pieces together with every possible scenario, but to no avail. Finally, Juan looked at Bill.

"Okay, one last shot. Maybe there was no dog."

"We don't see any evidence of a dog. That is the only thing that makes sense. Go on."

"It makes no sense how a dog got in and out of the house and we will need only one piece of evidence to prove or disprove my theory."

Bill nodded, eager to hear Juan's outside-the-box theory.

"Okay, Mr. Harper went to the kitchen after getting all spiffed up for his wife. She is such a classy and adorable Latina woman, and I mean that. He went to the fridge to get another beer, when suddenly, he began to lose control of his bladder, which is not unusual for a man his age."

"Go on."

"He started to wet his pants and it went down his boxers, down his trousers, and onto the floor. He ran for the bathroom, but slipped on his urine puddle, fell, and broke his shoulder. As he lay there with his bladder emptying, he struggled to think of a way to avoid telling his wife he pissed himself like an old man. You heard him say how important it is for his wife to respect him. So, being a professional fiction writer, he untied one shoe and made up the dog story. That would explain a lot. Remember, he is a fiction writer. He lies for a living."

"How about the knife on the floor, Juan?" Why did he have the knife?"

"He wanted some cheese or bread or something, I don't know, but that's easy."

Bill grabbed his phone and called the hospital. "Only one way to test that theory. Sounds the most logical so far, Juan. Hello, can you give me the ED, please? This is Officer Caine of the Westerville Police Department. I am looking for a paramedic named Howie Freeman. He just brought in a 'Michael Harper' with a broken shoulder. Can I speak to Howie right away, please?"

"Yes, Officer, I'll transfer you to his cell phone. I believe he is still here," responded the operator. One minute later, Howie answered.

"Hello, Howie, this is Bill Caine. You just brought in Michael Harper from Clineview. Is he still in the ED?" asked Caine.

"Yes, he is. They are just now cutting his wet clothes off him and cleaning him up. He's doing fine. What can I do for you, Officer?" Howie asked.

"I need you to put his clothes in an evidence bag and hold them until I arrive. Don't throw them away, and don't give them to Mrs. Harper. This is important, Howie. All his clothes, pants, shirt, socks, shoes, underwear. Everything. Got me?" said Caine.

"Gotcha, Officer. Mind if I delegate that one to the new kid to touch those nasty things, and I just supervise?" Howie said as he laughed.

"Sure, Howie. Be there in ten."

3

ON THE BRINK

Maria sat quietly in the waiting room while the team worked on Michael for his admittance. It felt strange for her to be on the other side of the fence. The room was recently remodeled and carried the fragrance of sterility. On the walls were several magazine racks along with a television at each end of the room. They both were tuned into a boring home rehab channel. Periodically, a nurse would stick her head out the door and tell Maria that Michael was doing fine and making them laugh with some dog tale. She could join him shortly. Maria smiled. She knew Michael could not miss a chance to impress the young men and flirt with the young nurses. At his age, she encouraged it.

As Maria waited, she stared blankly at one of the televisions. She reviewed what happened in the last three hours. She analyzed the timeline, starting with when she left the house to the time the ambulance took Michael away. She pictured all the doors and windows, wondering if any were left unlocked somehow. But mostly, when did she leave her prayer room door open?

After several rounds of obsessive thought, Maria let out a big sigh and buried her face in her hands. *Or maybe, none of the above,* she thought. *Michael has been acting peculiar in the last few weeks. Oh, please God, not Alzheimer's. Don't let that brilliant mind go out that way.*

Finally, a young woman with a stethoscope around her neck, opened the door and called, "Mrs. Harper?"

"Yes," said Maria.

"You may come back now. We have your husband clean and comfortable," said the nurse with a soothing smile. "He is a very entertaining man." Maria smiled.

Maria gathered her things and followed the nurse to an area curtained off from the other patients. She heard the sounds she heard every day; pumps, clicks, and moving chairs, along with voices too low to distinguish what was being said. She heard an occasional grown of pain and she saw people passing in tears. The nurse turned. "Before we get to your husband, and for HIPAA reasons, I must confirm he is your husband, correct?" Maria nodded. "I want you to be aware, we were forced to cut his clothing off his body to avoid more injury."

Maria gave a light grin. "My husband has been wearing that shirt with the half-naked biker babe on the back every Sunday since we lived in Panama twenty years ago. It's about to fall apart on its own, and frankly, I always hated it. But he loved it and told me the girl looked like me, so I never said anything. Good-bye biker babe."

The nurse smiled back at Maria. "My husband wears a Jerry Garcia Grateful Dead T-shirt with a big marijuana leaf on the back. Do these boys ever grow up? You can have the clothing back if you wish, but for now, the police officers from your crime scene confiscated them. They left with them a few minutes ago. We can let them know you want them back when they're finished with them."

"No, I have no need for them, but I am curious why they took them. What do you mean when they are finished with them?"

"Mrs. Harper, it seemed odd to me as well, but I don't know much about what happened to your husband," said the nurse. "I heard the officer say something to the paramedic about the crime lab and a DNA test so they may be able to ID some pit bull. Does that make sense to you, Mrs. Harper?"

"Okay, that makes perfect sense now. Thank you for your explanation," said Maria. She followed the nurse to Michael's bedside.

He lay uncomfortably in a bed, curtained off from other patients, his arm in a sling. His body was strapped from the waist up in a slightly angled bed, making him unable to move his arms or torso. The sight made

Maria claustrophobic. It was as if he was in a straitjacket. She had a fleeting premonition but pushed it out of her mind immediately.

"Hola, mi amor. You appear exhausted, and your eyes are droopy, like the little hound dog in the cartoon. They gave you lots of pain meds, my sweet?" asked Maria.

"Si, señora, straight in the old vein. I can't sit up far enough to drink. And I can't use the bathroom, so they put a freaking catheter up my penis. Oh my God, I hate that. They want me almost flat on my back. The only good news is, whatever they're injecting in me, the pain is gone, except when I forget and try to move my torso or take a deep breath."

"Or try to be entertaining to all the little cuties, right?" smiled Maria. She knew him too well. "Have they performed any diagnostics yet, X-rays, CT scan, blood work? What do they think is broken? Do you have a concussion?"

"The doc said he will be in to talk to us soon."

"That's good. Is he responsive, or are you just a piece of meat? I feel sorry for a lot of my patients. But that is why those docs with no social skills become hospital-based physicians. They are brilliant and are good doctors, but not a lot of fun." She was right, the doctor was cold.

"Have you called Allie yet?" Michael asked. "He probably went to the football game with his amigos and is still drinking down by the stadium. I miss those days of taking him and Cantor to the games. I doubt, over the bar noise, he'll be able to hear his phone. We should wait until the doc tells us what is happening to call him."

"That's a smart idea considering the condition you are in, Michael," Maria stroked his messy gray hair and kissed him ever so gently on the forehead. "It is one thing when I take care of patients in the ED, but to see you as a patient is unnerving." She felt emotional, so she teased him instead. "How will you ever get a date with one of those cute little nurses with messy hair like that?" Michael knew Maria was trying to show him that her strength and confidence were intact.

"Did they find that freaking dog roaming the neighborhood? The more I ponder what happened, the more I think a person was controlling that animal. How else could that dog possibly have gotten in or out of our house? It has paws, and paws can't push buttons or turn doorknobs.

Hell, what am I saying? They can't remember codes, even if they could push buttons." Michael rambled, moving only his eyes to see Maria in his peripheral.

"I agree, honey. I've been going over and over it in the waiting room. And not only how, but why. Why would anyone sic a pit bull on you? Don't take this the wrong way Michael, but there was a day when you got yourself in trouble with questionable people, like the dealers and my sister. Has your mischievous streak returned? Gambling debts on football games, Michael? You don't have some young woman's boyfriend after you, do you?" Maria rubbed Michael's head and kissed him on the lips with a look of comic relief on her face.

Michael rolled his eyes with a silly smirk. "Maria, stop please, don't make me laugh. That would hurt a lot. The answer is no on the gambling debts, and maybe on the boyfriend part."

"Oh dear, I'm sorry. I didn't think of laughing pain. I'll stop. I just feel so relieved you look safe and comfortable. Seriously, why would someone do this to you, and why did they wait until I left the house? It was almost like they knew our routine and have been watching us."

"Makes no sense to me whatsoever."

Just then, a doctor entered and introduced himself. "Good evening, I am Dr. Sung."

"Well, hello, Dr. Sung. I am Michael Harper, and this is my wife, Maria. Are you from the psyche ward? Are you the one that strapped me down like I'm looney tunes?" Michael made a silly face, sticking out his tongue to the side.

"Well, no, Mr. Harper. I am…"

"I know, those cops have me strapped down and drugged, so I don't rip that pit bull to pieces with my fangs," Michael said with a growl.

"Michael, stop it or they will think you're crazy," said Maria, although she was giggling. "I'm sorry, Dr. Sung. I think whatever pain meds you gave him are working too well. He rarely takes anything seriously for very long. But he probably wasn't kidding about the dog part."

Dr. Sung found no humor in Michael whatsoever, but then again, he had no sense of humor. He waited for the frivolity to end so he could continue.

I MURDERED YOUR MOTHER, I THINK?

"There are a few things I need to explain, and it is good you are both here so there is no confusion. First, I assume you are Mrs. Harper, Mr. Harper's spouse?" said Dr. Sung in a light Chinese accent.

"I just introduced you, doc. Were you not paying attention?" Michael said, suddenly not in a happy mood.

"Doctor, if we do have any confusion between us, I was taught Mandarin by my mother as a child. I am Mrs. Harper, and I signed papers earlier, since they didn't want Michael to move. And they said his verbal permission was enough." Maria answered. "I'm an RN in the ED at St. James. I never realized until now how annoying all this legal paperwork is to a patient and his family in times of trauma. Can we get on with it, Dr. Sung?"

"I would enjoy that, Mrs. Harper. And English is fine. I was raised in New York City. Well, Mr. Harper, the first thing I want to say is, right now, none of your injuries are of a serious nature. But at your age, we want to be cautious. We can see you have a displaced clavicle from the protrusion at the top of your shoulder, however, we are not sure if anything else is going on in there. We also want to check your scapula to see if it is dislocated or fractured. And we deduce most of your pain emanates from a few broken ribs, since you claim you're having a problem breathing. And we see no sign of concussion from that minor bump on your head."

"Sounds good so far, Doctor. Continue please." Maria motioned, then put her hand on Michael's forearm.

"We want to be sure none of these fractures have splintered and might puncture your lung or your heart or any vessels. Because of your age and the probability of a minor surgical procedure, we would like you to have a CT scan instead of an X-ray. We want to do an EKG and blood and lab work tonight. Do we have your permission, Mr. Harper? Your hip is bruised as well from the fall today. We will check that," explained Dr. Sung.

"Well," Michael said as he glanced over at Maria with a peculiar look in his eye. "Do we really need to do the CT scan? X-rays of my bones should be enough." Maria was confused by Michael's hesitation.

"Mr. Harper, I assure you, there is no pain involved in any of these tests. Claustrophobia for some people is the only issue with the CT scan, and if that's a problem for you, we can give you a light sedative along with your current pain medication. The worst thing after that is, you'll probably doze in and out of sleep the rest of the night. I'm sure you've had an EKG, and you know that's nothing, and a few needle sticks. Normally, we could do the surgery tonight, but unless the CT scan shows any displacement or breakage threatening your lungs or heart, then, due to your age, we would like to perform the tests tonight and wait until morning for surgery."

"Why in the hell do you keep referring to my age? Shit, I'm probably in better shape than you." Michael was upset, especially at his age being referred to in front of Maria.

"Honey, where I work, we do this routinely with anyone over sixty. That means they would take these precautions with me as well, at least soon. This is just another experience you can base a book upon, so settle down. Continue on, Dr. Sung." Michael settled down, for now.

"Is there a specific surgeon you prefer? We can refer a few to you who have privileges here and can probably have a spot for you in the morning. I really don't think we should wait past noon." Dr. Sung looked at Maria as he made his suggestion.

"Michael, the testing is a good idea, just to be sure. Dr. Sung did not mentioned an MRI, so that means it is not serious. Yes, Doctor, go ahead with the testing. We're fine with that," said Maria. Michael stared at the ceiling with a faraway look, not saying a word for a few moments.

Then Michael spoke, "Let me contact my primary care doc tonight. I have his cell phone, and I'll trust him to make the decision about the surgeon. I'll wait until all the tests are done and my wife has gone home for the night. How long do I have until the CT scan?" he asked.

"Oh, thirty minutes or so. You can call him now, you have time. Or Mrs. Harper can talk to him while you're having your CT scan. Just tell him you need an orthopedic surgeon, one that specializes in shoulders. We'll give you names from which he can choose. But remember, they must have privileges here, and it has to be done tomorrow by noon." Maria listened intently to Dr. Sung.

"Honey," Michael said, "I think I should talk to Stein myself tonight, after you leave. He knows what I need. And the gods know I have put you through enough today." The doctor gave him a funny look over that statement. "I also want you to call the officers from this afternoon and have them meet you at our house when you go home. Let them take another look around. And tonight, keep their number cued up on your cell." Michael shifted his eyes to look at the doctor. "Sincerely, thank you for your help. It has been a trying day, and I was attempting to lighten up. I'll let you know about the surgeon later tonight," said Michael. Dr. Sung bowed politely and walked out through the curtain.

"Michael, why are you being so insistent about talking to Stein yourself? Think about it. You can't dial the phone, and there's no reason I'm not capable of calling Dr. Stein sooner rather than later. Let us get this ball rolling before it gets too late to make arrangements. No more discussion. You can be stubborn sometimes." Maria smiled at Michael as she looked over the top of her glasses. "But before I call and before your tests, I think now is when we should call Allie."

"You're right. Let's call Allie and at least leave a message."

Maria proceeded to dial Allie on her cell. Oddly enough, her son answered on the second ring.

"Hey, Mom, checking up on me?" Allie answered in a happy tone with just a slight hint of a slur.

"Where are you, Allie? I hear a lot of noise in the background. Did you go to the game?" she asked.

"I'm at a bar downtown by the stadium. Yeah, went to the game. Great game. Did you see it?" asked Allie.

"Well, not today. That's why I'm calling you." Maria's voice began to quiver. "Can you go somewhere a bit quieter?"

"Something wrong, Mom? I can tell something's wrong when your voice sounds like that. What is it?" Allie was now concerned.

"Go outside or at least someplace where I don't have to talk loudly. We're in the ED, and I have to keep my voice down," Maria said firmly.

"The ED. Oh my God, what happened? Hold on. They have a back room that's empty." The background noise disappeared as Allie hurried to silence. "Okay, is that better? Now what's going on?" he asked nervously.

"Well, it's a long, peculiar story, and I'll fill you in on all the details later. But like I said, I'm at the hospital with your father and…"

"What happened? Is Dad okay? Or is it you? Or both? Did you have an accident? Heart attack, stroke? C'mon, Mom, tell me." Allie rambled too quickly for Maria to slide in an answer.

"Stop, Allie, you're worse than your father. Let me talk," Maria said, raising her voice slightly. "If you would be quiet and stop the panic, I'll tell you." Other than the mechanical noises and quiet mumblings of the ED, silence prevailed.

Maria took a deep breath. "It's your father. I'm fine. No heart attack or stroke. He slipped and fell on the kitchen floor, and he broke his collarbone. They're going to do a CT scan and maybe some X-rays to be sure he doesn't have any splintering near his lungs or heart or anyplace else. He bumped his head, but there were no concussion symptoms. And he bruised his hip, but I think he did that some other time, so no problem there. We're scheduling surgery for tomorrow morning to set his collarbone. He's not in much pain due to the medication, they have him pretty doped up."

"What hospital? I'll be right there," Allie blurted. Michael could hear Allie's responses faintly on the cell.

"Give me that phone, Maria. I want to talk to him, before he does something stupid," Michael barked.

"Michael, really? Where will you hold the phone, between your toes? I'll put the phone on speaker. Allie, did you hear that? Your dad wants to talk to you. I'm putting you on speaker." Maria sat in a chair by the bed and put the phone on the nightstand.

"Dad, can you hear me? You okay? You in pain? How did you fall?" Allie rattled off his series of questions in rapid succession.

"Hey, hey, hey, slow down, kid. I'm fine. Just angry. I played football, basketball, baseball, I skied down mountains, not to mention four-wheeling through jungles. And I never broke a goddamn bone in my body. Now I'm almost eighty years old, and I broke my freaking collarbone stepping on my freaking shoestring. You laugh at me, and I swear I'll get you in a headlock and give you noogies next time I see you."

Allie chuckled at hearing his father's attitude, which told him his dad was going to be fine. Michael was proud of all the crazy stuff he had done in his life, and this would be just another story he could brag to his friends about.

"And if they keep up with the 'we need to be cautious because of your age' crap, somebody's getting their ass kicked."

"Michael," whispered Maria, "people can hear you. Watch your language. I've seen you kicked out of bars for less than this. Let us not do an ED." They both heard Allie chuckle on the phone.

"I'm strapped in this stupid-ass bed, and you know I can't sleep on my back. And I'm hungry and wearing these silly hospital bottoms. What's on them, teddy bears or something, Maria?"

"Winnie the Pooh, to be accurate, Michael."

Michael was starting to feel better, and the pain medication was pumping him up.

"Dad, Dad, settle down. Mom is right. Just because you're going to be okay doesn't mean others in the beds around you will be. You have been lucky all your life. You should have broken a bunch of bones, or worse. I'll be there as soon as I can. Which ED are you in?" asked Allie.

"I'm at Mercy Westerville, but you're not coming here tonight. I know you and your buddies. I have been to games with all of you and picked up many a tab. You guys have been together drinking beers all day, and probably none of you, and especially you, can drive out here right now."

"Easy, Dad, I have no intention of driving. I was going to grab a taxi, then I'd stay with Mom tonight."

"No, come out in the morning," said Maria. "They have your dad doped up and are running tests tonight. Come to the house tomorrow morning before his surgery; he would like that." Michael nodded as much as he could in agreement.

"And if you have classes or an exam tomorrow morning, that takes priority. But your mother's right, no reason tonight. It's not like I'm dying. Your mom will let you know if we need you. Promise us, no driving or finding your way here tonight," Michael said in a stern and loving way.

"You're right, Dad. Mom, call me when you know something, anything. I'll be there in the morning."

"Will do, honey," said Maria. "Go have fun. Your dad will be back to his old obnoxious self sooner than we want. The drugs and adrenaline have him all fired up. He is far from being in a coma, but I will put him in one if he doesn't behave." Maria and Michael could hear Allie laughing on the speakerphone. "See you in the morning, Alejandro."

"See you, Mom. Love you both. A shoestring took you down Dad, a shoestring?" said Allie as he belly-laughed. "Wait until I tell Cantor and the guys." Michael smiled. He loved to make his son laugh.

"Allie, don't tell Cantor yet. Let's get your dad past this surgery tomorrow morning before we tell the rest of the family. It's a minor surgery. Let's not have a crowd here at the hospital. He may be home tomorrow night. We must schedule the surgery. See you in the morning."

"Bye Mom, bye Dad." Maria ended the call.

"Maria, I think Allie staying with you tonight could keep you safe. You want to call…"

"Michael, we still have the gods protecting us from the spell I cast twenty years ago. No person, and certainly no dog, will hurt me. You did this to yourself on the kitchen floor. All that dog did was piss on you. Not even my Voodoo can stop that. Could have been worse if you know what I mean." They both smiled while Michael held back a painful laugh.

"I'm proud of that boy," replied Michael. "Can you believe he will graduate with his bachelor's degree in chemistry this June, then be off to med school? This is all because he has you."

"Michael, if it weren't for you, he might be under the care of Andrea, and never would have made it through grade school. You did this for him, not me."

"Maria, we both did, along with my family's support and acceptance of both of you. Your powers saved his life and continue to protect him, along with your unconditional love. The gods freed us from Balboa for this very reason." Maria kissed Michael gently and continued to groom his messy hair with her fingers.

"Give me Stein's number and I will coordinate the surgery tomorrow. I want to make it early so you can eat by noon. They will be here any moment to take you for your CT scan. And stop acting like a tough guy in front of your son. He knows who you are, and I do too. We have heard your stories many times, but this is one is a keeper." Maria kissed him. She couldn't kiss him enough.

"Maria, he hasn't heard all the stories, but the time is drawing near." Otherwise, he can read it in my next novel under the *nom de plume* of Robert Arthur, even though I did embellish it a bit." Maria gave an unemotional nod and grabbed Michael's phone. At the same time, two nurses took Michael away. He smiled and waved, "Let's go girls."

Maria called Dr. Stein to schedule the surgeon. She shared the situation and the prognosis. "Is Michael with you now?"

"No, they just now took him for a CT scan."

Stein hesitated. "Why not just x-rays. He doesn't need a CT scan."

"The doctor said that would be better. You can ask him tomorrow when you meet him. Now what about the surgeon?"

"Edward Rowekamp is an excellent choice. He's a general surgeon, not necessarily shoulders, but he has done his share," Stein suggested.

"Whatever you say, Bob."

"Let's go with Rowekamp. You'll like him. He's a funny guy and Maria, it's not like Michael's going to pitch for the Reds someday."

"No, he isn't, but he probably thinks he could. You know him. Will you warn him about Michael's sense of humor?"

"I will handle that and see you in the morning, my dear. Be safe tonight. Have the police check your house before you go inside. Call me anytime you need me. I will coordinate everything. Go get some rest." The call ended. Maria held a tissue to her nose. Her emotions were attacking from all directions.

With a sigh, Stein went to the desk in his home office. He opened the top drawer and called Rowekamp. Since Michael was having a CT scan, there was another call he needed to make. *Tomorrow is not going to be easy for anyone*, he thought. He took off his reading glasses and stared at the picture of himself and Michael next to his WWII glider. They loved those flights together and he realized how much love he felt for Michael and his family. He put his glasses back on and sighed once more. "Here we go," he said aloud.

* * * *

It was 7:00 P.M. and Michael's tests concluded. Dr. Sung entered the waiting room and sat next to Maria. "Tests are complete. We will have the radiology report and lab results first thing in the morning. I am on a seventy-two-hour shift, so I am going to take a nap. We admitted your husband to a private room, and he is sleeping peacefully. We have an OR scheduled for 10:00 A.M. Keep your phone on, please. Arrive two hours before the procedure, so we can explain what's going to take place, and you can visit him before we take him back. Nothing you can do here tonight. Go home and get some rest, Mrs. Harper?"

"Thank you, Doctor. You have been kind and very patient with us, especially my husband."

"I do my job. See you in the morning, Mrs. Harper."

Maria gathered her things but before she left the waiting room, a text came from Dr. Stein.

I'll meet you in his room at 8:00 tomorrow morning. We are scheduled for 10:00. I checked with the hospital. He is resting peacefully. Talk to you then.

Good and thanks, Maria returned.

She went to the car and called Alexandro. "Allie, I'm exhausted, so no questions, please. He is asleep, thank God. Test results have not come back, so we won't know anything until morning. The surgery is set for 10:00 A.M., but they want us there at 8:00. Can you pick me up at 7:30? We can ride together."

"Sure Mom, I'll pick you up at 7:30 sharp. I'm going back to sleep. Love you," Allie said in a groggy hoarse voice from yelling all day at the game.

Maria needed to make one last phone call to the police station. "Hello, Officer Bill Caine speaking."

"Officer Caine, this is Maria Harper. You helped my husband and me this afternoon. It was the injury and the dog. Do you remember?"

"Of course, Mrs. Harper. Is everything okay? Are you safe?" replied Caine.

"Oh yes, all is fine. My husband is resting and will have surgery in the morning. He has a broken collarbone and two broken ribs. No concussion."

"That's great. Sounds minor. What can I do for you?" Caine asked in a serious voice.

"Well, you said if I needed any help, to call. I'm leaving the hospital, and first, I wanted to know if you found the dog. And if not, would you look around my house one more time before I go to bed to make sure I am safe?"

"Well, I can't, but I will call the officers on duty. They will help you. When will you be home? I want you to pull into your driveway and wait for them with your car doors locked. Don't go into your house unless they go with you. I'm assuming twenty minutes?"

"Perfect," said Maria. "I'll wait for them. And ask them not to turn their flashers on, please. No sense disturbing the neighbors again. Thank you for everything today. And I understand you took my husband's clothes to test for DNA. Good thinking. I would like to retrieve his shirt with the biker babe on the back. He loves her as much as he loves me. I hear the rest is nasty. You can pitch the rest." Caine laughed with a guy's kind of understanding.

"I'll make sure he gets his girlfriend back safe and sound. I'll make the call right now. Good luck tomorrow. And no, we have not found the dog. Still looking." They exchanged goodbyes.

Maria pulled into her driveway. Two officers were already there on the sidewalk. They instructed Maria to open the garage door and wait while one officer, with gun drawn, entered. No garage door game tonight. Maria parked, then opened the door to the house. The first officer entered, while the second officer with gun drawn had Maria's back.

"Be careful, officers. The floor may be slippery from the spoiled groceries and the dog urine." The whiff of both was potent.

"There scoots a little baby roach, Mrs. Harper. It just went under your sink. They don't waste any time finding garbage, do they? I'm not going to waste a bullet on him, but you might want to get some traps."

Maria followed the first officer, turning on light switches in each room before he entered. The officer yelled "Police," before he entered each room with his gun aimed to defend. He checked the closets, under the beds, and in the showers. The other officer covered Maria the whole time. They checked all the doors and window locks and closed the flue on the chimney.

"All checked except for the bedroom that's locked. Could you open it for me, Mrs. Harper?"

"Officer, there is nowhere to hide in there, but if I open it, I need to check that room myself. If I see anything, I will call for you right away. Nothing illegal in there, just personal." Maria didn't want any unnecessary questions.

"Sure, Mrs. Harper, if you think you are safe. This is for your protection. But I understand. I would not want anybody to see my workshop either. The officer stood next to Maria as she opened the door. A gust of warm humid air came out from the room and into the hall. The officers glanced at each other with puzzled looks. Maria flipped on the light, and within seconds called "All clear." She came out and locked the door behind her.

The officers placed their guns back in their holsters. "Appears all is clear, and locks secured. Here is my card, Mrs. Harper. We are on duty all night and will drive by at least every hour to watch your house. We will not come onto your property unless we see something, and we will let you know it's us. If you hear someone or somebody outside, call us directly, not 911. We're here to keep you safe. And just to be sure, do you have a gun? We don't want you to shoot us accidently."

"No, but I am sleeping with my machete next to the bed, and I can wield it with the best of them."

"I think we can handle that, Mrs. Harper." The officers smiled, not realizing how good she was with that weapon.

"Thank you. You are fantastic." Maria showed them out, checked all the chains, deadbolts, and doorknobs for herself, then set the alarm. She cleaned up the groceries she dropped earlier. She checked to see if the ground beef was eaten or if she saw more roaches. Both were negative. Next, she pulled out the mop, cleaned and disinfected the kitchen floor. She thought it was truly a blessing there was no sign of blood. But with that, her imagination took over, picturing the pit bull tearing Michael to shreds and ripping his throat out. "Okay, stop," she said aloud. "That didn't happen, and it can't happen, so don't do that to yourself, Maria Blanco."

Maria finished, grabbed a glass from the cabinet, and snagged a half-full bottle of wine from the refrigerator. She went to the bedroom.

I MURDERED YOUR MOTHER, I THINK?

She locked the door and shoved Michael's nightstand in front of it. She showered, brushed her teeth, and picked up Michael's towel he always left on the bathroom floor. In her warm robe, she sat in her comfortable chair and grabbed Michael's new novel. But she couldn't concentrate.

She thought back on all the curious events that happened today and in the last month; roaches, bats, and now a pit bull, but all according to Michael. Suddenly, her demeanor changed. She moved the nightstand from the door and unlocked the door. She turned off all phone ringers and went to her prayer room. She changed into her black Priestess vestment, lit candles and sticks of incense on the altar, and began praying in poetic creole. She perceived a presence she had not felt in a long time. She needed wisdom and protection from a place few people could understand.

Maria prayed and chanted without a break. She held her pentagram necklace inside her folded praying hands. When she finished, she blew out the candles and returned to her bedroom. She locked the door, slid the table back in front of the door, primed the officer's cell number, and finished the bottle of wine.

As she lay in bed, she sent out a group text to Michael's children and grandchildren, now scattered around the country developing their own precious families and careers. She told them only of his fall, accidental of course, his minor injuries, and his surgery in the morning. She explained how exhausted she was, and she would keep them informed after the surgery, but for now, she needed sleep. She sent the text, stared at the ceiling, and dozed off into a light sleep.

TWO WEEKS BEFORE THE DAY OF THE ATTACK

Maria worked three days a week. On those days, she came home at 5:30 P.M., playing her little garage door game, and listening to the same CDs over and over, year after year. In a fun way, Michael wanted to hear, just once, the garage door smacks the roof of her car.

Maria grabbed her purse and a bottle of wine from the front seat. She unlocked the deadbolt, the doorknob, and turned off the alarm. She opened the door, but it stopped. She gently bumped her forehead. From inside, Michael's foot stopped it. "Stay out there, honey. You can't come in yet."

"What is it, Michael? You baked me a cake. That is sweet, but it is not my birthday or our anniversary, love." She played it with a touch of her innocence.

"Bats. We just had a swarm of bats flying around the house. They were flying and darting in every direction, dozens, maybe more. Remember those hollow bat trees out by the point in Panama. That's what it was like. I think it is safe now. It's been fifteen minutes since they left."

When she entered, she burst into full laughter. Michael wore a pair of boxer shorts with palm trees on them and he held a warped tennis racket in his hand. "What's with the court jester outfit, Puck? I think that is a good look for you. Have an audition tonight?" Maria couldn't stop laughing. She could hardly catch her breath.

"Okay, smartass. But I hear those nasty bastards carry lice and get in your hair. Bald is not a good look for me. I think I have chased them off, but I want an exterminator right away. I don't want them to come back while we are asleep. And I want a bat expert, not one of those termite guys. He needs to discover where they are getting in and eliminate them right now." Michael was in a panic. "I hate bats. I mean it. I really, really, hate bats."

"But why do we need an exterminator, when you have that doomsday tennis racket?" Maria continued to laugh.

"Knock it off, I'm serious. I hate bats with a passion. And I heard they carry rabies too." Michael did not find Maria funny. "Come on, love, I'm serious."

"Absolutely, honey. You're right. It's just your outfit." She laughed again. "Okay, let Jane put down purse and wine in kitchen while you and Cheetah stand guard, Tarzan. Is Boy safe?" Maria couldn't leave it alone. Michael moved aside with a "not so funny" smirk on his face. "Okay Michael, seriously. I hate bats too. Let's call, but if an exterminator can't come tonight, we will stay in a hotel." Maria was concerned.

Maria found a number and called Nisner's Exterminators, the owner being Jim Nisner. She asked him if he knew anything about bats, and he assured her he was remarkably familiar. She relayed Michael's story.

It was less than an hour and the doorbell rang. Maria looked out the peephole and saw two men wearing baseball caps and work shirts with logos that read *Nisner's Exterminators*. She opened the door with the chain still latched and asked, "Are you Mr. Nisner?"

"Yes, I am. And you must be Mrs. Harper?" he responded as he handed her a card through the crack in the door. Maria let Mr. Nisner and his young assistant into the house. She led them to the kitchen.

"This is my husband, Michael, who saw the bats this afternoon." Michael and Mr. Nisner shook hands. Michael crept around the kitchen like a cat ready to pounce, staring down the hallways for bats, with the boxers still on his head and his tennis racket still in his hand. Comically enough, Mr. Nisner had seen this before.

He wasted no time. "Mrs. Harper, you gave me enough details on the telephone, so we can start right away." Michael continued to play defense. "You want to keep these things from coming back into your house tonight, right? I don't blame you. The evidence of their presence is usually obvious, so we should easily find where they're getting in." He and his assistant immediately took out their flashlights and nets and began their search through the house. They searched each room thoroughly then came to Maria's prayer room.

"Mrs. Harper, the one room is locked down the hallway. That is the only room we have not investigated, then we will move to the rest of the house."

"Oh, of course, Mr. Nisner. Please be aware, it is my prayer room. It makes some people uncomfortable, but I assure you, it is a slice of peace in the world for me." Mr. Nisner smiled and assured Maria of his respect. Maria unlocked the door, and a warm humid breeze filled the hallway. No one said a word.

After searching the room, Nisner came back into the hallway and Maria relocked the door. "Do you have a basement, Mrs. Harper, a crawl space or an attic?"

"No crawl space or basement. But we do have a small attic. You can get to it through the trapdoor in the ceiling of the garage. It does extend over the entire house. And you can check the fireplace. I hear they sometimes come down chimneys."

"Have you had a fire in the fireplace this year, and have you had it cleaned since last year?"

"No, we haven't had a fire yet this year, and honestly, we haven't had it cleaned for a few years." Maria felt scolded.

"Well, the fireplace is not suspect, since you have those glass doors covering it and I assume your flue is still closed from last year. But if they did come down the chimney, and you haven't cleaned it in a year, we would see soot everywhere. I want to start in your attic. That is where they usually nest and make a mess. Can you move your car from the garage, Mrs. Harper, so we can get to the attic door?"

Maria backed her car onto the driveway and the exterminator set up his ladder. Each held a flashlight in their hand and one on their head.

After thirty minutes, the men returned, and they all sat at the table to talk. "Okay," said Michael, "what did you find? Can you get rid of them tonight?"

"Well," said Mr. Nisner, "we looked at your roof and saw no signs of leaks or gaps, so we assume you have had no roof leakage lately. Is that correct?"

"Correct," said Michael.

"And your eave vents are screened. Then we went outside and climbed on your roof to look at your heating and plumbing vents. Plumbing vents are not an issue, because that means the bats would need to come through your drainpipes or toilets, and we saw no sign of that. And your hot water heater closet door is tight, so they couldn't squeeze through there either."

Maria raised her eyebrows in confusion. "So…what are you saying, exactly?"

"What we're saying is, if there's an infestation, we usually see lots of guano, or bat feces. They poop often. You know they can eat up to twelve hundred mosquitoes a day?" Mr. Nisner sat with a puzzled look on his face.

"You mean you saw nothing? Not one bat? Not a trace?" Michael balked. "They swooped in here for ten minutes, then just disappeared, gone? I'm sorry, Mr. Nisner, but I saw them flying around in my house. Maria, maybe we need to get a second opinion. I told you not to get one of those termite guys." Michael spoke to Maria in a degrading tone, really aimed at Nisner.

"Well, sir, I'm so sorry if I'm upsetting you, but I have been an exterminator for thirty-five years. I'm not doubting what you saw. Let me clarify, I said we *usually* find an abundance of guano. I've seen attics with up to a foot of the stuff." Then Mr. Nisner pulled out a tightly sealed specimen jar. "But we did find this guano, and it does look fresh. However, this little amount was in that room with the altar. I found it on the back corner of the altar."

"So, we do, or we don't have bats?" Michael asked.

"Mr. Harper, if you had multiple bats flying around down here for fifteen minutes, we would see some evidence of that. So even though that's odd, what's really odd is that this guano has small fish bones in it." Mr.

Nisner pointed to them in the jar, then he took off his hat and scratched his head.

"So, what does that mean?" Michael said, frustrated again.

"There are only a few species of bats in the entire world that eat fish, and none in North America. Our bats are all insectivores. The bat that dropped this is probably a Noctilio leporinus, also known as the Greater Bulldog bat. They only live off the coast of Mexico on the Pacific side, or in Central and Latin America, especially the Caribbean side around Panama and Columbia. May we take this sample to the zoo and have them test it for us? I don't have the same knowledge base or equipment those zoo kids have. This certainly has my curiosity, Mr. Harper. I have not seen anything like this before." He put his hat back on and gazed at Michael, then Maria.

"Again, what are you trying to tell us?" Michael demanded. "No sign of bats, except maybe one that happens to come from Central America? What the hell was I chasing, giant butterflies? I want your home phone, sir, because if they come back, I want you here right away."

"Michael, settle down. I'm sure this man will help us in any kind of emergency. Gentlemen, I'm sorry for taking your time. We will call you again if we need you," Maria said in an apologetic and understanding tone.

"No problem, Mrs. Harper. This has me stumped as well. I can understand Mr. Harper's frustration and fear. I've never seen guano with fish bones. We will wait for your call. And if it happens again, I will understand if you would like to use someone else. I will drop this off at the zoo regardless, if that's okay with you?" Maria nodded. And with that, Mr. Nisner and his assistant extended their hands for shaking. Maria accepted, but Michael just turned, ripped his boxers off his head, threw them in the washer and made his way to the bedroom. Maria thought, *that impoliteness doesn't seem like my husband.*

When the exterminators left the house, Michael returned from the bedroom. He and Maria went into the living room and poured themselves a drink. "I'm telling you, Maria, I'm not crazy. They were all over the kitchen, flying through the hallway, and then they just disappeared, boom, gone."

"I must admit, honey, I would have a problem believing it, if it weren't for that fish bone guano. Anyway, how was your day? Get any writing done? When are you going to tell me about the new plot line? Not like you to keep so hush, hush."

Michael said nothing. His only response was a slight smirk.

"Well, nobody died in the ED today," said Maria. "That is always a good day in my line of work. But in yours, people die all the time, because you kill them. Cheers, mi amor." They both toasted, sat back, and chatted about petty things, but not about Michael's new manuscript.

MORNING OF THE SURGERY

"Alejandro Harper, I am quite surprised. You are half an hour early." Maria said as she hugged Allie at the front door with her deep feeling of love and support. "From you, I expect on time or a bit late. But never early. Did your watch stop?"

"I don't know, Mom. Something told me last night, we need to be at the hospital early. I have had premonitions before, and this one is telling me Dad needs us as soon as we can get there. What room is he in?" Allie asked as he and Maria moved from the front door to the kitchen.

"I'm not sure. We'll ask one of those elderly ladies in the lobby when we get there," "Here, take a travel mug with you in the car, and let's go. I'll drive."

"No, Mom," Allie interrupted. "We must take two cars. I have a class at three and an exam at four o'clock today. I'm hoping to leave the hospital in time to make them. I can miss the class, but not the exam." Allie walked with his mother through the garage and out to his car, while Maria kept a careful eye out for anything strange in the garage without mentioning her cautiousness to Allie. He still didn't know anything about the dog. "I will follow you, Mom."

They walked into the hospital lobby. An elderly woman at the reception desk, wearing an aged, flowered dress, was fiddling with the controller of her hearing aid when Maria and Allie approached. "Can you tell me what room Michael Harper is in, please? He was transferred from the ED last night," Maria said, but the woman didn't look up.

"This is the best hearing aid money can buy, Missy," said the woman in a feeble voice and still working on her controller.

Allie and Maria looked at each other and smiled. She was so cute.

"How much did it cost?" Allie asked.

"Thursday." said the woman. "Hooper you say? Don't have a Hooper, sorry."

Maria leaned over the desk to get closer. "No, ma'am, Harper, Michael Harper. It's right there," Maria said loudly. Allie was trying to keep from laughing.

"You're not allowed to be on my side of the desk, honey. Scoot, Scoot. Federal laws you know. They told me they could arrest me and put me in prison if I let anybody back here," the lady's head shaking in fear as she looked to see if she was caught. "And they're not kidding. I heard of a receptionist in California..."

"I'm sure, ma'am, but what room is Michael Harper in presently?" Maria interrupted as she and Allie continued to smile at each other.

"Oh yea, there she is. Michelle Harper, Room 233. Just take those elevators right over there to the second floor and turn, uh, left, I think. Let me tell them you're on your way up. There's a note here that says to call when you arrive. They are expecting you, Mrs. Harper," said the receptionist.

Maria and Allie took the elevator to the second floor and hung a left, then shortly realized Miss Information in the lobby needed to tell them to take a right. Smiles again. As they walked down the hallway looking for room 233, they approached the nurses' station. What appeared to be the head nurse stood in the corridor like a tour guide in an art museum. *What a nice gesture of concern to greet us,* Maria thought, but the closer their approach, the less friendly she appeared.

"You are Mrs. Harper, correct?" said the nurse.

"Yes, I am. And this is my son, Alejandro. This is so kind of you to greet us and help us find my husband's room. He is fine, I assume?" Maria asked, her voice rising in pitch.

"Yes, your husband is fine at the moment. I told the receptionist to let me know when you arrived. I wanted to catch you before you talked to him. Will you two join me in the room across the hall? It is about your husband's behavior last night. We need to talk," said the nurse, her voice trembling, contemplating a confrontation.

"I must admit, you have me concerned." They followed the nurse.

"You introduced this young man as your son, and therefore, I assume he is Mr. Harper's son as well. It's nice to meet you both. I wanted to tell you about last night. We had an incident with your husband and had to call security."

"Security? I don't understand. He could hardly move when I left last night." Maria shared a perplexed glance with Allie.

"Security called the police station to ask what exactly happened to your husband yesterday afternoon."

"He tripped on his shoestring," said Allie. "Why would you need to bring the police in on that? I know he was angry last night about being so clumsy. But security? He couldn't have gone off that bad. That's not like my dad, unless it was the drugs you gave him." Allie spoke loudly, upset, and confused.

Maria turned to him, put her hand on his forearm, and calmly said, "Allie, I need you to be quiet right now and just listen. Remember when your dad said, 'You don't know the half of it?' Well, you don't. I'll explain it to you in detail while your dad's in surgery." She looked at the nurse again. "Please, tell us what happened."

"Well, Mrs. Harper, even with the medication, your husband drifted in and out of sleep due to his pain and discomfort. But every time he woke up, even a little bit, he would ring for one of us in our station. And every time, he told us he was awakened by a man with a pit bull that wanted to kill him, and he needed protection. After his first ring, we immediately called security, and two of our in-house guards came to the floor, while one called the police to see what had happened. They told us the story about the intruder and the pit bull attack that caused his injuries."

"Pit bull attack? What?" Allie exploded.

"Wait a minute," Maria said, ignoring the look of shocked confusion on Allie's face. "How could someone with a dog that size roam the hallways in the middle of the night without anyone spotting him? I don't understand. How could you let this happen? I want to talk to your administrator right now." She stomped her foot in anger to get her point across to the nurse.

"Mrs. Harper, give me time to finish the story, there is more. From your husband's first call, Security started to scan the hallways and the rooms, but we figured the man and the dog had escaped down the stairwell. The remaining security guards began to look on other floors. But this is a big hospital, with a lot of empty rooms and closets and places to hide. They watched the security footage, but there was no sign of a man or a dog."

"Well, maybe the man came here and was hiding in his room when you took Michael there after his tests. Like maybe in the bathroom," Maria suggested.

"Well, we thought about that, but he would have had to know the specific room we were taking him to before he was admitted."

"Do you have elderly ladies or anybody working in the lobby or in registration at night?" asked Maria.

"No, anyone entering the hospital after ten must go through security for a room number, and visiting hours are over at ten except for the Emergency and Intensive Care departments. No one is allowed up here. Why do you ask?"

"Oh, no reason." Allie and Maria glanced at each other quickly then back. "Then Security would have seen someone with a pit bull even if they did give out a room number?" Maria continued her interrogation.

"No doubt, that is a tough one to miss. So, we placed a security guard outside his door all night, along with someone watching the security cameras."

"And somehow, this predator got past your security and your cameras? Now I really want to talk to an administrator."

The nurse looked straight into Maria's eyes. "Mrs. Harper, if I were you, I would feel the same way. What kind of place is this, you must be asking yourself? But your husband pushed the help button for us two more times after that with the same problem. The guard was outside the door. All of us in the station kept our eyes and ears open, and nothing was recorded on the cameras all night. I assure you, no man with a pit bull could have gotten past us, the guard, and the cameras. Your husband went through a lot yesterday. I blame it on the trauma and the medication. It sounds like a hallucination. I wanted to warn you. He is not happy with any of us right now."

Maria looked down at the floor as Allie stared at his mother. "Let's go see your father," said Maria. "Thank you, for the information. I'm sorry I got upset before you finished. There are a lot of strange things happening lately." Maria and Allie walked down the hall toward room 233, but the nurse called to them.

"Mrs. Harper, I must request you do not allow anyone to sneak cigars into your husband's room. I heard you're an ED nurse so you know how dangerous that can be with oxygen. Every time we were called to his room, the aroma from his cigars was strong."

"Mother," said Allie, "I have never seen Dad smoke anything except that old corncob pipe when he would take me fishing. Does he smoke now?"

"No, he doesn't, but leave it alone. I will explain it to you when your dad's in surgery. But Allie, I am not sure I understand it myself. But there might be something else happening with your father."

As they entered Michael's room, he was still strapped down with tubes and IVs. "Hi, honey. How was your night? Uncomfortable, I'm sure," Maria said as she kissed him on the forehead.

In a groggy and angry tone, Michael snapped, "That son of a bitch with the dog came here three times last night. What kind of security does this place have, goddammit? Like I haven't had enough of this bullshit. I can't even close my eyes without that bastard and his freaking dog trying to kill me. I want to see the administrator as soon as I get out of surgery. And that asshole was smoking a cigar right here in my room. The room stinks big-time, and I hate cigar smoke. And, he could have blown us both up. I didn't think you could smoke in a hospital?"

Maria and Allie looked at each other. They both picked up a twinge of cigar smoke in the air. And neither of them was used to the profanity Michael was using in front of them. He was more refined than that. Allie was worried his dad was losing it.

"Yes dear, that is horrible," said Maria in a soothing tone. "We will get to the bottom of this." She leaned down and kissed Michael on the lips.

He did not smell or taste like a cigar. "I will call the two officers on the case, then talk to the administrator. You didn't say hello to Allie, mi amor."

"Oh, hey, kid. I'm sorry I ignored you. I'd give you a hug if I could move my arms. But you can give me one."

Allie approached Michael, placed his cheek to Michael's face and gave him a gentle hug. "I love you, Dad," Allie whispered in his father's ear. The sight of his dad in a hospital bed, weak and helpless, was disturbing to him. His Dad was his idol and image of strength. Thoughts entered Allie's head, thoughts he never had before.

"Love you too, my not so little guy. Thanks for being here," Michael told his son. "And sorry I'm so grumpy."

"No, it's okay, Dad. I get it. But I don't know much about what happened yesterday, except that you tripped on your shoestring. I'm so confused now about some dog and some man, not to mention police officers, but Mom will fill me in after you hit surgery."

"Michael, the nurse told Allie and me about the man and the dog visiting you last night," Maria stated. "When your meds wear off, we'll talk about it. Something is odd about the last two weeks. But for now, you're safe and healthy. Let's get through the surgery."

Just then, Dr. Sung came into the room. "Good morning, Mr. and Mrs. Harper. Thank you for getting here early, Mrs. Harper. It will give us time to talk. And this is who?"

"This is our son, Alejandro. Allie, this is Dr. Sung, the ED doctor following your father's case. Our son starts med school next fall. We are so proud of him. What would you like to talk about, Doctor?" asked Maria.

"Well, can we talk outside the room. Michael needs to be prepared for surgery, and the OR nurses prefer to work without distraction. We need some final paperwork, since your husband can't sign anything in his condition," said Dr. Sung. "And your husband's general practitioner paged me last night and explained a few things of which I was unaware." Dr. Sung's mood was even colder than last night. He seemed agitated. She told Michael they'd be right back. But as she kissed him, Michael had a look on his face she had never seen, not even in those early Panama days when they met. Her intuition said fear, a deep-down kind of fear, like a little boy keeping a secret from his mother and about to be exposed.

They went down the hall to a small conference room, where Dr. Stein and another doctor, unknown to Maria, were already seated.

Introductions and greetings were exchanged. Dr. Sung closed the door and sat around a powerful oblong conference table. Dr. Sung looked at everyone in the room, then began to speak. "I don't know where to start. I am not permitted by law to start this conversation. But I would be remiss if I didn't say I feel extremely uncomfortable. I must insist, however, that I obtain more information before this surgery can begin."

Maria and Allie, as confused and perplexed as they had been all morning, took their eyes off Dr. Sung, glanced at each other, then both, simultaneously, stared at Dr. Stein.

"What is he talking about, Bob? You've been his doctor, no, you've been more than that. You've been his friend and confidant since way before I met Michael. He put his life in your hands via telephone in Panama, as well as that piece of junk glider you guys flew around in. What is this all about? You boys are keeping something from us." Maria asked, her eyes squinted, and head tilted in a state of bewilderment. Allie began to speak up, but Maria held his forearm tightly, their long-time signal for him to stay quiet. Allie didn't know how much longer he could remain in this unenlightened state with puzzle pieces scattered and missing as they lay all over the floor.

Dr. Stein spoke first. "Well, Dr. Sung, I knew this day would come, but I, as well, cannot give you any information. You have what you have from your testing last night. And if Mr. Harper wishes to proceed with the surgery, he has that right, after signing a release and disclaimer holding you not responsible. You and I spoke on the telephone last night. I have been Michael's general practitioner and dear friend for many years. And this is Dr. John Knarr, another one of Michael's doctors."

"Come on now, Bob, this isn't right," Maria blurted. "Who are you, Dr. John Knarr? I thought you were the surgeon, Edward Rowekamp. You're not? Speak up, somebody, and say something meaningful. I have had enough of this silly-ass dance." Maria was furious. She stood with her palms flat on the table, leaning across at Bob Stein and this 'Knarr' guy.

John Knarr, M.D., a middle-aged man with a calm somber face and wire-rimmed glasses, began to speak. "Dr. Stein called me last night after

Mrs. Harper requested a recommendation for a surgeon. But like the other two doctors, Mrs. Harper, I am unable to breach confidence in this situation without Mr. Harper's permission. Dr. Sung, unfortunately, we were confident you would discover what we already knew when you ran tests last night, especially the CT scan. We were hoping to talk to you much earlier this morning but couldn't get hold of you. Bob and I decided it best to come here and talk to you personally before his family arrived."

"I was sleeping and gave instructions not to be disturbed unless it was an emergency," said Sung defensively.

Knarr was all business. "I'm sorry, Dr. Sung, but I told your assistant on the telephone I needed to talk to you personally before seven o'clock and it was urgent. I believe your staff may need some additional training." Knarr and Stein stared at Sung.

"You could have contacted me earlier, Drs., like last night." Knarr went on.

"Our plan was to consult with you at 7:00 A.M. when you had Mr. Harper's test results, but it was meant to be in private, not in front of Maria and Alejandro. You brought them in here without our permission and started this conversation that has now led the Harpers into mystery and grave concern. And before I say anything more, and before you say anymore, Dr. Sung, I will need to consult with Michael. I promised him total confidentiality in this matter. Before HIPPA laws, we simply called it ethics, and it was respected. I'm sure all the health care providers in the room, and Alejandro, who is about to be an M.D., will respect my position, and Alejandro will learn a valuable lesson." Knarr looked seriously into Alejandro's eyes. They all agreed, and Alejandro realized he was officially in pre-med. "Congrats, by the way, son," said Knarr. "Your parents must be proud, as well as Dr. Stein." Alejandro smiled showing him his respect, but wanted answers, not congratulations.

"Yes, sir, we all respect your position," Maria responded to the room, her passivity was over. "I understand all of your situations, legally and ethically. But if I don't get answers soon, and I mean real soon, I will march down that hallway and squeeze the answers out of my husband with my bare hands, no matter how hurt he is. He will ask me why I think something is wrong, Dr. Sung. You breached confidentiality when you

MORNING OF THE SURGERY

brought Alejandro and me into this room, Dr. Sung. Let's hope Michael is reasonable whatever this is about." Silence reigned over the room after Maria's push. Sung was aghast, sweat formed on his forehead.

Dr. Knarr pointed his index at Dr. Sung, "Mrs. Harper is correct. You breached confidentiality. I'm sure Dr. Stein agrees when I state that we are not pleased with you. Until I return, no more discussion about Michael, unless it's about his fracture repair this morning."

"Okay. Go quickly," said Sung "or we will need to postpone or cancel the surgery. I don't think the hospital, or the surgeon will be too happy about that," said Sung. Knarr got up, gave a disgusted glance in Sung's direction, and left the room.

Stein took over, "I would be careful with what sounds like demands and threats, Dr. Sung. You are in no position. I know Michael. You may have the 'Wrath of God' about to come down on your head, not to mention some of the most bad-ass lawyers you have ever met. And I will talk to Rowekamp if I need to."

"What's going on, Bob?" Maria asked.

"I have had enough," said Allie. "Everyone tells me to sit quietly like a good little boy. I am not a boy anymore, and my father and I are very close. Mom's tough, but I think it is time for me to get involved and become her protector." Maria smiled on the outside but thought how beautifully naïve that was coming from the young mortal with the Archangel Michael protecting all of them.

"Maria, Allie, be patient for a few more minutes. Knarr will be back soon, and I have a feeling you will have all the answers." said Stein. Maria sensed this was not good. She turned white as a ghost. Allie grabbed her hand and put his arm around his mother's shoulder. She reached for a tissue in her purse and dabbed her eyes. Allie pinched his nose as the tears threatened to fall and thought, *in a few years, when I'm a doc, I'll be on the other side of this table. Please God, don't let me be as cold as Knarr or as stupid as Sung.*

Knarr returned. He sat back in his chair and sighed deeply. "Dr. Sung, I just spoke to Michael and explained to him that when Bob told me last night you were going to do a CT scan, I called your radiology department. They told me what they found. I came in and studied the results myself.

They were consistent with what I already knew. Nine months ago, we did a routine screening to make sure his prostate cancer was still in remission. That's when we found a small mass on Michael's lung. We attempted to talk Michael into chemo and radiation again, but he refused. Alejandro, I'm sure, remembers bringing Michael to the hospital last April. Allie, he told you it was a routine diagnostic procedure, didn't he? Well, it was, and he knew what we were going to find, he knew his cancer was back with a vengeance, because he could feel it in his lung this time."

"I remember that day well. Our discussion was deep. He talked about his fantastic life and how, as he said, 'Something gets all of us.' He told me how proud he is I am his son, but I thought he was speculating and being philosophical. Dad can get a little corny sometimes. I had no idea he knew what he knew." Alejandro put his index finger to his nose and looked at the ceiling, holding back the reality of the moment.

Knarr continued. "After we confirmed it, he told me he had no desire to go through the nausea, pain, and weakness again. And he did not want the two of you to go through taking care of some 'old sick invalid,' as he put it. He would rather die sooner than later. He made me promise I would not tell anyone except Stein how bad it was, not even him. He didn't know how bad it was until I told him ten minutes ago. That's a promise I kept until today, until right now."

"How bad is it?" asked Maria.

"The cancer is throughout his body, in his lungs and his spine. A few cells have moved to his brain. Even if he changed his mind now to have chemo, it would be useless. He has six months to a year, tops. And from here on, he'll be in a lot of pain, lose a lot of weight, and get weaker every day. He told me he only has one reason to live. He wants to see his son, Alejandro, and his grandson Cantor, graduate in June."

Alejandro's tears no longer just threatened; they came roaring out. Stein got up and Maria buried her head in his shoulder. She sobbed.

"He still wants to go ahead with the surgery," Knarr continued, "and I agree, so he can at least be mobile for his remaining months. He said, after the graduation, if he must be taken care of like a child, he will deal with that problem himself."

MORNING OF THE SURGERY

Maria came out of Stein's shoulder. "He really said 'He'll deal with that problem himself'? Oh Bob, I know what he means and so do you. I'll kick his stupid ass myself if it means what I think it does."

Knarr didn't say a word. They all knew what he meant.

"And while he's in surgery and under anesthesia, I will drain his lungs again. It will help him breathe as he rehabs his shoulder."

"Again?" said Maria, "what do you mean, again?"

"Maria, with this kind of cancer, it slowly fills his lungs with fluid. This makes him short of breath. You may have heard him wheezing from time to time."

"Yes, I've heard him wheeze, but he tells me it's his allergies. But it goes away." replied Maria, again not knowing what she's about to learn next.

Knarr answered her question. "Maria, when you're at work, we have one of our RNs pick him up, about every week, and brings him to my office. I stick a needle through his back and into his lungs."

"Oh my God, doctor. He has shown no sign of pain from that procedure," said Maria.

"Maria, it doesn't hurt, well maybe a little. I drain the fluid out of his lungs to allow his body to get the oxygen it needs, and it relieves the pain and pressure. That cough and wheeze he tells you is an allergy, is his lungs filling with fluid. You probably notice a change in his behavior, for the good. It's an incredible relief to him. We've been doing this for six months." Knarr spoke seriously. Alejandro's imagination shot into the future, and he realized how tough this doctor thing was going to be.

Maria and Allie hugged, trying to talk. Maria ran her hand through her son's hair. "Allie, your father has told us many times, when he becomes a burden and is no longer useful, he wants to die. That time is drawing near. I know he is still able to write, and he is working on a book he will tell me nothing about. He has never done that before. So, he has one last novel to finish and you and Cantor's graduation to attend."

Allie turned to the doctors, "What did he tell you he wants right now?"

Knarr jumped in again, this time scratching his head. "He said he wants to have the surgery, then go into rehab, so he can kill some 'bastard' and his fucked-up dog before they hurt your mother.' Makes no sense to me, and dementia is not part of this type of cancer when there are no masses in his brain. But he is hell-bent on protecting your mother. I assume that makes sense to someone?"

Maria was starting to get an idea of what was happening. "I have had him protected for years. I will continue to take care of him and love him until the end. I just didn't see it coming this fast."

"Allie, Maria," said Stein. "Your father is one tough cookie. I have never had a patient handle pain and inevitable death like him. He has been preparing for it all his life. The last time I saw him, he told me he has special protection from angels in his life, but he said this was different. He talked about the wonderful life he has had, 'one that people can only dream about' to quote him. He wanted to keep this quiet, so you all could enjoy his last days without fear or pity. He wants love and happiness right up to the end and beyond. Now that you know, try to respect his wishes. Enjoy each other in the upcoming year."

Allie thought, *That is the type of doctor I want to be.*

Before leaving the room, Maria and Stein hugged and thanked each other. She forgave Dr. Sung for his misunderstanding and thanked him for his help. Sung continued to be aloof. And she thanked Knarr for his loyalty and respect for Michael's wishes. Allie was proud of the way his mother handled the morning in such a forceful, but graceful way.

Michael went to surgery. Maria explained the last twenty-four hours to Allie. He hung on her every word, barely managing to keep his flood of love for his father at bay.

"Mother, in the conference room, you had a look on your face like you know something nobody else knows, not even me. What is it?" asked Allie.

Maria put her hand on Alejandro's cheek and smiled. "I do, and your father and I will reveal it to you when he is stronger." Alejandro accepted her response for now. They both sat quietly.

6

ONE WEEK BEFORE MICHAEL'S SURGERY

It was the routine in the Harper's daily life. Maria played her garage door game and entered the kitchen with a bottle of wine and groceries. She called to her best friend and husband "Hola, mi amor. Did your day go well? Did all your characters survive your wrath, or did some poor soul get devoured by a wombat or a zombie?"

But rather than responding in his usual jovial fashion, she heard, "No, goddammit, the day did not go well. They're back, Maria, and they brought their friends and family."

"Who's back, love? The people calling again to tell us it's our last chance for an extended warranty on our eight-year-old car?" Maria laughed at Michael's impatience.

"No, no, not those clowns. Remember what I told you this morning?"

"No, I don't remember you telling me anything. But go on, tell me again."

We have cockroaches? After you fell asleep, I went to the kitchen to get a glass of milk, and when I turned on the light, I caught a glimpse of them out of the corner of my eye. They scampered across the kitchen floor and down the hallway, and I'm talking huge. I could have strapped them to my feet and won a race. We have never had roaches in our house here in the states. But I figured tonight, I can run after them and stomp them dead. I played a stompin' game in our kitchen in Panama. My record was nine. Maria knew Michael was dreaming, because then was then and now is now. She kept her humor locked inside.

"Honey," Maria laughed, "I think roaches are faster in this cooler weather. Traps or an exterminator will work better, and I don't want you tracking the goop from your shoes on my floors," Maria said, trying to save Michael's ego.

"But just when I heard the garage door, I came into the kitchen to greet you, and the ugly bastards were back, along with at least a dozen littler ones. The littler ones hightailed it under the cabinets, but the two big ones ran down the hallway like last night. Somebody leaked to them my nickname was 'The Smoosher'." Michael gave Maria an impish smirk.

Marie had one lip raised and her eyes wide open. "Seriously Smoosher, they sound as horrid as the bats. I won't go near the kitchen tonight. We're ordering out. But I didn't think they bothered you, Michael? You played your game and sometimes you didn't wear shoes. That was disgusting."

"I know it was disgusting and I did it just to tease you, but I always washed my feet before bedtime. And they didn't bother me down there. I figured the roaches were there first, and we were living on their land, so I respected their rights."

"'Roaches Rights' Michael? So, what is different now, Squasher?"

"Smoosher, not Squasher, my love. Those names mean two different things," Michael said, again with a boyish grin, "but what is different, honey, is these roaches are behemoths. They look like lobster. If we had a dog, they could eat him. They are creeping me out." Michael was getting into imagination mode.

"Alright, sci-fi guy, enough." Maria could enjoy his rambles, but there was a limit.

Do we still have the name of the bat guy we used? I liked him. He knew his stuff. Let us call him and ask if he knows anything about roaches?"

"I am sure he does. But I thought you didn't like him. You were rude to him. You didn't even say goodbye," Maria fastidiously tiptoed into the kitchen and unpacked the groceries.

"I wasn't after he finally explained himself. I was embarrassed for myself. Call him right now, not after dinner. Tell him to get his ass over here right away." Maria found Michael's change from humor to anger puzzling. "I will not have those things crawling on our food or on our faces in the night. I flung many off my face in Panama. Do you understand me, Maria? I want these monsters gone." Michael pounded his fist on the counter, eyes wide open, nostrils flaring.

"What is wrong with you? You never speak to me that way. I will call him now if you insist. Put the groceries in the refrigerator for now, so your roller skate roaches can't get to them."

Maria went to the desk and got Nisner's card. She was baffled by Michael's explosive behavior.

"Hello, Nisner's Exterminators, Jim Nisner speaking." Maria could tell he had a mouthful of food and was eating dinner.

"Oh, Mr. Nisner, I'm glad I caught you. I'm so sorry I am interrupting your dinner. This is Mrs. Harper on Clineview. You helped us with a bat problem last week."

"Of course, I just finished the research this afternoon and wanted to talk to you. Is that why you're calling? Are they back?"

"No, sir, they are not, but we have another problem. We had roaches in our kitchen for the first-time last night, and my husband saw them again right when I got home. When my husband and I lived in Panama, we were used to them, but now that we live in America, we are freaking out. Can you help us soon, like tonight?" Maria asked.

"Sure, I will be there in two hours."

"My husband is scared they will crawl on our food and our faces as we sleep. Can you come sooner?" Maria pleaded.

"Well, I could but that won't work..."

"I'm sorry," Maria interrupted again. "I will tell my husband it can wait until tomorrow. You have been working all day, and you are eating dinner, and you need to spend time with your family. We can stay in a hotel tonight."

"Mrs. Harper, I live alone and have only a dog. She is a sweet pit bull and defends me. I got her as a rescue. My point is, I must come after dark. They are most active at night. I want you and your husband to prepare dinner and drop some food and crumbs on the kitchen floor, preferable lettuce, or some rotten gunk from inside a garbage can. Leave the lids off the garbage cans so they get the scent. Then take your food into your bedroom and eat there. Turn off the lights in the rest of the house. Make it as dark as possible."

"We could eat by candlelight," said Maria with a chuckle.

"I like your attitude, Mrs. Harper," Nisner said with a chuckle as well. "Turn your phones to vibrate and when I arrive, I will call you from my truck. Blow out your candle. Have Mr. Harper go quietly to the kitchen light switch and stay motionless. You tiptoe to the front door. I will have my cell phone ready. At the same time, you open the door, Michael turns on the light and I take pictures. Sound like a plan, Mrs. Harper?"

"Fantastic, Mr. Nisner. You're the best. We'll expect you two hours from now, at 8:25. I will explain the plan to Michael. He will love it." Maria hung up and explained the course of action to Michael. She was right, he loved it.

At 8:25 P.M. Maria's cell vibrated. Before she could speak, Nisner whispered, "Here we go."

Maria blew out the candle and tiptoed to the front door. She quietly unlocked the door and removed the chain. Michael moved to the light switch.

Maria opened the door. Michael turned on the lights. "Got you, you nasty creatures," Michael yelled as Nisner flashed away at the kitchen floor. Michael looked anxiously over the wing wall and into the kitchen.

But to everyone's surprise, there was nothing, nada, not anything but the food and garbage on the floor. "Shit," yelled Michael, "I'm telling you; they were there earlier. Next time, I'm stomping as fast as I can. I'm going to squish one so you will believe me." He walked back into the bedroom, shaking his head with embarrassment.

"What do you think, Mr. Nisner?" asked Maria. "After the bat thing, you must think we're crazy. I am so sorry."

"No, no, Mrs. Harper. I want to talk to you about the bat situation when I finish. Something is happening I have never seen before. Let me check on this roach problem, first." Nisner went to his truck to get his flashlights and specimen jars.

Maria unlocked her prayer room, then went into the bedroom. She found Michael sitting in his chair, shaking his head, and staring at the floor. She walked over to him, sat on his lap, and gave him a big kiss.

"You both must think I am looney tunes. First the bats, then roaches. Hell, what next, Donald Duck dancing on the countertop? T. Rex in the backyard? Maybe those acid flashbacks from the sixties have finally arrived," said Michael. Maria kissed him again and started laughing.

"No, honey, Mr. Nisner told me he wanted to talk to us tonight about the bat situation. He told me it is something he has never seen. Before you flip out and play 'Kool-Aid Acid Test' on me, let us hear what Mr. Nisner has to say." She got off his lap and gave him one more peck on the cheek before going to the kitchen.

Maria settled into her favorite chair in the living room while Nisner searched the kitchen cabinets and looked under the sink. He inspected the bathrooms to see if the problem was water bugs. When he went into the bedroom to check under the bathroom sink, Michael didn't look up, he was too embarrassed. Nisner assumed Michael simply didn't like him.

Finally, Nisner checked outside around the foundation. When he returned, he spoke to Maria. "Mrs. Harper," he said in a reserved voice. "I found only one thing that could be roach related. I saw no sign of actual roaches, and I was about to tell you they were gone, but that would be unusual, especially with the quantity your husband saw. But I did find this in your back room near the altar." Nisner held up a specimen jar.

"What is that?" said Maria. "It looks like something left from the cicadas last summer."

"Well, it might be, but I doubt it. It looks like a molt from a roach nymph. Roaches go through a metamorphosis from eggs to numerous stages of nymph and molting as they grow to adulthood. But this was the only one I found."

"Is it a roach, Mr. Nisner? I really hope so, for Michael's sake. He thinks you question his sanity. I think he is suspecting Alzheimer's. Tell me it is from a roach."

"I can't say for sure. And I found only one molt. There would have to be more with the quantity your husband saw. I was going to tell you about the bat situation tonight, but now I need to wait. I took the guano to the zoo to have it tested, and they said they needed to double check something. Let me drop this off tomorrow. They can give me a report on both. In the meantime, I don't want to spray, because if the roaches die in your walls, the odor will be around for quite some time. I will put roach traps in your kitchen tonight. Maybe we can trap a few to see what we are dealing with."

"Sounds great, Mr. Nisner. I will tell Michael about your plan. And thank you for being so responsive and considerate."

"And tell Mr. Harper to stop worrying. Tell him I am as confused as he is until we get the report back from the zoo." Nisner set the traps under the sinks and in the middle of the kitchen floor, said good night, and left.

Maria went into the bedroom and kissed Michael on the forehead. "What did he say, Maria?"

"We both agreed you are as crazy as a cuckoo clock and he suggested I sell you to the circus," Maria said giggling as she fell back on the bed. Then they both started to laugh. "No honey, he said he would get back to us with results from the zoo. Michael, be easy on yourself; he has a strange feeling about this as well."

Michael and Maria both got ready for bed. They grabbed their books, read for a bit, and soon fell asleep, but both remembered experiencing the disturbing feeling of a roach crawling across their faces in those Panamanian nights.

The following morning, Maria arose and prepared for work. Michael continued sleeping. She went to the kitchen to grab some breakfast and noticed something was different. She went back into the bedroom and wanted to tickle Michael's face like a roach creeping across it, but decided he would not find that funny.

"Michael, Michael." She shook him gently. "Did you go to the kitchen last night and move any roach traps?"

"No, honey," he said in a groggy fashion. "Why would I do that? I kept a bottle of water in here, so I didn't have to deal with any roaches. Why?"

"Well, he put five in the middle of the floor. Two were still there but three were pushed all the way into the dining room. How did they get moved?" Maria and Michael stared at each other.

"Did you shake the box to see if anything is inside?" asked Michael.

"I did. They're empty," said Maria. "I think I should let Mr. Nisner know about this." Maria called, left a message on Nisner's cell. She grabbed a bagel and a cup of coffee and left for work. Perplexity was beginning to be a way of life.

7

OUT OF OR

As Maria and Allie talked, the man and the dog became a secondary conversation to the not-too-distant death of Michael. They cried intermittently and hugged each other often. They spoke of alternatives to keep him alive: diets, clinical trials, medical marijuana. Maria was thinking about something she might be able to do with her powers. Michael ruled out chemo and radiation when he finished his last bout of prostate cancer. Plans needed to be made for the next six months to a year. And Michael's children and grandchildren needed to be informed immediately.

"Mrs. Harper?" said a nurse as she stuck her head out the door. "The doctor talked to you both, correct? Your husband is doing fine. He's a strong man for his age. He'll be as good as new soon."

"Yes, he's stronger than you imagine, and thank you." The nurse was doing her job, but Maria became angry inside. *He is not doing fine*, she thought. It was going to be tough dealing with this grief.

"You and your son can go to Mr. Harper's room now. He is in a twilight so go slowly with him." Maria and Allie made their way to Michael's room.

He was, for sure, in the twilight. He looked pale and fragile. And now that Michael's condition was exposed, different sentiments were invading their psyches.

Maria pulled a chair to Michael's bedside and kissed him gently. She held his hand, her cheek pressed against it. She thought, *He kept this from us so we wouldn't treat him differently in his remaining days, but how do I do that? I can't lose him. I just can't.* She remained quiet.

"Hey, Dad, are you awake?" asked Allie, trying to appear upbeat.

"Sort of, Allie," Michael answered with a cottonmouth. "Can you get me some water?"

"I got it, Mom." Alejandro filled a plastic cup with ice water. He opened the bendy straw, but before giving his dad the straw, he gave him another gentle, placid hug. Looking directly into his face, Alejandro said confidently, "Doc said all went well. You could be back pitching for the Reds this Spring." Michael gave a weak smile.

Maria was struggling. As Michael emerged from anesthesia, his blanched and cadaverous appearance gave her the unfathomable prelude to his future deathbed scene. She felt nauseous. But she knew he needed her strength, not her pity. She knew Allie understood what needed to be done, though she caught glimpses of disquieting woe on his face as he glanced at the ceiling when his dad wasn't watching. The expressions betrayed his outward humorous actions.

"Your color is returning, love. Are you in pain?" asked Maria.

"No, no pain at all, unlike yesterday. But I haven't moved yet," said Michael, his voice scratchy but his mind becoming lucid. His mouth, however, was still like the Sahara. He could barely talk or swallow. "Can you ask the nurse if I can have some water, Maria?"

"Allie just gave you some, but you want more?" Allie grabbed his father's cup of ice water and again held the bendy straw to his father's dry, chapped lips. "Maybe sneak in some scotch for later, Dad?" Michael giggled.

"That would be nice. Come back after your exam and have a drink with me?"

"You can't have alcohol in a hospital, bad boys. I mean, you could sneak it in, but really, not this soon after surgery. Are you ever going to get serious, Michael?" Maria knew he loved to be scolded for his free spirit and rebellious nature.

"You both know what's going on, so the answer is no, my love. My name is Michael Harper and I do what needs to be done. And a glass of scotch with my son is what needs to be done, and every other member of my family; end of discussion." Maria and Allie understood what Michael was going to be like from here to the end. All three smiled, because they loved his playful attitude.

They made small talk as Michael consumed an all-liquid lunch. Then Maria spoke earnestly.

"Michael, I must call work to check my schedule this week, then inform the family about the success of your surgery, but I will not mention the cancer although I suggest we do it soon. Will you please excuse me?" She forced a smile and left the room. She knew her role in the next year would be difficult. And she would be helpless to protect him from natural forces, unlike her protection by the Archangel.

After Maria left the room, Allie gave Michael a goof-ball smile. "Okay, Dad, now that we're alone, what's going on with this dog thing? Do you have gambling debts I don't know about? Or did you feel stupid in front of Mom and couldn't leave it at the fact you tripped over your shoestring?"

"Gambling? Oh God no, boy. You have been around me. I am small potatoes. They would pay more to feed that ugly beast than what they would collect from me. And I win most of the time, so remember to whom you are talking." They both laughed and wanted to shadowbox like always, but not yet. "I must tell you, kid, there is something going on. It is real to me, but not others. I am questioning my sanity. I am getting around that age when minds go and with this cancer, who knows? Dogs and bats and roaches, weird events all month," Michael shook his head. "Allie, I don't want you all to remember me that way. I have always wanted to make you all laugh, but mental illness, that is different. My strongest trait has always been my brain. In my youth, what I lacked in size I made up by being a student of the game, and that followed me into the business and writing world." Michael's face looked concerned.

Alejandro put his hand on top of his father's. His voice was choking, and he was holding back deep emotions. His father taught him to be strong in the face of overwhelming odds. 'Always find a way to make things come out the best for your loved ones and you will be fine,' Michael would say, and all Alejandro knew was the basic of his Panamanian heritage. He knew his father needed him strong. Allie always knew his father was going to die someday, but he was having a problem with reality.

"Dad we were given all the details about your cancer and how long you have."

"Son, you and I must have a talk very soon when we will not be interrupted by anyone, especially your mother."

"Mom said she had something to tell me as well. Is it the same thing?" asked Allie.

"Don't know what she wants to tell you, son? I will ask her."

Outside in the waiting room, Maria was talking to her boss. On the other line, she received a call. It was Officer Caine. "Betty, I have a call coming I must take. I will call you back." Maria switched lines.

"Hello, Officer, how is your day? Do you have any news for me?"

"I do. Where are you now, Mrs. Harper? And how is Mr. Harper?"

"He is fine. He is out of surgery. My son is with him. Tell me, sir, I'm anxious to hear if you found anything."

"I am in the lobby with my partner. We want to speak with you in person, alone. Is that possible? If you could come down now, that would be great, but if you need to stay with your family, we understand. We can come back at later."

"I can meet you now." Maria poked her head in the room and told her boys she would be back shortly. She headed for the elevators. When she reached the lobby, the two officers were standing with an obese hospital security guard. He escorted them to a private conference room.

"Good to see you, Mrs. Harper. We hope everything went well with the surgery and expect Mr. Harper will be back on his feet in no time. But make sure he ties his shoes." They all smiled except the security guard; he was lost.

"Well, it's not as simple as a shoestring, gentlemen," said Maria. "We were informed this morning, before the surgery, that Michael is in an advanced stage of cancer, and he has less than a year. We are doing our best to hide our shock. Now, what do you want to tell me about last night?" Maria's eyes began to water yet again, though she had cried so much this morning, she was surprised her body was able to produce even one more tear.

"First, Mrs. Harper, accept my apologies for that unfeeling remark about the shoestring. He looks healthy, especially for an eighty-year-old man." Caine was blushing from his embarrassment.

"No offense taken, sir. You didn't know."

"Thank you, Mrs. Harper, and you have our prayers. But to the point, before you joined us, the head of hospital security seating across from you, informed us of Michaels' claim of the man and his dog entering his room numerous times last night. And cigar smoke lingering in Michael's room. Mr. Harper didn't smoke a cigar last night, correct?"

"Heavens, no. He hates cigars. He has always been a rebel, but that's not his style. My son and I did get a whiff of the smoke this morning in the room."

"The guard showed us the security footage, but the intruders were nowhere to be found. And the guard and nurses outside his room saw nothing." Caine revealed.

"I understand. They explained it to me before Michael went to surgery. But Michael vehemently swears they were here last night." Maria looked down and squeezed her forehead in bewilderment. "The cancer's in his lungs and spine, and a few cells in his brain. The oncologist highly doubts this is dementia or hallucinations from the cancer."

"Mrs. Harper, again we're so sorry to hear about Mr. Harper's cancer, but that is not why we are here."

"Well, what is it then? I am assuming we are all coming to the same conclusion, he is losing his grip on reality," said Maria.

Officer Caine looked at the security guard. He kept looking at his watch anxiously. "You may leave us, sir." It was lunchtime and he was relieved to be excused.

"Mrs. Harper, we will not rehash details since we did that ad nauseam at your house. Frankly, Officer Daniels and I took a walk around your house and found nothing. So other than your husbands claim that a dog urinated on him, we have no evidence of anyone or anything being in your house."

"So, what do you want to tell me?"

"Well, the only plausible explanation was your husband took a shower, got dressed, and went to the kitchen to get another beer. But he had to urinate badly and due to his age, he lost control. It ran down his legs onto the floor. He made a dash for the bathroom but slipped and fell, injuring himself. Then, when you came home, he made up a story because he was too embarrassed to tell you, especially since he adores you."

Maria was quiet. She didn't want to think about Michael that way. And now that she knew about his cancer maybe it was the truth. Michael told her many times he was too old for such a beautiful young woman and was ashamed he could not satisfy her anymore. His royalties still carried his financial weight, and his notoriety was still fun. He was a powerful, virile man well into his early seventies, but then came prostate cancer eight years ago. He then was unable to be the romantic lover from the past. It made sense, but something was still missing. Where did the cigar smoke come from? What about the cigar smoke?

"Officers, you may be right. I am so sorry if we put you through such wasted effort." Maria sighed, her expression depressed and apologetic. "But what about..."

Caine and Daniels glanced at each other, and Caine continued. "Mrs. Harper, we are not done yet."

"No, gentlemen, please. Can we leave it at that?"

"Mrs. Harper, after you left for the ED, I called our friend Howie, the paramedic, and asked him to save Michael's wet clothing, so we could take it to the crime lab."

"And?" said Maria.

"Mrs. Harper, it was, without a doubt, canine urine," said Office Daniels, scratching his head. Silence invaded the room. They all took turns staring at each other.

"How could that be? Last night, there were no signs of the man and the dog in the hospital on the security tapes, but Michael swore they were there. I must admit, I was sure at that point, like you, that he was making the whole thing up and going 'loopty loop.' And then this morning, after his cancer was exposed, I was sure of it. But canine urine?" Maria got up from her chair and began pacing the room. After a minute, she sat down and stared at the officers across the table in an imploring nature.

"I know you both could get in trouble for what I am going to ask, but I throw you myself at your mercy. For now, please go with the story that he wet himself. But if you must report your findings, say he mixed it with the coyote urine we use to keep deer from eating our flowers."

"But how did he get up and..." Caine started to rethink what happened.

"Officers, we don't have any coyote urine yet, but I'll pick some up at the hardware store tomorrow. I beg of you, leave your story at human urine for now. I beg you."

"The lab tech knows nothing about this case. That kid only cares about getting off work and going for a beer."

"Good, consider the case closed. With my husband's impending death, and for other reasons, if you explore further, bad things will happen. Please promise me. I have an idea which I have denied until now. And it has nothing to do with me or my son or anyone else." Officer Daniels now had his own ideas and agreed with Maria.

The officers stood up, they both gave Maria a hug, smiled, and left the room. Maria sat alone with a pensive look on her face, then went back to be with Michael and Allie.

As the officers left the hospital and got in their cruiser, Juan looked at Bill. "Bill, she has an altar and a crown."

"I know, Juan."

When Maria entered the room, Michael asked, still having doubts about his sanity, "What did the police say? Did they find that freakin' dog and his master? Are we safe to go home?"

"No, Michael, they didn't find our new little pet, but they talked to our neighbors and to the security guards here. There seems to be no sign of them anywhere. Let's let it go and see what happens. I feel safe, sweetie, and I have the machete." They all laughed. "How are you feeling?" asked Maria.

"Better, and really hungry. I want a strawberry milkshake, God, I love strawberries." He then became serious. "Maria, you think this dog thing is connected to the bats and roaches, don't you?"

"Bats and roaches, what does that mean?" asked Allie. "Hold on, what do bats and roaches have to do with this? When does all this end, elephants, and dinosaurs, as you used to tease me with 'Look Allie, there is a T-Rex in the back yard?"

"Oh, Allie, your father's just kidding you," said Maria. "He saw a couple bats in the garage and a roach or two in the kitchen, and I teased him about his housekeeping skills. Don't blow it out of proportion, Michael." She gazed into his eyes, telling him to be silent in front of Alejandro.

"Yeah, you're right, Maria. Two bats and two roaches. And only one T-Rex. Not exactly overrun, are we?" Michael dropped the subject in a hurry.

"Mom, I must leave in half an hour. I can skip my three o'clock, but I have an exam at four. I will be back tonight for that scotch."

"Allie, no need to come back tonight. Your dad will go home tomorrow. And he does not need a drink tonight. But come to dinner tomorrow night, remember, it's Taco Tuesday at the Harpers,' as always. But no friends this week, except Cantor. He's family. We love your friends but give it a week for your father to get handsome again and flirt with your girlfriends." Maria and Allie laughed. Michael smoked a fake cigar, raising his eyebrows up and down like Groucho Marx. Maria hugged Michael and Allie and left the room.

Maria sat in the waiting room, answering emails, returning phone calls, and arranging her upcoming work schedule around Michael. Allie came through the waiting room and, seeing Maria was on the phone, gave her a hug and kiss on the cheek. Maria smiled and waved goodbye. As Allie walked away, her line was again interrupted by an incoming call. It was Mr. Nisner.

"Mrs. Harper, Mr. Nisner here. Can you talk? I have some news for you. I hope you and Mr. Harper are well."

"We're fine, Mr. Nisner. Thank you for asking. Michael had minor surgery today, but he is fine. By the sound of your voice, it sounds like you have something interesting to tell me. What's up?"

"First, I want to apologize for taking a week to get back to you, but do you remember how I said something seemed very odd? Something I never experienced? I'm assuming you haven't seen any more bats or roaches, or anything else unusual since our first inspection?" Maria stayed quiet. "Both those incidents only happened once, right? That is one of a few things that confused me from the beginning."

Maria didn't want to go into the dog incident. "Right, Mr. Nisner, they only happened once, but please, keep going."

"I just left the zoo. They had the bat guano analyzed but forgot to call me. They analyzed the roach nymph molt. Are you ready?" Mr. Nisner said, rather excited.

"Please continue," said Maria.

"In regard to the bat guano, it was strange to find so little of it, with the number of bats your husband claims he saw in the house. And how would a Panamanian bat, or bats, get into your kitchen when we are a thousand miles from any ocean and three thousand miles from Panama?"

"Agreed," said Maria.

"And the molt from the roach is equally odd. It's called Blaberus Giganteus, better known as the Central American giant cave cockroach. Its habitat is mostly Panama as well, and it will molt many times as it grows. This nymph is in its early stages. The female will grow to be about four inches long. You told me the traps I set were empty but were pushed into your dining room. Well, that's because something moved them there. I think those roaches attempted to get in, but they were too big."

"Mr. Nisner," said Maria, "this all sounds crazy, but I'm not doubting you, I promise."

"I know, Mrs. Harper, but have you been to Panama lately? Maybe you brought back roach eggs or a bat in your luggage. Or have you had a visitor? I mean, that might make some sense?"

"We haven't been back to Panama in twenty years. We left never to return. And we have had no visitors. Nothing could be dormant for twenty years, correct?"

"No, they're not like cicadas, but I'll run it by the people at the zoo."

"Well thank you for your help. You have gone above and beyond." Maria was about to say goodbye, when she had a strange thought, like a voice from afar. "You say you were in my prayer room when you found them?"

"Yes, both were in the back-left corner of your altar. I am sorry if I disturbed anything," Mr. Nisner said apologetically.

"No, all is fine. I was curious. Thank you again and good night, sir." Maria disconnected the call, then peered into space. She needed two more answers to make this all make sense. She stood and stretched, then went into Michael's room, where he was dozing off.

"How are you, my sweet, feeling better? You look amazingly better than this morning. How was lunch?" asked Maria.

"Not bad, but still hungry as a horse. They told me I could have real food later. Did you hear from the exterminator? Did you see anything last night, bats, roaches, grasshoppers, King Kong maybe? How about Bugs Bunny dancing down the hallway?" asked Michael with a sarcastic smile. "If I was home, I would have seen them all."

"Stop, crazy man. No, not really. The exterminator is still researching," Maria said, not looking Michael in the eye. "I have a question for you about last night. You said the man and his dog came into your room, right?"

"I know, everyone thinks I'm bonkers, but I saw him, as plain as day, just like you are standing there now." Michael stared seriously into Maria's eyes.

"What did the man look like and last night is the only time you have seen the man, right? Not in our house?" Maria asked.

"Correct, last night, the light at the head of my bed was on so I got a good look at him."

"Describe him for me, Michael, in detail."

"He was a tall, skinny man dressed all in black. His skin was black as black can be. He wore a tall black hat with a red ribbon around its base and dreads down to his shoulders. And he had a grin on his face, not evil, it was mischievous. And his teeth were so bright white, they lit up the room."

"And he smoked a cigar?" asked Maria. "Allie and I could still smell the smoke when we came in this morning. And the nurses complained to me about it this morning. They thought you were smoking it."

"Maria, there is another strange part. He would take a puff of the cigar then lean down and let the dog take a puff. That was really weird. I thought I was dreaming. But I wasn't."

"Honey, it's all weird, but it must have been funny to watch," said Maria and they both smiled.

"Back to what he looked like, I didn't recognize him, but that dog was familiar like when I saw it in the kitchen. I have seen that dog before, or at least it's expressions. It has a wickedly playful smile. And they both knew something I didn't." Michael hesitated. "Maria, is he 'Death' coming to take me?" Michael turned pale. He was not joking.

"Michael, he is not 'Death' coming to take you. But due to Allie being here and nurses coming in and out, I have dodged the conversation of your future. Tomorrow night, after Alejandro and Cantor leave, let us climb into bed like we did after my sister's funeral, cuddle, and talk."

"Maria, I will say this only once. I am scared, very scared. The lack of treatment was my decision for the sake of all of us. You are my true love, the love of my life. Without you and Alejandro, a would have a gaping hole through my heart, through the middle of my soul. I have learned so much from you. Let us cuddle and talk until the sun comes. Let's reminisce, cry, and laugh. Then together, let us escort my mortality to the gates of heaven with love and courage towards all our friends and our beautiful family."

Maria laid her head gently on Michael's chest as he petted her soft black hair. She moistened his gown with her sadness. "Michael, we have had a wonderful life together. You made my life, and all around you special. You filled us with your wisdom and your affection. You have entertained millions with your literature and your movies. Let us cry it out tomorrow night in each other's arms, in our bed, then wake up and show everyone what a great man and a courageous couple we are. My powers can't save you from this natural act of nature, but my powers can help ward off emotional pain." Maria lifted her head from Michael's chest and looked him in the eyes. "If you are curious about the man with the dog, the bats, and the roaches, I think I may have the answer. So, if anything strange happens tonight, don't call the nurses. If the man and his dog show up, laugh at them, make fun of them, smile back at the dog. Tell the man he looks like a black Abe Lincoln. Have fun. It's not real. You are not going crazy."

"Maria, I have cancer cells in my brain. I understand. But if I accept the reality that these are only illusions, I can live with it. They may give me some fun short stories. I am okay, my love."

Maria leaned over and gave him a long, gentle embrace. "I want to crawl into your bed and hold you right here and now." Maria kissed two of her fingers, pressed them to Michael's lips, and left for home.

She arrived home at eight o'clock, playing her garage door game. She went directly to her prayer room. Crawling on her knees, she inspected the back-corner of the altar where Nisner found both the molt and the guano. There it was, on the side of her altar; the wood was scratched. That scratch was never there before. It was from a dog's claw. The officers missed it. Kneeling on the floor, she leaned back and reached her arms to the sky. As she gazed upward, she roared in her eerie Voodoo voice:

"MIRIAM!"

8

TELL ME WHY, MOMMY DEAREST?

After Maria's realization of Miriam's continuing contempt for Michael over the last two decades, she was enraged. She needed to talk with her mother and insist she end this needless aggravation in his remaining days. Maria remembered her mother's threat after her sister's death. Her mother promised to leave him alone only until her grandson, Alejandro, was grown and on his own. That time had arrived. Both mother and daughter knew the spell cast many years ago with the Archangel protected Michael, Alejandro, and Maria from human injury and death, but the spell was never able to block the Supreme Deity when he made his decision to bring someone to him in the heavens.

Maria took a long hot shower while sobbing in her solitude. She brushed her teeth and put on her pajamas and robe. She grabbed a glass of wine, sat in her chair in the living room, and called Sadie to begin the communication process among the family. Sadie wept on the phone over her father, as Maria's role as matriarch was strengthening in benevolence.

"Your father loves you all, Sadie, and we will miss his love and his charming childlike behavior. He is in good spirits and looks forward to seeing you all as much as he can in his short future. Alejandro and I love all of you. Let's pull together and celebrate the last days of this incredible man's life. And it's time for us to tell Alejandro the truth."

"Maria," said Sade, "I must end this call. Please send me a detailed email tomorrow. I cannot talk any more tonight. I need to cry a lot right now. I deeply love my father. And we all love you as well." Sadie hung up. Maria sat in silence. The final act had begun.

She called Allie to say goodnight. He also wanted to cry in silence. Maria went to her bed and propped herself up on her pillows. She gave a deep sigh as she looked at her empty bed. She looked at the ceiling and said aloud, "Time to call mother. This will be a different conversation than the last two. I need another glass of wine." Maria went to the kitchen. She thought, '*no bats, roaches, or dogs. Maybe Miriam will send a family of sloths next time.*' She shook her head and laughed, now that she had figured out the mystery and she was relieved Michael wasn't insane. Maria pictured Miriam's prayer room with an army of sloths in single file, ready to invade her kitchen in slow-motion. As angry as she was with her mother, she could still find some humor in all this. She was ready to lie in bed with Michael and laugh about it tomorrow night. She took a sip of her wine, picked up the phone, and made the call. Her mother answered.

"Hello Mother, it's Maria," she said.

"Why Maria, you haven't called me in over a year. How are you and Alejandro? And how's the old gringo fart? Not well I hope."

"You couldn't wait, could you? You just couldn't wait. I am sure you will be glad to hear Michael has cancer all through his body and has six months to a year."

"Oh honey, I'm so sorry for you and Alejandro."

"And how about Michael, and his family, and his friends? How can you still be so unfeeling towards my husband?"

"You know what I meant. I'm sorry for all of you, but especially for the two of you." Miriam was backpedaling.

"You said you would wait to challenge my powers and put a curse on him until Alejandro was grown. Well, he is graduating with his degree in chemistry in June and has been accepted into medical school here in town. He will still need our support, only his father will be dead. Do you think Andrea, you, or me, could have done this for him without Michael? Alejandro would have been a drug dealer in Balboa, or in jail, or dead. How did you get through the Archangel Michael's sword? I guess I'm not as good as I thought I was. This is our last conversation." Maria was about to hang up.

"Maria, wait please." said Miriam quickly. "I promised you I would not cast a banishing curse on him. First, I could never get through your spell and the Archangel, and I never thought Michael deserved death. I testify to you from the depth of my heart, the cancer has nothing to do with me. That is nature's way of the omnipotent. I am sorry for all of you, and that includes Michael."

Maria paused. She considered how sincere her mother sounded, and somehow, her intuition and inner sensitivity knew she was telling the truth.

"I believe you for the first time in a long while. Daddy is the only one that I know of you purposely made suffer and die. But we have weird occurrences lately, emanating from my prayer room. A pit bull accompanied by Papa Ghede, smoking one of his cigars stalks Michael, along with a cauldron of bats swooping at him as they flew through our house, and an intrusion of giant cockroaches dancing through our kitchen. All species, probably even the pit bull, are found only in Panama. And tonight, when I returned from the hospital, I saw the dog's claw marks on my altar."

"Hospital?" Miriam interrupted. "Is Michael that far along, honey? What stage is…"

"No, Mother, your cute little pit bull scared him so badly, he tried to escape, tripped, and broke his collarbone. Not funny, Mother."

"Oh dear, let me explain," said Miriam.

"I'm not done yet, Mother, so hush. I wasn't there to witness your tricks, just Michael. I just figured it out myself this afternoon."

"How did you figure it out," asked Miriam.

"The top hat and cigar smoke inside his hospital room. Michael honestly thinks he's losing his mind due to the cancer cells they found in his brain. Please, Mother give me, Alejandro and Michael's family love and compassion in his last days. Stop being silly. Let him die with respect. Mother, Alejandro is going to be a doctor. He wants to specialize in Pediatric Oncology at the Children's Hospital. Do you know what kind of heart and love is necessary for that specialty? Think how proud Etienna and Jesula would be."

"Maria, stop, let me explain. This whole thing comes from a spell I cast the night of Andrea's burial. I know I promised you I wouldn't, but I was so angry I needed to blame someone, anyone, but Andrea. I returned to the cemetery and cast it as I knelt at the foot of her grave. But as I aged, I realized the person to blame for Andrea's death was myself for being sexually irresponsible and exposing you girls to your drunken pervert of a father. I removed the spell many years ago, after hearing how happy you and Alejandro were on our infrequent phone calls, at least I think I did. I knelt by my bed and asked for removal ten years ago. I always write them down. Hold the line, honey, please." Miriam went to her prayer room to find the original spell she had written. Maria waited patiently.

Her mother returned to the phone. "Okay, I found it, Maria." Maria could hear her mother reading aloud in Spanish. "Oh no, Maria, here it is, I made a terrible mistake. I asked Ghede Nebo to remove the spell from Michael, but he was the one I asked to protect Andrea in the underworld. It was Papa Ghede I asked to place the spell on Michael. I asked the wrong god to remove it, Maria. That's why it was never removed." Miriam was feeling horribly guilty and thoroughly ashamed of her incompetence that caused such pain to her daughter and Michael.

Maria wasn't ready to absolve her mother's mistake. "Remove it now, Mother, the spell must come off now to protect Michael in his hospital bed. Send both the curse and the removal to me first thing in the morning. I must prove to Michael he is sane. And I will, sometime soon, unveil all to Alejandro. But for now, I will tell Allie it was a reaction to a new medication."

"I will cancel it tonight, but I will need a day to retype the original. I always wrote my spells and curses on witches' parchment."

"Thank you, Mother."

"Honey, I am sorry for everything I put you and Andrea through, and now Michael and Alejandro. Unlike Andrea, you made such wise and healthy decisions in your life. And now my grandson is going to be a doctor. Are you going to tell Alejandro everything including our powers before Michael dies?"

"Mother, I believe everyone needs to hear the whole story someday soon. Michael's three children are the only ones who know we are not Alejandro's biological parents. But they don't know about my powers. For now, I need to set Michael's mind at ease. I will expect your email tonight." And without another word, not an 'I love you' or goodbye, Maria hung up.

She finished her wine, turned off the light, and cried into her pillow. Time was waning for her hero and the love of her life. And the bed felt so, so empty.

* * * *

The next morning, Michael was unable to reduce his pain medication. But he did regain his appetite with a vengeance, and sadly, weight gain would never be a problem. But the good news, Maria was a great cook and family dinners would become special and prevalent.

As Maria awoke, a scan of Miriam's spells came via email. She printed them so she could read them to Michael and ease his mind. When she entered the room, she began, "Michael, you know all those demented episodes you claim to be experiencing here and at home, did anything happen last night?"

"No, in fact, they did not. Maybe Abe Lincoln had someone else to spook. Come on, honey, now that we know about the cancer cells in my brain, let's accept my lunacy as part of the last act of my life, like King Lear, only let ours be a comedy, not a tragedy. Let's have fun with it." Michael sort of laughed. But Maria had a few questions before she sprung the truth on him.

"Did Dr. Sung tell you when you would be discharged?"

"He said tomorrow, because of my age. You know how that makes me angry. Call Stein and put him on speaker." Maria called and Stein answered. "Bob, it's Michael, I need your help."

"Sure, what do you need?"

"This Sung guy is telling me he wants me to stay one more day, because of my freaking age; it's not going to happen. I have a date with my charming wife tonight as well as my son and grandson for Taco Tuesday. Get me the hell out of here."

"Done. I'll call Sung and insist you must leave. He will do as I say. And if he fights us, just walk out and we will press charges for HIPPA violations.

Have a fun time tonight. You sound great, Michael," Stein complemented his good buddy.

"Thanks, Bob, see you soon. Have any mild pain meds to prescribe? I want to be coherent and enjoy every remaining day."

"Be at your pharmacy on your way home, but don't drink the whole bottle of scotch with them. Keep it under control, like maybe half a bottle. You have a couple graduations to attend."

"Thanks, Bob." The call ended. "There you go, honey, I will be out before noon."

Maria pulled a chair to the bedside and grabbed Michael's face. "Michael, what I'm about to tell may make you laugh, and your ribs might hurt, but you must be told."

"I must be told what?"

"Remember last night I told you to pay no attention to Abe and his dog? When you described him, that is when I figured it out. Then the exterminator called, and it all came together. The bats and roaches were from Panama. This all must be a spell cast upon you by my mother twenty years ago, after Andrea's burial in Panama City. I thought it was to be benign until now."

"Why until now?"

"Mother promised not to challenge the powers of my protection spell until Alejandro was on his own. But I called her last night to take her on. It got a bit nasty."

"She still wants to blame me for your sister's death?"

"Listen for a minute. When I came at her, she swore she removed it ten years ago. She got the original spells she wrote on witch's parchment. It was then she realized she prayed to the wrong god to remove it. You could call it a High Priestess malpractice."

"Sorry babe, not laughing. Will she ever grow up? I genuinely thought I was going to the rubber room and leaving this earth an embarrassment to my family, friends, and fans. If she wasn't so vengeful, it might be funny?" Michael was relieved, but not amused.

"Michael, I realize this may be hard to accept, but she told me to convey her deepest apologies to you. She told me she realized ten years ago Andrea's death was because of her marrying our father. She takes the blame."

"But why did she, and why does she still, hate me. There is no reason. I have never met the woman."

"Simple, you are a man and that is the only reason she needs."

"Okay." Michael accepted that.

"Allie knows nothing of my powers, or his ancestor's powers. We must tell him these hallucinations were a reaction to a new experimental pain medication prescribed by Stein."

"He has a degree in chemistry. He will want to know what it is. He already wants to study my case file and find ways to help me."

"Tell him, you can't remember, and you threw them away. Do you want to read the spell? She sent a copy to me." Maria handed him the paper, but Michael handed it back.

"Sounds interesting, but it's in Spanish. I can sort of read it, but not with an accurate interpretation. Remember, that was why I had Vanessa." Maria took it back and started to read, but in her regular voice so the gods would not get confused.

> *(1998 at midnight in Panama City at gravesite of my loving daughter, Andrea.)*
>
> *Oh, to my beloved family of Ghede, hear me now.*
> *Before you, I kneel and humbly bow.*
> *My daughter, who has left this mortal Earth*
> *Two years ago gave her son his birth.*
> *And from that point her health did fall*
> *With drugs and poisons, sex, and alcohol.*
> *It started when the American she claimed as the father*
> *With political power stripped the child from his mother.*
> *Then a spell was cast upon her by her sister so kind*
> *Because the American distorted and twisted her mind.*
> *The spell caused Andrea's addictions to drain and to rot*
> *The soul in her body and to die, for what?*
> *So he could remove our child to his foreign land*

To have the boy and my daughter join his own family clan.
So I ask from you for this to me
When the boy is from his childhood free,
When his years approach age twenty-three,
Let the white man see through his very eyes
Things that will come forth for his demise.
To see things that are not truly there,
So his family believes he can no longer bear
His aging brain that begins to swear
The attacks come from animals, bats, and roaches
And they all become his haunting hostess.
Until all will cry and mourn his suffering
As he is put alone in a world that's buffering
The true respect he has always had
Until he lives in his own torment, totally mad.

Ghede Nibo, my beloved psychopomp, take loving care of my daughter who is dead. And Papa Ghede, I pray to your wisdom to grant or rebuke my wish. I bury this doll at the foot of my beloved daughter's grave. And pray that my other daughter and grandson you protect and save from this selfish foreign man.

Maria looked up. Michael reached for the document. Maria handed it to him. "That is beautiful. And it worked. But did she inflict this cancer on me?"

"No, my sweet, she has nothing to do with your cancer. Witches cannot override God's ultimate plan for us. Like my father, it was God's plan to agree with mother's curse. But you are dying at this time for a reason, and none of us will know for a while, if ever. But the timing, I feel, has something to do with Alejandro and Cantor. Mother is deeply sorry and embarrassed over her mistake, not removing that haunting curse. I wish you two could talk someday, but now I'm afraid that will not happen. And Michael, I do not feel good about lying to Alejandro."

Michael was released from the hospital by noon. Sung hid like a frightened ground hog. Maria brought him clothes since his were cut off from his body. They would wait until they got home to shower together.

Michael was slowly beginning to resemble the charming gentleman who appeared at dinner every Sunday night, but without his favorite shirt.

Maria and Michael spoke little to each other all day. They were saving it for the evening. This was the beginning of the end. It was a precious twenty-two years. Their discussion was to be in their bed that night, their bodies intertwined in each other's love like their first night of intimacy, the night of Andrea's death and the night Alejandro survived death with the help of the Archangel Michael and his soldiers.

THE LIFE OF WHICH PEOPLE CAN ONLY DREAM

As difficult as it was to accept, everyone knew this was their final holiday season with Michael, the patriarch of the family, the husband, father, grandfather, brother, uncle, and even great-grandfather. Because of the hectic celebrations amongst families and in-laws, Sadie organized a family reunion the second week of January. Michael lost only ten percent of his body weight, and his white hair was still thick, and he still had his captivation grin. The pain medications caused him to be forgetful, but not confusing his mind. He would limit the medication during the reunion, as uncomfortable as that was. But in the end, he had one reason to stay alive; make it to June, for the graduation of Allie and Cantor. His plans after that were known only to him.

In the last few years, the family spread out over the country. Maria and Sadie planned a unique day for the reunion. The family had grown to twenty-one, just the right size for Michael and Maria's home. Rooms were reserved at a nearby hotel, with an indoor pool, playground, bar, and restaurant. Maria and Sadie requested the family send family photos and videos of their lives. Maria and Sadie would arrange them into albums. On the day of the reunion, all would be presented with the collection for all to remember for generations.

The day arrived. Everyone gathered at Michael and Maria's home. Maria kept her prayer room closed and locked. Sadie brought out the albums. There was laughter and hugs and tears. There were children sitting on the laps of their aunts and uncles, their parents, and grandparents. The stories flowed. Michael remained in his chair, but all were glad to come to him. The children sat at his feet. He received lots of hugs and love, and was approached many times with 'Remember this, Dad,' or 'Remember this, Grandpa?' Sometimes they wanted to laugh, sometimes they wanted to cry.

Suddenly, the doorbell rang. Nobody stopped their storytelling, so Maria answered the door. She opened it. Her face became flush. She threw her arms around the new guest and would not let go. Maria started crying, her chest heaving. She was in shock.

Maria grabbed the elderly woman by the hand and led her through the living room to Michael. The room went silent. The woman was dark and wrinkled. She walked with a cane.

Michael rose to his feet. "Hello, I am Michael Harper. Maria, who might this be? Do you work with my wife at the hospital? You are welcome to join in on our family fun," he said politely.

"You are Michael. It is wonderful to finally meet you. I am Miriam, your mother-in-law." The silence continued. Michael gasped. "I know I wasn't invited, but I landed this morning from Panama City. I had to see for myself this beautiful, loving family who adopted my daughter and grandson twenty years ago, the one she has been bragging about all these years."

With that, Miriam, eighty-two years old, dropped to one knee at Michael's feet. "Can you ever forgive me, Michael? You never deserved the way I have treated you. I was wicked. You are the man I promised Andrea she would meet someday, but she was too far gone. You and Maria are so loving to each other. I am happy for both of you."

Michael embraced Miriam. "Miriam, once I learned the horrific story about Andrea, and even though I knew how you felt towards me, I understood the grief stabbing at your soul. I took your heart in my hands and held it gently, my Priestess." The family was confused but sensed this was a moment long past due.

"Oh Michael," Miriam said with a tear running down her cheeks.

I MURDERED YOUR MOTHER, I THINK?

"I want you to meet my family, but first..." He took Miriam's arm on one side and Maria's on the other and led them across the room. "Miriam, this is your grandson, Alejandro. Alejandro, this is your loving grandmother."

Miriam and Allie said something to each other in Spanish. Miriam held Alejandro in her arms. Allie was unsure how he felt. He knew almost nothing of his grandmother, but he could not help but weep. Then Allie and Maria took her around the room to introduce her to everyone. Michael returned to his chair. Everyone was gracious. Only Michael's three children and their spouses knew why it was twenty years since Miriam saw the son of her long-passed daughter.

It was approaching eight o'clock. The party was winding down. The room was filled with love intertwined with darkness in everyone's heart. They realized they would see each other in June at the boys' graduations, but perhaps not Michael. He was aware of that possibility as well. He shared all his favorite experiences involving each one of them and told them how they enhanced his life. And with each encounter, they laughed and cried at the same time.

When all left, Allie and Maria finished cleaning up the loose ends the caterers had left behind. Michael yelled into the kitchen, "Maria, see any giant cockroaches out there?" Everyone smiled, even Miriam. Allie smiled as well, but he didn't know why.

When all was finished, Michael, Maria, Miriam, and Alejandro sat alone together in the living room, beautiful flames danced in the fireplace.

"I have a lot of questions about my family and its history in Panama, Grandmother. How long will you be here?" asked Allie. All three of them glanced at each other.

"Oh, I am a retired OR nurse and live in a government retirement home, so I have no reason to hurry back. It is depressing, nothing like the energy here today, a couple of weeks, maybe. I would love to see as much of you as I can while I'm here," responded Miriam.

"I would like that, Grandmother. But I must leave now. I have early classes tomorrow. We have Taco Tuesday every week, so I'll see you then." Alejandro gave everyone a kiss on the cheek and left gallantly through the front door.

"What an incredible young man," Miriam said, filled with pride and happiness.

Michael, Maria, and Miriam sat quietly in the living room, emotionally and physically drained from the best day of their lives. Michael broke the silence.

"Miriam, we haven't told him much. He knows he was born in Panama and is half Panamanian because of his mother, Maria, who he believes is his biological mother. He knows Maria is religious. Catholicism, he assumes, because of her prayer room. He has no idea he comes from an ancestry of Voodoo Priestess.' Maybe while you are here, we' will talk. I'll leave that up to you and Maria. I have authored a book about your family history, including Andrea's life and death. Only my publisher knows it exists. He is instructed to publish it after my death, and the royalties will be split equally between Alejandro and Cantor for the boys' education. It is not all pretty, especially the parts about our beloved Andrea, but it is true. And all the names and locations are changed, so only our family knows it is about us."

"Michael, Maria told me the day of Andrea's funeral, you would give Alejandro advantages Andrea's other boyfriends could never give him. She was right. He will be a doctor, and Maria is loved and taken care of well. You love them both so deeply and sincerely. Thank you, and again, I'm so, so sorry." They both smiled.

Maria drove to the hotel where Miriam checked in and gathered her things. She returned and made her mother comfortable in the spare room.

As it was time for bed, Michael poked his head into Miriam's room. She sat in a chair. "The bats and the roaches were unnerving, but the dog, that was Andrea, wasn't it? I could tell by the smirk on its face and the way it walked as it bounced back to the prayer room."

"Yes," said Miriam. "At her gravesite, she wanted one more shot at you. I granted it at the time, but Maria cast that protection spell on you. That dog couldn't hurt you, only pee on you." Michael laughed. "You know she would have killed you somehow, or had you deported. My heart was tortured. If it weren't for her self-inflicted overdose, this day with your family would never have happened."

"You're right, Miriam. When she came after me, it always turned out to my advantage and her disadvantage. Even her dog character was funny in the end. She couldn't hurt me, but I am sure she loved pissing on me. There was a time when I was truly in love with Andrea. We were good friends. She had a sweet side in there somewhere. And she made me laugh."

"The gods realized they needed to protect you and Maria for Alejandro's sake, and ultimately, your entire family. They protected Alejandro for this time, so he may care for sick and innocent children. He must be taught the powers, Michael, from his kind and untainted mother. Add those powers to his knowledge, intelligence, and huge heart, and many children's lives will be saved. Good night, Michael. Wonderful to meet you and your family. Remember, many people are blessed, but you are truly a blessing to so many."

Miriam rose with her cane and walked to Maria's bedroom. "Maria, may I pray at your alter before I sleep?"

"Mother, I would be honored."

Miriam prayed and asked for love and forgiveness, then climbed in her bed, and rested more peacefully than she had in years in the home of her precious daughter, Maria Blanco.

10

THE BOOK OF REVELATIONS

Over the next two weeks, Maria and Miriam spent as much time together as Maria's job would permit. She took her to the hospital and obtained permission for her to tour the OR. Miriam was astounded by the advances made since her retirement many years ago.

Michael, Miriam, and Maria agreed not to inform Alejandro about his witchcraft ancestry or his mother's death until a more appropriate time. They let him concentrate on his relationship with his grandmother. Miriam shared the status of the Blanco family with Maria, and Maria shared the events of the Harper family, which created a new respect for Michael and Alejandro. Miriam prayed at her daughter's altar every night before retiring to her bed. She thanked the gods for her daughter who escaped the odious decisions of her mother so long ago. As it would turn out, Miriam would move from Panama into the house with Maria after Michael's death, but only for a fleeting time. Miriam would die in six months from a fatal stroke.

* * * *

Four months passed since the impassioned reunion of the Harper family. They were challenging times for Michael's powerful character as his pain intensified. But his will was resolute. In two weeks, he would watch his son Alejandro, and his grandson Cantor receive their bachelor's degrees from the same institution. Then Alejandro would be off to medical school at OSU and Cantor to law school at NYU. And although Michael was weak and frail, he made himself fun to be around. Perhaps because Maria spent more time at her altar.

"Allie," Maria said one Tuesday as they finished the dishes at the kitchen sink. "Your father is fighting hard. In the last month he has been in a lot of pain and has lost a lot of weight. I am afraid the end is drawing near. He and I want you to join us on Sunday for brunch. We want to share a few things about your ancestry and your life in Panama. Would you do that for us, my love?"

"I will spend the entire day with both of you. There are missing puzzle pieces in my head from when Grandmother was here. I assumed it was her memory leaving her," responded Allie. "I am glad we are having a talk before it's too late. I want to learn more about why we left and never went back to visit." Maria felt anxious. She did not know how he would react to the truth. He was unaware of the gravity about to be unveiled upon him.

* * * *

It was a splendid spring day in May. Maria decided to have brunch on the patio in the shade of the sovereign oak tree that ruled the neighborhood for decades, its new leaves Sherwood green from the spring rains. Maria planted her flower beds, splashing varying hues of color into her backyard. She made a delectable brunch of Huevos Rancheros, guacamole dip and chips, honey-glazed bacon, and Bloody Marias made with tequila. Michael and Alejandro made small talk as they enjoyed their cocktails. Michael was still coherent and a good conversationalist. Maria served a genuine Latin breakfast. Michael and Maria shared with Alejandro the breakfasts on their porch in Balboa, with the heavenly mixture of food and ocean breeze. And they shared the mess he made throwing his oatmeal from his highchair.

Brunch was perfect. Alejandro and Maria cleared the dishes. Then, as Alejandro sat back at the table, Maria pulled her chair over and sat close to him, took his hand, and stared into his eyes. She wiped the corner of her eye with a napkin. She began to shake, enough that Alejandro noticed. He was confused.

"My son, from the moment you were born, I loved you more than words can express. I held you in my arms, I fed you, I changed you, and protected you in mystical ways which we are about to explain to you."

"Protected me from what, Mom, like snakes and scorpions and rain forest diseases? You are confusing me like Grandma's stories." Alejandro's tranquil demeanor changed to a befuddled expression with a nervous laugh.

"Yes, those too, but I protected you from people. And your father protected you from people who wanted to hurt you and use you for their own criminal gain."

"Whoa, I was four when we moved here. People wanted to hurt me. Like, who? And why? Why would anyone want to hurt a little kid?"

"Your mother. We had to protect you from your mother and her felonious partners."

"Mom, now I am really confused" Allie's eyes squinted, and his face frowned. "You're my mother, the only mother I have ever known. You aren't losing your grip like Dad, are you? No offense, Dad."

"None taken, son. But let your mother continue. You are right when you say you don't remember another mother." Michael knew Allie was about to enter a realm of reality he could never have imagined. From this point there was no turning back. Only pure truth could save their family. Allie looked back at Maria.

"Allie, I may be the only mother you have known, but I am not the only one you had. I am your aunt, your Aunt Maria, not your mother. You are my adopted son. Your mother, Andrea, was my sister." Alejandro sat quietly, with an expression of deception on his face. It was serious.

"*Was?* What do you mean *was?* Who or where is my mother today?" asked Allie. He held back his tears.

"She died when you were three. She was a drug smuggler, a dealer, and a con artist. She became a heroin addict while she traveled with her boyfriend on his sailboat for a year, and the day she returned, she almost let you drown. She was in one of her drunken, cocaine ridden states and supposed to watch you at the beach. But when I went to the bathroom, she forgot about you. I saved you from a riptide before it pulled you out to sea and performed mouth-to-mouth to force the sea water from your lungs. Your legs were bleeding from coral cuts. That was when, drunk and high, your mother ran off and overdosed on heroin that night on her boyfriend's boat."

"No, this can't be true. Who knows about this? Why did no one tell me? Everybody has kept this secret from me all my life?"

"Only people in Balboa and your grandmother know. That is why we never went back, to keep this from you until the right moment. And your dad's three children and their spouses. We had to tell them when your father returned permanently from Panama and brought you and me with him. None of his grandchildren know, not even Cantor."

"So, Dad, you and Mom kept this from me all these years? Why?"

"Son, there's more. I'm not your biological father either. Andrea and I were together. We were in love and had a lot of fun until her drug and alcohol use got really bad. It is a long story, but she became pregnant and tried to trick me into believing I was the father. But I already had a vasectomy. but I played along. I realized her baby would be in such danger and the father would never care for you. So, I went along and signed the birth certificate. Certainly, there have been times you wondered why you have all Latin features and none of mine.

"But if you and Mom were around, how was I in danger?"

"All she wanted from me was child support and to confiscate my hotel."

"So how was I in danger?"

"She used you to attract surfer kids, like a puppy dog in the park, so she could sell them cocaine and pot, but I wouldn't allow it. Your biological father was probably a drug dealer or bar fly, but nobody knew who he was, not even Andrea."

"So, she was a whore too?"

Maria held out her hand to Alejandro, but he refused to grab it. "I was your nanny for two years before your father and I expressed our love for each other. It was the night your mother died of a heroin overdose, but we didn't know that yet."

"So, what kept her from hurting Dad and me?"

All three of us were protected from your mother and the drug dealers by a Voodoo protection spell, and the legal custody agreements, which your father handled brilliantly."

"Okay, so Dad obtained custody of me because she was a bad person. And I understand, how this mother of mine cheated and tricked you into thinking you were my father but…" Michael interrupted.

"She never tricked me. I played along to protect a child. I knew her child would not have a chance and wind up like his mother, or dead." Michael stared at his son with no expression on his face.

"Okay, but Mom, why would you have somebody cast a Voodoo spell on us. Did you think that would help? I'm studying to be a doctor, a scientist. Voodoo is hocus-pocus silliness. Come on Mom, you're smarter than that." Allie was insulting Maria to the core, but Maria accepted the innocence from a child raised in a white American suburb.

Maria looked at Michael, and he nodded with his permission. "Son, come with me." She led Alejandro by the hand to her prayer room. "Ever wondered why this room is always locked and you have never seen inside?"

"Always. Every time I walk past it."

Maria unlocked the door and pushed it open. A gust of rainforest humidity came into the hallway. She led him to the altar. He looked around at the masks and effigies and the ceremonious crown on the altar. He looked at her as if he had never seen her before.

"Alejandro Harper, I am a Voodoo High Priestess, from a long line of High Priestess dating back to my great-grandmother in 1916, who was trafficked to the Canal Zone from Haiti. And her mother before her and so on and so on."

Alejandro didn't know what to say. He looked around, then walked out of the room. He went to the door of the patio, looked at his father, then at Maria. "I'm leaving now. Thank you for all you have done for me over the years, but I don't understand any of this except I have been lied to all my life by the two people I love and admire most." Allie turned coldly to leave the house.

Michael struggled to his feet. "Son, turn back around and look at me." Allie stopped and turned with no expression. "Do just one final thing for me before I die. Take one of these chairs into your mother's prayer room and pray to whatever god you have in your heart. And if your science studies have left you without a god, then don't say anything, just sit and listen for thirty minutes. Then we can either talk more, or you can leave us and make your own way in life. If you don't ever want to see us again, that is your choice. Your mother and I have taken you this far. And we will always, unconditionally, love you and so will the rest of your family."

"I will for you Dad, but my mother is not who I thought she was all these years. She is a witch, isn't she? Or at least she believes in devil worship." Allie went into the prayer room with a chair and closed the door.

Maria ran to Michael, fell to her knees, and bawled in his lap. Michael cradled her head and her soul with every ounce of love within him. "Give him time. The gods know the whole history. And the Supreme God of all of us will touch him and open his heart to you. Have faith my dear. Remember why he gave us Alejandro so many years ago." Maria continued to cry and did not leave Michael's embrace for a moment. *'How could a man with such little mortal strength remaining have such powerful spiritual courage inside his soul?'* she thought. But Maria never understood where his strength emanated.

Alejandro remained in the prayer room, but not for thirty minutes, he remained there for an hour, attempting to absorb all he learned about the bitter reality of his life. His mother was his aunt and a witch and even a High Priestess. So was his grandmother and all the matriarchs before her. His biological mother was a criminal, a liar, a whore and a dead drug dealer and addict. Who knows who or what his real father is or was? His father wasn't really his father, but some man who adopted him for some unknown reason.

Finally, his nausea and anger began to subside. He gazed at himself in the reflection of a silver urn on the altar, pondering his past and, for now, his future life. Then something convinced him his life was spared and led down a path to become a blessing to many others. His life was not about himself. His life was protected by the two righteous people on the other side of the door. Alejandro emerged from the room. He began to speak, but his voice had a different tone. Michael recognized it as the same voice Maria uses in her Priestess mode. Alejandro had been touched by divinity.

"Mother, Father, I love you both and am ready to hear the unimpaired truth of my life." Alejandro sat across from Maria and Michael. Maria wanted to run and hug him, but Michael lifted her off her knees and pulled her chair next to his, motioning for her to sit quietly.

"Well, son," Michael began. "This woman and High Priestess sitting next to me is why you and I are alive today. Why you will be alive to help millions in a labyrinth of medical and spiritual encounters. Your mother put a protection spell on the three of us to keep your biological mother from killing us. She was selfish and had no regard for anyone but herself. She was an addict and a con artist. She was dangerous. The gods realized that. They decided the only way to protect us was to remove her from the earth. That allowed her to leave her own terrible pain and suffering behind."

"Is that it, or is there more?" Alejandro was pale. He wanted to hear it all, but at the same time, he wanted to run again.

"Yes, one more thing," said Maria as she grabbed both Alejandro's folded hands on the table and looked into his eyes. "I cast the protection spell on you and your father. I take responsibility for your mother's death. *I Murdered your Mother, I think.*"

"What do you mean, you murdered her? You catch bugs and throw them out the back door. You save people's lives for a living every day. You couldn't kill anybody or anything. But now you're saying you murdered my mother, your very own sister, you think?"

Michael jumped in, "She didn't, Allie. She didn't murder your mother, but she has carried that guilt around with her for twenty years. She protected us with her coven of witches and an esoteric spell. The gods, headed by the Archangel Michael, accepted the role as our protectors one mystical night on a deserted beach in Panama, because he knew your destiny and needed us to leave Panama and give you a family. Twenty years later, you will become a pediatric oncologist, probably the saddest, but most loving, of all specialties."

Alejandro squeezed his eyes shut, holding back his tears.

Michael spoke again. "Your mother used her powers to help and protect the innocent, never for harm. Your grandmother and I spoke. She suggests you allow your mother to train you in the powers to help the precious children you will treat in the future. Let the Supreme God, Christ, the saints, and the Voodoo gods help you fight for those children's lives and help their parents endure their grief."

"Mom, Dad, I expected none of this today. I thought it would be finances and funeral arrangements. But this is different, and I think I understand. You saved a helpless child from a terrible street life or worse. You raised me and have given me a blessed future. I love you both and the rest of the family. I will make you proud, but two more questions. One, why was my birth mother so evil?"

Maria spoke, "She was highly intelligent and studying to be a classical pianist until our father raped her at age fifteen and she became pregnant. But the child was stillborn. She laid her dead baby on her chest and stared coldly. Your grandmother and I were with her. From that day on, she was in such emotional pain from her unforgiving hatred towards our father, her only way out was the saturation of drugs and alcohol, and her torturing of men. She was a dejected tragic figure, and the gods protected many from her soul, a soul possessed by Satan," said Maria. "And your second question?"

"Dad, why did you keep your cancer situation from us, and why did you not try to save yourself a second time with chemo and radiation? Don't you know how much we're going to miss you? This is the only time I have ever thought of you as selfish."

"Allie, to be alive is one thing; to live life is another. I wanted to see you and Cantor make it to the finish line, or should I say, starting line, and I will. In my first bout with cancer, I sacrificed two years of the quality lifestyle. During those years in chemo and radiation, I gave up laughing and traveling with my love. That wasn't fair to her. I gave up drinking and playing golf with my buds. I was nauseous and tired. I ached all over, yet I pretended to be my happy-go-lucky self. I took years from your mother, as she took care of me. This time, other than the pain, I am myself, and no one will need to take care of me for long. I have told you; I have lived a life people can only dream about. Something gets all of us in the end. The internal pain from a stillborn child got your biological mother, a heart attack got my mother, and this cancer will get me. Living is more than a heart beating. It's about smiles and making those around you feel loved.

THE BOOK OF REVELATIONS

Remember that Dr. Harper. At my funeral, you will all cry terribly, because you all love me and will miss me. But when you come back here for the wake, I want you to laugh and tell stories about all the crazy things I did in my life. Celebrate my life. I do."

They all stood and hugged together at the same time. They kissed each other's cheeks. They could taste each other's tears, bubbling up from their hearts.

Before Alejandro left, Michael retrieved two manuscripts from his studio. "I have authored my last novel beginning with Miriam's grandmother in Haiti and will end with my death. I have already written the closing chapter. It will be added after my death." Michael handed Maria and Alejandro prepublication copies. "This is my graduation present to you. I would like for you both to read it before the graduation ceremony, so we can discuss it. I'm not going to be around much longer. I want you to understand your history thoroughly, so you can pass it on and add to it someday."

As Alejandro turned to leave, Maria stopped him. "I have a present for you, Michael, and I want you to have it when I die, Allie." Both Michael and Allie were puzzled. Maria went to her prayer room and came back with a present wrapped in tissue paper. It was an art print. "Open it, Michael."

As he did, Michael laughed with all the strength he could muster. He turned it around to show Allie.

"I can't believe you did this, Maria. I thought it was gone." It was a matted and framed piece of art. It was the 'biker babe' from the back of Michael's favorite Sunday shirt, the one they cut off his body the night of the pit bull Andrea's attack. Michael hugged Maria. Alejandro was again puzzled.

"I don't get it, Mom, Dad?" asked Allie.

"It's in the book, son." Michael sat down as he was laughing uncontrollably.

11

LOVE COMES IN MANY FORMS

Michael, frail but proud, was wheeled into the University of Cincinnati Arena for the graduation ceremony of Alejandro and Cantor. All Michael's children, grandchildren, and even great-grandchildren were in attendance. Everyone cheered as they announced Alejandro Harper, then Cantor Randall. Maria and Sadie helped Michael to his feet each time he clapped. Both young men acknowledged Michael's courage with a wave and a bow.

An open house was held at Michael and Maria's home. Over one hundred people streamed through the house that day. Many of the boy's high school and college friends came to pay their respects and say their good-byes to Michael. He had been a coach, a confidant, and a respected friend to these children now reaching their adulthood. The guard was changing in this circle game.

As the day went on, Michael sat in his wheelchair. He asked his family to stay after the non-family left.

When the last friend bid their farewell, Michael, in his wheelchair, looked tired and weak, but peacefully happy. He began to speak. "Many times, I shared my father's wisdom with you. He said something will get all of us someday. This cancer got me. I cannot go on any longer. This day was my finish line, and I thank God, he allowed me to cross it. I am proud of every one of you." The entire family stood and clapped as tears ran down their faces. Then they turned to each other and shared hugs and kisses of respect. Then they became still.

"I am in pain, kids, severe pain. I am useless now to you, my friends and to my fans. I performed my job on this Earth. I am now a burden to my lovely wife. She is a beautiful soul who picked me up in midlife and made these final twenty years as happy as my first sixty with all of you. Tomorrow, I will be admitted into hospice care. They will relieve me of my pain, and I will fall asleep. Within three days my body functions will shut down. I will be gone."

"But never forgotten, Dad," said Sadie. The room was quiet except for sobs and sniffs.

(No one knew, except for Michael and Dr. Stein, when admitted to Hospice, Stein would ask to be alone when he examined Michael. At Michael's request, he would euthanize him, so he was sure to die a painless death within three days. Michael would donate his cadaver for cancer research in the name of 'Michael Harper's Family and Friends' and there was to be no autopsy for cause of death. Michael wanted his family to move on as soon as possible.)

Michael continued his speech. "Arrangements have been made. An open house will be here on Saturday, and my ashes will be spread on Sunday. I will be unable to communicate with any of you past noon tomorrow, so tonight and tomorrow morning, we must say our goodbyes. Let my legacy be that you all know I love you."

Everyone sobbed as they exchanged hugs. No one could speak, just cry. One by one, they said their goodbyes to Michael and left the house, all but Maria and Alejandro.

"Can we talk about your book, Dad? I have some questions, but first let me say the book is correct. I would not be here on this path if it weren't for the two of you. You are my true parents. Dad, you saved my life and I love you for it. I also know it has been a long day, so if you are too tired…"

Michael interrupted. "This is my last day. I can't think of a better way to spend the entire night than with both of you. We can stay up all night. I have no problem dying tired." Michael smiled at both. He would take his wisecracks to the grave.

I MURDERED YOUR MOTHER, I THINK?

Suddenly, they heard a strange flapping coming from Maria's prayer room. They all looked at each other with curiosity on their faces. Marie walked down the hallway. As she opened the door, Maria was knocked backwards by a rainforest breeze and a thousand vibrant blue butterflies. She made her way through the swarm to rejoin her loves in the living room.

"Blue Morphos" said Maria with a smile. They filled every room of the house, landing on Michael, Maria, and Alejandro's heads and shoulders. The fluttering was a symphony. Michael and Maria recognized them from their days in Panama. They sat in awe, especially Alejandro. then in turn they spoke,

"Thank you, Mother," said Maria.
"Thank you, Miriam," said Michael.
"Thank you, Grandmother," said Alejandro.

An important question was answered for the doubting Alejandro. His grandmother's way of saying goodbye to Michael convinced him the woman placed in his life at birth, had a power far beyond textbook knowledge. Maria taught him the meaning of love, now she would teach him the healing powers of God. Alejandro would become a blessing to everyone he would meet, just as his grandmother in Haiti foresaw one hundred years ago when she sacrificed her only daughter, Etienne, to be the seed for the future of her family.

(to be continued)

www.ingramcontent.com/pod-product-compliance
Lightning Source LLC
LaVergne TN
LVHW091616070526
838199LV00044B/813